YEAGER'S MISSION

— AN ABEL YEAGER THRILLER —

SCOTT BELL

Yeager's Mission

Copyright © 2016 by Scott Bell. All rights reserved.

First Print Edition: May 2016

ISBN-13: 978-1-940215-71-6
ISBN-10: 1-940215-71-4

Red Adept Publishing, LLC
104 Bugenfield Court
Garner, NC 27529
http://RedAdeptPublishing.com/

Cover and Formatting: Streetlight Graphics

This one is for Earl Bell, the inspiration for Abel Yeager.

CHAPTER 1

THE DOG HEARD IT FIRST.

Six months old, the German shepherd pup already weighed forty pounds and had feet the size of a pony's hooves. Rascal's radar-dish ears came to attention, catching Yeager's eye as he sipped from a cooling cup of coffee.

"What is it? What do you hear?" Yeager was rocking on the porch, putting off another trip to the hardware store. He measured remodeling projects by the number of trips for different—or replacement—supplies. So far, the bathroom remodel was a three-trip job with no end in sight.

The dog flicked a look at Yeager, and his tail thumped the wooden porch. *Silly human*, his look said, *can't you hear that?* And then Yeager could. The *whump* of a helicopter's rotors beat the air somewhere over the hills to the south. Yeager tilted his head, trying to catch more of the sound. The chopper was heading their way, flying low from the sound of it. Only one guy he knew would come to visit in a chopper.

"Hey, Charlie," Yeager called over his shoulder at the screen door.

"Yeah?" Charlotte's voice came from several rooms away.

"Company coming!"

Rascal trotted to the edge of the porch, planting his front paws on the top of the railing, tail swishing in time to the beat of the rotors. He *woofed* and twisted a look back over his shoulder at Yeager, tongue lolling out as if to say, *What fun! Company!* Yeager joined him at the rail and tossed out the cold dregs of his coffee.

To most people, the view from the porch wouldn't be anything special. Low mesquite-and-oak-covered hills surrounded the house

1

in all directions except for a flat field in front. A gravel drive ran from the barn-slash-garage to his left all the way to the main road, fifty yards across the field.

The screen door banged, and Charlie came out. The sight of her slugged Yeager in the chest whenever he wasn't expecting it—a little tap under the sternum that made his heart jump. How a woman of her quality and beauty would want anything to do with a beat-up trucker, an ex-sergeant who'd made it through high school more by luck than application, was a mystery he pondered every day.

Today she wore jeans and running shoes and had thrown one of his old flannel shirts over a blue tank top. She brushed back her red hair, the color of old pennies, with one slim hand. Long legged with a loose, rolling stride and a sunny smile that wrinkled her nose, Charlie could stop a parade by walking past it.

"Who is it?" she asked.

"Victor, I think. At least, Brainless here thinks so."

"I'd better put on another pot of coffee."

The shepherd *woofed* again, more emphatically, and a Vietnam-era Huey topped the hills, thumping the air with a percussive beat. Rascal went berserk, dancing in circles and barking. The dog liked his Uncle Victor. A lot.

A heavy, sharp-toothed demon curled up in Yeager's stomach. Victor "Por Que" Ruiz visited every couple of months, but he never arrived unannounced only two weeks after his last visit. Yeager frowned, and his eyes narrowed.

Rascal made a dash for the front yard, but Yeager had a hand on his collar by then. "Hold up, Brainless." He had to yell to be heard. "That chopper will squash you like a tomato."

"He knows what you mean when you call him names," Charlie said, covering her smile with a hand. "He's very sensitive that way."

"Sensitive. Yeah. That's the word I was thinking."

The Huey settled in the field in front of the house, flattening the grass and blowing dust into a minihurricane before shutting down with a long whine. Victor Ruiz waved from the pilot's seat, flipped some switches, and hopped out while the rotors were still winding down. He held up a finger and ran around to the other side of the helicopter to open the door for his passenger.

"Who's he got with him?" Charlie shaded her eyes against the early-morning sun.

Yeager shrugged and held Rascal's collar. "Sit!" he snapped. The big pup looked hurt but complied, though his tail wagged so hard it threatened to come loose. Uncle Victor alone was cool, but Uncle Victor with company was a romp in a doggie-biscuit forest.

"I don't know," Yeager said. "Looks like... a *priest*? What the hell?"

"Maybe he's here for a wedding."

"Hah. Funny. He's probably taking the itemized version of Vic's confession. That right there would take a month at least."

"Victor's moving well," Charlie said. "His leg's not bothering him at all anymore."

"Take more than a bullet to slow him down," Yeager said. Victor was built like a nuclear reactor: short and powerful, as if somebody took a shrink ray to Arnold Schwarzenegger and made him a tiny Mexican muscle man.

"Hola, amigo!" Yeager called out with a wave.

"Hola, yourself, you ugly gringo!" Victor and his companion straightened up when they were past the arc of the slowing blades. The muscular man wore a standard green flight suit with a myriad of insignia patches, no two of which matched. The man walking beside him stood a head taller and fifty pounds lighter with a narrow face and dark hair combed straight back.

Rascal whined, and his entire body quivered. The mournful look he cast at Yeager could have won him an Oscar. *Best Ham Actor in a Dog Suit.*

"Go on, mutt." Yeager released the dog, who launched off the porch and bowled into Victor with the momentum of a furry freight train. Yeager and Charlie followed the dog at a more adult pace, holding hands. Yeager studied the priest. He wore a black shirt with a white dog collar, a black blazer, and blue jeans. Though thin and young, he carried a solemn expression more suited to a man twice his age.

While the dog barked and cavorted around his long-lost friend and the new playmate, Yeager glanced at Charlie with a raised eyebrow.

"Don't look at me," she said, keeping her voice pitched low. "I didn't ask for a priest. Rascal! Don't jump on company. Get down!"

Victor wrestled the dog away, worrying the shepherd's ears and telling him that he really was a very good dog. Rascal rolled over for a vigorous chest rub, wiggling his butt into the grass.

"Stop corrupting my dog," Yeager said while Charlie told the priest how sorry she was for Rascal's behavior. Up close, the man looked even younger than Yeager had first suspected.

The boy's barely out of college, if that. And why is he hanging around with Por Que Ruiz, of all people?

"No need to apologize, señora," said the priest. "Your dog is very… exuberant."

"Yeah, exuberant." Yeager shook hands with the priest. "And he's sensitive. Abel Yeager."

"Of course, Señor Yeager." The priest looked confused but smiled anyway. "Dominic Yglesias."

"So what brings you out to see us?" Yeager asked.

Charlie jabbed him with an elbow. "I'm sure that can wait until we're inside, Father Yglesias."

"Please. Call me Dominic." He smiled as Victor snagged a stick off the ground and threw it across the yard. Rascal was off in a flash. "And it is a long story, I'm afraid."

"No, it ain't." Victor joined them, brushing grass from his flight suit. He grinned at Yeager. "It's simple, hombre. Some people down in Mexico, they need their asses kicked. You up for it?"

———————※———————

Charlie gave Rascal a beef bone and left him outside while everyone else gathered around the kitchen table. She tried to ignore the ice-cold ball of dread expanding under her chest. She rinsed the coffeepot, refilled it with water, and got the machine going again. A plastic container of yesterday's scones took a minute in the microwave to warm up and soften. She arranged them on a Blue Willow serving plate and set it on the kitchen table along with a butter dish, a pot of fresh strawberry jelly, and four small dessert plates. Her pulse thumped so hard she could feel it in her neck. *Get a grip. It's only Victor.*

But he wanted Abel to go back to Mexico—back to a place they'd barely escaped with their lives. And Victor wouldn't ask for help if it was going to be easy. So no matter what his friend wanted, it meant Abel would be in harm's way. Again.

And he'll go. He'll go in a heartbeat just because Por Que is the one asking.

She set mugs, milk, and sugar on the table and went back for the coffeepot.

"Thank you, Señora Yeager," Father Yglesias said when she poured a cup for him.

Victor cackled his silly laugh. Her heart warmed, and the block of ice in her chest melted a little.

"No, Father Dominic, not Mrs. Yeager. At least..." She hesitated and looked at Abel, who gave her a rueful smile.

"You might as well tell him," Yeager said.

She smiled and laid a hand on Abel's shoulder. "At least not until the spring."

"What?" Victor jumped up with a comic look of surprise. "You're gonna do it? You're getting married? Holy fu—uh, hot dang!"

He tackled her in a bear hug that squeezed the breath out of her lungs then dropped her and thumped Yeager on the back.

"How'd you do it?" Victor grabbed her by the arms and shook her. "Was it drugs? Mind control? Hypnosis?"

"Just an iron skillet to the head once or twice," Charlie said, laughing. "You know, he gets pretty agreeable with a concussion."

"Man, that's awesome!" Victor punched Abel in the arm then paced across the kitchen. The short man brushed his hand across his flattop, making the hair squish down and spring back up. He jerked to a halt and pointed a finger at Yeager. "I know, *esse.* Your first kid, you need to name him Baker. Then your family, you could be Abel, Baker, Charlie, and David. A, B, C, D, huh?"

"Yeah, I don't think so, buddy."

Father Dominic leaned across the table to shake Yeager's hand. "Congratulations. A marriage is a beautiful thing."

Charlie shooed Victor back to the table and went to check on the coffeepot. The ball of ice returned to her chest, replacing the happy glow lit by Victor's enthusiasm. She finished stacking the breakfast dishes in the dishwasher. Earlier that morning, the day had promised nothing more exciting than watching Abel battle the bathroom remodel. But that was prehelicopter. She ran a dish towel across the counter with quick, jerky motions.

She looked at Abel from the corner of her eye while pretending to stare at the coffeepot. Strong enough to pull a stump out of the ground with his bare hands, Yeager was built like the diesel engine of the semi he once owned. He had mallet-like hands that could drive a fence post—or caress her cheek with a tenderness that left her breathless—and the saddest, most brooding pair of eyes that could melt her insides when he smiled at her.

Stop being such a... such a wuss, Charlie. Jesus, woman, get a grip. He's not gone yet, and you don't even know what's going on. Get some control of yourself. Six months ago, you were running your own business and raising a son single-handedly. Falling apart isn't your style.

Charlie forced a smile and snagged the pot. "Anybody want some more coffee?"

CHAPTER 2

J UAN GUERRERO DECIDED TODAY WOULD be his thirteenth birthday and that his name would be Artemis d'Artagnan—Artemis for the hero Artemis Fowl in Colfer's books and d'Artagnan for the bravest musketeer of all. Esteban, the janitor, had once told Juan he could decide such matters because no one knew his real name or birthday anyway.

He hiked the mountain trail high above the village of Rascón, scuffing his sandals in the dirt and pine needles along the trail. A swishing to his left, downslope, snapped his attention to the fleeing tail of a mountain goat, flashing between the trees before disappearing in the thick brush. Juan shifted his burlap knapsack to his other shoulder and continued on. The sun had risen over the horizon and burned away the mountain chill. He wanted to make the cave before the day got much warmer.

"I can make my name whatever I want, right?" Juan said to his dead brother, Armando. He spoke with Armando from time to time, especially when he was alone. Something else Esteban had taught him: Armando was with God, and you didn't have to get on your knees to talk to God. And He was everywhere. That meant Armando was everywhere, too, and could hear Juan anywhere he happened to be.

"The priests, they chose my name when they took me in," Juan told Armando, not for the first time. If Armando was tired of this story, he didn't have to listen—he could go sing with the angels or whatever. "They picked Guerrero because the people found me there after the *narcotraficantes* killed you and our parents."

He negotiated a fallen log in the trail by first hopping on top of it then jumping off with both feet together to land with a *whump* three feet farther on. "But why *Juan*? Such a boring name! The priests have no imagination, Armando. None at all."

For the twelve years he'd lived at the orphanage in Rascón, Juan had found the lack of imagination among the priests to be their one great failing. Except for Father Pepe. Juan smiled. *Father Pepe can find an adventure in a simple trip to the toilet.*

He kicked a pinecone down the trail, and something twisted and chattered a dozen feet away. He froze and studied the black-tailed rattler blocking the trail. Easily two meters long, the snake aimed his wedge-shaped head at him, flicking his tongue and ticking his tail in warning.

"So, Señor Snake, you think to challenge me for the trail, hey?"

He set his pack on the ground and dug into his pocket for the handful of rounded stones he kept there for a need such as this. Juan zipped one, two, three rocks in a row at the snake. The first three were hardly out of his hand before he had another three ready. They were not necessary. Juan's first volley scored three out of three hits, one directly on the snake's nose. The rattler knotted into a spaghetti curl and rolled more than slithered as it tried to get away. The snake surrendered the trail, clearly beaten.

"Hah! Take that, devil snake," he shouted as it slithered into the brush, moving as fast as it could through the thorny acacia and flowering manjack trees.

Father Dominic had told him once he had the arm of a major-league pitcher, like Nolan Ryan. Whoever that was. He also said he would take Juan down to Ciudad Guerrero to play baseball when he was older, perhaps enroll him in the local school so he could play with other boys his age.

Boys with a family.

"Hmmph," Juan said. *Who needs that, huh?*

With the sun still two hours from noon, Juan turned right from the main trail at a place he'd marked with a piece of white quartz. He followed a much narrower path heavily overgrown with species of bushes he had no names for. The trail ended in fifty meters at a sheer cliff face. The only feature in the rock wall was a vertical cut as wide across as a large car and as tall as two men.

The floor of the cave was solid rock with a scattering of dusty, dead leaves and a blackened ring of stones at the entrance. Juan found the scat of some animal and studied it in minute detail, picking apart the dried clods with a stick.

He sat against the wall of the cave and placed his knapsack between his knees. Juan retrieved a water bottle and took a long drink before setting it aside. Next to that he set a cloth bundle with several stolen tortillas and a small plastic container of beans. The thought of lunch made his mouth water, but he resisted the impulse to eat everything at once.

"You will just be hungry later," he told himself. Instead, he dug a book from deeper in his sack. *Los Tres Mosqueteros.* He was halfway through the book and couldn't put it down. He kept it hidden because the other boys would make fun of him if they knew he was reading books for more than just schoolwork. This was the reason he escaped the orphanage and made his way to this small cave high in the mountains. Here, no one would bother him while he read, and better yet, none of the priests could find him and give him chores or more schoolwork. He was safe from algebra, at least for the day.

Today, as for the past several days, the priests had been too busy to notice where he went or what he did. The earthquake had disrupted their routine, and they squawked around like angry chickens. He found it much more pleasant to stay out of the way and not be drafted into extra chores.

Juan had just cracked the book open to where he'd left off when a sound drew his attention to the forest outside his cave. His first thought: *fireworks somewhere near the village.* But then his brain caught up with his ears.

Gunfire—many miles away but gunfire for sure. Juan had heard that sound so often it had become background noise. The narcotraficantes killed each other, or fought the army throughout these mountains, all the time. One way or another, the battle would hopefully mean fewer drug runners in the world.

Juan's jaw hardened. *Good.* One thing the world had too many of was drug runners.

Yeager waited until Charlie had joined them at the table before he turned to Victor. "Talk to me, Por Que. What's this about Mexico?"

"It's a small country south of here. Lots of handsome, dark-skinned people."

"I've heard of it. They talk funny there." Yeager sipped his coffee. "Now, tell me why I want to go back there? Seems like last time you and I went to Mexico, we nearly got our asses shot off."

Victor patted the priest on the shoulder. "Probably best I let Father Dom tell it."

Yeager glanced at Charlie, sitting next to him. Her sky-blue eyes were a tad brighter than usual, and her normally effortless smile was superglued in place. Yeager shifted in his seat and studied his coffee; black ripples shimmered across the surface when he set the cup down.

Father Dominic cleared his throat and patted his lips with a napkin. He'd eaten half a scone and, as far as Yeager could tell, had not a single crumb on his black outfit.

"Have you heard of the earthquakes in the state of Chihuahua, Señor Yeager?"

Yeager nodded.

"Three in the past two weeks," the priest continued. "The first was centered very near Ciudad Guerrero. The results there..." Dominic shook his head, lips compressed. "It has been very bad."

"Wiped out a hospital." Victor was slathering his third scone with butter, having dispatched the first two with extreme prejudice.

"Sí." Father Dominic nodded. "The main hospital for the area was, for all practical purposes, rendered unusable."

"Oh my God. That's awful," Charlie said with feeling, leaning forward. "What happened to the patients?"

"That is where my part of the story comes in," Dominic said. "I am the... headmaster, I think you would call it, of a mission school and orphanage in a small village called Rascón, just to the west of

Guerrero. San Filipe de Cristo. We occupy a former monastery that's quite large. Too large for our number of charges."

"They got, like—what, forty kids?" Victor brushed crumbs off his flight suit and eyed the last scone on the plate. Yeager pushed it over in silent invitation, and Victor said, "Yeah, okay, don't mind if I do. These are good. You make these, Charlie?"

"I'm learning to cook again since I sold the bookstore and moved to the country. I'm learning all kinds of new things like dusting and mopping too. Maria didn't want to leave her family and come this far from Austin, so I'm experimenting on David and Abel." She tugged at her waistband. "I've put on five pounds in the last month alone."

"Experiment on me anytime," Victor said around a mouthful.

"Monastery?" Yeager asked.

"When the hospital in Guerrero was damaged, patients were evacuated to wherever they could be sent. We opened an unused wing of our facility and took eighteen patients and some support staff. Two nurses and a doctor."

Yeager nodded again and waited for the other shoe to drop. His coffee had gone cold, but he didn't feel like getting up for a refill. His hand found Charlie's. Her fingers were chilled, so he covered them with his other hand.

"Then the second earthquake hit," Dominic said. "And this one closed Highway 16, which is the main highway that joins the road to Rascón. We have been cut off from the rest of the world except by air."

"That would be me," Victor said.

"Good that you have God on your side," Yeager told the priest. "Relying on Victor as your lifeline, you're gonna need Him."

"It gets even worse." Dominic frowned. He appeared to carry the weight of the world's sins on his slim shoulders. His narrow, ascetic face had a drawn look of exhaustion. "Some men—former cartel people—have blocked all the small back roads through the mountains, including ours. They loot everything that comes through their territory. They have been stealing all the aid and supplies that are sent by the Church to help us through this crisis. We are running desperately short of medicine, food, medical supplies. When the hospital was evacuated, many of the machines—diagnostic and treatment equipment—were left behind. Verdugo's people have stolen every shipment in the last two weeks."

"Who's Verdugo?"

"He is the leader of a group we think broke off from La Línea. They have taken his name and call themselves Grupo Verdugo."

"Okay, so airlift it in," Yeager said. "You've already said that Dumbo here can fly in and out."

"Stingers, dude." Victor sat back and picked off a couple of the larger crumbs that lingered on his plate. "Somehow, the bad guys found some Stingers—"

"Stingers?" Charlie asked.

"Surface-to-air missiles, man portable," Yeager supplied.

"I barely made it out this last trip." Victor sat up, and his eyes widened in exaggeration. "The warhead must have been old, you know? It hit the windshield and didn't go *boom*." He mimicked an expanding fireball with his hands. Adopting an airline-pilot tone, he said, "Attention passengers. That nasty smell would be your captain having crapped his pants. Please sit up, tense up, and scream all the way home."

Dominic manufactured a tiny smile. "In this case, his passenger spent the entire remainder of the journey on his knees, figuratively speaking, in a close conversation with God."

"So how about an airdrop? Fly over, out of Stinger range, and drop the stuff by parachute."

"We would like nothing better, Señor Yeager. The day I left with Victor, our only dialysis machine broke down. We have three patients who depend on dialysis to survive. A replacement machine is available, but it would never survive the drop from the air. Without another machine, these patients will die within a few days. A week at most."

"Also," Victor said, "the orphanage has forty kids, three or four support staff, and four priests to feed. That's a big airlift, amigo. You need a C-140, and we can't get one."

"The Mexican army?"

Father Dominic shrugged. "I'm sure they are doing the best they can, but an entire region is devastated. They have no time for such a small crisis. This is why I reached out to Victor, here." The padre clapped a hand on the stout man's shoulder and broke into a shy smile.

"I have a feeling I know what's coming," Yeager said. "But tell me anyway. How do I come in?"

"Easy, man." Victor spread his hands and beamed. "There's a truckload of supplies sitting on a dock in Madera. We got food, medicine, and machines ready to roll. All we need is a pigheaded truck driver with giant cojones and no brains to ram the stuff past the blockade and save the day." The pilot leaned back and put his hands behind his head. "Naturally, I thought of you."

CHAPTER 3

THE GUNFIRE IN THE MOUNTAINS had peaked then dropped away to nothing. Juan Guerrero had heard none in the last hour. He used a grass stem to mark his place and laid aside *Los Tres Mosqueteros* then yawned and stretched. Lunchtime had come and gone, and the tortillas were a distant memory, but Juan wasn't hungry enough to pack up and head down the mountain to the monastery. With this much light left in the day, the priests were bound to find schoolwork or chores for him to do.

"Okay, Armando, it is time to explore."

Juan had not been able to find a flashlight for any of his previous trips. By default, his exploration of the cave had been tentative and shallow; he had only gone as far as he could see. The cave measured exactly one hundred and twenty paces up to the spot where a slight dogleg blocked the light from the entrance. Twenty paces beyond that, the darkness had become so profound and menacing that Juan had turned around and hustled back to the light.

Today, he had a different plan. From his knapsack, Juan removed a plastic bottle filled with gasoline filched from a can in the maintenance shed. Next to this, he laid a bundle of rags he'd found in the same place.

Now, to find a stout stick. Juan wandered outside the cave and kicked through the underbrush until he came upon a fallen limb that was the right size for his purpose. He stripped off a few small limbs and tested the stick for weight and balance. *Nearly perfect.* About as long as a baseball bat, only slightly crooked, and as thick as his wrist, the stick would make an excellent torch.

Back in the cave, Juan wrapped and tied a heavy bundle of rags around one end and soaked the cloth with all the gasoline from his container. The first of his three wooden matches broke in half when he tried to strike it. The second fizzled and died before it caught. Holding the third with the utmost care, Juan scratched it across the rock wall of the cave and was rewarded by a healthy flame.

Taking care to keep the gas-soaked rags far away, Juan set the match to the torch and nearly dropped the thing when the rags went up with a *whoosh!*

"And I have made fire!" he cried in imitation of a movie he once saw about a man lost on an island. His glee turned very quickly to disappointment, however, when the flame flickered and nearly died. Clouds of smoke made him cough and his eyes burn.

In moments, his fine torch had all but burned out, the rags charring and falling apart, leaving little more than glowing embers at the tip of his stick.

"Why didn't that work?" On TV, torches always lasted for hours with a big, bright flame. On his, the fire burned out within minutes, making the whole thing completely useless. He waved the stick around, the ember on the end flaring and trailing a line of orange light in figure eights as he swung it.

That was fun for a while—using the stick like a sword with which to slay dozens of the cardinal's men. But the game ceased to be interesting when the last ember withered away. He tossed the stick down.

"Well, Armando, I guess no exploring today. We will need to find a flashlight after all."

Juan packed up his containers, book, and trash, shouldered his backpack, and started down the mountain.

After Victor had laid it out there, asking him to ramrod a shipment of supplies past an outlaw gang, Yeager grabbed him by the arm. "Let's go see the pond. I want to show you the new dock."

"Is not a gangplank, is it?" Victor asked, one eyebrow cocked, looking skeptical.

"Excuse us, Father," Yeager said. "We'll be right back." He gave Charlie's shoulder a squeeze as he went by.

She flicked a glance at him, flashing a smile that stuck for only a moment, then turned to the priest. "More coffee, Father?"

The back door shut out the response. Rascal pelted around the side of the house and ran ahead of them. Yeager and Victor cut through the trees behind the house.

"So how'd you get involved in this?" Yeager asked. "What's this priest to you? Don't tell me he's another cousin."

"Oh, hell no." Victor shrugged. "He's my mother's cousin."

"How did I not guess?"

They skirted the banks of the stock pond, following a beaten path through the tall grass. A gust of chilly air riffled the water and rattled the few remaining leaves on the surrounding oak and pecan trees. A turkey buzzard drifted in slow circles, dark against the leaden gray sky.

A wall of bruised clouds to the north promised frigid air before much longer. Already, the temperature had dropped ten degrees since Victor and Father Dominic landed in Yeager's front yard.

The dog spooked a squirrel from the water's edge, and the chase was on, Rascal barking to warn the humans of imminent danger from such a fierce predator. When the squirrel juked left, the dog's big feet got tangled, and he tumbled into a heap, legs churning for purchase. By the time he recovered, the squirrel had rocketed up a tree and disappeared.

"So I want you to look around." Yeager dug a stick of gum out of the pocket of his jean jacket and paused to unwrap it and start chewing. Peppermint tingled his nose. "I am living with the best woman on earth—"

"No doubt about it."

"—I'm getting married to that woman. We live on a goddamn ranch in the Hill Country of Texas with woods and trees and... and fish in the pond." Yeager gestured to indicate the stock tank in case Victor had missed his point. "I'm teaching my fiancée's son—who, by the way, is a terrific kid—how to hunt and fish and shoot guns."

"Very important life skills." Victor nodded.

"I have a dog," Yeager said, pointing to Rascal, who'd found something interesting to roll in near the squirrel's tree. "Not a smart dog, but a dog anyway."

Yeager shoved his hands in his pockets. "The insurance finally paid off on my rig, so the bank's off my ass. Between selling my business and my house, I paid off my debts and even came out a little ahead. Enough to live on for a while, anyway." The clay soil around the pond was damp, and it stuck to his hiking boots. Yeager grimaced and moved to drier ground, following a path through the trees, away from the pond.

"Too bad the Feds wouldn't let you keep all the cash what's-her-face hid in the bookstore." Victor grinned and made a half-assed gang sign. "So whatchu sayin' here, *esse*? You sayin' you don't wanna go?"

"Watch out. You're slipping into Mexican gangbanger speak."

"Is what I am, *pendejo*!" Victor struck a pose, head back, arms crossed.

"No, I'm not saying I don't *want* to go. I'm saying I'd be *stupid* to go."

"Well shit, man; I know you stupid. Why else would I come?"

Yeager cocked an eyebrow. "Charlie's looking pretty freaked out."

Victor nodded. His voice turned serious, and he grimaced. "I know that, bro. I'm sorry, man. I wouldn't have come if I had another truck driver handy. Dom called me, said he needed help. He knew I flew a helicopter, so he thought I could get in, y'know?" Victor shrugged. "He's family, dude. What could I do?"

They walked without speaking, catching glimpses of Rascal as he bounded through bushes, creek beds, and deadfalls. The crunch of their footsteps and an occasional bark of the dog broke the cathedral-like silence of the forest.

"I can't deny it," Yeager said into the stillness, looking straight ahead. "When you said let's go, something jumped up inside me, happy as all hell. I believe sometimes powder smoke gets in your blood, you know? Poisons you like a drug. Once it's in your system, you can't help but crave it."

"Too deep for me, bro." Victor picked up a stick and held it like a machine gun. "I just wanna shoot guns and fly helicopters."

Yeager whistled for the dog and turned around on the forest track, facing back the way they'd come. He waited for Victor to come up beside him.

"You should see the kids, man," Victor said. "They all bright and shiny. Like new pennies, y'know?"

"So you're saying I should do it for the kids?"

Victor shrugged. "Maybe so. That's why I'm doin' it."

"More likely I'd do it because you're the one asking."

"Hey, if that works, it's okay with me."

"All right, Por Que. Let's go tell Charlie."

"Absolutely." Victor grinned and slapped him on the back.

"You go first," Yeager said.

Juan sucked his right index finger and shook it in the air to cool it. He'd roasted it when he lit the torch, and it had turned reddish and begun to sting. Playing in the cave, he hadn't noticed the sting, but halfway down the mountain, it started to bother him.

Maybe it is bad enough I won't have to do lessons.

Every cloud has a bright lining, as Father Pepe said. Maybe he was right. Juan studied the finger to see if he could make it look like a nearly crippling injury that would keep him from writing math problems.

"Ay, stupid," he muttered. "Then they ask you how you burned it." Juan could see how that conversation would end, and the results were not pretty. At best, he'd be confined to the mission grounds for a month. If Father Dominic was really angry with him—which seemed likely given the theft of gasoline and shop towels—he would be forced to write a three-page paper on how it was bad to steal and another paper on the dangers of playing with fire.

"Bullshit on that, Armando." Juan looked around to see if anyone had heard the profanity, a gesture so automatic he didn't realize he was doing it until he did it.

He came out of the tree line a hundred meters upslope from the village, on the far side of the river from the mission. He could go south and use the paved bridge and stay dry, or circle north and wade across the shallow ford, thus guaranteeing his feet would get wet and muddy.

Juan angled north, cutting across the loose talus at the base of the mountain, avoiding spiky thorn bushes and the few scattered, shrubby trees. Forced to keep his eyes on his footing, Juan paid no attention to the village until he heard loud voices from the road.

He stood high enough on the hill to see over the roofs of the buildings between him and the highway through town. The only paved road, called Rascón Road to the best of his knowledge, ran from south to north, paralleling the river as it wound through the valley. Any other day, he would cut between the cluster of buildings below, cross the road, ford the river, and climb the opposite hill to the mission.

Today, something was wrong. Dead center in the middle of town, in front of Tia Bonita's store, two pickup trucks idled, blocking the road. In the back of one truck, three men stood with cowboy hats and machine guns. Another leaned on the hood by the driver's door, smoking a cigarette. His rifle was slung over his shoulder.

The other truck stood empty, both doors open.

Juan crouched down behind a scraggly tree and peered between the sparse leaves. His heart thudded, and his tongue tickled with fear. Even though he'd peed not ten minutes before, he had a demanding urge to go again.

A shallow arroyo cut the earth only a few feet away from where he crouched. Juan charted it out in his mind, and it looked as though he could duck into the shallow ditch and follow it all the way to the back of Tia's. From there, he could creep around the rear of the building to the left and watch from behind a board fence. The fence had numerous gaps and knotholes. He and his friends had used it as a makeshift fort in many different battles.

Juan took care of the urge to pee. He dribbled a few drops on the dusty rocks and managed to splatter himself, his attention more focused on the bandits hanging around the second truck than his own business.

"*Madre de Dios!*" he hissed and shook his wet foot.

With that need met, curiosity itched like a fever under his skin. The gunman by the hood went back and spoke to the men in the truck bed. A trickle of remote laughter came from the men, who were talking together and facing away from the hill.

Juan slipped into the arroyo and scooted down the dusty channel, keeping his head low and covering ground like a desert roadrunner. After two minutes of heart-pounding scrambling, he reached the back wall of Tia's, breathing harder than the short run warranted.

Gunmen in the village were not unheard-of, in Juan's experience. He'd seen them many times. Typically, the gunmen were narcotraficantes moving product or supplies via the main road. At times, they would stop to get petrol or food then move on. They hid in bases deep in the mountains, and sometimes soldiers would come and try to root them out. The gun battles were fierce, and the mission children would listen to the distant popping and try to figure out who'd won. Juan always rooted for the soldiers.

He slipped around the side of the store on ghost feet and crouched behind the worn, toothless fence. As if his arrival cued the action, the front door of Tia's banged open, and two men came out, their arms loaded with boxes of liquor and other goods. The boxes were so heavy the men had to carry them straight-armed.

Behind these men trailed Old Arturo, who ran the store for Tia.

"Please, señores." He held his hands up as if beseeching God. "Do not take so much. I cannot afford to buy more."

"Shut up, old man," grated one of the thieves, a short, squat man with dark, greasy features and an unshaven face. "Be grateful we are not taking your women and your life."

The men hefted the boxes into the back of their truck with grunts of effort. The truck bed was already full of a similar collection of boxes, all stuffed to bursting.

"But señor, please!" At this, the old man in the red apron dropped to his knees and held his hands out, striking the pose of a beggar in the street.

The fat gunman laughed and kicked Arturo in the belly with the point of his Western boot. The old man made a sound like a goose and doubled over, head to the pavement, making awful retching noises that tore at Juan's heart.

Juan moved without consciously realizing it. He stepped through a gap in the fence and came out from between the buildings. His hand, without guidance, closed around a throwing stone in his pocket.

He cocked his upper body, drew up his left leg, and coiled his muscles into a tightly wound spring. His arm came back, the rock fitting into his grip as if made for it. In one long, fluid motion, Juan took a step and whipped his arm forward, zipping a fastball with more velocity than he'd ever thrown in his life. The target had grown to the size of a moon in his pitcher's eye. No way he could miss.

Nolan Ryan couldn't have done it better. The rock hit the fat gunman just below his left eye with a *thock!* The man's hands flew up to his face, and he crumpled without a word, falling to the ground like a sack of grain.

Juan's first thought: *I killed him!*

Some kind of battle madness had taken over his body and filtered his senses. Colors were crisper, details sharper. Sounds were muted by a ringing in his ears, and he became hyperaware of his own breathing and thudding heartbeat.

Another rock zipped from his hand.

The second bandit—fatter than the first—tried to duck away. The rock skipped off his forearm and shoulder then ricocheted into the man's ear. The fat gunman yelped and pulled a pistol from his waistband. "Damn you, boy! You are going to die!"

CHAPTER 4

VERDUGO, LEADER OF THE NEWLY formed Grupo Verdugo, stubbed his cigarette out in the forehead of the emissary from Los Zetas. The little fucker clamped his jaws shut, hissed and gurgled between his teeth, but did not scream. Tied to a chair, the emissary showed some balls, which one would expect from a group trained by former Mexican Army Special Forces.

Vincente Miguel Espinoza, the emissary, now sported a swollen, blackened third eye in the middle of his forehead. Clear fluid leaked from it, trickling along the man's brow.

"Tell Marco," Verdugo said, "that I am no longer aligned with La Línea. Los Zetas and the Fuentes people can go fuck themselves together if they love each other so much. I have no use for their alliance."

He paced around the man in the chair, seated in the guest room of the modest, one-story house in the mountains west of Ciudad Guerrero. The bare room contained no furniture beyond the single seat. A dusty sixty-watt bulb in a fly-specked socket left deep shadows in the corners in the windowless room. He occasionally used the house for meetings and kept this room empty of adornment for the purpose of… entertaining guests.

Verdugo ran a hand through his mop of unruly blond hair. He'd learned long ago he could use his height advantage to scare the shit out of people. His strong brow and unusual green eyes could make anyone uncomfortable. He flexed the heavy muscles under his Tommy Bahama shirt. The ugly scar on his throat where his chief rival had tried to decapitate him forced him to speak in a near whisper. On the whole, Verdugo's presence was intimidating, and he used it to make men like this piss their pants.

And if that didn't work… a machete with a stainless-steel blade rested against one wall. Verdugo picked it up and gave a fancy double swish through the air in front of the emissary's face.

"Tell him," he continued, "that Grupo Verdugo owns these mountain routes."

The emissary kept his attention fixed straight ahead as Verdugo continued to circle like a shark sensing blood in the water. He dragged the flat side of the machete over Espinoza's shoulder. Raul, Verdugo's lieutenant, lounged in the corner, eyes glittering in the dim light.

The smell of burnt flesh stung Verdugo's nose. *A little like bacon.*

"Tell your boss we own everything from Highway 17 in the west to Highway 45 in the east and from the border to Highway 16 in the south—all of the mountain roads of the Sierra Nevada range, from Sonora to Chihuahua."

This pronouncement broke Espinoza's vacant stare. He snapped his head to the right and fixed Verdugo with a wild look. "You're crazy!"

Verdugo pulled a pack of Dunhills from his shirt pocket and made a production of lighting one with a steel Zippo, machete dangling. Espinoza watched, one eyelid twitching. Sweat banded the emissary's collar and tracked down his cheeks.

"It's simple," Verdugo stated, smoke puffing with every word. "Due to the earthquake, normal routes are, ah, disrupted. Grupo Verdugo controls the ones that are not. My men and I are no longer part of La Línea. We are aligned with no one at this time." He shrugged. "Although, I admit, we have been in touch with the Sinaloa people. Negotiations are, ah, ongoing."

Espinoza flinched, locking gazes with Verdugo.

"Am I going too fast for you?" Verdugo flicked ash into the emissary's lap. The prisoner looked away and shook his head. "Where was I? Ah. Tell Marco the rates for protection and shipment through this area are now doubled."

Espinoza gave a half-hearted gallows laugh. "Sure. And then Los Zetas will muster in force and destroy you."

Verdugo laughed and clapped a hand to the man's shoulder. "Los Zetas step into our mountains, they will leave their bones. Speaking of which, there's no sense leaving you with the ability to pull a trigger, hey?"

Thock! The force of Verdugo's blow left a half-inch of blade in the arm of the prisoner's chair. It took a full second for Espinoza to realize his right hand had been cut off. He screamed a second later.

"And in case you are left-handed..." He swung, carving another glittering arc of stainless steel. *Thock!* "Not so good," Verdugo said dispassionately. "I didn't get a good angle on that one."

To his displeasure, it took two more hacks to separate Espinoza's left hand from his arm. Verdugo frowned at the chopped-up mess. Poor workmanship displeased him. *If you're going to do a job,* his father had once told him, *do it right.*

"So before you die from blood loss, let's see what else I can cut off."

Yeager found Charlie and Father Dominic on the front porch when he and Victor came back from the pond. Father Dominic looked stiff and drawn, sitting in the glider with one hand on the chain.

Charlie had thrown a light jacket over her flannel shirt, and her cheeks were flushed from the chilly air. The big rocking chair creaked as she moved. "Where's Rascal?"

"Squirrel patrol." Yeager propped his rear on the porch rail. "The vicious beasts have taken over the forest."

"C'mon, Father," Victor said. "Let's go take a look at that dock."

"Of course." The young priest stood and stretched. "It must be very impressive. I'd love to see it."

Yeager waited while the pair disappeared around the house. He waited some more.

Charlie's electric-blue eyes jolted him with live voltage whenever he took a moment to really look. He'd seen blue topaz in jewelry-store windows that sparkled less.

24

"So," she asked, pinning him in place with her stare. "When are you leaving?"

"Who said I was going anywhere?"

She huffed a laugh. "Can't fool me, big guy."

"What's your take on this deal?"

"Are you kidding?" Charlie tried to smile. "Father Dominic here has been telling me about his orphans. Did you know most of them are victims of the drug war in Mexico? The cartels kill the parents, or the street gangs do, just to make a point. Terror tactics. And now they're victims again."

Charlie looked away and swiped the back of one hand across her eyes. She came off the chair and in one step had her arms around him. Her voice was muffled from speaking into his chest. "He showed me pictures. How can I say no to helping save little kids from starvation? But this goddamn pisses me off."

"They can drop food from the air."

"I know, but the patients…"

"People die all the time." Yeager stroked her hair. "You are more important to me than those folks. Por Que asked me to go, but I'll tell him no if…"

"Goddamn you, Yeager—don't you put this on me." She pushed back and glared at him. The anger in her eyes took him off guard; he couldn't remember ever being on the receiving end of that type of look from her. She punched him without force in the chest once, twice, and would have done it a third time if he hadn't grabbed her and pulled her in close.

"Stop it," he said. "This ain't your fault." Warm moisture seeped through his shirt. He held Charlie and rocked against the porch railing. Words wouldn't come through the ache in his chest.

"You wouldn't be who you are if you could stand by and let people suffer." Charlie leaned back and snagged clumps of his shirt in both hands. Her blue topaz eyes were red rimmed. "I know you, Abelard Yeager. You hate a bully worse than you hate a thief. And these people—these bastards—are the worst of both. No." She released his shirt and straightened the material, patting it flat. She drew in a shuddering breath. "I'm not going to be the person responsible for letting those people die. I couldn't live with that." Charlie played with the buttons on his shirt until the top one came loose. The next two followed soon after. "Oops. Look what I've done. How long do you think it will take them to tour the pond?"

"Long enough," Yeager said.

Juan froze, and a chilly sensation seeped into his muscles, replacing the heat of anger. The men in the other truck were laughing and pointing at their stricken *compadres*.

"Shoot him! Shoot the vigilante!" one cried out from the bed of the truck, doubled over from laughter.

Juan bolted. With the speed of a jackrabbit, he squirted through the fence and ran for his life. The bark of a pistol shot spurred his feet to fly faster than they ever had before. Juan pounded down the alley, leaped over a pile of cardboard boxes, then dodged the hulk of a rusting Fiat with no tires. The gunman's curses receded behind him. Too late, he remembered to take cover in the ditch he'd used coming down.

The ditch is too far away now, back the way I came. But there's no way that fat slob can run after me. He'll die of a heart attack!

The crashing of fence boards made a liar out of Juan before he finished the thought. He risked a look and wished he hadn't. The narco rounded the corner with surprising speed and shouted a curse at him.

Juan skidded right and ducked past the rear of Pedro's Garage. A bullet smacked the wall as he passed, and a puff of brick dust blew into the air. The rough gravel road slapped at Juan's sandals as he ran. He crossed the road at full tilt and made the corner, slipping a little in the loose footing, going left this time.

No great plan came to him as he ran. In the movies, there was always something handy that the hero could use to save his life and turn the tables on his pursuer. In Rascón, nothing like that existed. Juan ran past the front of Marta's house, Antonio's house, and Mariposa's house and saw nothing but lawn furniture, kids' toys, and clotheslines. No laundry, no huge concealing sheets hanging

26

from the sagging ropes suspended between tired poles. Nothing to hide behind.

The hill he'd descended only a few minutes ago rose to his right—a deathtrap if he was caught in the open trying to make the tree line. But that same line of trees provided a powerful degree of safety. If the gunman tried to climb after him, Juan could pelt him with rocks or escape into the forest.

He glanced back. *No sign of Señor Fatso. Good. Maybe there's still time.*

He took the hill, legs churning in the loose soil. At twenty-five meters, he came to the first of the scrubby trees that eked out a living on the rocky slope. Panting and dripping with sweat, Juan risked a glance behind him.

And stopped running.

The gunmen were piling back into their trucks. The first one he'd struck held a rag to his face and slumped in the passenger seat while the second stomped around to the driver's side. He paused at the door.

"I find you," the fat man yelled into the empty street. "I find you, I'm gonna cut your dick off and skin the hide off your stinking ass!" He got in as the other men laughed. The door slammed with a dull thud, and both vehicles pulled away.

Juan struggled to catch his breath, sitting on the hillside with his head between his knees. While he sat, the sun disappeared behind the mountains overlooking the mission school. The school's dinnertime bell rang, its lonely dinging the only sound louder than the rasp of his lungs.

For the first time he could recall, Juan wanted nothing more than the safety of his bed in the orphanage.

CHAPTER 5

YEAGER REPOSITIONED HIS BUTT IN the metal jump seat against the bulkhead, between the flight deck and the cargo space. Father Dominic had the copilot seat because, Yeager reasoned, his prayers would carry more weight. Aside from his go-bag, the cargo bay was empty. A couple of bolts rattled and danced across the metal floor of the rugged chopper. He hoped they didn't belong somewhere important.

The thrum of the Huey's rotors and the vibration of the aircraft blanketed Yeager in an isolated cocoon of sound. His eyes drooped, and his thoughts wandered. He tried not to think about how many times the Huey's Lycoming T53 engine had been rebuilt since its initial service date, sometime around the Civil War. He also tried not to think about how many times he'd ridden to war in helicopters. He'd lost count during his first tour in the sandbox. Two dozen? Fifty? No way to know.

Too many was the obvious answer, but a part of Yeager disagreed. Flying to battle, smelling the stink of burnt avgas and hot oil, feeling the thump of rotors like a bass drum in the chest—

Yeager's nostrils flared, and his blood ran hot as if mixed with Tabasco sauce. Colors burned brighter, sounds more distinct. No doubt about it: he loved this shit.

"Are we there yet?" he asked over the headset plugged into the intercom.

"What?" Por Que's voice crackled and buzzed even though he sat less than a foot from Yeager's back. "You needa go to the bathroom? I tole you to go before we left."

Yeager chuckled and closed his eyes. *Charlie...*

Getting out of bed had been harder than chinning a barbed-wire fence. Charlie, her coppery hair tousled and hanging over one eye, propped herself on an elbow to look down at him. A pink-tipped breast, sprinkled with freckles across the top, slid free of the sheet. Her scent filled his world, and it took all his effort to draw a steady breath.

"Goddammit," she had told him. "You'd better come back before Thanksgiving. You know my parents are coming down, and don't you dare leave me alone with my mother. There will be blood."

"Thanksgiving's three weeks away. Plenty of time to deliver one truckload."

"Through bandit-infested mountains?"

"Sure. Hey, Por Que and I blew up an entire cartel stronghold in one night."

"And nearly got your asses shot off."

"That was Por Que. And it was his upper thigh."

"Shut up and listen." She poked him with a sharp-nailed finger.

"Ouch." He laced his hands behind his head and put on an attentive look. "Okay. Listening."

"David called you Dad the other day."

"Say what?"

"It was a slip, and he corrected it right away, but I was talking with him about going to the movies last Saturday. Remember, we decided to stay in and watch a DVD instead?"

"Sure."

"Well, I asked David what he wanted to see, and he said, 'What does Dad say?' I'll tell you I nearly cried right there."

Yeager tried to swallow and found it harder than normal.

"He's starting to think of you that way," Charlie said. "That's how much you mean to him. So the story is this: I don't care about me; I could take you or leave you, no matter. But you better come back for David. Otherwise, I'll hunt you down and kill you again."

"You don't want me?" Yeager gave her his best hurt look. "Not what you said a few minutes ago. I think you kept saying—"

"I know what I said." She hit him with a pillow. "Shut up. You can't hold what I say during sex against me; that's not fair."

Charlie could turn the prettiest shade of red at times.

"You know," he said, fumbling to say it right. "You know I feel the same way about David. Right? He can call me Dad whenever he wants. And that..."

He'd ground to a halt, unsure how to tell her how much he needed them in his life, Charlie and David both.

"I know," she'd whispered and laid her head on his chest.

Yeager smiled at the memory. Somewhere south of Galveston, he fell asleep, still smiling.

❈

The Beechcraft lifted off the airstrip, leaving twin swirls of dust behind as it climbed into a purple eastern sky. Verdugo stood by his Hummer H3 and waited until the blinking lights from the plane disappeared.

At this altitude, the coming of night brought a nippy bite to the air that reminded him of his childhood, camping in the mountains with his father and brothers. He and his brothers would sit around a campfire on nights like this and shiver while their father told them scary stories of the chupacabra and Mayan ghosts. He had been a gentle man, his father—a teacher, too gentle to keep Verdugo, then known as Emilio, from joining the police. And too gentle to stop him when he joined the enforcement arm of the Juarez Cartel.

The stories Verdugo could tell would have scared his father until he pissed his pants. Mayan ghosts had no chance against the enforcers in La Línea—"The Line." Police officers turned into protectors of drug smugglers—and now, owners of the mountain routes to the United States.

"El Diego was right," he said to Raul.

Raul, Verdugo's slim, dark-eyed lieutenant, materialized out of the brush-covered rocks near the road. He wore ostrich boots, fashionable jeans that were bleached out in the thighs, and a blue satin shirt, open at the collar. A gold cross the size of a tarantula hung from his neck. He'd slipped off for a piss and was still working at his zipper. "How's that, jefe?"

"El Diego said that there's nothing like a liberal application of brutal violence to get people's attention."

Raul grinned, the gold in his teeth shining in the last of the daylight.

The plane would fly over the Zetas compound to the east of Guerrero and drop the emissary from about a hundred feet up. Verdugo had gotten... carried away with the machete, and Espinoza had died. The man's dead body would be the message, along with a detailed note pinned to his chest.

Raul's cell phone rang, and Verdugo waited while his lieutenant answered it. Raul spoke a few words, listened for a moment, then covered the phone with one hand. "Our man in San Felipe—at the mission—"

"The priest?"

"No, the other one. He is calling to say another shipment of supplies is being sent. Tomorrow night."

"Where is the shipment now?"

"In Madera, he thinks. The drivers will stop at de la Cueva's first then go for the supplies."

"Put some people on the old man's ranch. Hit them when they go for the pickup."

"Sí." Raul brought the phone back up to his ear.

"And tell them to send a message: kill everyone."

The slim man nodded and repeated Verdugo's orders.

"We will squeeze those damn priests until I get what I want."

Raul flashed white teeth as he clicked off the phone.

"Come," Verdugo said. "Let's get back to Tomochi. If we hurry, we can catch some football before dinner."

The thump of the landing skids hitting tarmac jarred Yeager from an awkward, neck-twisted sleep. He blinked hard and yawned while Victor shut down the engine. The clatter of harness buckles came from the flight deck, prompting Yeager to unlatch his own and climb out.

Full dark greeted him when he pulled back the sliding door of the cargo bay and hopped into the muggy air of McAllen, Texas. The reek of exhaust and hot engine washed over him as the rotors wound down overhead. Out of an old habit, Yeager hunched over and trotted clear of the blades.

"You know that's a myth, right?" Victor stopped beside him at the door to his small hangar in the private-terminal side of McAllen International Airport. "The rotors are too high to chop your head off. Mostly."

"So says the midget."

"What now?" asked Father Dominic, joining them. Yeager noticed he'd bent low until clear as well. The priest addressed Victor as he spoke. "What is the plan?"

"I was trying to think of one." Victor jerked a thumb at Yeager. "But with this guy snoring all the way, I couldn't concentrate."

"Snoring? I don't snore."

"Amigo," Victor said, "I thought the tail rotor was coming loose."

"Father Dominic, help this man to see the light. I didn't snore, did I?"

The priest held his palms out. "God does not want me to take sides."

"It don't matter anyway," Victor said. "I drive the chopper; he makes the plans."

They went through the cramped and untidy office into the main hangar, Victor clicking on lights along the way. A twin-engine plane, partly disassembled, was lit up by the greenish fluorescence as the overheads flickered on. The smell of oil and solvents tainted the air.

"Cujo modifying his plane again?" Yeager asked, nodding at the aircraft.

"Yeah, the .50 cal broke a wing strut. He bought the Skyknight here, and I think he's looking for a coupla rocket pods he can hang off the wings."

"Sweet Jesus," Yeager said.

"Amen," the priest added, crossing himself.

In the middle of the remaining space, two folding tables had been pushed together. A topographical map was unrolled in the center, weighted down at the corners with engine parts. Scattered around it were blurry satellite shots, printed on plain paper, from Google Earth.

"Let me show you what we got," Victor said, coming around the table to lay a finger on the map. "This is the state of Chihuahua, right next to the border with Sonora. See this road? This is Highway 16, which runs from Hermosillo in the northwest through the Sierra Madres to the city of Chihuahua and continues east until it hits Texas north of the Big Bend here."

"Uh-huh. Keep going." Yeager traced the route, noting the density of squiggly red elevation lines along the border of Sonora and Chihuahua. Rough, mountainous country.

"Highway 16 is the only road from the Hermosillo that will take you to Chihuahua. The city, not the state. The objective for the drug runners is to get to this road—45D—here in Chihuahua. That is the only straight route from the western and central part of Mexico to Juarez. This is important to the Juarez Cartel, since it goes right through their stronghold."

"With you so far." Yeager straightened from the map and stretched his back. "What about this road to the west that goes up the coast then cuts east to Juarez?"

Father Dominic said, "Since the death of Amado Carillo Fuentes, the Juarez Cartel has diminished in power. Their territory has been, ah, confined, I think you would say, to certain areas. This road of which you speak, it is controlled by the Sinaloas, with whom the Fuentes people are at war."

"And so the problem with getting to 45?"

"And so the problem," Victor said, "is that Ciudad Chihuahua is a clusterfu—a real mess. Roads buckled up, buildings tumped over into the main streets, bridges down. The earthquake hit 'em hard, dude, I'm tellin' you."

"And even more of a problem, from our perspective," Father Dominic added, "is that three bridges on Highway 16 are down, between here"—he pointed to a spot where Highway 16 dipped into a cup-shaped curve then to another place a tiny bit farther east—"and here. This means a truckload of anything, including illegal drugs, cannot take this cutoff at Guerrero and go north to Madera and then over to 45."

"The druggies got three roads through the mountains. Here, here, and here." Victor stabbed three spots in the heavily lined terrain. Yeager frowned when he realized the tiny gray lines his friend pointed to represented roads.

"And our village of Rascón is on this one." Father Dominic indicated the center of the three. "And all three roads are controlled by the narcotraficantes—Grupo Verdugo."

"Can you even get an eighteen-wheeler down those roads?" Yeager scrunched up his face in disbelief.

"Yeah, sure. No problem." Victor shrugged. "Most of the time, they don't even fall off the mountain at all."

CHAPTER 6

Juan waited until lights started coming on inside the houses before he came down the mountain. He rubbed his arms to keep warm on his way down. He slipped once in the loose gravel and skidded on his butt for a meter, swearing under his breath. Something to add to confession on Saturday.

"I see many, many Hail Mary's coming, Armando. Do you think I can slip all the cursing into one lump? God won't mind, will he?"

Señora Mendoza's chickens roosted on the lower limbs of the tree in her backyard. Juan skirted wide of their roost because the hens would raise a ruckus if he got too close but also because they gave him a crawly feeling. Like creepy dead vultures they were, or worse, gargoyles crouched on the limbs, waiting for their prey to pass.

And of course, Señora Mendoza was a witch of uncommon power. Everyone knew that. If disturbed, she would cast a spell and make you sick or make all your hair fall out.

Juan drew comfort from a stone clutched in his right hand. Slipping into the pitch darkness between the witch's house and Señora Reynosa's house was like going into a cave. Not far away, a dog barked and kept barking as he emerged from the gap and navigated to the gravel road by the spill of lights from nearby houses. From there, it was easy to follow the road.

White sheets billowed from the clothesline in front of Mariposa's house. Where were those when he needed them? Perfect cover, wrong time.

Although he'd seen the narcos leave, Juan kept his eyes peeled, staring into shadows and jumping at every movement. The smell of frying food made his mouth water. Several men gathered around the open hood of Antonio's pickup, drinking beer by the light of a camping lantern, laughing and listening to music.

When he passed, one of the men, Jorge Rojas, stepped away from the truck and raised his can of Budweiser. "Hola! Here he is! The famous David who slew the gangster Goliath with a rock. Come here, boy, come here."

Jorge put his arm around Juan and led him into the circle of light. The man's eyes were red, and he wobbled a little, but his excitement at seeing Juan seemed sincere. Juan allowed himself to be steered into the group, where he received a round of backslaps and handshakes.

"Well done, Juan. I saw what you did, and it was very brave." Antonio, an old man, had strong laugh lines and bad teeth. Juan didn't know Antonio's age but suspected he was at least forty. He worked in Madera, building houses and doing carpentry and tile work.

Juan smiled for the first time in many hours. Antonio's praise did more to restore his spirits than a cold drink on a hot day. He ducked his head and studied his feet, unable to think of anything to say.

"Juan!" a female voice called. "Is that Juan? *Madre de Dios*; I thought they'd killed you."

Juan had no sooner registered the presence of Tia Bonita than he was swallowed by a giant pillow smelling of strong perfume and cigarettes. Tia Bonita was not her real name, but Juan had never heard her called anything else. She'd run the only store in town, called Tia Bonita's, for so long that the name stuck to her the same way as had every pan dulce she'd ever consumed.

She held him at arm's length and shook a finger in his face. "That was a very silly thing to do. What were you thinking, hey? Aiee! Those men are very bad."

"I—"

"No, you listen to Tia," the big woman admonished. Stopping her when she got going was like holding a boulder on a slippery slope. Tia's hair exploded from under the band she wore, jutting out black with burnished red highlights. "You were very brave to stop the narcos from hurting Old Arturo, but you mustn't do that again, okay? If you see those men, run and hide. They have killed so many..."

The men shuffled their feet and sipped from their beers. The boom box playing from the porch steps changed from music to a commercial, the announcer excited about a sale on pickup trucks.

"Tomorrow," Tia said, "you come to the store, and I'll give you a reward. What do you want? Some candy? Some soda pop?"

Juan thought a moment. "Can I..."

"Yes, what is it? A toy?" Tia smiled with encouragement and cupped his face in her hands.

"Can I have a flashlight?"

"A flashlight?"

"Sí. With batteries."

Dr. Alexandra Lopez sipped her coffee and waited for Father Sebastian to do the same. She couldn't rush the man or else he'd give her The Look—the one priests perfected after taking their vows, an expression that said how disappointed with you they were. Father Sebastian appeared old enough to have taken his vows directly from John the Apostle, so he'd had many years to practice The Look.

Dr. Lopez was thirty-two years old and had received a Doctor of Medicine degree from Stanford University, graduating sixteenth in her class. She had undergraduate degrees from Universidad Autónoma de Guadalajara and Universidad de Monterrey under her belt, not to mention an internship at CIMA in Hermosillo and a three-year residency at Adolfo Lopez Mateos hospital. She'd gotten top marks in every class and in every review.

So how is it these priests make me feel twelve years old?

"They have been gone for two days. Just last night, armed men were in the village, looting the store. Any word yet, Father?"

Light streamed from the window to her right. Outside, rugged mountains, colored by God's palette as the deciduous trees began changing for fall, reached for an azure sky. The adobe-lined walls of Father Sebastian's office radiated the chill of a stone castle. A fireplace to her left provided the only heat.

"I have spoken to Father Dominic this morning," the old priest said in a thin, reedy voice that could turn sharp when needed. Father Sebastian had the eyes and nose of an aged hawk. He missed very little and was amused by even less. "He and Señor Ruiz have found the man they sought. A truck driver, by the name of Yigger. He has been engaged to drive the supplies past the bandits' roadblocks."

"How do they plan to do that?"

The priest frowned at her interjection. "He did not say. Nevertheless, he says the man seems competent, and Father Dominic wants you to know you should have your dialysis machine and the other supplies in two to three days."

"That is cutting it very close," she murmured to herself, already thinking about how to stretch the medication she had to keep her patients alive. *I need to inventory how many bags of saline IV we have. We'll need to ration it out. And check the stock of pain medication.*

"It is in God's hands at this point, Doctor."

"Yes, Father." She spoke by rote, her mind focused on medication and dosages. If only... how many times had she said that since the earthquake? *If only.*

After the quake had knocked out the power and the emergency generators had run out of fuel, the hospital evacuation had been a nightmare. Many, many things she wished she had remembered during the mad scramble to get patients loaded on ambulances and buses and transferred to functional locations.

Just her luck to wind up in the most remote facility in Chihuahua, cut off by terrain and the cartels. *No medicine, very little food, stone walls, and a gaggle of priests who are well-meaning but not medically trained.*

Her coffee had gone cold, but she drank it anyway. No telling how long the supply of coffee would last. It would be a shame to waste a drop.

"And the helicopter pilot?" she asked. "Will he be coming back?"

Father Sebastian didn't shrug—he never shrugged, to her

knowledge—but he made a face that suggested a shrug. "Who is to say? He is the friend of this Yigger person, so I suppose."

"Oh. Of course."

The brash, muscular pilot had impressed her with his nonchalant bravery and grinning, happy disposition. He struck her as the type of man who would kick the devil in the nuts and laugh about doing it.

"We should pray for their safety," the priest said. "Don't you think?"

He bowed his head over clasped hands and waited while she did the same. The words came back to her even though she hadn't used them in many years, bringing more comfort than she thought they could.

"Our Father, who art in heaven, hallowed be thy name..."

———————❦———————

The dog would have to die first.

Oscar Cruz resettled his eye behind the lens of his Bushnell Trophy spotting scope and reacquired the image of the two-story farmhouse. The damp leaves crinkled under his belly when he moved, and his breath fogged around him. At a kilometer's distance, he didn't worry about being seen.

He itched all over and his nose leaked from an allergic reaction to the bushes he'd crawled through to reach this spot. Or maybe just from being outdoors. Skulking through the woods, tripping on vines, tree limbs scratching his face and hooking his jacket, cold seeping up from the ground and wetting his clothes—aiee! It was disgusting.

His brother had done the outdoor work. Oscar had become more suited to pushing a mouse than pulling a trigger. He had lost his edge, grown fat, relying on Humberto to do the ugly jobs and shoulder the burden of risk. But Humberto was gone, killed by those who lived in the house below—Señor Abel Yeager and his whore, Charlotte Buchanan. Oscar had to find his edge and recover that hot-blue flame of killing lust he'd known as a youth. He was the only one to do the trigger pulling now.

For six months, he'd been dodging assassination attempts from the Sinaloas, who somehow believed him responsible for the destruction of their truck full of money. He'd spent two more months searching the records and tracking down the man who'd killed his brother then two days driving, followed by an hour on foot, battling the forest and the briars and the biting chill. Now, with the sun nothing but a weak brightness behind heavy clouds, he got his first look at the house where they lived.

Oscar felt a warm tingle start in his belly and work through his chest. A black-and-tan shepherd lay on the porch, chewing something. Not some little lap dog; this one would fight to defend his people. So the first thing Oscar needed to do was kill the dog.

The sound of a diesel engine drew his attention to the road. A yellow school bus stopped in front of the house with a squeal and hiss of brakes. A child charged from the house, the banging of the screen door carrying to where Cruz lay. The boy pulled a backpack on over his jacket as he ran to the bus.

More motion at the front door. A red-haired woman stepped to the front of the porch in a T-shirt and jeans. She cupped her elbows and hugged herself, rubbing her arms for warmth. She called something to the boy, her voice a tiny sound in the distance.

At last, he had found one of the people responsible for Humberto's death.

So this is the woman. Now, where is the man?

CHAPTER 7

Yeager and Victor flew together. Or rather, Victor flew, and Yeager watched. He occupied the left seat in the cockpit of the Huey, taking care not to touch anything that might interfere with the operation of the aircraft.

They dropped Father Dominic at the departure terminal of McAllen International at first light. The priest would take a commercial jet to Mexico City for an audience with the archbishop. There, he planned to ask the highest church official in Mexico to exert some influence and maybe get the army to break the siege in the mountains.

"You think he'll do any good?" Yeager asked after the priest had gone. "Dominic, I mean."

"Maybe yes, maybe no." Victor shrugged. "Say we do get the army to come. Look at it this way: Pancho Villa hid in those mountains, and Black Jack Pershing never could root him out. Apaches—they lived there for years. Shot the finger at *everybody*. No, the army comes, they're gonna get their ass handed back to 'em. Especially with all the guns and shit these people got."

Yeager grunted. The green ribbon of the Rio Grande Valley curled to their left, two thousand feet down and a mile south. Below them, an arid landscape, patched with the green of irrigated farms, scrolled by at a hundred miles per hour.

Before leaving McAllen, Victor raced the clock to get all the requisite forms and flight plans filed. "It's gonna suck if the DEA or Border Patrol shoots us down, thinking we are smug drugglers."

Yeager studied the ground and hoped everybody got the message. "Did you get ahold of Riley?"

41

Victor nodded and gave him a thumbs-up.

Riley Amick, ex-marine chopper pilot and another of Por Que's running buddies, had agreed to sign on. A notch of tension went out of the belt around Yeager's chest. Having another pilot on board for the long flight to Madera would be comforting. If Victor had an unexpected heart attack and keeled over dead at two thousand feet with no copilot to take over, all Yeager would be able do was watch the scenery gyrate on the way down.

The first leg, they wanted to stay on the United States side of the border, hopping up to Del Rio to fill the main and auxiliary tanks to the brim—so full that Victor said the Huey would fly "like a pregnant yak."

From there, it would be a grueling six- or seven-hour haul to Madera, Chihuahua. Riley could spell Por Que at the controls and make himself useful once they got on the ground.

"Hey," Yeager said. "One thing we didn't talk about with the priest around."

"What? Sex?"

"Guns."

"Oh, yeah, fire sticks." Victor flashed his trademark toothy grin. Yeager's image reflected back at him in the pilot's sunglasses.

Yeager failed to return the smile. "Preferably fully automatic fire sticks with high-capacity magazines. And NVGs, tactical armor, knives, grenades, sidearms, C-4, timers, det cord, and anything else we might need to create shock and awe in the hearts of our enemies."

"Be they few and dead. Amen."

"Be they *none* is okay with me."

Victor slapped him on the arm. "Hey, I heard your future mother-in-law was coming. Wouldn't you rather fight a bunch of cartel gunslingers in a lawless land than face down the Queen of North Dallas?"

"Any day, brother." He smiled, remembering Charlie, bare from the waist up, stabbing him with a fingernail. Trying to be stern. *There will be blood.*

"Well, there you go." Victor broke off to toggle the radio and exchange technical gibberish with air traffic control. Yeager tuned out, holding on to the memory of Charlie's blue eyes and red hair for as long as he could.

"No, seriously, dude," Victor said, snapping Yeager back to reality. "You think I would go into a combat zone with nothing but my massive swinging dick? And my penis, too?"

"As if you *had* a penis."

Victor laughed. "Well, while the good father and I were touring your pond, for what? Like an hour, bro? Come on, man. Anyway, once I knew you were, ahem, excuse the pun, *coming*, I got on the phone with a friend of mine who owns a gun store in Uvalde."

"Gun store in Uvalde's not gonna do a damn bit of good. You want to fill out 4473s for some hunting rifles?"

"Keep your shirt on, killer. This friend of mine does some other business on the side. Sells things to some people south of the border."

"A gunrunner?" Yeager stared at his friend, expression set to: *Are you serious?* "A goddamn gunrunner? That's what you're counting on?"

"Hey, you know." Victor shrugged. "Beggars can't be choosers, amigo. He's got good connections down there. Solid. Not like the cartel people, just honest citizens who want protection from all the gangs running around. We hook up with him in Madera. He has a van; the insides look like an issue of *Guns & Ammo* magazine. Weapons galore."

The chopper bucked in a heavy air pocket, and Victor adjusted the cyclic, gaining a few feet of altitude.

"And who's paying for this?" Yeager asked.

"The Catholic Church of Mexico."

"You're shitting me."

"I told Father Dom I needed money for gas and supplies. He wrote me check with a bunch of zeroes."

"Where does a poor missionary orphanage come up with that kind of cash—and not ask for a receipt?"

"Is a mystery."

"You should be used to that feeling."

Victor scrunched his face into a frown. "Now you just being mean."

"Something about this deal strikes me as hinky."

"Hinky?"

"A condition of not normal, unusual, weird, FUBAR'd, or just plain *off*."

"Ah. I got that feeling too."

———————◆———————

Juan Guerrero's punishment for skipping school included enough lessons that his hand cramped into a claw from writing. The instructors kept him in a separate room, away from the other kids, and watched his every move, perched like Señora Mendoza's chickens.

After that, Father Sebastian sent him to the kitchen to wash dishes and clean up the dining room. The head cook—a vile, skinny man who reeked of cheap cigarettes—supervised his work. The cook smacked him with a ladle whenever he slacked off then giggled like a girl when Juan flinched.

He didn't finish cleaning until long after the end of television time in the rec room. The cook released him with a grunt then whacked him with the ladle when he didn't move fast enough. Juan glared but kept his hand in his pocket, covering the twelve packets of sugar he'd squirreled away when the ladle monster wasn't looking.

A few steps from the kitchen, he passed the door to the basement. He had never been in the basement, but he had heard from the older boys that the priests kept a torture chamber down there—fully equipped to drag confessions from small boys. Every time he passed the basement door, he pictured being chained to the wall, a spike-filled metal cage clamped to his face.

It was late at night, and light pooled around wide-spaced fixtures. He heard nothing but the shuffling of his own feet, so the spookiness factor pegged the needle on the creepy meter.

The basement door swung open as he passed it. Juan jumped back like a startled cat, both fists raised and heart pounding. A tall figure in black robes floated from the darkness of the basement and loomed over him. At first he thought—well, he didn't know what he thought except that maybe Death had come for him.

"Juan," Death said. "What are you doing out of your room this late?"

Juan swallowed and blinked. The tall figure in black robes resolved into Father Dietrich, the German priest. Not Death, but someone who looked a lot like a dead man. With pale skin stretched tight over a bony face and deeply sunken eyes, the priest reminded Juan of a monster from a horror movie.

"I... I, uh..."

"Speak up, boy."

"Kitchen duty, Father," Juan managed at last. He waved a shaky hand in the direction of the kitchen.

"Well, get to your room." The priest jingled a ring of keys in his hand and turned to the basement door. "It is after lights-out."

"Yes, Father." Juan wasted no time hanging around. He took off while Father Dietrich fiddled with the lock. It wasn't until he was almost to his room that he wondered what the spooky priest was doing down in the basement this late at night.

━━━━━❖━━━━━

At four o'clock in the afternoon, the school bus hissed to a stop in front of Yeager's place, the squeal of brakes coming to Oscar's ears moments after the yellow vehicle stopped. A ginger-haired boy got off, and Oscar trained the spotting scope on him as the kid shouldered his backpack and headed toward the house.

The dog bounded around the boy in wide circles, barking.

The woman came out, wearing a denim shirt over a T-shirt. Oscar refocused on her magnified image. She said something to the boy that was lost in the distance.

They went inside and closed the door. And nothing else happened for two hours except for some lights coming on inside the house.

With nightfall, the temperature dropped to almost freezing. Oscar's nose was cold and running constantly, and all his muscles

45

were stiff. He had waited throughout the day but saw no indication that the man, Abel Yeager, was present at the home or would be anytime soon.

Oscar could see nothing beyond the curtains. He waited another hour, just to be sure, but Yeager did not come in or out of the house. At seven, Oscar packed up his gear. He got out a tiny flashlight and used its feeble illumination to guide his way back through the woods to his car.

Creepers tried to trip him, and once he cursed aloud when he blundered into a spiderweb and spent several panicky moments brushing it off.

How long? How long do I wait?

That thought continued to loop through his mind. If he moved too soon, chances were he'd lose the man, Yeager, whom he wanted to kill more than anybody. The woman was a secondary prize, and the boy just an accessory.

But still, if there was a relationship there, maybe killing the woman and kid would hurt Yeager more than death itself. After taking everything Oscar owned from him, Oscar would return the favor. There was a certain... *justice* there.

He found his car where he'd left it behind an old barn, and he started it up, turning the heater on and cursing again at the cold air blowing through the vents. It was time to make a decision. How long should he wait? Blowing and chafing his numb fingers, he came to a decision.

Two days. I'll wait two more days. Then I kill everyone at the house and see what happens from there.

CHAPTER 8

YEAGER CHECKED THE TIME WHEN the skids touched down at their final destination in Mexico, north of Ciudad Madera. His watch read 19:20 hours. The Huey settled into the soft soil of the pasture turned landing field, the engine whining as Victor and their new copilot, Riley Amick, flipped switches and shut down power. Yeager pushed out of his seat and worked the kinks from his back by twisting and stretching.

Father Dominic had arranged with a rancher to provide a lighted landing zone for the Huey. The rancher had promised no one would bother the helicopter. A ring of trees concealed the pasture, and his men would stand guard until Victor and Yeager completed the delivery.

Riley handed a small satchel back through the cabin divider. Many years ago, Victor had fashioned a concealed compartment under the copilot's seat to carry anything he might want to keep away from the prying eyes of Customs officials. He called it his Han Solo hole. Before leaving Del Rio, Victor had packed the compartment with three pistols, including Yeager's, along with all their spare magazines and ammo.

They'd made a brief stop across the border from Del Rio, in Ciudad Acuna, to clear Customs and Passport Control and to file a flight plan for Madera. Mexican Customs officials barely glanced into the Huey before stamping passports and wishing them a nice day. Yeager had breathed much easier when they lifted off again. Smuggling the sidearms was a risk, but landing in unknown territory, in the dark, on a mission contrary to the cartel's enforcement goons was a bigger one.

Yeager seated his Springfield XDM in a high-rise clamshell holster under his plain green hoodie and snapped the magazine pouch on the other side. He didn't need to do a Hollywood chamber check. He never carried a weapon without one up the spout. After six hours of riding in a noisy chopper, drinking coffee from a thermos, and peeing in a plastic jug, he was happy to be on the ground and just wanted to get far away from helicopters. He popped the cargo door and slid it back, to be greeted by a blinding bright light.

"Obtener esa cosa fuera de mis ojos!" He covered his face with his forearm. *Get that thing out of my eyes.*

"Oh. Pardon me, señor." The man spoke in Spanish, his tone deferential. All Yeager could identify was a shape in the darkness wearing a cowboy hat. He squinted and made out several human silhouettes standing by headlights of three vehicles.

Yeager slung his bag over one shoulder and hustled from under the spinning rotors, aiming for the pickups. Victor and Riley joined him a few seconds later. The guy with the flashlight pointed it toward the ground and trailed behind.

In the middle of the group, a single figure stood a step apart from the others. By their body language, the others seemed to defer to this man, and as Yeager approached, he could see why. The man's age was impossible to read in the darkness, but Yeager would have guessed he was over sixty. The man was about six feet tall and wolf lean with predator eyes and black hair combed back. The leader of the pack, without question.

Yeager held out a hand and introduced himself. The man's grip was strong, firm, and dry. He flashed a white-toothed smile and spoke with a powerful voice.

"Mucho gusto, Señor Yeager. My name is Raphael Martinez y Beltran de la Cueva." He paused for a beat. "You may call me Ralph. Come, let us go to the house. My men will take you into Madera once we've had some coffee. Bueno?"

"Muy bueno," Yeager said. "This tall, skinny boy here is Riley Amick, and the short, ugly one is Victor Ruiz."

Everybody piled into the vehicles: an old Jeep Cherokee, a GMC, and a Dodge Ram. The Ram carried more chrome than a 1966

Cadillac. Yeager rode shotgun in the Ram next to a dark-skinned Indio with a bushy mustache. A short, bumpy ride along fence-line trails brought them to the main house… although calling this place a house would be like calling Buckingham Palace an old fixer-upper.

Yeager whispered under his breath, "Oh my God."

The driver chuckled and said in Spanish, "Yes, everyone says that the first time they see casa de la Cueva."

A wall, twelve feet high, circled the property. Redoubts anchored the corners, obviously there for defensive purposes. A cleared dead zone of land surrounded the wall for a hundred yards in all directions. The caravan lined up at a steel gate that moved open like a massive garage door.

When they entered the protected area, the full scope of the compound came into view. Four stories tall, the main residence had been built of native stone with a terra cotta roof in what Yeager would call medieval Spanish style. Two outbuildings flanked the main house, built of similar material.

The drive led to a lighted courtyard with a garage to the left of the house. Except for the driveway, some stone paths, and the courtyard, the remaining space was given over to a garden full of trees and flowering bushes.

"Why the wall?" Yeager asked, though he suspected he knew the answer.

"This land is very lawless these days." The dark-skinned man's face, lit only by the dashboard, held a sad expression. "The cartels and the troublemakers run everywhere, killing who they want. Don de la Cueva built the wall many years ago, when the narcos started taking over more and more of the police and the army."

"Have you been attacked?"

"Not yet." The man shrugged. "It is only a matter of time."

Yeager remained silent, feeling as if he'd fallen through a magic mirror to another world—one of those movies where the aircraft travels through a rift in the space-time continuum. Some things weren't adding up. First, the supposedly poor orphanage could afford to write a blank check to a small-time helicopter pilot. The same priest then arranged a secure landing zone in the backyard of a megawealthy landowner, who offered them coffee as though they'd just dropped in for a visit.

Inside, de la Cueva led his guests and another man he introduced as his foreman to what he called the Gun Room. Yeager froze and stared in open-eyed awe.

The room resembled a hunting lodge with a Southwestern flair. A timber wolf snarled from a corner, preserved by a taxidermist of tremendous skill. Other museum-quality trophies—from a pheasant to a sailfish—were mounted throughout the room, each one frozen midmotion. Four gun cases were spaced around the walls, each lit by its own low-wattage bulb. Other firearms, both vintage and modern—a utilitarian M-16 to the left of the fireplace caught his eye—were displayed on custom-made dowels driven into the walls.

A coffee service waited on an antique buffet against the far wall, its silver urn warming over a blue flame. A slender girl in a maid's outfit stood at attention next to it.

"Please," de la Cueva said. "Sit. Costanza will pour your coffee. The washroom is through that door if you'd like to freshen up. Then we can discuss logistics."

"Sounds good," Victor said. "Talk to the ugly one. Yeager likes logistics."

Yeager scowled at Victor. "If it's a *short* subject, you should handle it." Smiling at their host, he said, "Pardon me, señor, but I think I'll go wash my hands."

"By all means."

Yeager fought a yawn and went through the door to the washroom. Inside was a toilet with a polished wooden seat, brass fittings, and the smell of money. Yeager took a leak, feeling almost sacrilegious for soiling such a beautiful fixture.

He washed his face and hands and dried off with a velvet-soft towel. Cleaning up didn't do much for the grittiness in his eyes and weariness caused by a day's worth of traveling in a noisy, vibrating helicopter. The idea of finding a place to take a nap seemed really appealing.

"You're getting old, buddy," he told the man in the mirror. "Time was, you could fight all day and party all night. Now look at you. How'd you get into this mess anyway?"

The tired-looking guy in the mirror had nothing to say.

From his front yard, Cristian Guzman had an unobstructed view of the orphanage-cum-hospital called Mission San Felipe de Cristo. He lit a new cigar with a wooden kitchen match then passed the box to his oldest son, Herman, who fired up a Marlboro. The aluminum lawn chair creaked, and the webbing dug into his butt when he shifted. He sucked on the cigar, the tip brightening to a glowing orange and the smoke wreathing his face, working its magic through his pores.

The night air of Rascón had grown chilly, cool enough for Cristian to wear a jacket these last few nights, sitting under the stars in front of his clapboard two-room house. His son shook out the match and flicked it into the rocks at the edge of the dirt road. Insects danced around the light over his porch, not as many this time of year as in the summer but enough to draw the occasional swoop of a bat from the darkness to nibble the edges of the swarm.

"The truck will come soon?" Herman asked. Again. Impatience was a weakness of the youth.

"So said the priest."

"Good. I'm tired of waiting. I want out of this stinking little town."

"Some places are worse than Rascón." Cristian drew another mouthful of smoke and puffed it into the air.

"Are you going to tell me again about how you went to jail in America for six years? How you drove a truck for the coyotes and they caught you with twenty *indocumentados* and sent you to prison? This I have heard before."

Respect for their elders was another virtue lacking in the youth of today.

"Yes, you have heard that story." Cristian moved and spoke with deliberation. Herman, in contrast, was a long and lanky boy with hair to his shoulders, jerky movements, and machine-gun speech. "Have you also heard the story of how we came to be in this country? Of what we did to survive Somoza's people in Nicaragua?"

Herman scowled but remained silent. For a change. He knew those stories very well because Cristian had told the whole family the story of that journey through hell. Forty years later, he still jerked awake two or three times a week, bathed in sweat from half-remembered dreams of those days.

"Not long, my son. The priest said the truck will come. Once it does, we have but a few hours' work, and we will be gone from this place. Gone to somewhere much better."

"Seems funny." Herman snapped his cigarette away, spiraling it into the dark, trailing sparks.

"What?"

"Working for a priest, for a change."

Cristian remained silent for a long time, so long the coal on his cigar almost went out. When he did speak, it was slower and more deliberate than ever. "Yes, this is true. But I don't think we are on God's side."

CHAPTER 9

THE DIM GLOW OF THE Ciudad Madera lights lay across the horizon, an ochre haze against the backdrop of a clear mountain sky. Yeager's eyes followed the twin beams of the Suburban's headlights bathing the road in silver at 80 kph. De la Cueva's foreman, Rudy Aguilar, drove in companionable silence. A hatchet-faced man with hooded eyes bracketed by deep laugh lines, he smiled often but said little. He kept an ancient straw cowboy hat affixed to his head, its brim curled up and stained.

Riley and Victor rode in the middle seats while two more of de la Cueva's men squeezed into the jump seats in back, each carrying a Heckler & Koch UMP submachine gun. Aguilar introduced them as Dino and Miguel, but Yeager forgot which was which in a second.

A lot of firepower for a simple trip to town. He repeated the thought out loud to Aguilar, who shrugged.

"Madera is controlled by the cartel people, Señor Yeager. The police, they are pigs. Those who don't work for the cartel are too afraid to interfere. At times, gunmen have roamed the streets at will, taking what they want." He shrugged again. "It is best to be prepared, yes?"

"It's like the Wild West down here," Yeager muttered, not intending to be heard, but Aguilar's ears must have been pretty sharp.

"Very much so," he said. "These mountains have been refuge to many outlaws, revolutionaries, and Indians. The narcos are the newest and best armed of all."

"Tell me about the supply truck," Yeager said.

"What would you like to know?"

"First off, what kind is it?"

Rudy shrugged. "Red. That's all I know."

"Eighteen-wheeler?"

"Yes, big. The box in back is many meters long. Many wheels, although I did not count. It has a bulldog on the hood, you know? In chrome?"

"A Mack truck, then."

"If you say, señor."

"Who owns it?"

"Señor de la Cueva," Rudy said. "He owns many things in town. He once owned a timber company there before the cartels started fighting so much, then he sold it and... how do you say in English? Retired, yes?"

"Retired."

Yeager remained silent for a time, watching the road unspool ahead of them. A jackrabbit flashed to the right, bounding away from the road, there and gone in the blink of an eye.

"What about the supplies?" he asked.

"Supplies?"

"The stuff in the truck we're taking to the mission."

"Ah, sí, sorry." Aguilar grinned. "Many of the things were donated by people in the town or sent by another hospital to the one that was destroyed, yes? One that is, how do you say it? Affixed?"

"Affiliated?"

"Sí. And Señor de la Cueva donated many things, of course."

"Of course."

Victor spoke from the back for the first time since they started. Yeager thought he had been asleep.

"How does Señor de la Cueva fit into all this?"

"Que?"

Victor switched to Spanish. "Señor de la Cueva has gone to a lot of trouble and expense for this effort, correct? I mean, a truck, supplies, a landing strip..."

"Ah, sí. The mission was founded many years ago by an ancestor of de la Cueva. The ancestor grew rich from mining silver from the mountains and donated much money to the church to build the mission so that the people where he lived would have a church, yes? My boss, he has a strong sense of tradition and believes this is the right thing to do, to carry on his great-great many-times-great grandfather's work."

"How do you—"

"Excuse me, Señor Victor," Aguilar said. "We are coming into the outskirts of Madera. We need to be alert here, for the narcos would be very happy to kidnap three gringos and three of de la Cueva's people. They would think the ransom would be... very large."

"Buckle up," Yeager said. "The fun's about to start."

━━━━◆◆◆━━━━

Dr. Alexandra Lopez pumped the bulb of the blood-pressure cuff strapped to Señora Gutierrez and noted the result when she released the pressure. One-fifty over one hundred. Very high. She worked to keep her sigh to herself. Señora Gutierrez snored gently in her sleep and wouldn't notice any sound she made, but Alexandra had been a doctor too long to let her professional mask slip in front of a patient.

Five days off dialysis.

When the dialysis machine went down, the poisons started to build in the old lady's blood, killing her a little at a time. The discomfort had gotten steadily worse until Alexandra had sedated the woman to help her get some rest.

If the replacement machine doesn't come soon, I will have to attempt peritoneal dialysis. Not a good alternative.

Peritoneal dialysis would require that she insert a catheter into the abdomen and pump the patient full of dialysate then drain and refill to keep the poisons out. She had read about the practice in med school but had never seen it done, let alone attempted it.

Alexandra left the room, easing the door shut to avoid waking the elderly woman. A beneficial side effect of the evacuation to this remote mission was they had almost an entire wing vacant. Six of her most critical cases had their own rooms, while the remaining patients were doubled up. She and the nurses each had a private room.

In a previous evacuation, due to a gas leak, patients' beds had been lined up in the showroom floor of a local car dealership. By comparison, the facility here was Mount Sinai.

As she closed the door, the sound of a footstep behind her and a hand on her shoulder made her jump. "Oh!" She twisted to find Father Dietrich towering over her. "I didn't hear you come up."

The tall, blond-haired priest gave her a tiny bow of his head. "My apologies, Doctor. I didn't mean to frighten you."

She had learned Father Dietrich emigrated from Germany to Mexico sometime in the past few months. "For the climate," he'd said. Of all the priests, Dietrich stood out not only for his height—well over two meters—but for his Frankenstein demeanor.

The man gave her the creepy crawlies.

"It's just so late," Alexandra said, keeping her voice low. "I wasn't expecting anybody else to be about."

He gestured her away from the patient's door and then fell in step beside her. "I am often up late." His German-accented Spanish was textbook correct but hard to understand. "With a house full of boys and girls, it is wise to remain vigilant."

"I'm sure you're right." A nervous smile twitched at her face. Her heart was still pounding from the spooky priest sneaking up on her.

"I came to ask you a favor. One of our charges, a young girl named Emelita, has been complaining of some stomach problems. I was wondering if you might stop in to see her tomorrow morning."

"Yes," she said. "Of course I will. What are her symptoms?"

"Excessive schoolwork, I suspect."

A laugh bubbled out of her unexpectedly. *So Frankenstein has a sense of humor after all.*

"Is there anything you need, Doctor? Anything I can provide you with, I mean." The tall priest spoke with all the emotion and warmth of a frozen zombie, completely at odds with his solicitous words.

"No. Nothing, thank you." Alexandra paused at the next patient's door, her hand on the knob. The nighttime hush in the deserted hall made her feel as if she had been stranded in a *Twilight Zone* episode with a strange android in priest's clothing. A corpse sitting up in bed waiting for her in the next room wouldn't surprise her at all.

With a grave tilt of his head, Father Dietrich moved on, ghosting away on near-silent steps. He went through the stone arch at the end of the corridor and disappeared around the corner. Alexandra let out a breath that she did not remember taking.

"We're here," said the foreman, Aguilar.

Here turned out to be a gate in the middle of an eight-foot-tall board fence topped with concertina wire. The fence surrounded a warehouse in the industrial part of Madera, one of a number of similar places Yeager had seen coming through town. Other than a stray dog slinking away, nothing moved along the fence line.

Aguilar got out and stood in the beam of the headlights, flipping through a ring of keys until he found the right one for the padlock. When the gate swung open, the wiry foreman jumped back in the Suburban and gunned the big vehicle into the warehouse yard. He parked next to an eighteen-wheeler backed up to an overhead dock door. Over the door, insects danced in the light of a humming security bulb.

On the other side of the truck, a beat-up, dusty Toyota Corolla with mismatched fenders and no hubcaps deteriorated in silence.

Yeager was the first out, scanning the yard for threats, hackles raised. For the past twenty minutes, Aguilar had transmitted nervousness like heat waves. Yeager adjusted the pistol in its high-rise holster, confirming the gun wouldn't snag if he had to draw it.

He checked his watch again—22:04. Early for a town in Mexico. People would be finishing their evening meals and getting ready to go out, if that was what they planned. For all that, not much seemed to be going on. In the distance, a car's horn beeped, and tinny Latino music drifted from several streets away.

The warehouse itself wasn't much: a tin building about the size of a restaurant, with a corrugated metal roof, three loading docks, and an office door. The fenced-in gravel yard was big enough to turn a Lincoln Towncar around in, if you didn't mind scratching the fenders. A single security light glowed at the peak of the building's eaves.

Victor climbed out of the car and went through a series of stretches and deep knee bends. Riley Amick, the image of a lean, lanky Texan, tamped a can of Skoal against his palm and pinched out a dip. Both of Yeager's companions had visible sidearms on their hips, and both were in surveillance mode. Their eyes never rested in one place or looked anything less than alert.

The two de la Cueva men with machine guns slipped out to the street entrance and took up positions by the gate, holding their weapons down by their sides. Each man seemed relaxed, but Yeager noted they kept their index fingers extended against the trigger guards of their submachine guns. They didn't laugh or joke or so much as crack a smile.

Aguilar went to the office door and fumbled through his ring of keys again. He disappeared inside, not bothering with lights. Moments later, the big overhead door rattled up.

"Señor Yeager, please, you will find some bags of ice in a cooler in the back of the car. We need to keep some of these medications cool."

"You hear that, Por Que?" Yeager called. "Get the man his ice from the back."

"Heh. You a funny gringo." Victor opened the back hatch. "Remember, you the minority in this country."

Victor reached into the compartment, grunted, and deadlifted an ice chest that probably weighed a hundred pounds. His arms stretched across the top of the cooler, cantaloupe-sized biceps swollen with effort. Riley moved to help, but Victor shook him off.

"Nah, I got this." Victor waddled, stiff-legged, to the loading bay.

"This truck belongs in a museum," Yeager muttered and went to get a look at the tractor-trailer rig. Riley met him there. Riley had flown helicopters with Victor in Afghanistan, but Yeager didn't know much about him except he made a cigar-store Indian seem talkative.

"Why do y'all call him 'Por Que'?" Riley asked with a dusty Texas twang. The question surprised Yeager, coming as it did from a man who acted as though each word he used cost a dollar.

"When we were kids in McAllen," Yeager said, "every time

somebody would tell Victor he shouldn't or couldn't do something, he'd ask 'Por que no?'" Yeager inspected the driver's front tire then went around to the passenger side of the Mack. "Means *why not* in Spanish. That little phrase got me in more trouble than a preacher in a whorehouse."

The tall man smiled and turned his head to spit. Yeager went on to inspect the rear tires, checking the rubber for cracks in the tread or bulges in the sidewall. Losing a tire on this beast in the ass end of the Sierra Madres would be… annoying.

The trailer had two sets of dual wheels under the cargo box, which made a total of eight tires to inspect there and ten more on the main tractor. He was on the last tire on the passenger side, wishing for a flashlight, when a squeal of brakes from the front gate froze him in place.

Men shouted conflicting demands in Spanish, so fast Yeager couldn't tell who said what. He pulled the XDM and swept off the thumb safety. With both hands supporting the weapon, Yeager stayed in his crouch and duckwalked to the front of the truck.

The shouting escalated in volume to the feverish intensity of imminent violence:

"Drop your guns!"

"Go away, or we will shoot!"

"Drop it, now!"

Yeager came level with the front wheel of the Mack and took a quick look. A Toyota 4Runner and a midsized sedan of some kind blocked the gate. All the car doors were open, and eight men, wearing masks, confronted the two guards, Miguel and Dino.

The Mack had a flat fender over each front wheel, which made a perfect gun rest. Yeager braced the pistol on top of the fender and picked out a target: a young man in a plaid Western shirt and jeans. His hair slicked to a peak on top of his head, the man wore a bandana over his nose and mouth and pointed an F2000 bullpup submachine gun at the men by the gate. The FN F2000 held a thirty-round magazine and could shred Dino and Miguel into hamburger in seconds. Yeager settled the front sight on the middle button of the man's shirt.

"Hey!" Yeager had trained his sergeant's voice in the United States Marine Corps. When he barked a command, men paid attention. "Shut the fuck up!"

The masked men flinched when he spoke, eight heads snapping in his direction. They appeared taken aback by the confrontation from an unexpected flank. Yeager planned to use that moment of surprise against them.

Take the initiative. If he could exert enough command presence, he might be able to back these guys off without firing a shot.

"You boys ready to die today?"

CHAPTER 10

THE FRONT HALF OF THE San Felipe mission housed the dining hall, kitchen, and cathedral. The back section was built in a square around a central courtyard, each side lined with dormitory-style rooms or teaching facilities.

Alexandra didn't have far to go to find the room with Emelita, the sick child Father Dietrich wanted her to see. Emelita and another girl slept in a small but comfortable space, not unlike a college dorm, in the same wing of the quadrangle as the refugees from the hospital. No posters of rock stars decorated the walls; however, plenty of childish drawings and other school art were taped to the plaster.

"How long has it been hurting, *mi hermosa?*" Alexandra asked after she'd introduced herself and taken the girl's temperature. Emelita had delicate features and the eyes of a fawn—the kind of girl Alexandra's father would have called a little heartbreaker, although at the moment she looked quite ill and her hair was lank and damp from perspiration. She had a mild fever of 101.

"Since yesterday, Señora Doctor."

"You know, Emelita..." Alexandra leaned close and whispered like a conspirator. "You know, I don't let many people call me Alex."

Emelita nodded as if she knew that for an absolute fact.

"But you, my angel, may call me Dr. Alex. Okay?"

The little girl giggled and pulled the covers up to her chin.

"No, sweetie; I need to feel your tummy." Alexandra palpitated Emelita's abdomen while keeping up a stream of questions. "How old are you, Emelita?"

"Nine."

"Have you been throwing up? Or going potty a lot?"

"I threw up after lunch. Father Dietrich was angry."

"Nauseated? Sick to your stomach?"

"Sí. All the time now."

"Does it hurt when I push here?" Alexandra pressed under the girl's rib cage.

"No."

"How long have you lived here?"

The girl paused and looked at the ceiling as if seeking the answer there. "Uh, I don't know. Since forever, I think."

"Aw, my little one; I'm so sorry."

"Don't be sorry, Dr. Alex. I will have a new family soon. Father says so."

"How about when I push here?"

"No."

"Well, I hope it's true that you are adopted very soon. I'm going to poke you some more, okay?"

"Oh, I know it will happen, Dr. Alex. All the girls find new homes before they are twelve."

"All of them?"

"Yes. My friend, Beatrice"—she indicated the empty bed next to hers—"left with Father last week, before the earthquake, to go to her new home. He said she went to a nice family."

"How about the boys?"

"Boys are icky. Nobody wants the boys. *Aieeee!*"

"Oh, sorry. That feels very tender there, huh?"

"Ow, it hurts!" Emelita sniffled and moaned again.

Alexandra eased the covers up and patted the girl's shoulder. "Well, little dove, it may be your appendix is acting up a little bit, or you could have a nasty tummy bug. I am going to have a nurse come by and take some blood, okay? We need to know your blood type in case we have to pop that mean old appendix out."

"Will it hurt?" Emelita looked ready to cry.

"Would Dr. Alex hurt you, sweetie?"

"Nooooo." The tiny girl seemed unconvinced.

Alexandra talked with her for a few more minutes before patting her hand and promising to be back in a little while to check on her. She closed the girl's door behind her and let out the sigh she'd been holding on to. She was ninety percent certain Emelita's appendix was infected, and the only known cure for appendicitis was surgery.

"How in the hell," she muttered, "am I supposed to operate in the ass end of nowhere with no spare blood, no operating table, and no anesthesia?"

That truck better come soon, or we'll be digging two graves instead of one.

If Yeager had to pick an alpha dog of the pack facing them, he would choose the kid in the Western shirt with the F2000. Yeager thought of him as Mohawk because of the peak in his hair and because he seemed the most aggressive. He stood the farthest forward and, before Yeager had intervened, had been doing the most yelling. When Yeager asked if they wanted to die today, Mohawk fixed him with a hot stare of pure molten *fuck you.*

In the hesitation after his challenge, the silence stretched for a heartbeat, then two.

"You in this, Riley?" Yeager called out, never taking his front sight off the leader.

"Yep." Riley's laconic voice placed him down low, probably under the truck's engine block. *Smart man.*

"What about you, Victor?"

"Por que no?" Victor called out from somewhere near the warehouse doors. "I got the two on the left. Riley, take right."

"So, boys," Yeager said in his border Spanish. "You have a choice."

The armed thugs shifted, some pointing weapons in one direction, some in the other, all of them confused and off balance. With each new voice from Yeager's side, they seemed to grow uneasier. What started out as an eight-to-two slaughter had turned into an eight-to-five firefight with the gang standing in the open. Anybody would be a mite uncomfortable in similar circumstances.

Except Mohawk, who unleashed a torrent of Spanish too fast for Yeager to follow.

"Come again?" he asked.

The man switched to harshly accented English. "I say, you the one gon' die, *cabrone*. You give truck, we no kill. No give truck, we kill ever'one."

"Well, podnah," Yeager drawled. "That just ain't gonna happen. Now, I ain't got all night, so you got three seconds to back off before I shoot you where you stand. Go home. You're too young to die tonight."

The tableau held for a silent moment, and the gang leader's eyes narrowed. Yeager had time to think, *He's not going to back down.*

Mohawk made his move, twisting at the hip and bringing the submachine gun up. His trigger finger spasmed, and the gun spewed a line of fire. Like many inexperienced shooters, Mohawk fired too soon. Bullets splattered and sparked into the gravel yard, racing in a line toward Yeager's position.

Yeager double-tapped Mohawk in the chest. Two .45 jacketed hollow points blew the thug's heart out and punched him back and down, shutting off the torrent of fire from his weapon.

The rest of his gang reacted by cutting loose, filling the night with bright flashes and the percussive beat of weapons on full auto. Yeager picked another target. This one was down on one knee, firing a pump shotgun at de la Cueva's men. The XDM bucked in his hand. The shotgun whirled away as its shooter spilled to the ground. A section of his skull departed on a different trajectory.

Yeager registered the pulse of fire from Riley's position and from the warehouse even as he sought another target. Four of the opposition were down, and the remainder were scattering for cover behind their vehicles. Dino and Miguel were blocked from sight by the truck, but the firing from their UMPs had gone silent.

The XDM held thirteen rounds in its double-stacked magazine, a wealth of ammunition for Yeager. He found it almost obscene that it had nearly twice as many rounds as his old 1911 .45 semi-auto.

Yeager fired at a man ducking around the front of the sedan, noting a solid hit when the bandit stumbled. He fired again, and the man went down for good. Either Victor or Riley took out one by the SUV with a well-placed shot to the face. The last two thugs abandoned their positions and pelted away, vanishing into the alley across the street.

Ears ringing and with the reek of gunpowder burning his sinuses, Yeager safed his weapon but didn't holster it. *No way to know if we're out of the woods.*

"Victor?" he yelled. "You good?"

"No problema! Me and Rudy are good."

"Riley?"

"Yo."

Yeager came around the truck and helped Riley get to his feet as he slid out from under the vehicle. One glance confirmed his suspicion that Dino and Miguel were dead. Both men were peppered with bullet wounds. Caught in the open, they hadn't stood much of a chance.

"Uh, Yeager?" Riley said.

"What's up?"

"Problem."

The skinny Texan pointed to the front of the Mack, where a steady stream of greenish-brown liquid drizzled from the grill.

Oscar finagled the folding canvas camp chair back into its tubular carrying case, struggling in the darkness and working hard not to spew a long stream of obscenities. He had stayed in the woods much later than the previous night, watching the farmhouse until after ten.

Last night, after cleaning up in his motel room, he'd driven into the suburbs of Austin to a sporting-goods store. There he'd bought the camp chair—which, theoretically at least, was supposed to fit back in the carrying bag—a camouflaged winter coat, heated socks powered by small batteries, and a giant thermos for coffee. If he had to sit in the woods, at least he wouldn't freeze his ass off and catch a chill from the wet ground.

But that day had proven as fruitless as the last. No Yeager— indeed, no man at all—had shown up. The boy, the dog, and the woman had been there. No one else.

All day he had brooded, feeling the anger bubble up, remembering the pounding of a bucking pistol eliminating his enemies, the smell of their blood rich in his nostrils. How had he buried that away for so long? He itched to let the demons run free again.

Tomorrow night, he decided once the goddamned chair had gone in the bag. *Tomorrow night, I go down there and kill them all.*

He felt the Taser in his coat pocket, not for the first time that day. He would shoot the dog first, of course, with his pistol. No sense in taking chances there. Then he would Taser the woman and secure her with plastic ties. He wanted to destroy her in the most awful way he could imagine so that Yeager's soul would burn whenever he thought about the pain she had suffered.

The boy? That would depend on circumstances. Maybe he could be restrained easily and, if so, share the same fate as the woman. If not? Then Oscar planned to shoot him like the dog and avoid complications.

His brother, Humberto, may have been the operational arm of their partnership, but both of them had grown up on the same mean streets and learned their trade at the feet of the most brutal men in Mexico. Oscar remembered how to instill terror and fear in the minds of his enemies. It was all coming back to him. The acts he planned for the woman would rip screams from her throat.

Oscar grinned, bundled his supplies on his back, and crunched away into the dark forest.

CHAPTER 11

"**R**ILEY," YEAGER SNAPPED. "GET THOSE bodies out of here. Dump 'em in the 4Runner, and drive it off around the corner. Hide it as best you can. Put our guys in the Suburban; don't cart them off with the trash. Victor!"

"Yo?" The pilot appeared at the front of the Mack truck and pulled up short at the puddle of coolant. "Aw, shit."

Rudy Aguilar joined them. "Fucking cartel pigs."

"Scavenge all the weapons and ammunition you can find," Yeager told Victor. "Sort out what fits what and consolidate."

"You got it. What about the...?" He pointed at the coolant-soaked ground.

"I don't know yet. Rudy, your boss got any more diesel trucks this size?"

The foreman gave a miserable shake of his head, panning it from side to side in slow motion.

"Okay, help me get this hood up," Yeager said, going to the latch on the driver's side. "See this? Go pop the one on the other side, then help me tip the hood up. It tilts forward from here. Then get me a goddamned flashlight!"

"Sí!"

With everybody moving, Yeager concentrated on working the problem in front of him. He and Rudy tipped the hood of the big diesel until it rested against its stops. The foreman hustled to the Suburban and ducked into the open driver's door.

Yeager crawled up onto a strut and, squinting in the dim light from the security fixture mounted to the warehouse, tried to find the leak. He found one spot right away at the top of the radiator. A bullet had ricocheted off the grill and angled up, tearing an inch-long gash in the top section of the radiator reservoir.

"How is it?" Rudy asked when he appeared with a plastic flashlight.

Yeager took it and focused the dim yellow beam on the radiator coils. "We may have gotten a little lucky. If a bullet hit the coils, we ain't got a snowball's chance of fixin' it. If this cut on the top is all..."

Yeager forced himself to slow down and pan the light across the face of the radiator. He didn't allow a sigh of relief until he'd covered every square inch of cooling coil and found nothing leaking and no other holes. Then he checked it again. The coils were dinged and battered, filled with all the species of dead bugs known to science, so it was slow going. Missing a puncture in all the mess would result in a lot of wasted effort.

"Rudy, can you bring me a jug of water?"

"Sí, señor." The man ran for the office on his spindly legs.

While he was gone, Yeager used the flashlight to inspect the rest of the engine for damage. Once done there, he checked the air canisters and tires then crawled underneath the engine compartment to look for leaks in the oil pan, transmission case, and anywhere else a bullet might have punctured something vital.

Satisfied the radiator was the only casualty on the Mack, Yeager waited for the foreman to return. Rudy came back with a two-liter plastic Coke bottle, holding it with a palm over the open top. Thanking him, Yeager took it, poured the water into the radiator, and watched for leaks.

Two minutes ticked by. Nothing drained from the radiator in any unexpected places.

"Well, maybe we can still make this puppy run," he said. "It all depends on you, Rudy. We need an acetylene torch, or an arc welder would be better. That and some brazing rods or silver solder. What about it?"

Rudy pursed his lips in thought. "We have a torch." He enunciated with care. "It is at the ranch, in the tool shed. I can have someone bring the torch and the welding supplies you need."

"Do it," Yeager said. "And tell them to haul ass. Those two boys that got away are probably going for reinforcements. No telling how long until they get back."

Rudy nodded, snapped open his cell phone, and stabbed the keypad. Yeager glanced at his watch; it was 22:32—an hour and a half before midnight—and they hadn't even left Madera yet.

Victor straightened up from his chore under the tailgate of the Suburban when Yeager came up.

"What are you thinking, hombre?" Por Que asked.

"We only lost whatever coolant was in the top section. Maybe a quarter gallon? Maybe less. I'm thinking I can solder a patch on the radiator that'll hold it long enough to get to the mission. After that..." He shrugged. "When does your gunrunner get here?"

Victor glanced at his watch. "Twenty minutes, give or take."

"Call him. Tell him to bust open a can of quick."

"You got it. In the meantime, we got a wide and varied selection of firearms for your shooting pleasure." Victor pronounced "shooting" with a *ch* sound. He spread his arms like a game-show host doing a reveal of Door Number One.

Besides the two UMPs that Miguel and Dino had carried, there was also the bullpup used by the late Mr. Mohawk, two M4s, and three AK-47s. Victor stacked the extra magazines for the tactical weapons next to their respective guns.

"Well, that ought to hold us for a little while," Yeager admitted. He picked up an M4, cycled the action, and checked for barrel obstructions. Satisfied, he snapped a full magazine in place and pocketed two more. The extra mags made his hoodie sag at the waist.

"Look atchu!" Victor said. "Rambo of my double-wide trailer."

"Don't you have a phone call to make?" Yeager left him and went to the truck. He rooted through the cab and found a metal box with a selection of rust-covered tools. Taking out a flat-blade screwdriver and a ball-peen hammer, he attacked the tin door of the warehouse office. Minutes raced by faster than they should have. He kept checking his watch. Time was sliding away, moving them toward another collision with the cartel thugs.

He used the flat-blade screwdriver as a punch, knocking out

a ragged two-by-two-inch piece of aluminum. Start to finish, it took him twelve minutes to cut out the square. Once he had his makeshift patch cut free, he spent another four minutes hammering the edges flat.

Riley came back from ditching the bodies, and Yeager had him hold the flashlight while he crawled into position and worked at wrapping the small piece of tin across the top of the radiator, ensuring that it would completely cover the gash.

"What'd you do with the bodies?" Yeager asked.

"Ditched the car. Two blocks away, behind a vacant building."

"You wipe it down?"

Riley gave him a look.

"Sorry," Yeager said. "Just checking."

Too much liquid near the joint would keep the metal too cool to bond, so he had to drain more coolant from the radiator stopcock. Eighteen minutes were wasted looking for a pan to catch the runoff.

"Just use water," Riley said.

"Could do, but I'd rather have coolant."

In the medical supplies, Rudy turned up a bedpan, which worked better than expected.

A battered white Chevy step van with Mexican license plates and a primer-gray driver's door pulled in front the warehouse gate at 22:54. The van's headlights switched off. Elapsed time since the gunmen had run off: forty-six minutes. Victor went to the driver's side and spoke for a second, then the van pulled in the rest of the way, parking on the far side of the Suburban.

"Getting to be a traffic jam in here," Yeager said to Riley. The thin Texan nodded and spat a stream of tobacco juice. He had taken possession of the F2000 and held it at the ready, loosely pointed toward the newcomer. The *Star Wars*-looking weapon jarred with Riley's cowboy hat and boots.

"Rudy," Yeager said, "por favor, would you keep an eye at the gate? I hate getting snuck up on."

The foreman nodded and moved away.

A man dressed in biker gear popped out of the van and gave Victor a backslapping bear hug. "How're doing, ya crazy Messican fuck?" The gun dealer's voice bounced off the walls of the warehouse lot, too big to be contained in such a small space.

Victor winced. "Ssshhh! Dude, come on. We just, like, committed major felonies here. Can you turn it down a notch?" Standing beside the man, Victor looked like a baby bear next to a fully grown North American beer-belly grizzly.

"Yeager," Victor said. "This is John Wayne Smith. Smith, Yeager."

Yeager took a giant paw in one hand and felt the big man hold back from crushing his bones to powder. J. W. Smith would have to duck and turn sideways to get through a door. He wore a bandana over his hair, had a scruffy beard—more white than brown—a leather jacket over a Grateful Dead T-shirt, and saggy jeans that were old when Carter was president. The leather jacket had patches covering every surface and cause, from *POW-MIA* to the US flag to Harley-Davidson motorcycle logos.

"Hoo-wee," Smith said, dialing his voice down to a more normal level. "It sure weren't easy findin' you ol' boys out here. Call me Smitty. Everybody calls me Smitty."

After the rest of the introductions, Smitty threw open the double doors in the back of his van. Inside the cargo space, six containers, labeled "Medical Waste" in Spanish, lay stacked in two rows. Smitty pulled one loose and set it on the ground near the rear bumper.

"Now, Vic here didn't spefically say what y'all wanted," Smitty said, mangling *specifically*. Yeager couldn't decide if he spoke more like Foghorn Leghorn or Yosemite Sam. "So I brung ever'thing I could think of."

Opening the clasps, Smitty threw back the lid. "This ratchere is a Ruger SR-556 rifle with a Slide Fire grip. If y'all don't know what a Slide Fire does, it allows you to simulate burst and full au-toe. These are completely A-T-and-fucking-F legal. 'Cept here in Messico, of course, where ever'thing in mah truck is illegal."

Rudy whistled from the gate. Yeager looked up in time to see a Silverado pickup wheel into the driveway and stop. The driver cut the engine and climbed out, exchanging volleys of Spanish with the foreman. The passenger door opened, and a white-haired figure stepped out.

"Damn," Yeager said to Victor in a low voice. "De la Cueva's here. He's probably pissed about his men gettin' killed." He looked at the big gun dealer. "Sorry, Smitty, I don't have time for the sales pitch. Vic's in charge of armaments; he'll decide what we need. I have to go patch a radiator before the cartel shows up with reinforcements."

"Reinforcements?" said Smitty. "Reinforcements for what?"

Nurse Marta Beltran joined Alexandra in the hallway outside Emelita's room. She slipped a small tube of blood into her light-blue medical scrubs and gave the doctor a shake of her head. The nurse's expression—more sour than normal—snuffed out Alexandra's tiny spark of hope.

"I agree, Doctor. I think it is appendicitis."

Barrel shaped and battle hardened, Marta had been a nurse for more years than Alexandra had been alive. If there were a trauma, disease, or condition she hadn't seen, then the book on it had yet to be written. Alexandra would look at the blood sample under a microscope anyway and see if she could determine if the girl had an elevated white-blood count, but if Marta said appendicitis, that was as good as a lab confirmation.

"Please prepare the slides for me, Marta. I'll look at them later. Can you keep an eye on Emelita as well as the other patients?"

"Of course." The big nurse huffed and waddled away.

Since their evacuation to the mission, the two nurses had divided the day into twelve-hour shifts. Marta took nights, and Estella had the day shift. Estella was a sweet girl with a sunny disposition, but Alexandra would rather have Marta next to her—sour expression, battle-ax temper and all—in a medical emergency.

She sighed and rubbed her eyes. *Now, where can I find an operating room?*

CHAPTER 12

Y EAGER SET UP THE TORCH and the supplies he needed in the cramped space between the hood and the radiator. While he worked, de la Cueva ordered the loading of Dino and Miguel into the Silverado. Yeager climbed out as they settled the last body in the bed of the pickup.

"I'm sorry." Yeager shook de la Cueva's extended hand. "They were caught in the open and didn't stand a chance."

"I understand," the older man said. "It is hard, this land. I have known Dino since he was born. This will break his mother's heart."

Yeager escorted the rancher to the passenger side of the pickup, where he paused.

"Señor Yeager, these cartels..." De la Cueva put a hand on Yeager's shoulder and gave it a firm squeeze. His voice turned hard and feral. "These cunts! They are a plague and pestilence on my homeland. If you have any trouble from them, please señor, please call me, and you will find a ready ally."

"Good to know, sir. I appreciate it very much."

"Bueno." De la Cueva got in the truck and closed the door. The driver backed out of the lot and drove away, moving at a funereal speed.

Yeager went to work. The time was 23:03.

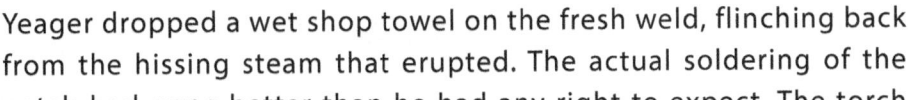

Yeager dropped a wet shop towel on the fresh weld, flinching back from the hissing steam that erupted. The actual soldering of the patch had gone better than he had any right to expect. The torch supplies came with sandpaper and flux paste, which made cleaning the weld area a simple task. Once he got the metal hot enough, the soldering rod melted and sucked into the joint just as it was supposed to with only a small amount of globbing up.

Yeager gingerly lifted the towel off with the tip of a screwdriver and inspected the joint.

"How's it look?" Victor asked.

"No holes, no cracks. Looks like the patch took." Yeager glanced at his watch. Half an hour till midnight. "Now the question is: will it hold under pressure?"

Riley handed him the bedpan full of coolant, and Yeager splashed it into the radiator then followed that with water from a plastic Coke bottle. He replaced the cap and tightened it. Handing Riley the tools, Yeager clambered out from the rabbit hole he'd squeezed into between the tilted-forward hood and the radiator.

His lower back screamed at him for being twisted into an awkward position for so long. Yeager stretched and twisted, trying to loosen up. Riley, Victor, and Smitty gathered around him in a semicircle without speaking. Rudy kept watch at the gate.

"We need to get moving," Yeager said. "I feel like ants are crawling up my spine, waiting for those cartel boys to come back. Victor, you and Riley take that beat-up Toyota. You have the GPS and a map, so you run point about a mile ahead of me. If you hit a roadblock, give me a sitrep on the radio. Keep your weapons out of sight, and do your dumb-Mexican routine."

"Sí, señor." Victor struck a gangbanger pose. "Obey-Juan says: nothin' here to see. These ain't the badasses chu lookin' for."

"Right. You get all the ordnance loaded?"

"Back of the truck."

"We should know within a few miles whether or not the radiator will hold, but one way or another, I plan to be as far from here as I can get. Smitty? What's up with you? I figured you to be gone by now."

"I'm all done. Just fixin' to leave. Good luck heppin' them kids and all."

"Thanks. Okay, let's—"

The roar of engines and the squeal of brakes shot a bolt of blue lightning through Yeager's heart. Rudy whistled, but it was unnecessary. The foreman crouched by the gate and jabbed a finger outside. His eyes glowed white in the darkness.

Rudy hissed, "They're coming!"

A *snap* from the fireplace jerked Charlie Buchanan from her light doze. For a moment, she struggled to separate her dream—a jumble of random images that dissipated into mist—from the reality of her own living room. Rascal lifted his head from the rug and regarded her for a moment then lay back down. A single lamp by her chair, and the dying embers of the fire, provided the only light in the room. The book she had been reading lay tented on her stomach.

The grandfather clock near the front door chimed its little song, and Charlie counted twelve dings. *Midnight.*

She shivered even though the room was warm enough. A Blue Norther had dropped temperatures to nearly freezing, but the house was well built and snug. So tight, in fact, she had to leave an upstairs window cracked so the fireplace would draw properly.

Yeager. Damn, I wish you were here.

The house seemed too big without him, as if his presence would take up the extra space. A pair of his work gloves rested on the coffee table, and under them lay a gun magazine, its cover ringed with impressions from a mug. The last remodeling project in the downstairs bathroom remained suspended—tools waiting, concrete floor bare, and walls half-covered with flower-print paper.

A strong gust of wind buffeted the house, and something rattled against the downstairs window, pulling Charlie from her moody reverie. She closed her book with a snap and set about getting the house ready for bed. She banked the fire, checked the door locks, set the alarm, and rinsed out the coffeepot.

Charlie couldn't remember a time she'd felt this blue over being alone. She had been alone seven years before she met Abel Yeager and, aside from grief over the divorce from her first husband, had handled the solitude without dipping into melancholy. At first, raising David had kept her busy. Then, as he had grown older, her son had become all the company she had needed. She never felt lonely when her son was around.

But now, for some reason, her mood had plummeted with the temperature. *Maybe I need some retail therapy. A trip to town would do us both good.*

The more she thought about it, the more the idea appealed. Tomorrow was Friday, so David would have the weekend off school as soon as he got home. She could pack them a couple of overnight bags and head for Austin. David could stay with Maria and Tomas, who would spoil him rotten. Charlie could maybe snag a room at one of the downtown hotels. One with a damn big spa. And, best of all, she could get some Christmas shopping done before the post-Thanksgiving rush.

Perfect. Already happier, she bounced up the stairs to get ready for bed, wondering what to get Abel for Christmas.

⊱✳⊰

"Rudy, get back from there." Yeager snagged his M4 from where it leaned against the Mack's front wheel and raced for the gate. While Yeager had been welding, Riley and Victor had pulled the first cartel group's Kia sedan inside the compound. They had maneuvered it across the opening to form a more protective barrier than the flimsy gate. Since a rifle bullet would punch right through the thin sides of an automobile, they had carried dozens of cinderblocks from the construction site next-door and stuffed them in the trunk and interior of the car. The Kia squatted on its springs, heavily overloaded.

The wooden slats in the fence were less than a half-inch thick and would barely stop a spit wad. The car and cinderblocks offered some solid metal and concrete as a barricade.

Yeager took up position by the trunk while Riley and Victor deployed to his left, bracing their weapons over the car's hood. Rudy faded back through a small gap between the car and the fence, circled around behind Yeager, and disappeared. The man was a ranch foreman, not a soldier, and Yeager had ordered him to get back to the warehouse if trouble broke out.

"Holy overkill, Batman," Victor yelled.

Smitty didn't join them, and Yeager had no time to look for him. Three SUVs were parked in a haphazard tangle across the street. The warehouse opposite de la Cueva's place had no surrounding fence, leaving nothing but thirty yards of open parking lot between their Kia and the cartel's vehicles.

A dozen-plus men bristling with tactical weapons boiled from the SUVs. The first wave lobbed random, unaimed fire as they scrambled for cover behind their cars. Yeager would be shredded by incoming fire if he tried to pull the truck through the gate, make a turn, and head west.

The good news: thirty yards was a picnic for a trained marksman. Yeager targeted the first gunman he found over his front sight and dropped him with a three-round burst. From there, it was shift-aim-fire, repeat, until the bolt locked back.

"Reloading!" He dropped behind the Kia's fender to swap magazines.

The cartel people had gotten warmed up. The incoming rounds spattered and thunked the Kia in a deadly hailstorm. The clatter of automatic weapons on full rock 'n' roll blended into a furious, monstrous barrage of sound as physical as the dozens of chunks of lead impacting Yeager's shelter every second. Glass shattered and spewed from the Kia's windows. The car settled toward the gate side as its tires blew out. Yeager sent up a quick prayer that a freak shot wouldn't hit the gas tank.

"This ain't good, Por Que." Yeager had to yell it twice. Victor and Riley had ducked for cover as well. "All they have to do is keep us pinned, then charge."

"Goddamn right!" Victor poked his AK-47 over the hood and fired a burst without looking. "We need a fucking plan, dude!"

The deluge of fire diminished. The attacking fighters had to change magazines, several at the same time. Yeager crawled to his right, by the back bumper of the Kia. He risked a quick peek. The cartel men appeared content to stay behind their vehicles and hose the Kia with enough lead to sink it through the earth.

One of the shooters ventured out from the protection of the middle SUV. He held something in his hand, cocked back to throw.

"Grenade!" Yeager snapped the M4 to his shoulder. He ripped off a quick burst, aiming by feel.

The man staggered and threw the grenade in a wobbly arc before collapsing. Yeager ducked and curled up. The *whump* of the explosion slapped him with the force of a mule kick. The concussion stung more than stunned, like an open-hand slap over his whole body.

"How many?" Victor called out. He fired without looking again. Riley stayed quiet, sitting with his back against the car. He spat between his knees, looking as calm as if he were waiting on a bus.

"Started with twelve or fifteen at most," Yeager said. "I count three down for good; another one or two I know are clipped."

The heavy thump of an enormous gun sounded from behind them. Yeager whipped around to follow the sound, and his eyes widened. "What the hell?"

"Yeah, go Smitty!" Victor screamed.

Smitty had not only climbed onto the peaked roof of the warehouse, but he'd also set up a Barrett .50-caliber rifle. The big man's booming laugh sounded over the next percussive beat of the Barrett. A deadly piece of machinery, the Barrett could rip through the flimsy protection of the bandits' vehicles like an ice pick through a beer can.

Yeager glanced around the back of the Kia again. The gunmen were in disarray, stunned and caught off guard by the heavy gun. One tried to take aim and fire back at their rooftop tormentor only to have his head taken off by a high-velocity .50-caliber round.

Four of the cartel men ran away, zigzagging across the parking lot. Another group remained, cowering behind the illusion of protection provided by their vehicles.

Yeager levered himself up. "I'm going to the right! Catch 'em in the flank." Smitty's laugh boomed out, and Yeager glanced up. He was stunned speechless for the second time that night. "Where the hell'd he get *that*?"

Smitty straddled the centerline of the roof. On his shoulder rested a rocket-propelled grenade launcher. One conical round was seated and ready to fire. The bearlike man lined up the simple sights and triggered the weapon.

Yeager dropped.

With a *whoosh* and a trail of smoke, the grenade arched over the warehouse lot. The grenade took the center SUV directly in the passenger door. A chest-slugging *crump* bounced Yeager off the ground. The cartel vehicle hopped up, and smoke blossomed from its mortally wounded body.

That was enough for the remaining opposition. The men huddling behind the other two SUVs bolted. They ran for the cover of the surrounding buildings... and kept going.

Victor jumped to his feet and screamed like a cheerleader. Smitty howled, and even Riley wore a big grin.

Yeager fist pumped the air. "All right, ladies. We're back in business. Let's get out of here before those yahoos come back with a tank."

"You're welcome," Smitty called out. "Now get the fuck outta here."

"You got it." Yeager ran to push the Kia out of the way.

He had a truck to drive.

CHAPTER 13

"**W**ELL, DON'T THAT JUST SUCK donkey balls," Smitty groused. They gathered in front of the big man's van, and Victor whistled. "Holy shit, cabrone; that's fucked up."

Shredded by the grenade, the front end of Smitty's van leaked steam and vital fluids from countless wounds. The body listed to the right on a flattened tire.

"I can't weld that back together, buddy," Yeager said. "Sorry."

"Hey, y'know what?" Smitty said. "When life hands you lemons, squeeze 'em into a glass of tequila, I always say. Y'all need some company on this here mission trip?"

Yeager clapped the man on one meaty shoulder. "You're hell on wheels in a fight, Smitty, but there's no call for you to get involved here."

"Why, shore they is. Little orphan kids—I love 'em as much as anybody. I was a sniper back in that little jungle exposition we called Viet-fucking-nam. Y'all need a sniper?"

Yeager sighed. "I don't have time to fight you over it. Get your gear. Pile in with Riley and Por Que. C'mon, boys, let's haul ass."

Ten minutes later, Yeager slowed to allow Victor to pull ahead in the Corolla then followed his taillights to the outskirts of Madera. They passed the main fork to the mountains, taking the split to the northwest. There wouldn't be another major intersection for sixty miles.

This particular Mack CH600 had been built in 1987—according to the stiff, yellowed manual in the glove box—and appeared to have suffered from indifferent maintenance and abusive drivers.

The cab smelled of wet dog and onions, the seats were cracked, and the windshield had a diagonal split from bottom left to top right.

Yeager fiddled with the power divider lockout switch and confirmed that it worked. Had it been inoperative, driving through slippery, soft conditions would be harder. The two-speed rear axle took some practice, as did the nonsynchronized transmission. Constantly having to double-clutch wasn't something he enjoyed.

"Admit it, Yeager—you're spoiled." Funny how easily he fell back into the old habit of talking to himself when he drove. A sense of peace seeped into his nerves from the vibration of the diesel engine and the view of an open road in front of him. Driving at night had always been one of his favorite things. Twin beams of light defined the world. A chilly breeze blew in the open window, mingled with scents of pine forest and a whiff of burned fuel.

The adrenaline high of the fight at the warehouse had drained away, leaving him drowsy. Yeager dug into his bag and found a warm can of Red Bull, which he downed in four long pulls. He had two more in the bag, but it was going to be a long night—longer if he had to fix the radiator again—so he held off popping another one.

The road changed from asphalt pavement to hard-packed gravel when they left Madera—solid enough that Yeager had no problem with traction, but as the road began to twist and turn, he constantly had to work the shifter, clutch, brake, and accelerator to keep the massive vehicle out of the ditch.

"How you doin' back there?" The squawk of the radio jolted him.

Yeager pushed the talk button. "Enjoying the view, amigo. Any company ahead?"

"Negative there, good buddy." Victor adopted a folksy tone, imitating a hick accent. "No smokies in sight. Come back."

"Behave yourself, you asshat, and pay attention."

"Ten-four," Victor said with a laugh. "Lookie here—we got ourselves a *convoy*."

Yeager shook his head in mock disgust. Everything Victor knew about trucking, he'd learned from *Smoky and the Bandit* movies.

"I'm in for a long night," he said to himself.

Verdugo and his men were watching the second cycle of replays by ESPN Deportes, waiting for the football highlights to come back around, when Raul's cell buzzed. Verdugo muted the sound on the fifty-inch plasma and watched as his lieutenant's expression turned dark. The thin man snapped and swore at the caller.

Paco and Gabriel Mendez, two of Verdugo's senior men, paused in their discussion of the four-four-two formation the Italians preferred versus the more aggressive three-four-three style of clubs like Barcelona.

Raul swiped the off button and made as if to throw the phone against the wall. He swore in a low monotone.

"Que?" Verdugo asked. A frown started at the corners of his mouth.

Raul drew a deep breath and turned to face Verdugo. "There has been a… setback in Madera."

"Go on."

"The men we sent to intercept the truck bound for San Felipe were fired upon by the people at the warehouse." Disgust dripped from his voice. "Of the eight, two survived. These idiots, instead of calling me, rounded up all our reserves in Madera and attacked again. Of the fourteen men in that attempt, seven are dead and six are wounded. All their vehicles are lost or destroyed."

"Holy Mary, Mother of God," murmured Verdugo. Thirteen men gone in one night. "Who are we up against? Is it the Army? The Sinaloa?"

Raul shrugged. "The two from the first fight, who got a close look, saw two Mexicans and two Americans."

"And the truck?"

"Gone."

"*A que la chingada!*"

"Sí." Raul nodded and held up his phone. "I told them to find the truck. Our man at the mission said they were bringing in many supplies, including a dialysis machine. With these supplies, they might be able to hold out against our demands."

Verdugo stared at the TV without seeing it. He was vaguely

aware of the Mendoza brothers sitting forward, holding beer bottles between their knees. Verdugo rarely made a big scene of shouting when he was angry. It hurt his throat too much to shout. Also, he'd found quiet to be more effective. He got the quietest of all when things were really bad.

He motioned to the phone in Raul's hand. "Tell them to follow the truck." He spoke so low Raul had to lean forward to hear. "We know where it's going, but tell them to catch up and lay eyes on it. I want to make sure it goes to the mission." Bright light from the TV flickered in his eyes. A car commercial replaced the promotion for an upcoming tennis match, "How many men can we pull together by morning?"

Raul pursed his lips and looked at the ceiling. "Ah, two dozen? Depends on if we strip the roadblocks and pull the protection from the current shipments and warehouses. If we do that, maybe another sixty, sixty-five. Call it eighty-five total."

"No. We will not strip our protection, not after sending Espinoza back in pieces. This is the wrong time to leave ourselves open. No. Gather the two dozen here at this house. Make sure they are all properly equipped. We will travel together to Rascón and find out who's responsible for this." Verdugo snapped off the TV with a jab of the remote. "I've had enough of the priest's bullshit. He will give me what I want, or I will send him to meet God in small chunks."

How much longer should I wait?

Oscar pondered this as he lay awake, staring at the ceiling of his cheap motor-court room. The place had more activity at night than some brothels he had known in Amsterdam. People came and went, talking and yelling. Cars pulled into the lot, their headlights washing through the thin curtains and stabbing his eyes. Diesel-truck engines cranked over then idled for seemingly hours at a time before the drivers left.

He would have changed locations, but this place was casual about asking for identification, and it was the closest motel to his target's house.

But Mother of God, how he hated it. *So why wait? Why not go now and take care of the woman and boy? What difference will a day make? Yeager will show up sooner or later, and when he finds his woman hanging from the ceiling, the skin stripped from her body...*

A tiny spark of lust prickled his groin. He'd never considered the possibility that he might become aroused by thoughts of torture. He had always stayed away from that end of the business, leaving the dirty work to Humberto. But now, lying in the dark, he snaked one hand under the covers and coaxed his erection to life.

Oscar's hand moved, and he was surprised at his own physical reaction to the perversion that crept through the dark corners of his mind. He allowed his imagination to wander down paths he'd never before traveled. One scenario after another played out in his head until he could stand it no longer and, with a grunt, spent himself into a pillow.

Afterward, breathing hard, he resolved to wait no longer. *Tomorrow. I will go tomorrow.*

Alexandra found a classroom that contained a high wooden table surrounded by stools. A science lab. The flat surface was not as elevated as a standard operating table, but it would do for Alexandra. Plus, she could sit on one of the stools and be about the right distance from the patient to operate.

"It will have to do," she told herself.

She retrieved sheets and blankets from the supply closet and made a pad for the tabletop and a cover for the patient. Alexandra went back to the hospital supplies they'd left stacked in a nearby classroom and rummaged around until she found a surgical kit, gowns, and masks. She carried the bundle back to her impromptu operating room. It took another trip to locate the box containing Propofol and some intravenous antibiotics.

The sanitary conditions weren't the best, and she lacked good lighting, proper monitors, and a whole suite of modern accessories to assist her.

Plus, let's face it: I'm a GP, not a surgeon. I've observed a total of— what, two appendectomies?

Nurse Beltran entered the classroom while Alexandra was organizing her limited equipment and trying to think through the stages of the operation. Laparoscopic was out of the question; she had never done one and...

"Ahem, Doctor," the frowning nurse said. "I have typed the little girl's blood. A negative."

"Damn." What else could go wrong? A negative meant Emelita could only receive whole blood from O negative or A negative donors and blood plasma from A or AB donors. They had none of these.

"The girl has gotten worse," Beltran said. "The right side of her abdomen is stiff, and she says it hurts very much. We do not have much time. If the appendix bursts, it will be much harder to keep her from getting peritonitis."

"Yes, I know this," Alexandra snapped. It came out sharper than she intended.

The squat nurse stiffened, and her face closed up even more. "I was just saying."

"Yes, I know. I'm sorry, Nurse Beltran. It has been... difficult for all of us. Do you know if, by chance, was there any A negative blood coming in the shipment?"

Beltran relaxed a little and gave her a nod. "Yes, we ordered all types of blood from the Instituto."

"We will wait as long as we can. I would prefer not to operate without adequate blood on hand. Thank you, Nurse Beltran. Please keep an eye on the girl. She can have three hundred milligrams of Tylenol to cut some of the pain. Please also find out when she last ate or drank."

"Of course." The big woman huffed and trundled away.

Alexandra rolled her eyes and then rubbed the grit away. She yawned and wished for a cup of coffee. Much more of this, and she would be popping amphetamines just to stay awake. A bitter smile tugged at the corners of her lips. *I never thought I'd be back in residency.*

CHAPTER 14

YEAGER'S LEFT LEG SHOOK FROM the strain of working the clutch, and his right hand had cramped into a claw around the shift knob. It was four o'clock in the morning, and all the Red Bull was gone. He had a newborn headache behind his right eye and acid bubbling in his stomach. And at least an hour to go.

The peaceful sensation of returning to the wheel of a big rig had disappeared two hours into the drive, sometime around the fourth hairpin turn that required backing and filling to get the Mack and its trailer around. At one point, he stepped out of the truck and went to the passenger side to take a leak. In the dark he kicked a rock from the side of the road, which skittered over the edge of the roadbed and into space. The clatter of it hitting bottom came three long seconds later.

Now it was all shift-clutch-gas-shift-brake in a never-ending cycle of gear changes and microcalculations of speed, distance, turning radius, and torque—the kind of computations that Yeager did at the cellular level, through the input of tired eyes and sore butt, as everything from the condition of the road to the feel of the traction provided data points.

And so far, no opposition. Part of his tension came from wondering when and where the cartel people would make an appearance. It didn't make sense they would just give up after the fight at the warehouse. Where were the roadblocks? Where were the chase vehicles?

The grade steepened, falling away ahead of him in a long hill, so Yeager downshifted and applied the engine brake to slow the Mack to a crawl. He realized about then that the grades had been mostly down for the last thirty minutes or so. Maybe that meant they were over the top and on the last stretch to Rascón. *One can only hope.*

Yeager shifted without using the clutch, giving his leg a rest. He yawned and twisted his head around, neck crackling like cellophane. *Can't be soon enough.*

Juan Guerrero slipped from bed before dawn, having skipped along the surface of an edgy and troubled sleep. The light from false dawn pressed against the single slot of a dorm window, purple and bruised. Their Big Ben windup alarm clock ticked away the last few minutes before six, an hour before its tinny bell would wake everyone for breakfast.

He dressed in silence, trying not to disturb the other boys, and slipped through the door. First stop was the toilet for a pee and to splash some water on his face.

In the mirror, reddened and swollen eyes stared back, the result of a night's worth of bad dreams about running from hordes of laughing cutthroats with guns. Every stone he threw at his tormentors missed or caused no damage, and Juan had jerked awake time after time as they closed in for the kill.

"What do you think, Armando?" he whispered to the mirror. "Should we run for the cave? Hide out for awhile?"

Armando stayed quiet, offering no opinion one way or the other. Juan dried off with a thin gray towel and ghosted into the silent hall. To the right, his room and three roommates waited; to the left were the kitchen and dining hall.

Juan went left.

In the chapel, the priests would be gathering for Prime. Once upon a time, the fathers made all the kids get up for the early liturgy, but since Father Dominic had come, they had only been required to attend Terce at nine in the morning and Vespers at six in the evening. But all the mission's staff members were still required to attend Prime and Compline, which meant one very good thing: the kitchen would be momentarily unattended.

Juan first went through the hall door separating the boys' wing from the main complex, took a short outdoor covered walkway, and entered the mission's administrative section. A quick right turn, and he pushed through the swinging metal door to the kitchen.

The smell of soapy mop water competed with the unmistakable scent of grilled tortillas. Drying streaks crossed the red tile floor, and it squeaked as Juan crossed it, despite his effort to remain quiet. Tiptoeing, he passed the baker's racks—which held giant-sized condiment jars—and the double steel doors of the big refrigerator. He passed through the kitchen entrance to the main dining hall and found the stainless-steel warmer containing the tortillas in its normal place. To his surprise, all the other metal pans were empty.

"*Carajo*, Armando—where's all the food?" Juan swore under his breath. He'd noticed the meals getting lighter and lighter lately, but this was ridiculous. *No huevos, no arroz, no pappas, no frijoles.* Just tortillas. "Where are they stashing all the food, hey?"

He opened the lid of the steamer and found it half-filled with warm tortillas.

This is barely enough for everybody to have a good snack!

Come to think of it, last night when he was cleaning up, he had found the big fridge and the walk-in cooler nearly empty as well. At the time, he had not paid much attention, but now he began to realize how deep a hole they were in, here at the mission.

Juan glanced around, checking for the sneaky cook with his ladle of death. Nothing. The lights of the dining hall were off, leaving the big room painted with shadows of tables and chairs—and a tense, expectant silence.

Intending to snag a good half-dozen tortillas, he settled for one. A strong twinge of guilt nipped at him when he rolled it up and slipped it in his pants pocket. "We're going to need more than this if we're going to make a run for it," he muttered.

Maybe some fish? Several cane poles with hook and lines were kept in a small shed behind the mission along with other tools and equipment used by the maintenance man, whom the children had named Mocoso because his nose was always running.

Juan would have to dig for worms for bait or catch grasshoppers, but that wouldn't be hard. Focused on his mission, he hurried through the creepy dining hall, his steps echoing, and made his way down twisty corridors, avoiding the chapel, until he reached the back door of the main complex. Slipping outside, he shivered. The mountain air had turned sharp overnight. Frost rimed the ragged grass and weeds, dusted the hill rising behind the mission, and outlined the shed in white.

Juan picked out a stout cane pole with a solid piece of fishing line and a whole, unbroken float. The brass hook was a good size for perch or catfish, which was about all he ever caught in the river. "We sure won't get a trout, Armando. No trout is stupid enough to fall for a cane pole."

Pole over one shoulder, Juan skirted the south side of the mission, intending to head downstream to a deep pool where he'd caught some fish before. He came around the front of the weathered stone building, eyes fixed on the grass, hunting for the spring of a grasshopper. The little bugs liked to fly up under your feet when you—

"Hola, amigo!"

The man's voice sent an electric shock of panic through Juan's body. He went rigid. *This is it. They found me!*

Fear buzzed through his tongue when he twisted to see who spoke. Two men stood by a beat-up old car: a thin strip of a gringo in a cowboy hat and a short Mexican man, built in a V shape with the most powerful upper body Juan had ever seen. The Mexican had a flattop haircut, brown eyes, and a pistol strapped to his hip.

"Who's in charge here, little buddy?" The Mexican-looking man spoke with a strange accent as if he came from the United States. The Anglo in the cowboy hat said nothing. He leaned over and spat a brown stream into the dust.

Juan's tongue remained glued to the roof of his mouth, and his heart hammered. There wasn't a single rock in his pocket, and the stout cane pole had shrunk to a skinny reed. It would be useless as a weapon. *Run!* his mind screamed.

The short man grinned and came toward him. "Don't worry, little man. We're the good guys. My name's Victor. What's yours?"

Juan trembled, but feeling seeped back into his legs. He was on the verge of bolting for the mission when a growl of a big engine sounded from the pass to the north of Rascón. In moments, a red diesel truck appeared at the cut and traveled the few hundred meters through the village, where it turned right onto the bridge and rumbled up to the mission's front courtyard.

Wisps of steam escaped from under the hood. That, coupled with the rattle of its power plant and the enormous size of the thing, made it seem as if a fire-breathing demon had come to call. Juan backed up, one careful step after another, ready to fly.

The truck jolted to a stop with a hiss and a gasp, and the driver cut the engine. Juan blinked in the sudden quiet.

A bull of an Anglo climbed out of the cab and hopped to the ground. He wore a denim work shirt over a black T-shirt and jeans and work boots. He had brown hair, tossed by the wind, and brown eyes. The Anglo checked his surroundings as if he suspected enemies to spring from the grass under his feet. He wore a pistol high on his right hip. "Going fishing?"

"Sí," Juan said then had to repeat it to make the sound come out. He was coming to the realization these men weren't narcotraficantes come to kill him. The cartel wouldn't send two gringos and a big diesel truck just for him.

Nodding at Juan, the man went to the one called Victor. He spoke in English, words that Juan didn't completely understand. "The needle on the temp gauge peaked about ten miles back. I thought she was gonna blow her top before we got here."

"But we made it," Victor said.

"That we did."

Juan's eyes bugged out again when the back door of the old car slammed open and the biggest man he'd ever seen sat up and rubbed his face. The car rocked when he got out. He looked big enough to eat a small child whole, without butter.

"Mornin' boys," he boomed. "We're in fucking nowhere now, for damn shore. You think they got beer?"

Juan dropped his pole and ran for the back door.

CHAPTER 15

YEAGER WANDERED ON RUBBER LEGS toward the river to get a better look at Rascón in the gray light of false dawn. The mission claimed the high ground on the west side of the valley, so he could see the entire town laid out before him.

The morning sounds were dampened by chilly air. Gravel crunched underfoot. When he yawned, his breath fogged.

Behind him, Victor laughed. "Dang, Smitty, I think you scared that boy half to death."

"What boy?"

Change the signs to English, and the village could have been any small town in South Texas or rural Alabama. An unnamed river flowed in a lazy twist from the mouth of the canyon to his left until it disappeared into a stand of trees to his right. A hundred yards beyond the trees, another canyon swallowed the forest.

Across the river, a short stretch of paved road took over from the hard-packed gravel, paralleling the river's course in a straight line. A half-dozen businesses lined up in single file along the main street. A general store centered the line—a place called Tia Bonita's, which proclaimed itself in bold red letters as a "super mercado." Beyond the main street, a cluster of buildings was stacked against a slope that angled toward a high ridge.

"Hell of a setting, huh?" Victor had come up to stand beside him.

"Beautiful country."

"Too bad it's filled with chumps carrying guns, hey?"

"Whose fault is that, hombre?" Yeager asked.

"Drug users, I expect."

Distant roosters crowed, and a car engine cranked and died,

then cranked and caught, idling rough. A red Dodge pickup moved across the front yard of a house near the back of the village. It made a right onto the main road and disappeared north, toward Madera.

Riley whistled, and Yeager turned; a white-collared priest in a black suit jacket and slacks strode from the front doors of the mission. The little boy he'd seen with the fishing pole slipped around from behind the priest and regarded them with narrow eyes and a lip curled in suspicion.

"Gentlemen," the white-haired priest said, arms held out as if giving benediction. Despite looking somewhere north of eighty years old, he spoke in a clear, unwavering voice—clearly, a man used to speaking in front of large crowds. "Welcome to Mission de San Felipe. We are most grateful you have come in answer to our prayers. God bless you all."

Yeager came back up the hill to shake the old man's hand and introduced himself and his companions.

"Ah, yes," the priest said. "Señor Ruiz; we know from before. The pilot. It is good to see you again, my son. I am Father Sebastian Felix Maria Rodriguez. And this," he said, gathering up the rake-thin boy next to him, "is Juan Guerrero, one of our... more spirited charges."

"D'Artagnan," the boy said, glaring. *"Mi nombre es d'Artagnan."*

Yeager nodded, careful not to crack a smile. *"Mucho gusto, d'Artagnan."*

"Finally!" A small woman in a white lab coat strode through the doors and into the courtyard. "I need blood. A negative or O negative." She came to a stop at the knot of men gathered in the courtyard. Her eyes skewered each man in turn, pausing at Victor. She gave him a tiny nod of recognition. "Well? Why are you standing here? I have a patient who needs an operation. This is no time for chitchat. Go"—she made shooing motions—"get the truck open; start unloading."

"Yes, ma'am." Yeager raised an eyebrow at the other men, who remained rooted in place, looking slightly stunned. "You heard her. Let's get the truck unloaded."

"Bring all the units of blood to classroom number twelve." And with that, she whirled on one foot and marched back into the mission, white coat flaring.

"Holy shiiii-oot," Smitty said. "She's a little fireball, ain't she?"

"Please, señores," Father Sebastian said. "It is best to do as she says. Where her patients are concerned, Dr. Lopez gives no quarter. I will bring the bigger boys and the staff to help with the unloading. Come, Juan. You may help me gather the boys."

"D'Artagnan," the boy muttered. He followed the priest back inside the mission.

"She may be a little-bitty thang," Smitty said after they'd gone. He held his hands cupped under his chest as if holding invisible grapefruit. "But man, did you see that rack?"

"Hey," Victor snapped. "That's a doctor, amigo, not some broke-down hooker. Watch how you talk."

Yeager snorted. "Looks like you hit a nerve there, Smitty."

The big man looked embarrassed. "Dang, buddy. I didn't mean nothing by it."

"C'mon." Riley clapped Smitty on the back. "A little hard work might help you get that size-sixteen boot from between your gums."

Oscar Cruz fumbled the phone off the nightstand and listened to the recorded wake-up message. He rolled over, went back to sleep, and didn't wake again until the housekeeper knocked at ten o'clock.

"Go away," he shouted at the door.

The maid said something he didn't hear, then came the sound of her cart squeaking away. Oscar sat up amidst tangled sheets and tried to get his bearings. The previous night's fantasies came back to him, and instead of the disgust he expected to feel, a sense of exhilaration washed away some of the sleepiness. The pillow he'd used, scented with dried semen, reminded him of how excited he'd become by the thought of sexual torture.

Now that his interest in torture had revealed itself, he felt a compulsion to indulge it, which added a degree of complexity to his original plan. Instead of simply walking in and shooting everyone, a more elaborate solution was needed.

Oscar showered and dressed, taking special care with each action, making sure everything was done with complete and deliberate attention to detail. He had plenty of time to kill before the boy came home at four o'clock, and he found the anticipation to be very pleasurable.

He packed his small suitcase, went through the room one last time to verify he had everything, dropped the key cards on the dresser, and left. Oscar had no intention of returning to this room, this hotel, or this town.

No, for the next few nights, I will be staying at Señor Yeager's house, eating his food, fucking his wife, and pissing on his son's dead body.

Oscar started the rental car and silenced the chiming dashboard by putting on his seat belt. He recalled seeing a hardware store on the road to Austin. A quick detour there would ensure he had the proper supplies for the job at hand. He wheeled out of the motel parking space and circled the lot to the exit.

Careful to signal, Oscar turned left into traffic and accelerated away.

"The truck is at San Felipe," Raul reported at 11:23 a.m. "Three men and a driver, all armed, came with it."

"Four men took out two of my teams?" Verdugo asked.

Raul shrugged. "Four men is what he said."

Verdugo folded his newspaper and set it on the coffee table in front of him. He took a last drag on his Dunhill and stabbed it out in the ashtray, blowing smoke through his nostrils. His men had been arriving by twos and threes all morning, assembling in the kitchen and dining room and some spilling into the living room. *Like a wolf pack,* Verdugo thought. *Predators ready to tear into the raw meat of their kill.*

"How many do we have?" he asked.

Raul did a quick count and came back with, "Twenty-one."

"Enough. Let's go see these four men and take what they mean to keep from me."

The men lounging in the living room showed their teeth in

matching grins. They filed out, gathering the others as they went, heading for the vehicles.

Verdugo asked, "Rascón is—what, two hours away?"

Raul glanced at the ceiling and wagged his hand. "Sí, about that. No rain, so it should be no trouble."

"So we should be there by lunch, you think?"

His lieutenant nodded.

"Good," said Verdugo. "I sense our wolves are hungry. We will give them lots of raw meat."

Raul looked confused but nodded anyway.

"Let's go." Verdugo holstered the HK pistol that lay on the coffee table next to his newspaper. "It's time to hunt."

"Hey," Yeager said into the phone. Cell service was nonexistent, so he'd borrowed the mission's landline.

"Hey yourself." Charlie's voice sent a tingle through his tired muscles.

"We're here." He sat in a guest chair in Father Sebastian's office and worked at staying awake.

The priests had assigned him a tiny room with no phone, of course. Victor, Riley, and Smitty had similar closets, each furnished with a narrow bed, a nightstand, and dust bunnies. It wasn't much, but at the moment, Yeager could sleep at a rock concert on a bed of nails.

"Where's here?" Charlie asked.

"San Felipe. You'd like it. Mountains, trees, pretty little creek. Cute little orphan kids."

"Thugs with guns?"

"No." Yeager kept his voice level. "Not yet, anyway. It's been pretty smooth."

"Thank God for that."

"Yep. This is the place to do just that. Thank God, I mean." Yeager listened to her breathe, satisfied to hear the sound echoing over the phone line.

"When are you coming back?"

"Tomorrow probably." Yeager rubbed his gritty eyes. "I need some down time. Plus, the truck sprang a leak, and I might have to weld it back together again."

"Again?"

"Yeah. Long story. Anyway, we got here at dawn. Just finished unloading. You should've seen it. We had this conga line of priests, boys, me, Victor, all lined up from the truck to the front door. Right now, the mission dining hall looks like somebody dumped a freight train in it."

Charlie laughed, a low, throaty sound that sent another tingle down to his belly.

"Oh, and I think Por Que's in love."

"What? For real?"

"Could be. There's this woman doctor here, even shorter than he is. About as big as a Barbie doll and about as cute. Anyway, our man Victor gets all goofy when she's around. This could be the highlight of the trip—just watching him follow her like a lost puppy."

Charlie laughed again, and they talked some more until Yeager yawned for the third time.

"Go to bed, big guy," she said. "You're going to need your rest when you get back."

"You say the sweetest things."

"Don't be a smart-ass. Just get yourself back here with all your parts attached."

"Especially that one."

"Well, sure," she told him. "Why else would I want you?"

CHAPTER 16

J UAN SLIPPED AWAY IN THE clutter and confusion of unloading the truck. The priests were busy running around, bumping into each other, and giving silly orders—*do this, no, do that, no, do the first thing*. Getting away unobserved proved to be easy.

He made a quick stop at Tia Bonita's for the promised flashlight, dodging her questions about why he wanted it. While there, he used all of his pocket money to buy food and soda. He wanted to stay out of sight until all the work of unloading the truck had died down.

The sun topped the ridge above him, and birds trilled and flitted from bush to bush as he climbed the slope behind the village. A bright-green lizard skittered across the trail and vanished into a split in the rocks. Juan breathed the sweet wine of free air and whistled to himself. The cave was less than an hour away.

The trail Juan walked on joined another path at a fork fifty meters ahead, marked by a head-shaped boulder. Running roughly parallel, the second path cut through the forest on his left like the branching of a crooked stick. He sometimes took that trail back to the village, though it was steeper and harder than the other, with more switchbacks and rough patches. As he approached the junction, stretches of the other path showed through breaks in the trees.

Juan whipped his head around at a sound from the second path—a man's voice, complaining in sharp, angry mutters. Juan froze, eyes roving. There. A flash of bright cloth. A dingy cowboy hat.

Juan squinted, and his chest squeezed when he made out a chunky, overweight man, carrying a rifle.

Pulling himself along by grabbing trees or touching the ground with one hand, the burly man cursed his way up the trail. He was farther away than Juan could throw a rock but close enough for a rifle bullet. Was the man a narco—one of Verdugo's men—or just a hunter seeking game?

Juan shifted for a better look as the climber passed behind a screen of trees. When the man appeared again, something—maybe Juan made a noise, or maybe a devil whispered in the man's ear—caused him to look up. The gunman's eyes pinned Juan to the spot, and a cold wash of fear washed him from head to toe. He swayed, and his vision blurred. It was the man from the trucks. In the village.

The one he'd clocked in the ear with a rock.

The one who'd shot at him.

The one who'd said he would track Juan down and kill him.

A smile split the ugly narco's face, which was made even uglier by an eggplant-colored ear. "Good day, little rock thrower." His voice had the hollow quality of distance, but it was unmistakably the same narco. "It's Miguel's lucky day, hey? I have been hoping we would meet again."

Juan's feet broke their bond with the earth, and he sprinted for the cave. Miguel's booming laugh followed him.

———※———

It took several groggy seconds for the sounds of running feet and shouting voices to register in Yeager's unconscious mind. The noise roused him from his dreamless doze. He rolled out of bed, snagged the M4, and slipped on his boots before fully understanding what he was hearing. Shouts in Spanish and barked orders echoed through the mission halls. Yeager couldn't make out the specific words, but the tone was clear enough. He finished lacing his boots, found his holstered Springfield, and clipped it on his right hip.

The cartel? Had to be. The guys from Madera hadn't run away after all; instead, they must have tracked the rig to the mission. But if they wanted the load, why wait until the truck was unloaded?

Yeager cracked the door open for a look. He had an inside-corner room, so he could see straight down the hall—closed doors on each side, nothing moving, and voices, muffled by distance, battering away in Spanish. Another peek to his left, down the other leg of the hall, revealed a similar situation except for the door next to his, which cracked open. Victor—wearing a muscle shirt and boxers—looked at him with a wide-eyed *what the fuck?* expression.

Yeager shrugged and started out of the room. Voices from the left, near the connecting door to the dorms and classrooms, froze him in place. Shrieks and screams of children spilled down the hall. Yeager motioned Victor to hold back and closed his own door to a razor-thin sliver, pressing his eye against the slit.

An avalanche of youngsters, ranging in size from toddler to teenager, tumbled into the hall as if spewed from a fire hose. They flowed through the hallway past Yeager's door, jostling and bumping through the turn, and headed away from him, toward the exit. A quartet of gunmen, wearing black bandanas for masks, shouted and pushed the stragglers. They passed by and turned the corner, disappearing. The sound of the group's passage diminished with distance.

Yeager's jaw tightened, and his pulse thumped with the power of a kettledrum. He had to concentrate on relaxing his hand around the grip of the M4, and worked on controlling his breathing.

Never fight angry. The rule, passed down from drill instructors and sergeants from the time Leonidas led the Spartans at Thermopylae, echoed through his head. Anger made you crazy. Anger made you do stupid things. Think first, shoot second.

So when I do shoot, I can shoot every fucking one of them.

Yeager and Victor came out of their rooms at the same time. Por Que had pulled on his jeans and running shoes but not his shirt. The musculature of his upper body looked as if it had been carved from granite, and he carried the same AK-47 he'd used at the warehouse, along with a pouch of magazines slung over one shoulder.

"What's the plan, Kemo Sabe?" the shorter man asked.

The door to Riley's room opened, and the slim Texan slipped out, armed with the F2000 bullpup. "'Sup?"

"Not sure," said Yeager, "but it looks like the cartel found us. Por Que, do a sweep of the back rooms. I didn't see the doctor or any of the nurses in that group. There could be more bad guys behind us, and I don't want any surprises sneaking up on our ass. Take Riley with you to watch your back. Go."

Victor nodded and took off, Riley behind him. They went in the direction from which the kids came, in good overwatch formation, leapfrogging from point to point, checking rooms as they went.

Yeager crossed to Smitty's door and rapped on it. When he got no response, he pressed his ear to it and was rewarded with the sound of deep, satisfied snores. Yeager shoved into the room and woke the big man with a kick to the bedframe. "Get dressed. We got company."

"Who? What?" Smitty blinked and pushed himself up.

"Get your Barrett, and find the highest point you can reach. Cover the front of the mission. The bad guys took a bunch of kids out front, and I need some high cover in case things go bad."

"You got it." Smitty moved quickly for a big man and had started the instant Yeager said "Barrett." He'd already pulled on his pants, grabbed his socks, boots, and gun case, and was on Yeager's heels as he left. "I'll see if I can get up in the bell tower from the cathedral."

"Go," Yeager said. "I'm headed to the front."

Smitty roamed down the same hall as Riley and Victor had, but at the far junction he went right—toward the cathedral—instead of left. Yeager moved in the opposite direction, back past his room to where the hall made a ninety-degree left turn. This hallway led to the administrative offices, storage rooms, and doors to places Yeager hadn't seen.

The mission's original whitewashed plaster walls and solid oak doors had been infected with modernization. Electricity ran through an exposed conduit fixed to the ceiling next to aluminum ductwork for the HVAC system. Doors were labeled with plastic tags in Spanish. The first tag Yeager passed said the room was a laundry.

Raised voices from the end of the hall drew his attention to the last door on the left—Father Sebastian's office. Yeager slipped forward, M4 held at the ready. He kept his eyes moving, sweeping the hall forward and back. His nose twitched with the need to sneeze. No matter how much modernization they tacked on, the mission retained a musty smell of age and dust.

He checked doorknobs along the way, senses tuned for people with guns who might pop out behind him. Every door he tried was locked.

As he crept forward, the high, clear, and very angry voice of Father Sebastian came through the partially opened office door. His excited Spanish rattled so fast Yeager had trouble understanding half of what he said.

"... a place of worship! What is wrong... people? Take your men and go! I will pray..."

In response came a whispering voice so quiet Yeager couldn't catch a single word, although he'd worked his way next to the door. Based on the sound, Yeager guessed the whisperer sat in the left-hand guest chair, facing Father Sebastian's desk—the same chair Yeager had used when he called Charlie.

Enough. Time to put an end to this bullshit. Yeager verified the M4 was ready to fire, stepped back, and kicked the door open with a size 12 boot. He went in hard and fast.

CHAPTER 17

"**N**URSE MARTA, PLEASE STAND BY with that unit of blood. The last time I did this was on a cadaver in med school. If I nick an artery..."

"Of course, Doctor. You will be fine."

Alexandra had made every preparation she could think of. Emelita was sedated and sleeping comfortably on a pallet of sheets stacked on the classroom lab table. More sheets covered her with the exception of a square opening over the right side of her abdomen. The skin retained swathes of the Betadine solution they used to sterilize the area, orange under the light of two gooseneck lamps positioned on either side of the child's body.

Dr. Lopez's instruments had been selected and laid out in the order she would need them. Scalpels, retractors, gauze wipes, and clamps lay in neat rows by the girl's hip. The only thing left to do was begin.

She glanced at Marta, who stood on the other side of the bench with her back to the classroom door. She somehow seemed less intimidating in her mask and surgical gown. Marta gave her an encouraging nod and gestured with one gloved hand then activated the blood-pressure cuff on Emelita's left arm and placed the tip of her stethoscope on the girl's chest. Her job would be to monitor the patient's vitals during the surgery and alert Alexandra if a problem arose.

Voices, raised and excited, drifted through the closed door, but Alexandra tuned them out. She picked up the scalpel, secretly pleased to detect no shake in her hand. With a sure, deliberate stroke, she made the opening incision. After cutting through the muscle encasing the abdominal wall, Alexandra spread the opening with a gleaming retractor and paused while Marta mopped away the blood with cotton pads. The ease with which the older woman performed her duty helped calm Alexandra even further, and she was soon absorbed in the surgery, the sounds of the outside world drifting away. One part of her mind marveled at how well she and Marta worked together, communicating on an intuitive level. Almost before she knew she needed it, Marta would extend the instrument or device she needed.

Bang!

The classroom door slammed back so hard Alexandra jumped and dropped the scalpel she'd just used to part the abdominal wall. It clattered to the floor with a metallic tinkle.

Two armed gunmen barged into the room, wearing masks and shouting at them to get out, to move, to go quickly or they'd be killed.

Marta shouted, "Get out of here!" and shoved the nearest intruder in the chest. He stumbled into his partner.

Alexandra's mouth went dry, and she couldn't form the words she wanted to speak to protest the intrusion. The introduction of violence and mayhem shocked her system so much it was all she could do to grasp the intent of the gunmen. Her heart rallied as the battle-axe of a nurse, the woman she'd least enjoyed working with at the hospital, showed none of the fear that Alexandra felt.

"Can't you see we have a sick child here?" Marta raised a menacing fist.

The first masked man recovered from his stumble. He slammed the butt of his weapon into Marta's cheek. It hit with a meaty thud, and the big woman yelped. She tottered on unsteady feet but stayed upright, bracing a hand on the makeshift operating table. Her attacker cocked his arms for another strike.

"No!" Alexandra shouted, finding her voice at last.

With a *thunk!* the masked man butt-stroked the older woman in the head, and she crumpled in a heap, making no effort to break her fall. She bumped the table, and it screeched out of position. Emelita wobbled in her anesthesia-induced slumber.

The second man pointed his rifle at Alexandra. "Come with us. Everyone outside."

"I-I can't," she said. "I am in the middle of surgery here. I can't leave my patient."

The two intruders seemed to take in the scene before them for the first time. They shared a perplexed look, clearly at a loss about what to do. The smaller man, the one who'd clubbed Marta, glanced around the room as if seeking a solution on the chalkboards and bookshelves scattered along the walls.

The taller one shrugged and stepped forward. "It is simple. Come with us, bitch. We will take care of these two."

The tall gunman aimed his rifle at Emelita's head, and for Alexandra, the world spun down to a single point then expanded to infinity. She could see everything in the room with a clarity beyond human senses, from the black muzzle of the rifle as it touched Emelita's hair to the tension in the gunman's finger as he took up slack on the trigger. In a larger scope, she could see the cruelty in the man's eyes and complete lack of a soul in the wasteland behind them.

"No!" She didn't know if she screamed it or if the word pulsed from her heart without sound. She reached across the girl's form, her bloody glove outstretched, intending to knock the barrel away. She had to lurch up onto the lab table, cursing her short stature, straining to reach the muzzle before it bloomed with fire—

The gunman's head came apart in slow motion, a melon expanding from within, first with one side cracking, eyes bulging from excessive pressure, then with shards bursting outward like pieces of fired clay exploding from within. Blood rained as if powered by a garden sprinkler.

The masked attacker spilled sideways, falling with a soundless thump that Alexandra felt through the soles of her shoes. The smaller gunman danced backward, plumes of red bursting from his shirt, looking like a marionette jerking in the hands of an inexperienced puppeteer.

He too collapsed, crashing into another lab table and taking several stools down with him.

Alexandra fixed stunned eyes on the man in the doorway, recognizing the short, muscular pilot who'd come with the truck. He held a smoking assault rifle to his cheek, surrounded by a gray haze. His fierce expression softened when he lowered the weapon and looked at her.

"Victor Ruiz, at your service." When he spoke, his eyes took on a merry glint. "Did you forget to fill out the insurance forms again, Doctor? Shame on you. Hey, maybe you should finish that—you know, what you're doing there?"

Yeager kicked open the door to Father Sebastian's office, followed it in, and slid left, pinning the door against the wall with his back to make sure no one lurked behind it. Father Sebastian sat behind his desk, stunned, his mouth open and eyes wide. Two men sat in the guest chairs, their backs to Yeager.

Both of them jerked at the intrusion and started up from their seats.

"Stop," Yeager barked in Spanish. "Move again, and I blow your head off!"

The men froze in place, half twisting to look behind them. To Yeager's right, a viperous man, slender with slicked-back hair and sharp, narrow features, glared laser beams of dark poison at him. The scene reminded Yeager of parents in consultation with the school principal—except for the Walther PPQ 9mm the man carried in a black hip holster.

"Who the fuck are you?" the man on the left hissed, standing up. This one's blond hair surprised Yeager. In a country dominated by Indian blood, light hair was rare. The blond man wore his hair thick full and slightly messy as though he combed it with his fingers, so carefully artless as to appear natural. He wore fashionable clothes: a snakeskin jacket over a black T-shirt, gray denim jeans, and black cowboy boots.

Yeager couldn't see a weapon but had to assume one was concealed under the sport coat.

"I'm the guy with an automatic weapon pointed at your head,"

Yeager said. "I'm tired, I'm pissed off, and I just woke up. You wanna fuck with me, that's okay. I'll just shoot you and go back to bed. Now, sit your ass back in that chair, nice and easy."

The blond guy hesitated. Yeager took two deep breaths, thinking Blondie would go for it anyway and damn the consequences. He steadied his sight picture on the guy's forehead and felt his shooter's calm flow through him. The dot-two-two-three copper-jacketed express train was ready to leave the station.

Blondie must have read something in Yeager's eyes, because he relaxed into his seat, turning the chair halfway around so he could see Yeager without having to look over his shoulder. The slender man did the same.

"Father Sebastian," Yeager said, "why don't you come around from behind there and stand by the wall?" Yeager flicked his head to the right. "You're in a bad spot right there."

"Sí, of course." The old priest had regained his composure. A coal of righteous anger tinged his voice.

"What's going on here?" Yeager asked once Sebastian had moved out of the line of fire.

The blond man opened his mouth to speak, but the priest cut him off, spraying words in staccato Spanish. "These men! These hoodlums! They have come to our mission and demanded that we resume our agreement. They say we must pay the toll! A toll? A toll? On God? What kind of men are these? And this one, wearing the cross of Jesus Christ our Savior around his neck."

"What agreement?" Yeager asked.

"I know of no agreement!" Sebastian was working up into a diatribe. His face had gone red, and he punctuated his sentences with grand gestures and a stabbing finger. The old man drew breath to continue, but Yeager stopped him.

"Hold on, Father. I got the picture." He brought the M4 off his shoulder but held it ready at his hip. With a snap of one hand, he could drop both of these characters with three-round bursts between one heartbeat and the next. He spoke to the man in the snakeskin jacket. "And who are you, Blondie?"

Dark-blue eyes under a heavy brow stared back at him. Razor-edged icicles in a cavern of frozen death would have more warmth. Hesitation in the face of the enemy often got a person killed, but Yeager took a second to try to figure the guy out. A dozen responses to the challenge inherent in that stare ran through his mind, but none of them seemed right.

Time slipped past, liquid mercury flowing through a drain. The children who'd been rounded up and driven like cattle preyed on his mind. His instincts screamed to take action, but his brain applied the brakes; making a wrong move could mean disaster for those kids. He needed to know the score, and quickly.

The blond thug bailed him out. He spread his hands as if the answer were obvious. "I am Verdugo."

"Verdugo, huh?"

The man in the snakeskin jacket inclined his head and made a small movement of his hand. Amused, like a king indulging a peasant.

"It means *executioner* in English."

"Hmmm." Verdugo grunted assent. "And I have twenty men outside, surrounding a group of children. One order from me, and they will open fire."

"It'll be the last order you give."

"Possibly." He inclined his head again, acknowledging the point. "Are you part of the group who killed my men in Madera?"

"They didn't give us much of a choice. Those supplies were under my care; I don't take that lightly."

"Who are you?"

"Just call me Trucker."

Verdugo cleared his throat and looked to the slim man next to him. His rough whisper turned gravelly as if speaking caused him pain. "Raul. Explain our position here to, ah, Señor Trucker."

"We own these mountains." Raul's Spanish had the harsh overtones of a street thug, giving the lie to his fancy clothes and dapper appearance. He sounded to Yeager like a hundred other Mexican tough guys he'd grown up with. "Anything that moves through here is ours to take, especially from people like these, who renege on their agreements."

"Agreements?" Father Sebastian could contain himself no longer. "We have no agreements with men like you. You mean to steal from God and from little children. Where is your religion? Why have you turned your back to God?"

"Religion!" Raul chuckled. "Your religion would have us on our knees, sucking the dicks of the rich and powerful for a few coins. No, Father, this is not our religion. You have failed us, so we have chosen a new god. One who rewards those who take what they want."

"Enough," Yeager snapped, shifting the weapon in his hand to more directly target Raul. In English, he said, "You *comprende* English? Good. Here's the deal, plain and simple. You, Raul, go outside and tell your men to send the kids back inside. You don't do that, I shoot this cockroach in the head." He gestured to Verdugo. "You send the kids back inside, put your men back in their cars, and drive off. Leave one vehicle for the executioner here. When everybody's cleared out, Verdugo walks away."

"And if you kill me, señor?" Verdugo rasped. "Then what? There will be a massacre. My men will not stop until everyone here is dead."

"They'll try," Yeager told him. "I've been down this road before, against tougher motherfuckers than you can bring. I'm still here. Point is, you'll lead the way to hell."

Verdugo steepled his fingers in thought. He cleared his throat and spoke in his scratchy whisper. "Here's the deal, as you say. We will take the supplies you brought in exchange for your lives and as compensation for the men you killed. If we walk away empty-handed today, I will have no choice but to come back and kill you, your friends, these priests, and everyone in the village. Then I will sell the children into slavery."

"Well, then," Yeager said. "It may be best that I kill you now and take my chances."

He raised the rifle and centered the blond man's heavy brow over the front sight.

"No, señor, por favor," said Father Sebastian. "Please, do not kill for the sake of some food and medicine. This man is not worth it. God will see us through."

"No, Father, I don't see it that way." Yeager curled his finger around the trigger. Verdugo arched an eyebrow, looking mildly surprised. Leather creaked when he shifted in his chair. "It ain't about that anymore. This little prick needs to understand there's a line you don't cross. This is it. Last chance, Verdugo. Walk away or die—your choice."

CHAPTER 18

R. Alexandra Lopez came back to the present with a rush. *Patient. Emelita. Operation.*

"Dios mío," she said. "Marta!"

"That the nurse?" Victor asked.

"Yes. She was struck…"

"We got this." Victor turned to another man who had come to the doorway, a lanky cowboy. "Riley, we good?"

"Clear," Riley said. "Got two more down the other hall, where the sick people are. They was busy trying to molest a young woman. A nurse. Didn't see no one else."

"Is the woman okay?" Victor asked.

"Yeah, they didn't get too far. She's shook but gettin' it together."

"Good. Get the trash outta here while I check on Marta."

Alexandra had to work at controlling the shake of unburned adrenaline running through her system. First Marta brutally beaten and her patient nearly killed. Now Estella almost raped! She shivered and clenched her teeth to keep them from chattering.

Victor, bending down to look at Marta, disappeared behind the table. From the corner of her eye, Alexandra noted the taller man dragging a dead gunman by the heels into the hall. He left a streak of blood on the white linoleum floor.

Focus, Alexandra. You have your hands in a little girl's stomach.

"You okay?" Victor said. It took Alexandra a moment to realize he was still crouched down, talking to Marta. "No, don't get up yet. You took a nasty whack to the head. Let me get you some ice."

The mumbled reply of Marta's voice sent a tingle of relief through Alexandra. She concentrated on isolating the inflamed and

110

infected tissue of Emelita's appendix, only vaguely aware of Victor Ruiz rattling around in one of the ice chests.

Motion caught Alexandra's eye, and she glanced up then did a double take. Victor had peeled off his T-shirt and was using it to carry ice. As he approached with the dripping white cloth, Alexandra noted the clear definition of every muscle in his upper body. If not for the puckering of scar tissue from an old wound in his side, the man's body could have been carved from stone.

Her cheeks heated, and she ducked her head back to Emelita's abdomen. The little girl stirred a little, coming out from under the anesthetic. Alexandra would have to finish soon, or her patient would wake at a really bad time. However, she could not resist another glance as Victor came closer.

He grinned and gave her a wink. Her cheeks went from warm to burning.

The priest lied. Verdugo didn't know they could do that.

He cursed himself for getting caught flat-footed. When they had arrived, the first person they'd encountered had been a cadaverous priest with white-blond hair and pale features. He had been in front of the main entrance, deadheading a rose bush, when Verdugo's convoy of vehicles pulled into the drive.

"Where are the men who delivered this load?" Raul demanded. "The men with guns."

"Gone," the priest said with a shrug, holding his palms out in a helpless gesture. His Spanish was heavy with some foreign accent. "They unloaded and left in another car."

"You lie!" Raul pulled his gun and stuck it in the pale man's face. "Our men have been watching this mission and have seen no cars leave."

"No, not from here," the priest explained with a calm reserve that gave no sign of a man in distress. "They went to the village and caught a ride there, I believe."

"Go to the village," Verdugo ordered two of his men. "Find where they went." He asked the priest, "Who is in charge here?"

"That would be Father Sebastian. He is in his office—through these doors and turn left. First door on the right."

"You"—Verdugo pointed to a group of eight men—"search the dorm rooms. Round up all the children and everyone else you find, and return here with them. If you encounter armed men, kill them if you can. The rest of you stay here, ready to react."

He and Raul had then gone inside the mission and found Father Sebastian right where the gringo priest had said he would be. Verdugo had—foolishly—accepted at face value the word of the priest that the armed men had escaped his net.

Now he stared down the muzzle of an automatic weapon with a man's finger tightening on the trigger. *Walk away or die*. That was the choice. But would Trucker pull the trigger?

He didn't look like much on first appraisal. Brown hair, brown eyes. Slightly less than two meters tall. Strong hands and an impressive musculature. Dressed like a workman, the man looked like the trucker he claimed as his name.

Verdugo had learned through his years how to read people, especially their willingness to kill. Most found the act distasteful. They hesitated or refused to do the deed even when pushed to the brink. A few would do it if the killing was distant or easy, such as dropping bombs from a plane or pushing a button. But to kill up close and personal... now *that* was a rare ability.

And this man has it.

"All right, Señor Trucker." The words came with reluctance. Verdugo resolved that he would live to fight another day; a tactical retreat wasn't a loss—no matter how much it felt that way. "Raul, go tell the men to release the children. Send them back inside. Leave me the Land Rover. Take the rest of the men with you."

Raul nodded once in a stiff motion, his lips compressed and his face red with anger. He jerked to his feet and turned to leave.

"Huh-uh. Leave the PPQ here," the trucker said. He gestured with the rifle. "Two fingers. On that couch over there."

Raul slid the weapon out and tossed it underhand onto the sofa next to Father Sebastian, who regarded it as though it were a live snake.

Verdugo smiled. The one called Trucker shifted.

"Who are you really?" Verdugo asked. "What are you? Army? CIA?"

Trucker chuckled. "No. I'm nothin' but a truck driver."

"You and your people killed thirteen of my men in Madera. Wounded several others. I heard an RPG was used. You are more than a simple truck driver. How much are these priests paying you to deliver their food, hey? Can't be much."

"Nothing. This one's on the house."

"A mercenary who works for free!" Verdugo snorted. "I doubt that."

The man shrugged and said no more. He watched Verdugo with hooded, cold eyes.

How dedicated to the San Felipe orphanage can he be? Verdugo tapped his steepled fingers against his lips. Whoever these people were, they wouldn't be getting much active assistance from the priesthood here at San Felipe. The Fathers weren't known for taking up arms. The twenty men he had with him should be enough. Once he was out from under the man's weapon, he would turn his men right back around and strike hard and fast. *No getting caught like a teenager with his hands down his pants. So embarrassing.*

This time, when he and his men came, they would start shooting and not stop until everything was dead, down to the chickens and pigs. Priests and children included.

Oscar wheeled his orange shopping cart through the aisles of The Home Depot. He had already selected a hundred feet of nylon rope as well as duct tape, rubber gloves, and a selection of brackets that he could use to secure the woman to the bed or the floor, depending on the situation.

Now he stood in the tool aisle and compared power drills. Should he ask the clerk which unit would work best for drilling holes in kneecaps? He chuckled aloud. He chose one that came with an assortment of bits. After that, he picked out pliers, a carpet knife, a hammer, and a saw with a narrow blade.

He struggled through the self-checkout process, reading each direction and swiping a credit card through the PIN pad device as the voice suggested. The card would not set off any alarms as it was part of his new, clean identity—one of several he'd established over the years, knowing that some day things might fall apart and he would have to run.

The clerk at the central cashier station said "Thank you," and he nodded in return.

He loaded his sacks in the trunk of the rental and paused a moment before getting in, pretending to stretch. He studied the parking lot to see if anyone had taken a special interest in him. Sinaloa cartel people would kill him on the spot if they found him. Even though months had passed since that trouble started, the Sinaloas had a long memory and a longer reach.

Seeing no one but shoppers, Oscar got in the rental and headed out of the lot, pointing his car toward I-35 North. The clock on the dashboard said 2:06 p.m. It was a thirty- or forty-minute drive to Yeager's place in the country.

The fun would start in less than an hour.

———————————◈———————————

Yeager stood in the shadows of the main entrance doors as Verdugo lumbered across the courtyard and got into the Land Rover. His men had withdrawn, and the children were back inside. The grupo leader's size surprised Yeager. He was at least six-two and on the heavy side, with the build of a heavyweight boxer and a kind of ponderous intensity.

Riley drifted up beside him as Verdugo drove across the bridge. "Building's clear."

"Good," Yeager said, "but it won't be for long. These jackasses will be coming back. Either right now, or sometime soon. Where's Victor?"

"Helpin' the doc."

"Helpin' her what?"

"Operate."

"Okay, here's what we need to do." Yeager paused to close the big double doors. "Smitty's armory is stacked in his room. Get into it and grab everything you can carry. Go find Smitty, and the two of you get up in the bell tower. That's where Smitty was headed when this shit started. You're gonna be his spotter and close-in protection."

"Gotcha." Riley took off at a loping run.

"Señor Yeager." Father Sebastian stopped in front of Yeager and held up a hand. "What are you doing? Why are you provoking this conflict?"

"Provoking?" Yeager studied the priest's eyes and determined that the man was serious. "Father, I don't know if you noticed, but those men invaded your school. They threatened your kids and the other priests. What would you have me do—let them take everything we worked so hard to bring to you? Hurt the children?"

"We have dealt with these types of men for many years." Father Sebastian's brown eyes watered with emotion. "They take things, yes, for they know no better. We always survive, with God's will. No one is hurt as long as we cooperate."

"But you were yelling at them. I heard you before I came in."

"This was nothing more than a bargaining tactic. I didn't say we would give them everything. Just enough to make them go away."

Yeager took a deep breath and clenched his jaw to keep back the first response that came to mind. He placed a hand on the old priest's shoulder. "Father, I don't believe you have a grasp of the current situation. This man plans to steal everything not nailed down, kill everybody, and leave you with nothing. Now, we could leave—get in that old Toyota and haul for the border. In which case, Verdugo waltzes in here and kills everyone, including the orphans and patients. I can't live with—"

"But—"

"Hear me out, Father," Yeager said, tightening his grip on the man's bony shoulder. "We fought our way here, risking our lives to bring you these supplies. In Madera, we shot it out with Verdugo's men twice before we could even get on the road. I've fought people like Verdugo before, and there's one thing I know." Yeager patted Father Sebastian and released him. "He will be back. He will come with guns blazing, and he will try to kill everyone here, you included. You may be ready to see God in person, but I'm betting these others aren't. Now, if you'll excuse me."

He pushed by the priest, ignoring his continuing protests. *Provoking the fight,* the old man had said. Yeager wondered if there was any truth in that. If they left, would Verdugo skim some of the haul and be satisfied with that? *Can I take that chance? And what is this agreement Verdugo mentioned?*

Yeager turned the corner and went to Smitty's room. He nearly collided with Riley, who was coming out festooned with guns and flak vests, his arms loaded with boxes of ammunition and magazines.

"Here." Riley fished out two tactical radios with earpieces and boom mikes. "One for you, one for Vic."

"Thanks."

"You think we got enough ammo?" the slim man drawled.

"I hope so, Riley. I truly hope so."

CHAPTER 19

JUAN GUERRERO STOPPED RUNNING WHEN he got to the cave.

The fat narco had not given up. Several times, Miguel's voice had floated up from the back trail, taunting and laughing. A bullet had snipped a twig from a tree next to Juan's ear at a point near the top of the rise. The sound of a shot followed a heartbeat later.

No, the fat killer had not given up.

Juan had paused to drink his strawberry soda between panting gulps of air. He sat a moment to rub his tired feet, but the threat of an angry Miguel appearing any moment drove him on. The cave beckoned: a dusty, dank-smelling black hole of possible sanctuary.

More than once, he considered slipping off the trail and disappearing into the underbrush, but fear that Miguel possessed the skills to keep tracking him kept Juan on course. No, best to vanish into the cave.

No way will that fat ass Miguel go more than two steps into the dark before he chickens out. Juan stepped through the crack in the wall and played the light around the space. Narrower than his room at the orphanage, the walls of the tunnel leaned inward to form a triangle. He would need to stand on a bigger kid's shoulders to reach the apex. The tunnel stretched away into the gloom, farther than the light's beam could reach. Juan froze as if the darkness itself pressed him back. He swallowed a lump the size of a jawbreaker and wiped damp sweat from his face. Was he crazy? Why did he think *he* could go into such a place? There could be animals. Bears. Mountain lions. There could be goblins and trolls, too, hairless, pale, and blind from living in the dark—and feeding off rats and small boys, chewing them up with large, blocky teeth stained blackish red from all the blood.

"Stop being stupid, Juan." His voice bounced around the tunnel walls with a hollow, echoing sound. "There are no such things as trolls and goblins."

A waft of air cooled the sweat on his face, and a rank smell of compost made his eyes water.

"Armando! What is that smell?"

Armando's voice didn't come.

Juan shrugged. "Well, let's go find out." He reseated the pack on his shoulder and took one step forward, then another, until the fear subsided, the stiffness left his legs, and the hammering in his chest slowed to a salsa drumbeat.

"Hello!" he called out. His voice echoed back, but nothing else made a sound.

Probing with the light, he crept into the darkness.

Charlie picked up David from school at a quarter past three rather than wait for the bus to come by the house. She hung out with six other moms that she knew from attending science fairs and school fund-raisers. Moms were a great source of intel about the school and the community: which teacher was good, which was bad, whose kid was a bully, and whose kid had untreated ADD and ran wild in the streets and would no doubt turn to a life of crime soon. The CIA could use a spy network half as effective as those moms.

"David," she called when he jetted through the door in a pile of boys, laughing and shoving and insulting each other. It seemed as though her son had grown three inches in the short time since she had seen him get on the bus that morning. Long and gangly with pale skin and reddish-blond hair, David wore round, wire-rimmed glasses, jeans, and a light jacket.

He looked up, acknowledged her with a nod, and disengaged from the pack.

"Hey, Mom. What's up?"

"Feel like spending the night at Maria's?"

"Tonight?"

"Yeah, tonight."

"Yeah, sure. I guess." David shrugged. He looked unimpressed, a façade that most boys his age worked on perfecting. Charlie could read the signs, though. David loved going to Maria's because both she and her husband, Tomas, spoiled the boy worse than his grandmother ever could. They also had a houseful of kids around David's age, and the Xbox tournaments that resulted when they got together could last all night.

"Well, let's go," she said. "I packed your things, and the car's loaded. We need to get a move on before Rascal chews my backseat to ribbons."

Rascal had a good time at Maria's too. What dog wouldn't, surrounded by six rambunctious kids? But when locked in the car, he tended to get restless and start gnawing on things. The alternative meant trying to control him with a rush of kids racing past.

David made a face. "Can we go home first?"

"Why?"

"I need to get some games."

"It's not really on the way…"

"Please, Mom?"

Charlie quirked her lips. "Using the eyes on me—that's not fair. All right, c'mon. Let's go home and get your games."

Yeager waited by the door as the tall priest with the German-sounding name—Dieter?—herded all the children into the dining hall and got them quieted down by feeding them. Included in the new supplies were dried milk and huge boxes of macaroni and cheese, both easy to fix. As the kids ate, they joked and jostled each other, but Yeager found it more orderly and quiet than the average school lunchroom in the States. Probably something to do with fear of Prussian discipline as meted out by the German ex-pat Father Dieter—no, *Dietrich*—who paced the aisles, arms behind his back, a wooden ruler in one hand.

Yeager caught the priest's attention and motioned to meet him at the dining-hall door. He took Dietrich aside and spoke to him in a low voice. "It's a strong possibility the bad guys will come back. If they're gonna do it, they'll hit us soon before we can get set. They wait too long, the sun will be in their eyes."

"Ja." Dietrich nodded. "This makes sense." The priest spoke Spanish with a strong accent, but when he switched to English, it was even stronger.

"Whatever happens, it would be best to keep the children here, away from the outside walls. Better yet, a basement."

Father Dietrich tilted his head back and looked at the ceiling for a long count of three. "No. The basement here is very crowded with equipment. Here would be better, where the children are comfortable and they know their surroundings."

"You know best," Yeager said. "I'll leave you to it. Just keep them out of the halls and away from any windows until we give the all clear."

Dietrich nodded once, a sharp inclination of his head, more of a bow than a nod. "It shall be as you say. I will have Father Pepe bring activity books, and we will conduct lessons here." He hesitated.

"What is it?" Yeager asked.

"There is one boy. His name is Juan. He has disappeared from the mission. He does this quite frequently, runs off to the mountains for hours and hours. I believe you met this boy earlier when you first arrived. His running away is a discipline issue about which we have had many, many discussions. However, I am concerned for him."

"All right, Father." Yeager patted the priest on the shoulder. "I'll have the guys keep their eyes peeled. Anything else?"

"No, Mr. Yeager, there is nothing else. Please. Go with God."

"Yes, sir, I will. God and my forty-five."

CHAPTER 20

ERDUGO FOUND RAUL AND HIS men beside the road, waiting for him. They stood around their cars, rifles propped on hips, or they lounged in the shade, passing around a bottle of tequila. Raul came up to the window of the Land Rover when Verdugo stopped.

"They caught me by surprise, Raul." Verdugo put the shift lever in park but left the engine running. Dust eddied and swirled in the open window. "We will not let that happen again."

"We are going back?"

"Of course," Verdugo rasped, anger coloring his voice. "I will not be treated this way, not by anybody. Especially not by truck drivers and priests."

"How do you want to do it?"

"How? *How?* I want to slam through the front door with everything we have and kill everyone in sight." Verdugo had learned tactics in the Villas de Salvacar attack, early in 2010, and the Horizontes del Sur massacre in October of that year. The La Línea team had used the same technique in both shooting sprees: armed with assault rifles and masks, Verdugo and his teammates had blocked off the street at both ends of the Juarez neighborhood and hit the location with maximum force. The targets were unarmed—teenagers for the most part—and the results were devastating: sixteen killed in the first and fourteen in the second.

How could anybody resist for long, given a full-frontal assault by his men, his veterans of murder and massacre? The people in the mission, including the mercenaries, would be overwhelmed in minutes. Yes, he might take some losses, but in the end, the message sent by the total annihilation of an orphanage would reverberate around the world. Grupo Verdugo's rightful place in the hierarchy of Mexican cartels would be guaranteed.

"Gather the men," Verdugo ordered through his tight grin. "Turn these cars around. We go back. Now."

———————————

Yeager went down the hall between the chapel and main building on his way to the bell tower. At the end, a door opened onto a closet-sized room with a ladder against one wall. Overhead, sunlight poured through an open trapdoor.

He climbed the ladder and found Smitty and Riley snugged down behind the parapet. A brass bell hung in the center of the cupola, green with age.

"You make one hell of a Quasimodo," Yeager told the big man.

Smitty laughed and waved a hand, indicating the vista as if he were a giant bearded tour guide. "And this here's one hell of a Notterdame."

"No shit." From the tower, they had a panoramic view of the entire valley, from north to south. The sun had edged down behind them, painting the red-rock cliffs and pine forest with a golden brush.

"Look here," Yeager said. The river ran left to right across their field of vision. He pointed to a spot at the ten-o'clock position. "See those rills? That's a low spot in the river, probably low enough to cross on foot. You'll need to keep one eye there."

"One eye, gotcha."

"Now here"—Yeager pointed to the bridge at their two o'clock— "is where I think they'll come first."

"Agreed."

"Well, good, cause here's the hard part. You think you can light up any vehicle that tries crossing? Stop 'em cold with the Barrett?"

"Aw, hell, Yeager." Smitty frowned and spat over the side. "That's, like, a hunnert yards. I could shoot a gnat's ass blind drunk on roller skates at a hunnert yards."

"Just be sure 'n stop the first vehicle that tries to cross. You disable a car there, it's as good as a roadblock."

"Why not let the first couple through?" Riley asked. "Stop number three, and the first two are cut off."

"Could do that," Yeager admitted. "I just didn't like the idea of anybody running around loose on this side of the river. This way, they'll all have to come on foot, and that means we can hold 'em at a distance. At least until nightfall."

"Even after." Smitty grinned like a drunken Santa Claus.

"Huh?"

"Didn't you see? I brung us all some NVGs. We can shoot them little peckerheads in the dark, and they'll never know what hit 'em."

"Smitty, remind me when this is over: I'm gonna buy you a cigar and a bottle of whiskey. Okay, keep in mind I'll be out there in the trees on the right. Don't shoot me. Riley, you good here?"

Riley nodded and tamped his tin of Skoal into one hand.

"You act any more excited," Yeager said, "and you could work at the DMV."

Riley twitched a smile, pinched out a wad of tobacco, and got it seated in his lip. Yeager clapped him on the back and started down the ladder then stopped. "Where'd you leave that midget Mexican?"

"Playin' doctor." Riley spat over the side. "Classroom twelve."

Yeager left them to it. As he descended, Smitty's voice followed him. "You don't talk much, do ya, Riley? Well, that's okay, 'cause I talk like there's only so many words left, and I gotta use 'em all afore I die. There was this time…"

Yeager smiled and closed the door to the access ladder. *Those two should get along fine. As long as Riley doesn't stick a knife in the big man's throat just to shut him up.*

He stopped a chubby priest coming out of the chapel—a happy little round man who reminded Yeager of a Hispanic Friar Tuck—and asked directions to classroom twelve.

"Sí, sí, sí," the man burbled and took his arm. He pointed down the hall with his free hand. "At the end of this hall is the connecting door to the dormitory quadrangle. Like a square, yes? Bueno. You and your people are in the hall nearest this building—call it the A hall, yes? Bueno. Now, the two side halls are B and C. The boys are in the B hall, and the girls are in the C hall, okay? Bueno. Also the patients from the hospital are in C since we have more room. Now, the last hall is—"

"D hall?"

"Sí, sí, sí, D hall. That is where the classrooms are."

"Muchas gracias, Padre."

"Eh bien. Vaya con Dios." The short man patted him on the arm and showed a wall of teeth in a happy grin. "If you have any trouble, just ask any of the children to come get Father Pepe. I will come find you and lead you to the light."

Yeager followed the connecting door and entered the quadrangle. He recognized the first hallway as the one with their rooms and found the boys' wing right where the tubby priest said it would be. He broke into a trot, his footsteps echoing in the empty hall. The doors were open, and he glanced in as he passed. Small dorm rooms, well kept, neat as pins with the exception of schoolbooks and some loose papers and pencils. Whatever else was going on here, the priests ran a disciplined operation.

At the end of B hall, the corridor made a ninety-degree left turn. Here the rooms changed from small bedrooms to larger schoolrooms. A blood trail streaked the hallway from a room two-thirds of the way down to one nearby. When he cautiously checked the end of the trail, Yeager found two dead gunmen in masks, one with half his head blown away.

Sometimes Riley carried his silent act too far; he'd not mentioned having any trouble.

At classroom twelve, Yeager found Victor holding a blood-spotted rag to a nurse's head. The woman looked woozy and more than a little worse for wear. On the table behind them, Dr. Lopez held a stethoscope to a tiny girl's chest.

The doctor snapped one finger up in a command for silence, and Yeager froze.

"Okay," she said after a long pause. "Emelita seems to be doing just fine." Lopez put the stethoscope away and fixed Yeager with a challenging stare. "No thanks to these people who keep barging in. What is it?"

"Actually, ma'am, I need this hombre here." Yeager hooked a thumb at Victor. "We have a little situation with Verdugo's people."

"Of course." The doctor came around the table and took the cloth. "Thank you, Señor Ruiz, for taking care of Marta. I... I appreciate it. Very much."

"Nah, *querida*, no worries." Por Que straightened and gave the tiny woman's shoulder a light squeeze. "And call me Victor. Or Superman if you must."

"C'mon, Stupor-man," Yeager said. "Your day's not over yet."

"Work, work, work," Victor groused but picked up his rifle and headed for the door.

"Señor Ruiz." Dr. Lopez seemed quite different from the bossy tyrant Yeager remembered from that morning. "Victor... uh..."

Yeager's stout friend paused and looked back, raising a questioning eyebrow.

"I... I wanted to say thank you also for... for what you did. Earlier. When they wanted to hurt my patient."

Por Que waved it off. "Hey, chica, what else would I be doing today?"

Yeager kept his silence until he closed the classroom door. Then, in a singsong voice, he said, "Victor and the doctor, sitting in a tree—"

"Shut up."

"Okay, lover boy, listen up." Yeager handed him his tac radio and replayed the scene with Verdugo and his men. "And this guy, Verdugo, looked pissed. I think he's coming back, and soon. I need you to cover the back and south sides of the mission, preferably from the roof of the quadrangle. They get inside the building, and we're toast."

"Gotcha. I saw a roof access when we swept the building earlier. I'm on it." He turned and trotted toward B hall.

"You want a shirt?" Yeager called.

"Nah, I'm good this way," Por Que called over his shoulder. "The bad guys get a look at my superior physique, and they will roll over and die right there. Won't have to shoot nobody."

"Die of laughter," Yeager yelled. Victor shot him the finger without looking back.

With the front covered by Smitty and Riley and the back by Por Que, that left Yeager the option of taking a position on the roof or inside the building. The other possibility would be to go outside and engage the enemy from the flank.

Although the building offered the protection of stout walls, the trade-off was confinement to a fixed position and fewer shooting angles. Yeager made his way through the narrow halls to the main doors without encountering another person. The volume of chatter from the dining room filtered through the space, reminding Yeager once again of an elementary school at lunchtime.

Two stout oaken doors stood at the main entrance to the mission complex, though to call it *secured* would have been an overstatement. A close look at the lock showed nothing more than a single deadbolt on one door and a floor peg on the other. A solid blow from a sledgehammer would split wood around the deadbolt latch and pop the door in an instant.

Stepping outside, Yeager took a deep breath of the mountain air. The shadows in the mission courtyard had grown longer in the short time since he had left the bell tower. From the village, a faint trickle of Tejano music played from somebody's radio, and an engine revved and stalled then revved again.

Yes, outside was better.

Yeager went right, carrying the M4 and a backpack of loaded magazines, bottled water, and some trail bars. On his hip rode the Springfield XDM, extra mags, and a Gerber knife. A short dogtrot from the mission, the forest sprang up from the red clay soil, a thick line of pine mixed with deciduous trees. The leaves on the latter had started turning, and two or three drifted past as he entered the tree line.

The light changed from a warm glow to dappled shadows. Birds scattered and danced through the trees, and a woodpecker rattled in the distance. Yeager soaked in the forest. The deeper he moved into the trees, the more his predator's nature replaced the civilized mask he normally wore. His lips skinned back, and he slipped between patches of sun, searching for a place to make his stand.

CHAPTER 21

VERDUGO'S SMALL CONVOY RACED INTO Rascón at high speed. The lead car, an Expedition, made a tire-smoking left turn onto the bridge to the mission. The red Hummer H3 followed, its big rear end sliding and fishtailing when the driver overcorrected. Verdugo, in the third of four cars, tapped the brakes, widening the gap between him and the skidding H3.

The Hummer's brake lights flared on, and the big SUV nosed down, tires squealing as it slid forward. Verdugo slammed on the brakes and skidded to a stop. The stink of burned rubber filled the air, and clouds of gray smoke eddied and swirled in the wind.

"*Tu madre!*" Verdugo shouted.

The lead car slewed sideways on the bridge, and its grille embedded in the right guardrail with a crunch of metal. The hood buckled, and steam fogged the front end.

Boom! A powerful rifle punctuated the shouting of his men. The Hummer thudded into the back of the wounded Expedition and knocked it farther sideways.

Men spilled out of the front two cars. Some fell flat as they ducked and scuttled toward Verdugo's vehicle, weapons clutched in their hands. It took a long second for him to realize his men were under fire. The trucker and his men had beaten him to the punch, taking first blood and throwing him on the defensive. Verdugo cursed again.

The rattle of small-arms fire came in quick bursts. Metal *pinged* and glass *cracked* with hits from high-velocity bullets. Verdugo ducked instinctively. His windshield spiderwebbed from three neat holes the instant after he dropped below the dash. They were being raked by bursts of automatic weapons. The heaviest fire was coming from the left. Probably from the tree line. There was also a very big rifle set up somewhere. On top of the mission?

A cacophony of tactical rifles on full auto ripped across the river as his men found their poise and returned fire. The steady boom of the big rifle punctuated the crack and chatter of smaller weapons.

I have to get out of here. Verdugo launched himself across the center console and punched at the latch on the passenger side. Shoving the door open, he tumbled from the Land Rover in a graceless heap, spraining his left wrist in the fall. He rolled more than ran to the back of the car, where he paused by the tailgate.

Glass shattered over his head and sprinkled down his collar.

Boom! The sound of the rifle came a split-second after the bullet pierced the Land Rover's rear window. Verdugo crouched by the bumper and peeked through the crazed glass.

The Expedition blocked the bridge at the midpoint, the Hummer jammed into its right-rear-quarter panel. His car had come to a stop with its front tires on the bridge, at a forty-five-degree angle. The car behind him—a black Suburban with Raul and four other men— had stopped six feet away on the main road. Its doors were open, and four men huddled on the right side, popping up at intervals to spray the forest, or the mission, with unaimed, undisciplined fire. The last car in line was in a similar position.

Men ran past him, heads down, seeking cover. Two, then three more. As the last in line came past the tailgate, his head disappeared in a red mist.

Boom!

Verdugo took a quick count as best he could from his current position. He estimated thirteen men left out of the twenty-one he'd started with. Four had never come out of the mission from their first trip. Which meant four more had gone down since the Expedition was hit crossing the bridge. Verdugo did the math again in his head and swore.

Fucking gringo truck driver. Twenty-one dead since yesterday. What a fucking disaster.

"Raul!" he shouted as loud as his throat would allow. "Raul! Goddammit, Raul, get over here!"

Boom! The Land Rover shuddered with impact. Steam hissed and billowed from the front of the vehicle, making at least a partially effective smoke screen. Verdugo gathered his legs and ran for the next vehicle in line.

A whine zipped by his head, and a bullet sparked off the road in front of him. Someone in the trees had targeted him. Verdugo dove for the protection of the car, scraping his hands and sending a shock of pain through his sprained wrist.

"Fucking whore bitch Mother of God!"

Pings and thumps answered him as the shooter peppered the other side of the SUV. Two bullets popped through the door. A man fell back with a cry of pain, clutching his shoulder. The others dropped to the ground and huddled there.

"Raul!"

"Sí! Coming, chief."

Verdugo cursed in a solid stream while he waited for his lieutenant to come forward.

How many of them could there be? Two? No, somebody said four. Who said that? I don't remember, and it doesn't matter. We have superior numbers; we can take them. They just caught us by surprise. "Again," he spat.

Verdugo peeked from behind the front tire and squinted into the trees. Maybe he could get lucky and spot the shooter. The setting sun threw light directly into his eyes. He could see nothing.

"No matter," he whispered to himself. "In a few minutes, the sun will be down, and we'll rush those woods in force." Once in the protection of the forest, the sniper with the big gun would be out of play. Then it would be down to the two or three men in the woods against his thirteen.

And then it would all be over for the truck driver and his friends.

———◆———

Yeager peered through a screen of leaves and tried to see where Verdugo had gone to ground. He stretched out on his belly, twenty yards into the forest, resting the barrel of the M4 on a brush-screened fallen log. He had an excellent field of fire, covering the entire length of the bridge and main road, only occasionally interrupted by trees.

A natural cut, more of a gulley or a drainage ditch, gave him a convenient egress path should he need to unass the blind and head for cover. All in all, the spot met his highest standards of approval for an ambush site.

Another testament to its effectiveness was the presence of three unmoving men, boneless heaps sprawled beside the tangle of cars on the bridge. When Smitty had uncorked the Barrett and decapitated the driver of the lead vehicle, Yeager had been in perfect position to drop the remaining three men in the car when they'd bailed out.

He had then shifted fire to the second car. Those men reacted quickly and well, and he recorded no hits. After that, he had one quick shot at Verdugo. Since then, nothing. The bad guys were keeping their heads down. Yeager wasted the occasional burst through the car doors to keep them pinned down. The thin metal door of a modern car would not stop a BB, let alone a .223 FMJ round, so his shooting had to be making them nervous and hesitant.

Smitty's voice crackled over the radio earpiece. "Papa Bear to Ugly Trucker. Come back."

Yeager twitched a smile. *Papa Bear?* He clicked his push-to-talk button. "Yeah, Papa; go for Trucker."

"Cowboy counted fourteen guys, repeat one-four tangos, behind them cars. Over."

"Confirm one-four tangos."

"What's the plan, Trucker man?"

"Any more RPGs, Papa?"

"That's a negatory, Trucker. I jest had the one."

Yeager remained quiet. Movement from car to car caught his eye, and he triggered a burst. Metal sparked, and he made more holes in the Land Rover but could see no other effect.

He keyed his mike again. "Break-break. Trucker to Midget, come in."

A pause, then a click. "Handsome Mexican Superman here. Wassup, boss?"

"I'm going to work my way across the road and try for their rear. Come up to the front of the mission. When I give the go call, you three lay down suppressing fire so I can pop out and ruin their fucking day. Over."

"Chu got it, homes."

Yeager eased back from the log and belly crawled into the cut, slithering around and under low bushes and creepers. He ignored the scratches and pokes from foliage and sharp rocks, focused only on moving with the best combination of speed and stealth that he could achieve. At the bottom of the cut, he came up to a crouch and was able to travel more freely, slipping through the shadows of the miniravine.

The sunlight had all but disappeared this deep in the forest. The last of it flared along the ridge behind the mission, cutting through the trees in long, diagonal stripes. A gust of chilly air stirred the pines and scattered leaves from the oak and poplar trees.

Yeager followed the cut for a hundred yards downslope, heading for the road. He started breathing hard about halfway there, from a combination of the altitude and lack of exercise.

"No doubt about it," he said under his breath. "I make it through this, I gotta get back in shape." He slowed when the river came in sight, a green slash through the trees ahead. Moving with stealth, Yeager hugged the embankment and followed it until he found a crossing, dotted with algae-coated boulders. He balanced his way across the water and made for the road, intending to cut across at least two hundred yards south of the attacking force.

The chatter of weapons had long fallen silent except for the occasional kettledrum thump of Smitty's Barrett. At the edge of the road, Yeager paused and scanned in both directions. The forest continued on the other side, climbing upslope toward another ridge. To his left, a curve blocked his view of the village and the invading Grupo Verdugo people. To the right, the pavement ended and hard-packed gravel took over, a narrow tunnel of red rock and dirt cutting through the greenery.

Yeager took a chance and dogtrotted right to put some distance between him and the bandits. When he was certain he was far enough away, he crossed the road and hit the slope on the other side at a run. He climbed in short, choppy steps, digging in and pushing himself upward. He started panting within seconds, sweat slicked with blood pounding in his ears.

Jesus, Yeager, this is embarrassing. He cursed his own tired body and forced it to move faster. He wanted to get high enough that he could lay fire directly down into the enemy rear from behind them and to their left. It would be a devastating surprise to anybody caught that way, forcing them into an awkward turn to counterfire. Verdugo's men would be caught flat-footed and chopped up like salsa in a Cuisinart.

"If… I can… only… get there in time," Yeager grunted under his breath. He had always hated running in the Marine Corps, frequently coming in dead last on the company runs. His jogging ability had not improved with age.

At close to fifty yards uphill, he cut left and slowed, following a game trail. He sucked air in deep, gulping breaths and worked at slowing his heart rate. Pounding as it was now, the chances he could hit a bull in the ass with a bass fiddle dropped to nil.

Six minutes of steady movement brought him to a gap in the trees. There, not eighty yards away, a cluster of men huddled against the sides of two SUVs, holding assault rifles and shifting nervously. The shadows cast by the cars reached all the way to the runoff ditch on the near side of the road. There wasn't much light left, but there was enough to spot Verdugo. His blond hair stood out. He stood at the far right near the wheel of the second-to-last car in line. He and his guy, Raul, had their heads together, talking.

Yeager mopped sweat off his face with the back of his sleeve.

Perfect. Now I need to find a good spot to set up so I can kill the bastard and put an end to this little party.

CHAPTER 22

JUAN FOLLOWED THE NATURAL TUNNEL into the mountain. It continued straight and fairly level for several hundred paces. The occasional dip in the floor, or rocky outcropping, made the footing treacherous and no walk in the park. Taken as a whole, however, Juan discovered that he could move quickly and easily.

And then he had to stop. The tunnel opened into a chamber so large he could not see the other side. The floor ramped down, and the ceiling disappeared into the gloom above. The cave had grown warmer the deeper he had gone; sweat patched his underarms and dripped from his nose.

And the smell. A rank stench from the moist soil underfoot made his eyes water, and he had to cover his nose with the crook of his elbow. *Madre de Dios, Armando. What is that stink? And how far down do I want to go to hide from Miguel? Is this far enough?*

Armando had no ready answer. Juan paused at the lip of the ramp and considered the best course of action. Move forward or stay still?

He played the flashlight around. The smell could be from a dead animal. Maybe even a dead human body. What if this was the dumping ground of the narcos? Maybe they used this cave as a place to discard their victims once they tortured and raped and killed them. Maybe Miguel came here all the time and knew this cave better than anyone. Juan shuddered.

In the darkness, it was easy to picture any number of possibilities, each more dreadful than the last. Images played on the movie screen of his mind: rotting skulls with lank strands of hair still clinging to them and rats and snakes crawling through their empty eye sockets. Bony hands reaching through the soil, waiting for the unwary to pass so they could grab an ankle.

"Shut up, stupid." His voice echoed in the chamber, bouncing back to him in double waves. "Armando's not afraid. Are you? D'Artagnan wouldn't be afraid."

Juan took a step forward, feeling with the toe of his high-top sneaker for firm ground. The slope wasn't bad—maybe about half the steepness of a playground slide. He took another step, then another.

The tunnel expanded. It felt as though he ventured into the belly of huge snake or, better yet, a dragon. Narrow at the neck, wide at the belly.

Juan took another step. Black soil squished under his foot. He checked with the flashlight and found the footing pretty firm. Halfway through his next step, something overhead rustled, and Juan pointed the flashlight at the ceiling.

And slipped.

His butt slapped hard on the ground then started to slide in the moist dirt. He grabbed at the floor with his free hand, holding the flashlight over his head. His skid slowed, and he breathed out a sigh...

Without warning, the slope went from a mild incline to a funhouse slide. Juan shot downward with a startled yell, tobogganing on his back, flashlight beam dancing in wild swings. The stink billowed up from all around him, smelling more and more like... *dung!*

In the space of a few heartbeats, Juan hit the bottom of the slope and tumbled into a reeking pile of damp earth. The flashlight jarred from his hand, arced across the gallery, and painted the ceiling with its yellow light. The flashlight struck the floor with a thump and went out.

Juan was left in a darkness so total and absolute that spots danced in his eyes. But that didn't terrify him nearly as much as the scene revealed by the last moments of the flashlight's flight through space. He had no problem seeing, in that one wild swing of the light, a colony of hundreds and hundreds of bats suspended above him. Their tiny, sightless eyes glittered in that one brief moment of illumination as they stirred at the intrusion into their domain.

When the light went out, Juan could no longer see the packed mass of tiny gray bodies as they woke and started to rustle and flutter in agitation.

Oscar Cruz approached Yeager's house from the side, using the barn to shield his progress. At the back corner of the barn, he drew his pistol and went to one knee. He risked a quick peek around the corner and then took a longer look.

The place appeared dead. Nothing moved. Only one light glowed from a downstairs window. After having watched the house for two days, Cruz expected to see more lights on. Clouds the color of an undertaker's frown hid the sunset, making it uniformly darker by the minute.

No TV played. No dog barked. They seemed to be gone. Was this a shopping trip for groceries, or a long vacation? Maybe they'd gone to meet Yeager. How ironic that would be. *I spend all this time waiting for Yeager, and they go off to meet him somewhere.*

Oscar stalked forward, reaching the house without raising an alarm. He checked one window after another along the sides and back of the house. Dead quiet. No people moved around and, more importantly, no dog. Aside from a single lamp in the den, the house was dark and silent.

He mounted the rear steps and peered in the glass pane of what turned out to be the kitchen. On the right-hand wall, near the door, an alarm keypad glowed a dull green. A red light on the panel blinked, indicating the alarm was set. Unfortunately, disabling alarms wasn't something he knew how to do. During their early days, he and Humberto had done a few smash-and-grab burglaries, but then they had drifted into extortion and prostitution and, from there, into hijacking. Oscar had never learned how to bypass an alarm system.

He stepped off the porch and checked the rest of the house just to be sure. He even stood on the porch and rang the doorbell.

Nothing.

What now? Oscar traipsed back to the barn and circled that building, looking for alarm connections. He did not find any. So it looked like the barn would be it. At least he'd be inside, out of the wind and chill.

He stopped in his tracks. A glance at the upper floor of the house brought a smile to his face. One window, on the side of the house, was cracked open a couple of inches. *Why not wait in even greater comfort?*

A handy trellis led to the roof of the wraparound porch. From there, it would be an easy reach to the window frame. As long as he avoided motion detectors, he could slip into the house and lie in wait for the woman and the boy.

Oscar chafed his hands for warmth and started to climb.

⸻ ⧫ ⸻

Charlie did not resent returning to the house for David's games; the time lost was not that significant. An hour's drive to Austin, drop David off at Maria's, then dinner with Martha and Tim, who worked at the University. She had a room reserved at the downtown Marriot—the same place she and Abel had first made love—and she planned to wallow in good memories.

That man better be on the way home. If not, I'll drive down to Mexico and get him myself.

Her headlights panned across the barn, and her tires crunched the gravel driveway when she pulled in. It was early to be this dark, even for November. A blanket of low cloud cover blotted out warmth and light.

"Okay, kiddo," she said. "Let's get what you need. Hit the bathroom, too, as long as we're here."

David mumbled something she felt sure was a sarcastic teenage retort, the kind that seemed to come as naturally as breathing to kids his age. Rascal bounded from the open car door as though he hadn't seen home in months. He ran a complete circle around the car, raced to an oak tree, and watered it then headed for David at a dead run.

The dog tackled the boy halfway to the front door.

"Get down, you moron." David laughed and tussled with the dog.

Charlie stepped around the wrestling match, flipping through her key ring. David and Rascal raced past her, headed for the porch. She toggled off the alarm with her remote then stopped in her tracks.

Rascal had gone stiff, no longer playing a game. All four legs were locked, the ruff around his neck bristled out, and he had started a low growl in the back of his throat—a chilling sound that Charlie had never heard the dog make.

David looked at her with his face scrunched. "What's gotten into him?"

The shepherd pup stared at the front door, lips skinned back and teeth bared all the way back to his jaw.

"Get off the porch, David."

"What?"

"Get. Off. The porch. Now."

David, looking bewildered, joined her at the bottom step.

"What is it?"

Charlie didn't answer. She grabbed his hand and backed away. With her free hand, she dug in her purse for her cell phone before remembering it sat in the charger in the car.

"Dammit," she muttered.

"Mom?"

Her gun was in the nightstand next to the bed, not in her purse. How could she have gotten so complacent that she stopped carrying a weapon?

"Mom, what the heck?"

"Ssshhhh. Not now, David. Go wait in the car. Get my cell phone and be ready to call 9-1-1."

Rascal continued growling and remained immobile, watching the door.

"Rascal!" she snapped. "Heel!"

The dog ignored her.

"Go to the car, David. Now."

"But, Mom—"

"No *buts*. Go."

Charlie went back to the porch and took a quick peek in the front-door windowpane. Nothing seemed out of place, but Rascal's attitude had every spidey sense she possessed tingling at full alert. *He's really spooked. This is something bigger than a squirrel.*

"C'mon, boy," she murmured, taking the dog's collar in one hand. Working gently, encouraging and cajoling, she pulled the dog back from the door. He remained determined to stay at his post, so she wound up doing more pulling than she wanted, but she finally managed to get him back to the car.

"Get in there, Rascal. Guard David."

She shut the dog inside, where he promptly jumped into the driver's seat, planted both paws on the dash, and growled murder at the house. David watched on the passenger side, frowning. He held her phone up so she could see he had it in hand.

Charlie made a perimeter check. All doors locked, and no windows broken. Everything seemed secure. *So, what the hell had made the dog go crazy? A solicitor? Did another dog, or a wolf, pee on the door?*

Wolves and stray dogs were not uncommon, but they tended not to venture near homes during daylight hours. Same with coyotes. Door-to-door salesmen and Jehovah's Witnesses came by every once in a while, and Rascal tended to bark at them, but more a warning than a threat. She had never seen him this spooked.

Charlie came back around to the front porch and mounted the steps again. She stuck her key in the door and unlocked it, swinging the door wide without going in.

Muffled by the car windows, Rascal barked. She glanced back. The dog was beside himself, his face pressed to the windscreen one moment, jumping into the backseat and returning to the front in the next.

"Okay," she whispered. "This is the part in the horror movie where the dumb girl goes into the spooky house and gets her face eaten off."

Charlie stayed at the threshold and took a long look around. Directly in front of her, a staircase led to the second floor. To her left, the den and living area. To her right, the dining room. Not a damned thing was out of place. Anywhere.

From where she stood she could see the entertainment center with an expensive receiver and Blu-ray player, both untouched. The dining room had a china hutch, inside of which was her grandma's silver set. The drawer wasn't open. *Decision time, Charlotte. Trust the dog and call the cops? Or take the mutt to the vet for a checkup on his paranoia bone?*

She wanted to blow it off. They were already late; any more delay would mean hitting Austin traffic at the worst possible time.

I need my gun. The staircase was directly in front of her. Six steps away. One quick run to the top, right turn into the bedroom, circle to the left side of the bed, and open the nightstand. Her Smith & Wesson N-frame .41 Magnum, lying in a cushion of a folded towel she kept there to stop the gun from sliding around.

Ten seconds, tops.

She glanced back at the car. David and Rascal sat there, eyes fixed on her, unmoving. At least the dog had finally stopped going nuts, though the way he stared at her through the safety glass of the windshield...

Charlie shivered. "This is ridiculous." Nothing moved in the house. There was no sound but the tick of an heirloom clock in the living room, one that required winding with an old-fashioned key. Yeager said the chimes sounded prissy, yet he wound the spring every morning.

Charlie gritted her teeth, crossed the foyer, and jogged up the stairs.

CHAPTER 23

YEAGER DUCKED AND TWISTED HIS way through the brush to reach a better overlook position. He wanted to be directly behind the cartel shooters when he opened up on them. Being taken from the rear was one of the most terrifying things for a force in the open. A swift, brutal attack should scatter Verdugo's men and leave them easy pickings for Smitty and his sniper rifle.

"Trucker, Trucker," crackled in his ear. *Victor.*

Yeager kept moving and pushed the talk button. "Go," he whispered.

"They're moving, Truckboy. Hitting the trees. You better haul ass if you want a shot."

"How many?"

A booming report from the Barrett punctuated Victor's transmission. A half second later, lighter weapons opened up from the mission rooftop as Victor and Riley got involved.

"Twelve, maybe thirteen."

Yeager abandoned stealth and crashed through the brush, seeking a clearing. Limbs swiped at his face, and vines grabbed his ankles. He cleared a boulder in the trail in one leap then skidded to a stop when he found a break in the trees on the other side.

Verdugo and his men had abandoned their position and were pumping hard for the woods on the opposite side of the road. They were storming the position Yeager had already abandoned. A figure lay sprawled in a lifeless heap, victim of Smitty's .50-caliber bullet. Even a close miss with one of those would ruin your whole day; a direct hit left a distinct mess.

As if to add an exclamation mark, the Barrett spoke again, and another cartel fighter was blown sideways, a spray of red exploding from his side.

Yeager sought the blond hair of Verdugo, but the last of the orange sun had dropped below the horizon, and all the running figures looked the same. Snapping the M4 to his cheek, he picked a target at random. He fired a three-round burst. Picked another. Fired. And another. Fired.

Then they were gone, lost in the trees. At least one of his rounds had hit a target. A man writhed on the ground, twisting in agony, moaning loud enough to be heard over a hundred yards away.

Shooting men in the back turned Yeager's stomach, but he willed the feeling away. These men were prepared to kill children. They were not worthy of a warrior's death. He had to keep that thought in mind if he wanted to survive this fight.

And it had just gotten messier. The enemy—at least eleven men—had reached the security of the woods, where they'd be under the cover of darkness. If he snuck into that same forest and played a little game of Knife Fight in the Dark, the odds were heavily stacked against him. He had done it before, against mountain fighters in Afghanistan, but never at ten-to-one odds.

Yeager hunkered down behind the nearby boulder and keyed his mike. "Listen up, kids. Trucker's coming home. I'll be crossing upstream through the ford on the north side. Don't shoot me."

"Ten-four, good buddy," Por Que drawled. "Bring it on, and we'll keep the smokies off your tail."

Yeager broke static twice rather than replying and headed north again. He planned to circle the village and come out on the other side of it. No reason to get the locals involved, or interested in his movements. There was no telling how many of them were spies for Verdugo or what the cartel leader might do if he thought the natives were fraternizing with the enemy.

Night came on with a rush; the first stars prickled the sky. A cold wind gusted from the north, drying the sweat on Yeager's face and chilling his body. At such a high altitude, snow this early in the year was not unheard-of though Yeager sensed no dampness on the breeze.

Still, it should be a long, uncomfortable night for Verdugo and his men.

Yeager grinned and picked up his pace, jogging along the mountain trail by a twilight sky.

The moment after he realized he was in a cave full of bats with no flashlight, a blind panic set in so deep and so severe Juan could not form a single rational thought. Images came to him in flashes. The San Felipe mission—no one there knew where he was. The slide down the incline—no way to get back up. He was trapped. With bats. They would latch onto his neck and suck his blood. He would die in this cave. Alone.

Juan struck out in a blind panic, thrashing through the loose soil—guano—of the cave floor, mewling a terrified whimper. No direction. No thought. He scrabbled across the floor on hands and knees, blindly searching for a way out.

Rustling from above fed his panic, stoking it to a white-hot flame of fear. Juan had no idea how long he stayed in that state of mindless insanity. Minutes? Hours? He had no idea which direction he traveled—toward the ramp or deeper into the cave.

After he'd exhausted himself, Juan sat still on the floor, forearms resting on his knees, head down. Snot clogged his sinuses and dripped from his nose. Heaving sobs wracked his body. He closed his eyes and tried to control his breathing.

"Armando," he cried into the darkness. "Help me. Help me, Armando." His words sounded hollow in the cavern.

Slowly, like water soaking into a sponge, calm and sanity returned. Juan kept his eyes closed and tried to block out the bats, the cave, and everything. He blew his nose with his fingers and flicked away the mucus.

"Armando," he whispered in a calmer, less desperate voice. "Talk to me. Tell me what to do, brother."

After a moment, Juan opened his eyes and panned the cave in a slow, methodical arc. Three-quarters of the way through his search, a glow near the floor arrested his attention. At first, he thought it was his eyes showing spots, like before—playing tricks on him. But the spot didn't move. A steady, yellowish glow held fast two meters away to his right.

At a snail's pace, Juan slid toward the glow, not daring to hope. When he got closer, he extended his hand toward the dim light. His hand brushed metal, and he sucked in a sharp breath. He groped with questing fingers and found the barrel of his flashlight, buried, lamp down in the guano. Only a small bit of light showed through the loam, lighting the soil with a tiny glow only discernable against the utter blackness of the cave.

Pulled free, the light bathed the cavern in so much brightness it hurt his eyes. Juan could not remember ever feeling such a sense of joy as he did in the moment that light sprang free. Tears ran down his cheeks, but he didn't care one bit. He cried and held the flashlight tight in both hands. With light, there was hope.

"Thank you, Armando." Juan rocked in place for a moment. "Thank you, God."

Barely daring to look, Juan glanced at the ceiling. By ones and twos, individual bats detached themselves and flicked away, dancing out of the light and heading back the way he'd come. As if his glance was their cue, the remaining mass of bats broke free and flooded away.

Their sudden movement caused Juan to duck down and scream. The rush of their leathery wings carried on forever, it seemed to him, a steady stream of bats. One of the creatures snagged his hair, and he screamed again. He beat at the thing, swatting and clubbing in a frenzy until it broke free.

All the bats in the world, it seemed, had roosted in this cave. The leathery flutter went on forever. But then the sound tapered off. Another glance confirmed the bats were gone. One or two stragglers flicked past, and then nothing.

Juan found and shouldered his pack, which had fallen off in his panicked scrabble across the cave floor, and pointed the light back at the incline down which he had slid.

The surface of the ramp was slick as grease, coated with a mix of water dripping from an unknown source and bat poop. He tried a couple of times to get enough purchase to climb back out that way, but it was no good. He took no more than two steps before sliding back.

Well, if I can't go back, maybe I can go in the other direction.

"Better than sitting here boohooing like a baby, hey, Armando?"

Juan swung the light around the cavern and followed the wall to his left for no particular reason. He had read somewhere that if you were ever lost in a maze, just pick one direction, either left or right, and keep turning that way. Eventually, if you kept going and didn't lose track, you would find the exit.

His pants were wet and chafed his legs. He was covered in guano, and the smell saturated everything. The stench had only gotten better because he couldn't smell it anymore. But he was moving forward.

"Hey, Armando, do me a favor. Don't tell no one I peed my pants, okay? We'll keep that to ourselves."

By the time Yeager worked his way back across the river and into the mission, full darkness had set in. He reported his position at frequent intervals so none of his companions would light him up if they saw motion. He keyed his radio. "Entering the mission. Everyone, gather in the bell tower. We need a council of war."

He came through the front doors, which he would have to find a better way to secure, and headed for the bell tower. He stopped along the way for a brief conference with Father Sebastian, who seemed no happier than he had before. During the conversation, the priest reported the phone lines were down.

"Cut by Verdugo?" Yeager asked.

Father Sebastian shrugged. "It is possible, though phone service here in the mountains is unreliable at best. Since the earthquake, even more so."

Yeager left the old priest and climbed the ladder to the bell tower, feeling every muscle in his arms and legs protest. No question about it: he needed to get some exercise when this was all over. He found Smitty and Victor sitting cross-legged against the inner wall of the tower. Riley stood watch, ATN night-vision goggles making him look like an alien with a single eye protruding from its forehead.

The air had turned crisp and cold. It was the kind of night when frost would form by midnight and a bucket of water would have a thin film of ice by morning—a cloudless, diamond-sharp sky salted with countless glittering stars. An owl hooted somewhere close by, and a mild breeze carried the scent of frying onions from the village.

"All right, boys." Yeager settled with his back to the wall, next to Victor, stifling a groan.

"Hey, El Toro," Por Que said, "you sound tired. That little bit of exercise wear you out?"

"What, that?" Yeager snorted. "No, but I think I might have pulled a hammy. Let me stretch it out for a bit, and I'll be fine."

"Sure," Victor said, drawing it out. "You go with that story."

"Hell, Vic," Smitty drawled. "Ain't a marine alive gonna admit that he's tuckered out. Marines have big heads, considerin' they's just a small department of the navy."

"Yeah," Yeager said. "The *men's* department."

"And there ain't no such thing as a ex-marine," Smitty said. "You can bet on that."

"Yeager bleeds khaki." Por Que held up his right hand. "Is true. I swear I seen it."

"Hey, Abbott and Costello, listen up. Riley, this speech includes you too." Yeager started to rub his tired legs and stopped. "We signed up to deliver a load of goods and to relieve this here mission. Bring food and medicine and whatnot to a bunch of kids. Supplies. Or at least Victor and I did. Y'all two just got pulled into it."

"Aw, hell," Smitty boomed. "I wouldn't have missed this here party for nothing. I only wish I'd brung more bullets."

Yeager nodded. "Me too, Smitty. And more RPGs. Anyway, mission accomplished. We did what we came for. Now it's time to decide to bet 'em or fold 'em. Smitty, Riley, y'all didn't sign up for an all-out war against the cartel. There's a car in the front court down there; I'm suggesting you take it and hit the road while you can. If you don't want to risk the road, you could probably hike your way through the mountains in a few days."

"Is this the part," Victor said, "where you get out a saber and draw a line in the sand?" He thumped his heel on the floor of the bell tower. "Well, in the wood, I guess."

"Remember the Alamo!" Smitty crowed.

"In all seriousness," Yeager said, unsmiling, "this could turn out to be just like that fight in San Antonio with Jim Bowie and them. We got damn lucky today, and last night as well. They've been underestimating us all along, and we managed to punch them in the nose pretty hard. Knocked 'em back on their heels. But that ain't gonna last. Verdugo gets his head on straight, he's gonna come hard, and he's gonna bring the kitchen sink."

"What about them kids?" Riley spit over the wall, never stopping his scan. "What happens to them?"

"And the doctor." Victor's white teeth gleamed in the moonlight. "Don't forget the pretty doctor lady. Person. Woman. You know."

"Ain't no use you askin' for volumenteers," Smitty said. "We ain't a-bailin' outta this here sit-che-ation. Not for all the beer in Birmingham."

Yeager looked at Victor, who said, "Doan lookit me, esse. I the one gotchu into this thing. Remember? I gotta bring yo' ass back in one piece. If I don't, Charlie gonna have a short but well-tanned skin hanging on her barn door."

"Riley," Yeager said, "you don't have to play this game with these idjuts. They're dumb and don't have an excuse. No harm, no foul if you pull up stakes and head for the border. In fact, it'd be a good idea if you could get out and get a message to de la Cueva. Maybe he can send in some reinforcements."

Riley had started shaking his head the moment Yeager mentioned his name. He spat over the side again. "Nope. I reckon you'll have to use that newfangled telly-phone thingy to call up the old man. I ain't going anywhere." The slim man squared his back and looked away, as movable as a fence post.

"All of y'all are stupider than God made a mule." Yeager sighed. "All right, then. Here's what I think we should do..."

CHAPTER 24

NO ONE WAITED IN THE bedroom when Charlie burst through the door. She quickstepped around the bed and reached her nightstand in two more long strides. The drawer slid open with a wooden rumble, and there, lying on the towel was... an empty place where her revolver should have been.

"Looking for this?"

Charlie spun, heart stuttering. A short, paunchy Hispanic man leaned in the bedroom doorway. He had salty hair, nondescript features, and a mustache. His brown eyes sparkled over the sights of a semiautomatic pistol in his right hand. In his left, dangling by one finger through the trigger guard, was Charlie's S&W.

"Who are you, and what do you want?" She kept her voice calm through an act of will, though her thoughts skittered and short-circuited, fizzy sparks going off behind her eyes. *How could I have been this stupid?*

"Oscar is my name." He pronounced it *OH-scar*, the Spanish way. "You will find out why that is important later, chica." The man grinned. "Now, we will both go back downstairs, where you will call your son to come inside."

"That's not going to happen."

Oscar shrugged. "Then I will just shoot you here and take my time making the boy suffer. It is all of no matter to me which way this goes."

"Wha-What?" Charlie remained rooted in place, her mind flipping through tactics, seeking something she could use as a distraction. Oscar was not big or physically overwhelming. It wasn't inconceivable that she could take him, given the right circumstances. "What have we done to you that you want to hurt us?"

"What have you done?" He frowned as if considering. "Nothing so much. Your friend, though, Señor Yeager, he has done much."

"Abel? This is about Abel?"

"Shut up, now. Move." He gestured with the gun. "Downstairs. Now."

Oscar straightened from the door and took a couple of steps into the room. He turned into a dueler's stance, holding his pistol straight out, squinting slightly over the sights. He held her gun in his left hand, behind him, away from her reach.

At a rumble from the hallway, Charlie's heart seized. Rascal streaked up the stairs in a black-and-tan blur. Silently. He didn't bark. He didn't growl.

He attacked. His jaws clamped on Oscar's left wrist, and forty pounds of adolescent dog hit the end of that arm with the fury of a mother wolf. Oscar yelped in surprise and triggered a shot that burned over Charlie's head close enough to clip a strand of hair. He jerked at the dog's flying tackle and flailed wildly, spinning in a half circle.

Rascal growled deep from his throat, a low, gutteral sound. His hackles were raised, and his eyes glowed with hatred. Oscar screamed. Man and dog fought a tug-of-war, with Oscar's arm as the prize. Until the man brought his pistol up. "No!" Charlie screamed.

Bang!

Rascal yelped and rolled across the floor, wild-eyed, slamming into the nightstand on Yeager's side of the bed. The lamp fell over and hit the floor with a crash, and the dog yelped again.

Charlie spotted her revolver at the foot of the bed and dived for it. She slid across the hardwood floor, snagged the weapon, and triggered off a shot, firing double action, aiming more by feel than sight. A chunk of plaster exploded over Oscar's head. He ducked, showered in white, and twisted through the bedroom door, avoiding her second shot, which ate a divot in the molding on the doorframe.

Ears ringing, Charlie scooted to her feet and snatched a quick peek, only to see Oscar's back as he turned the corner and thundered downstairs.

David! Charlie launched herself through the door, rounded the corner, and snapped a shot at Oscar that hit the floor in the foyer. "Goddammit!" she yelled. *Get control, Charlie.* It was Yeager's voice in her head. *Quit spraying rounds downrange.*

Too late. Oscar was through the door and out of sight.

Charlie took the steps two at time and ran onto the porch. A quick glance confirmed David was okay, standing by the car, cell phone pressed to his ear.

Oscar rounded the barn to her left too fast to get another shot off. She chased him, but by the time she reached the corner of the barn, he was already disappearing into the trees.

At four minutes till ten o'clock, Yeager had the watch. He scanned the greenish landscape through night-vision goggles, moving from one corner of the bell tower to another in a random pattern. His eyes traveled the open ground surrounding the mission and studied each section before moving on. He fought off the third yawn in as many minutes and slapped his cheek hard enough to sting.

Yeager's short nap that morning had been his only sack time since his catnap in the chopper on the crossing down to Mexico. Maybe three hours in the last thirty-six, total? He huddled under a scratchy blanket and blinked bleary eyes. The night had grown frosty, with a light breeze that sent icy fingers into every gap and chilled his nose, making it run. He sniffled and shifted position on the campstool Victor had appropriated from somewhere.

A wolf serenaded the crescent moon, lending the night an element of the surreal. A trio of mule deer ghosted from the tree line on the slope behind the village, on the other side of the valley. A buck and two does.

No other movement, human or animal, had disturbed the peace of the moonlit valley. The people in the town must have gone to ground when the shooting started, as not a one had come outside all night, nor was there any traffic on the road. No music or TV noises came from the houses, and all but a few lights were turned off, which was unusual for this time of night in a Mexican town, even a rural village like Rascón. Or maybe not so unusual, given the threat of violence misting the air like lingering gun smoke.

The buck snapped his head up and froze, followed an instant later by the does. Between one blink and the next, all three were gone, bounding into a gap in the trees and vanishing. Yeager drew a sharp breath and tensed. Something had startled the mule deer.

All night, he had assumed Verdugo would work his way into position for an assault on the mission, given that he did not seem the type of man to accept defeat once, let alone twice in one day. He had guessed wrong.

By twos and threes, the cartel thugs made their way out of the trees near the bridge at about the same point they had gone in. Crabbing like spiders, crouched low, the greenish shapes passed the wreck of the Hummer and the Expedition.

"What are you up to?" Yeager murmured. He poked the snout of the M4 downrange and settled his cheek against the butt. The automatic rifle had no thermal or night sight, so using it in conjunction with his NVGs would be... difficult.

He held fire and watched. Within seconds, engines cranked and caught. The two vehicles at the tail of the convoy roared to life, peeled around in a large circle—churning dust and gravel—and smoked away to the south. The hum of their motors faded to silence as they moved away without slowing or stopping.

Yeager let out a steaming breath and relaxed his grip on the M4.

So now what? Are they coming back tonight? Going for reinforcements?

Yeager did not believe for a second that Verdugo had given up. The luxury of kidding himself would only get a lot of people killed. He had to plan as if the drug runners would be back with an army, loaded for bear and twice as angry as before.

What was it about this place that drew the attention of a creature like Verdugo? Sure, they'd kicked him in the balls in Madera, but that wasn't enough reason to go batshit crazy and decide to murder everyone.

So maybe it was time to get everybody the hell out of Dodge. The problem was how did they evacuate forty kids, the priests, the doctor, and a bunch of sick people? Maybe stuff them all in the back of the trailer and use the Mack to haul everybody. The balky radiator would need another patch job. On the way in, the truck had started steaming from a pinhole leak and had run redline hot for an hour.

So fix the truck, pile everybody inside, and... then what? *Hit a roadblock, and the bad guys open fire, ripping the trailer into confetti along with everyone inside.*

Which left walking out. Yeager frowned and scratched the stubble on his chin. He pictured a line of kids hiking along a mountain trail, strung out for a quarter mile, old people hobbling along behind in hospital gowns, carrying their IV stands. Litters being carried by the priests for those who could not walk.

"Ugh. No thanks."

So that leaves option three: fort up here and call for help.

And try to find a way out that wouldn't get everybody killed.

The police officer who responded to the Hill Country Veterinary Clinic to interview her was pissed she'd left the scene before they arrived. He relaxed a notch when he saw Rascal in the recovery room, a bare patch shaved over his left ear, sporting a small train track of stitches in his pink and swollen flesh.

Charlie stepped into the hall, leaving David stroking Rascal's fur, the oversized puppy twitching in his sleep.

Deputy Worden of the Travis County Sheriff's Department delivered a short lecture about leaving the scene of a shooting. A tall cop with dark hair and thick black eyebrows, Worden chewed spearmint gum and had wraparound sunglasses on a cord around his neck even though it was pitch-dark outside.

"Could you identify the man in your house, Mrs. Buchanan?"

She shook her head. "No. He said his name was Oscar. Short.

Maybe five-six, five-five. He had a round face, plain features. No scars or tats."

"And you clearly saw a firearm? In his hand?"

"Yes, definitely. A semiauto of some kind. How do you think he shot my dog?"

"I... I, uh, I'm sure you're right, Mrs. Buchanan, but I have to ask."

"My fiancé will never let me hear the end of this. I killed the wall and the floor."

"Ma'am?"

"He's an ex-marine and a hell of a shot. My fiancé is. He would have drilled the guy dead center."

"You were lucky, ma'am, that you reacted as fast as you did. Most folks wouldn't have even gotten off a shot, let alone three. May I see your driver's license?"

Charlie dug in her purse, located her ID, and handed it over. Deputy Worden pinned the card to his metal clipboard and started copying information.

He wanted to take her gun—for evidence, he said—but she dug in her heels, telling him the only thing she shot was her house, and they didn't need her gun for that. With the intruder still on the loose, there was no way she would let them take her revolver, not without a fight.

He called his supervisor, who relented and agreed she could keep her weapon.

"Beg your pardon, ma'am," Worden said, "but that big wheel gun is about the most impractical weapon you could use. Why not get a 9mm, like a Glock, or a SIG?"

"My dad gave me this gun when I went to college," Charlie said. "I've carried this thing ever since, and it's always worked when I needed it. I don't trust automatics; they jam too much."

Worden raised a thick eyebrow. "You've had to use a gun before?"

"More often than I've wanted."

Fortunately, he let the subject drop. "Are you going back to your house tonight?"

"Only to set the alarm. I don't think either my son or I could sleep there tonight. I called a friend, and we'll stay at her house."

"I understand," Worden said. "I'll meet you at the house to check it over. You'll need to do a full search to see if you're missing anything. For insurance."

It took eighteen stitches to close the wound in Rascal's scalp. The vet wanted to keep him overnight, so Charlie drove home with David in a quiet car, the empty space left by the dog's absence crushing any conversation before it could start.

They were more than halfway home before David spoke, his voice subdued. "Do you think he'll be okay?"

"Rascal? Yeah, the vet seems to think so, and Dr. Randall is good at his job."

Twin halogen high beams raced ahead of her on the narrow country highway, and it took all of her waning concentration to stay focused on the road. The drainage of adrenaline from her system had left her tired to the point of being groggy and slow witted.

Very little traffic moved on that section of rural blacktop, but the road was a patchwork of various materials applied over a half century of poor county budgets. Asphalt lay in the cracks and over potholes, sometimes two or three patches in the same spot. The yellow lane divider was more of a memory than a reality—faded and washed out or patched over and not repainted.

Traveling on that rough road in a tunnel of blackness, Charlie reached into her purse and touched the walnut grip of the heavy revolver. She had reloaded the spent chambers with spare hollow-points she kept in a speed loader, giving her six chances to get it right the next time. *No more firing blind and taking snap shots without aiming.*

David kept folding a paper towel into a knot, unfolding it, and then twisting it into a new pattern.

Charlie had killed men before—men who'd wanted to hurt her. The memories of that night had dosed her with troubled and restless sleep on more than one occasion. She thought she'd never have to do it again, but now she wished she had. Oscar, the man who had violated the safety and security of her home, was still out there. And it seemed as though he carried a grudge of some kind.

David turned to look behind them. "Is the cop still there?"

"Yes, he is. He's going to follow us home. We're going to lock and set the alarm then go to Judy Loehr's house. You remember Mrs. Loehr, right? My friend from college?"

David mumbled a yes and went back to folding his towel. A minute later, he asked, "When is Abel getting back?"

"I wish I knew, David." She held back the sigh that came with the thought.

She and Yeager had moved to the country six months ago, a full eight months after he had bloodied the nose of the cartel people in Mexico and the two of them had faced down the invasion into her apartment in Austin and killed some men. It was possible that Oscar, a man with a grudge, was a remnant of that action.

And where was Abel? She had worn out the speed dial on her cell phone and only gotten the same out-of-service message over and over. Not knowing what he was up to or when he was due back twisted her stomach in a tight knot.

He should be here. It's his job to kill bugs, change light bulbs, and shoot bad guys.

She glanced at David. His face, always so serious, had gone positively bleak. Worried about the dog, no doubt—and about seeing his mother shoot at an intruder in their home. She gritted her teeth, and her knuckles, wrapped around the steering wheel, turned white.

One thing's for damn sure: if I ever get the bastard who shot our dog in my sights again, I'm going to take the extra second to line up, center mass, and squeeeeezzzze. No trigger jerking ever again.

CHAPTER 25

YEAGER GRABBED A SOLID SIX hours of rack time after he turned the watch over to Smitty. At six in the morning, he jerked awake with the sense that the bad guys had crossed the wire while he slept, hitting his firebase and killing everyone. His mind caught up to where he was, and he shook off the dream but not the sense of urgency. He missed Charlie something fierce. Dreams like that rarely came when he slept with her.

After a quick check of the perimeter, he returned to his room and picked up his toilet kit. After a hot shower and shave in the locker room next to the mission's small gym, followed by a change into clean clothes, he went in search of the priests. He found them lined up along one side of the head table in the dining room, supervising a rowdy mob of orphans as they finished off breakfast. The doctor sat at one end of the table, to the left of the priests, huddled over a cup of coffee.

The room fell silent when he walked in, like a saloon in the Old West shows on TV. Forty sets of small, dark eyes fixed on him as the boys and girls noticed the guy in the room with a gun. Yeager worked on looking peaceful and happy, smiling and nodding to several of the children as he passed. He approached the priests, running a gauntlet of frightened faces.

Yeager registered the presence of the young man in a dark sports coat at the center of the group. "Father Dominic! When did you get back? *How* did you get back?"

The slender young priest, looking as worn as a peasant's sandal, scratched up a smile and rose to shake Yeager's hand. "God saw me through, as he did you, Señor Yeager. Have you met all of my brothers?"

"Some." Yeager nodded at Father Sebastian. He got an enthusiastic handshake from Father Pepe and a more reserved one from Father Dietrich. "Good morning, Dr. Lopez. Your patient doing well?"

The tiny woman gave him a tentative smile. Her liquid dark eyes reminded him of his ex-wife, Martina, who had the same look of intense focus. "Yes, thank you. She is doing quite well, in no small thanks to you and your men."

"Glad to help." Yeager drew out a chair and sat across from Father Dominic, his back to the kids. The murmur of conversation edged back up toward its previous volume. Kids, being kids, would not stay quiet for long.

"So, what is the situation?" Dominic asked.

Yeager explained the events leading up to the attack on the mission and its aftermath. He also shared his thoughts about trying to evacuate the mission by truck or on foot.

"Impossible," Dr. Lopez said. "I have patients who are in no way ambulatory or ready to be jostled around by a big, moving truck."

"Understood." Yeager nodded. "Hey, anywhere I can get some of that coffee? And maybe some breakfast?"

Father Pepe jumped up. "Sit, sit, sit. I will get you something." He shot off before Yeager could say thanks.

"The first thing we must do," said Dietrich, "is get your truck repaired. We should at least have that option available to us."

Dominic nodded. "I agree with Emil. We need the truck ready to go, regardless. There is an excellent mechanic in the village. I will send a boy down to get him."

"Okay, I have no problem with that," Yeager said. "But what we need more than anything else is intelligence. We need to know what Verdugo's up to. Is he planning to hit us again? Is he bringing an army with heavy weapons? Also, we need to get word out that we're under siege here. Your guardian angel indicated he may be able to help. Maybe he can get the Army to intercede now that they know exactly where Verdugo and his boys plan to gather."

"None of this would have happened had you not challenged Verdugo to his face!" Father Sebastian, red spots flaring on his cheeks and neck, stood from his chair and pointed a finger at Yeager. "If you had stayed out of this, we would have paid Verdugo his tax and not be facing death and destruction at his hands now."

Yeager opened his mouth, but no words came.

Dietrich laid a hand on the old man's arm and attempted to calm him. "Do not blame Señor Yeager. He and his men risked much to bring us the supplies we needed."

"And I say he should take his truck and go." Sebastian made a shooing motion with his free hand. "Get out, and maybe Verdugo will settle for a small payment to save face and leave us in peace again."

"And maybe he'll murder all of you like he said he was going to," Yeager snapped. The kids in the dining hall had gone silent again, their murmuring shut off like a switch at Sebastian's angry tone. Yeager lowered his voice, very aware of all the big ears behind him. "He tried to get his hands on this truckload in Madera. When that failed, he came here. Somehow, he knew right where to go both times. Think on that for minute. How'd he know?"

"Bah! Why should we care?" Sebastian sat down with another dismissive gesture. "The cartel people have spies everywhere. They are so ubiquitous they can taste your food before you take a bite."

"What Father Sebastian says," Dominic said, "is unfortunately true. La Línea, the group that Verdugo broke away from, has riddled these mountains and villages with eyes and ears. A web of informants, both paid in cash and those looking to curry favor, convey information faster than the Internet."

"Verdugo mentioned an agreement," Yeager said. "Do you know what he was talking about?"

Dominic hung his head for a moment. "It is... it is shameful to admit this." The priest rubbed his face with a long-fingered hand and looked away. "Mission San Felipe has—had—a small reserve of silver. From the mines that operated here in the late 1800s to early 1900s."

Yeager waited while Dominic studied his coffee cup. Father

Sebastian shifted in his seat, his mouth set in a grim line, and Dietrich focused his eyes in the middle distance as if modeling for an Easter Island statue.

"For a time," Dominic said, "we... appeased Verdugo with a small payment to leave us in peace. A tribute."

"A bribe," Dr. Lopez stated bluntly.

Dominic acknowledged her charge with a nod and an openhanded gesture. "Just so. Except the... bribe... became more expensive, and soon our store of silver was exhausted."

"And Verdugo doesn't believe you," Yeager added.

"And Verdugo doesn't believe us." Dominic tried on a rueful smile, but it wouldn't stick. "He began taking our supplies instead, which is how we ended up in this fix. I used the last of our emergency fund to help Victor procure weapons for you and your men."

"Any chance we know who the local spy is?" Yeager stood and took a tray from a beaming Father Pepe. Tortillas, eggs, and sliced ham were piled on the plate. Next to that steamed a cup of stout coffee. "Muchas gracias, Padre."

"De nada. Enjoy, with God's blessing."

"Amen."

Dietrich and Pepe excused themselves to get the children to their assigned classrooms. Dr. Lopez went to the kitchen to refresh her coffee cup. Yeager addressed Dominic again. "If we knew who was ratting us out to Verdugo, maybe we could turn him."

"Turn him?"

"Make him a double agent. Supply false intel to Verdugo."

"Ah, I see. No, I don't know who this person might be. Or how many there might be."

"Well, Father Dominic, please think on it." Yeager sipped his coffee then attacked the mountain of eggs. He piled some on a tortilla, sprinkled on hot sauce, and rolled it up. After chewing down the first batch he said, "This is good. I don't care if they're dried eggs or not. Nothing like hunger to whet the appetite. Anyway, if we can find this person, or people, it would be a good thing."

"What will you do?" Father Sebastian huffed. "Torture him? Put him on the board of water? This is how you will get this information?"

Make him sit through Mass with you? Yeager kept the thought from passing his lips with an effort. The old priest had a way of getting under his skin that he normally only associated with the ex-Mrs. Yeager.

"Torture who?" Dr. Lopez frowned and sat back at the table, her mug full enough that some coffee spilled over the side. She muttered something fierce that he didn't catch and wiped at the cup with her napkin.

"No, Padre," Yeager said. "I thought we might try the honey before the stick if it's all the same to you."

"Never mind sending a boy, Dominic." Sebastian pushed back from the table. "I will go find the mechanic, Trevino, and bring him myself. The sooner this man's truck is repaired, the sooner he can leave."

Once the older man marched away and passed through the doors, Dominic said, "I'm sorry, Señor Yeager. Father Sebastian can be... quite difficult at times."

"I understand, Father. What about getting a message out? You got in. Maybe we could get a message out the same way."

"Out to whom?"

Yeager hesitated. If there was a spy, he didn't want de la Cueva's name brought up. "To the authorities."

"I rode in with one of the men of the village," Dominic said. "I'm ashamed to say I hid my collar and pretended to be just another laborer. We were stopped once by a formidable roadblock about two kilometers to the north, on the same road you must have used to come in?" Dominic made the last part of his statement into a question by inflection and a lifted eyebrow.

"Yeah," Yeager said. "We saw nothing. Didn't hit a single roadblock."

"Hmmmm. Interesting." Dominic paused, pinching his nose. "Anyway. The point is the men said we had better be comfortable staying in Rascón because Grupo Verdugo was shutting down all outbound traffic. If we attempted to leave, they said we would be killed. *Executed* is the word he used."

"We'll have to punch our way through, then, if it comes to that."

"Excuse me." Dr. Lopez fixed Yeager with a glare, the corners of her mouth turned down. *Just like Martina.* "I don't understand something. I believe as you say, that this Verdugo will come back with killing in his mind. If you go, we will have no protection at all. I saw the way his man looked when he pointed a gun at my patient. A little girl. He would have shot her without another thought." She looked at Father Dominic. "We can't evacuate again. I have three patients who are just now recovering from a week without a dialysis machine, and another just had an emergency appendectomy."

"Dr. Lopez," Yeager said, "we're leaving. Trust me on that. But only when we have safe transportation for everybody. All we need is to find the way."

He traded looks with Dr. Lopez and Father Dominic, but nobody had anything to say.

———————

Cristian Guzman—a former truck driver who was about to return to his old vocation—came through the side door of the garage and paused, letting his eyes adjust to the dim interior. An arc welder crackled, and sparks dazzled from the front of the Dodge Ram pickup in the middle of the garage. Herman crouched at the grill, a welding hood over his face.

Cristian closed the door behind him, shutting off the midmorning sounds from the village of Rascón. *"Como 'sta?"*

His son looked up from his welding and tilted the mask up. "Almost done. Another couple of spots, and it will be done."

"Bueno." Cristian inspected the new feature on the Ram, thinking about how appropriate that name was. Herman had affixed to the front of the dual-wheeled pickup a lattice of black iron bars, welded to struts sticking out from the frame. The struts, in turn, were welded to the unibody frame of the industrial-duty truck. He had also beefed up the springs and added knobby tires.

In the bed, twenty bags of concrete added mass and weight.

"Bueno," Cristian repeated. "You must hurry, though. Trevino needs his welder back. The truck is damaged."

"The truck?" Herman glanced at the pickup in front of him, puzzlement creasing his brow under the hood.

"Not that truck. *The* truck." Cristian pointed toward the mission. "The big one."

"Ah. Damaged? Damaged how?"

Cristian shrugged. "I think the radiator."

"Can it be fixed?"

"We can only hope."

Herman's face took on the look of a brewing storm. "It has to be fixed. I will not give up everything at this point. What did the priest say?"

"He said to be patient, that God will provide." Cristian shrugged again. "As if he can speak on God's behalf anymore after what he plans to do."

"How long? I mean, when we know?"

"We have all day today, so perhaps Trevino can fix the radiator and the truck would be ready to go tonight. We have to go at night anyway, so maybe tonight."

"What about the fighting men at the mission? Has the priest accounted for them?"

Cristian was wearing out his shoulders shrugging. He did it again anyway. "He says the open fighting with Grupo Verdugo complicates things, but he'd planned to... how did he say it? It sounded so nice. Ah. He said he planned to *make sure they did not interfere.*" Cristian waggled his hand. "Whatever that means."

"And if the Verdugo men come back while we're loading? Or before?"

Cristian forced himself not to shrug. "That, my son, is something else that is in God's hands."

CHAPTER 26

AN HOUR PAST DAWN, CHARLIE checked on David and found him still asleep in the tiny back room that Judy used as her office. Although only the back of his head stuck out of the blanket, her mommy instinct detected his breathing pattern and recognized he was in a heavy sleep cycle.

She eased the door closed and followed the smell of coffee to the kitchen. Judy sat at the table holding her e-reader in one hand and a mug in the other. With dark hair trimmed short, wearing a man's shirt and sweatpants, Judy Loehr looked more like a bum than a successful real estate attorney. Monday through Friday, Judy dressed in power suits, had every hair in place, and slipped through the shark-tank waters of Austin with such confidence the sharks gave way and let her pass.

She peered over her reading glasses at Charlie. "Hey, girlfriend. Glad you're up. Coffee's on. You know where the stuff is, right?"

"As long as you haven't moved it."

"Me? Move stuff? That would require housework, and you know *that* ain't happening."

Charlie brought her cup to the table and scooted some stuff around to make room to set it down. Law books, papers, and legal pads fought for space with bills, junk mail, and other... stuff. "I still don't see how a woman as shit hot as you are in litigation and negotiation can be so..."

"Disorganized?"

"Yeah, that's the word."

"Hah!" Judy said. "Tell me. It's been that way since college. You adapted, didn't you, roomie?"

"It was adapt or die."

"Poor thing."

"Hey, thanks again for letting us stay the night," Charlie said.

"Are you kidding? If it had been me, I'd be a basket case, blubbering all over your shoulder. You were always the tough one."

Charlie sipped her coffee, smiling with her eyes. Judy lived in a modest house in a high-dollar neighborhood north of Georgetown, a suburb of Austin. With the kind of bucks Judy pulled in, she could afford something much bigger, but moving would require time away from her job. And she'd have to pack and clean up. Staying put, she had told Charlie, was much easier.

Light streamed in from French doors overlooking a yard of dead grass—Judy did not garden well, either—and a wooden privacy fence. Tort, a fluffy Maine Coon cat with multicolored fur and white paws, curled up in the middle of the table, oblivious to the mess.

"So when's he-man coming home?" Judy put down her Kindle and went for a coffee refill.

"I wish I knew, Judy." Charlie allowed herself the sigh she'd held back in front of David. "He went charging off on his white horse, and I haven't heard from him since. His cell keeps going to a 'not in service' message."

"Would you ever have thought, way back when we were Dallas blue-blooded Hockaday honeys with country-club tans and Neiman Marcus credit cards, that you'd wind up living in the boonies with Paul Bunyon?"

"More like John Wayne, but yeah, I know what you mean." Tort woke up and stretched. He padded over to Charlie and butted his head into her hand. "But you know? I never thought I'd be this happy, either. Not after Steven and I divorced."

Judy smiled, crinkling the laugh lines at her eyes. "I'm happy for you, sweetie."

Tort climbed into Charlie's lap as if it were his due. "And something you'll never believe: I've been in some kind of fiendish Stepford Wives housekeeping trance. All I've been doing is cleaning and dusting and—and *baking*, for God's sake. I'm no Judy Loehr, but you know, housekeeping has never been big on my to-do list. I don't know what the hell's gotten into me lately."

"I know what's gotten into you." Judy had a merry glint in her eyes. She pulled off her reading glasses and leaned forward. "I know exactly what's going on."

"Huh? What?"

Judy giggled, sounding more like the girl Charlie went to college with than she had in a long time. "Oh, I don't believe this. You haven't even guessed yet, and I can see it plain as day."

"Goddammit, Judy. If you don't tell me what you're talking about, I'm going to stab you in the eye with a dull spoon."

"Oh, girlfriend." Judy bubbled through her giggles, which had grown to chuckles and threatened to hit a full-out belly laugh any second. "You. Are. Pregnant."

"What? No way!" A cold dash of ice water ran through her body. Pregnant?

"Yessir. Most women get all mother hen late in the game, but the same thing happened when you got knocked up with David. Plus, I can see it, plain as your freckled nose. Your cheeks are starting to fill out, your skin has this, uh, this luster... I'll bet you've started to feel the waistband get a little tight, haven't you?"

And as soon as Judy said it, Charlie had an uncomfortable urge to run her finger under her bra to loosen the snug feeling there.

"That's—that's not supposed to happen." Her words were wooden, coming out stiff and slow. "We used..."

"Even so," Judy said. "It's never one-hundred-percent perfect."

"Oh my God. I think you're right." The clues started piling up now that she knew where to look. The weight gain, the hormone-induced mood swings—all of it, just the same as twelve years ago when she found out she was pregnant with David. "What is Abel going to say?"

"If I know that man," Judy said with a smirk, "he's going to say 'Yeehaw!' That's how he rolls. He adores the hell out of you. Anybody with eyes can see that."

"Quick." Charlie deposited a ruffled Tort back on the table and stood up. "Where's the nearest drugstore?" She ran to the spare bedroom, found her purse, and scrabbled through it until she dug out her keys and wallet. She rushed back to the kitchen.

"Why are you just sitting there? I need a drugstore. Write me directions or something."

"Not gonna do it." Judy held a hand over her mouth and shook with suppressed laughter.

"What?" Charlie waited, keys in one hand, wallet in the other. "Why not?"

"Nope." Judy lost it completely, doubling over in a fit of laughter so hard she started crying. She struggled to catch a breath. "I... I'm not... telling you."

"Stop laughing, you dork. What's gotten into you? Never mind; I'll find it myself."

"Hah-hah! Stop. Please." Judy sucked in a breath and held up a hand. "Wait-wait-wait."

"What is it?"

"Don't you think—" She snorted and tried again. "Don't you think you ought to change out of that nightgown before you leave?"

<hr />

Alexandra Lopez, her nose buried in Señora Gutierrez's file, quick marched along the dormitory wing and rounded the corner without looking.

And thudded into a solid wall of flesh and bone.

"Excuse me—" she gasped.

"Hey, is no problem," Victor Ruiz said. "The mos' fun I had all day."

"Señor—Señor Ruiz." The warmth of a flush crept up her neck. "I'm sorry, I was..."

The man smiled, an expression he wore often, it seemed. "No, Señora Doctor, you can run into me any day. And call me Victor. Or Por Que."

He wore jeans and tennis shoes and an olive-drab T-shirt, stretched over granite-carved muscles. Over his torso was strapped a harness containing military equipment. Spare ammunition and the like, she supposed. He also carried an assault rifle, muzzle down, slung over one shoulder. His brush-cut hair gleamed faintly blue-black, and his dark eyes smiled even when his mouth did not.

"What...?" She cleared her throat. "What are you doing? Here, I mean."

"Chocking the doors."

"Checking? I'm sorry, my English is not always—"

"No, señora." He held up a canvas sack. "Chocking." Victor rummaged in the sack and pulled out a triangular piece of wood. "You hammer this into the doorframe—you know, at the floor? It blocks the door from being opened from the outside. See, all the doors here open inward, which is, you know, like a major fire hazard by the way, but at least we can keep out the bad guys. Unless they blow the door or break it down. This slows 'em down long enough for us to react. I hope."

"And if we have to get out—like you said, in a fire?"

"You just kick the chock out of the way, and *boom!* Home free."

"I see, Señor, um, Victor."

"Where you headed?"

"To see how Emelita is doing. The little girl I was operating on when you... when that... those men..." Alex heard the babble spilling from her tongue and hated it. Her normally commanding, articulate doctor persona had deserted her. *How could this be happening? I am twenty-eight years old, not some schoolgirl.*

"Sure, I remember," he said, grinning again. He had very white teeth. "Cute thing. Except for, you know, that big hole in her belly."

"Would you like to come see her? I didn't tell her what happened, but when she heard the shooting yesterday, she became very upset. I told her some brave warriors were here to protect us from the bad men. I promised I would show her when she was able to walk. But... this would be better. If you want to. Come visit, I mean."

"Yeah, sure. Lead the way. This chore is about done anyway."

Alex tapped on the door to Emelita's room and stepped in without waiting for a response. The little girl lay propped in bed with two well-worn, mostly naked Barbie dolls in her hands. The dolls were "talking" to each other in Emelita's singsong voice and jump walking on her chest.

"Hola, Emelita!"

"Hola, Dr. Alex." The girl waved a doll in greeting and grinned as if an old friend had come to play. "Marissa has been telling all about you."

"Marissa?"

"Marissa!" Emelita held the blond Barbie up. "And this is Chinka."

"Chinka? That doesn't sound like a real name."

"I made it up, silly." The girl's eyes widened when Victor came into the room behind Alex. He had removed the military gear and hidden his rifle, presumably in the hallway.

"Hey, I like that name," he said. "I like the name Dr. Alex, too."

Emelita blinked. She spoke with deliberate gravity. "You must not call her that. Only a very few people are allowed to call her that."

"Oh, I think it's okay for Señor Ruiz to call me that as well. He is one of the men I told you about. One who is fighting the narcotraficantes and keeping us safe from them."

Victor edged around her and squatted by Emelita's bed. "Last time I saw you, you were asleep with your tummy open. Did you know you had rabbits in your insides?"

"No... I do not." Emelita denied it but did not look convinced.

"*Sí. Es verdad.*" Victor held his hands a body width apart. "And snakes about this long."

"No, I don't." Emelita giggled.

"And spiders. Great big ones. And owls and turtles too."

Emelita giggled again then winced at the pull in her belly. "Don't make me laugh. It hurts when I laugh."

"Yes, Señor Ruiz, do not make her laugh." Alex gave him a playful shove, pushing him out of the way. "How are we feeling today, my little one?"

"Okay, I guess. My tummy hurts."

Alexandra continued her examination, conscious of the presence of the ex-soldier behind her. Once, Emelita looked over Alex's shoulder and started giggling again. The doctor spun around and caught Victor making silly faces, mocking her examination. She scolded him but had to press her lips closed to keep from smiling.

"Dr. Alex?" the little girl asked as Alex finished putting her stethoscope away. She had turned shy, and the question came out very timidly.

"Yes, my sweet. What is it?"

"Will this—" She gestured at her stomach. "Will this keep me from getting adopted?"

"What?"

"I mean..." The girl was nearly whispering now. "I mean, will parents still want me if I have no pendix?"

Alex brushed Emelita's hair back from her face with a gentle hand and forced a smile past eyes that wanted to cry instead. "Of course they will, my little darling; don't you worry. All we did was take out one of the bad parts you didn't need. Now people will want you even more."

They left the girl chatting with her dolls. Alex eased the door shut while Victor picked up his equipment.

"She's a sweetheart," the muscular man said. "She should have no trouble getting adopted."

"Yes, ah..." A thought struck her, and she stared into the middle distance. Her stomach twisted a little as she chased the thought down its natural path.

"What? What are you thinking?"

"Hmm? Oh, nothing, just something Emelita told me the other day. She said all the girls in the mission get adopted right after they turn twelve. It didn't strike me until just now that she meant only the girls got adopted. I've noticed there's like a five-to-one ratio of boys to girls here. It seems strange."

Victor cocked one eyebrow. His expression had turned serious, for a change. "That ain't just strange. That's downright weird. Macho country like this, people adopt boys before girls."

"I see that now. It *is* strange..."

"But is it...?"

"Bad?" Alex asked.

"Exactly," Victor said. "Is something going on that shouldn't be going on, or is it coincidence?"

"With little girls, the first bad thing I can think of, I can't even say it."

"Sex trade? That's what you're thinking, isn't it?"

"Yeah, that."

Victor compressed his lips and looked grim. His laughing eyes went obsidian hard and bitterly cold. Alex shivered.

"Who's in charge of adoptions here?" Victor asked.

"I don't know, but I can find out. What if it's one of the priests? What then? I don't know—maybe we're reading this all wrong."

"I hope we are," he said through gritted teeth. "'Cause otherwise..."

The powerful man shifted the weapon into his hand and tugged something—the bolt?—back a tiny amount, revealing the brass gleam of a cartridge. He said no more, but he didn't have to.

Alex shivered again.

CHAPTER 27

THE PRIEST'S BEDROOM RESEMBLED A monk's cell. No windows. Stone walls. A bare minimum of furniture and fixtures. A bed, a chest, a wardrobe, and a nightstand with a Bible. What else did a priest need?

When he closed the door and turned off the lamp, only a tiny amount of light seeped under the threshold. Even though it was daylight outside, his room changed from a dim cell to a tomb black as a raven's wing.

Black as my heart. The priest lay on the bed and stared into the darkness, not seeing the outlines of the ceiling above. His eyes sought answers from inside his soul. He wanted to dive into the past and find the *one moment* when it started—the turning point, the key decision, as small and insignificant—or gross and obvious—as it might have been, that had set his feet on the Devil's highway.

A fork in the road, he mused. A path had diverged from righteousness, the light straying farther and farther away so that the route to redemption was lost and the way back overgrown in a thicket of briars and razor-sharp thorns.

With the benefit of hindsight, he could see it had been a trap, skillfully concealed, laid with care and baited with temptation. And he had blundered in, disregarding caution, temperance, self-control... and God. The actors in this little drama of his were all human beings, venal and corrupt, but the director, the stage master, was none other than the Devil himself.

Had I trusted in God, listened to Him just for a moment, this would have never happened. Even now, I plan to commit more sin rather than repent and throw myself on God's mercy. How cowardly is that? I preach to others of a forgiving God, one who merely seeks your confession of imperfection to allow them to return to His grace.

But what I have done goes beyond spiritual cleansing and the sanctity of the confessional.

There would be criminal penalties as well. He had gone too far. His name and face would be public news, flashed on television screens across Mexico and perhaps even the world. People would revile his name and point to him as another example of a failed priesthood. More would turn away from God, using his weakness to bolster their own desire to be weak. He would suffer, but the Church would suffer more.

No, there was but one chance to avoid the indignity of a public confrontation. If he could get through the next twenty-four hours, he could retire in peace and anonymity, hidden from the world, the Church, and the consequences of his own awful acts.

The planning, the accidental good fortune brought by the earthquake, the manipulation of people, the lying... and the shame... all of it would be worthwhile if he could just disappear and live in relative comfort and peace and, in some small way, begin to atone for the weakness of his flesh. The priesthood was lost to him, but the desire to serve remained.

How much do I need for that? A bed, a chest, a wardrobe, and a nightstand. Not much. A simple life for whatever time I have left before I must explain myself to God.

Everything had finally come together. The earthquake. The vehicle. Cristian and his son. If the truck was fixed, it was time to go.

Tonight.

Yeager and Victor improvised a barricade while the mechanic, Trevino, worked on the radiator. He had pulled the entire unit and set it on the ground for better access. He used an arc welder, connected to the mission by a long power cord, to weld a new patch.

"Been meaning to ask..." Yeager paused, still holding a sack of beans. They were using crates and sacks from the supply shipment as a makeshift wall, stacking them in a semicircle around the entrance to the mission. "Where exactly did you get hit by the dud Stinger?"

"'Bout two klicks north of here. You go through that pass"—Victor pointed to the left—"into the next valley. Do you know where the road follows the ridgeline, coming down into that last valley? On top of that ridge. I was staying down low, keeping off the radar—you know, like I do—so I saw the smoke trail one second; the next second *bang!* The warhead hit the canopy, and I about crapped my pants."

"You think they knew you were coming from the mission? Or were you just a target of opportunity?"

Victor shook his head. "Uh-uh. Not for sure. My bird looks a lot like the choppers the Mexican Army flies. My guess is they thought I was with the Army, looking for smug druggling."

Yeager picked a thumbnail. Trevino toggled off the welder and sat back on his heels, lifting his hood and inspecting the seal. An older man, somewhere between fifty and sixty, Trevino wore blue mechanic's coveralls over a round, short body. Face flushed and dripping sweat from being under the welding hood, he reminded Yeager of a happy version of the Mexican actor from *Treasure of the Sierra Madre*, the one who uttered the famous line, "We don' need no stinkin' batches!"

"Why?" Victor asked. "What you thinkin' about doin'?"

Yeager spat between his boots. "I'm thinking about going up there and taking out the Stinger post. Can't be more than one, right?"

Victor looked dubious. "You *hope*. You gonna drive the chopper and find out, bro?"

"You should be fine, Super Mex. You keep telling me you're the best pilot this side of Chuck Yeager."

"You related to him?"

"Not a bit. And quit changing the subject."

Trevino used a damp cloth to cool the metal around his weld enough for him and his helper, a big kid from the mission whom everybody called "Ah," to lift the entire assembly. They manhandled the radiator over the Mack and started the arduous process of maneuvering it into place.

"My thinking is this," Yeager said. "You take the Toyota and haul ass for Madera and de la Cueva's place. Drop me off near where the Stinger crew was. Get the chopper and bring it back here. By the time you make the return, I'll have the anti-air out of action, giving you a clear route."

"Then what?"

"Then you get these folks out of here, starting with the critical patients and small kids."

Victor sat on the barricade and twisted his neck, making it crackle. He looked at the sky and frowned. Yeager let him have his time, not wanting to push his friend any further. He would have the hardest part of the assignment, driving all night, fueling and flying the helicopter, all the while with the threat of taking a surface-to-air missile up the rectum at any moment.

"What if Verdugo hits while we're gone?"

Yeager shrugged. "That would truly and completely suck." He said it flat, no trace of humor. "With enough men, Verdugo can crack this place like a peanut shell. No two ways around it, amigo. If we try to fort up, all of us are dead meat."

"Okay, modification to the plan. You borrow a vehicle from the village people down there. Village people. Get it? YMCA? Never mind. Anyway, use that to go after the Stinger crew. That way you can get back quick once it's done."

Yeager nodded. "Makes sense."

"It's three o'clock now. When do you wanna go?"

"Sooner the better. Now would be good. Sunset at the latest."

"Roadblocks?"

"Blow through 'em."

"Okay." Victor hopped off the improvised barrier and dusted his pants. "But this time, you get to go first."

<hr />

Juan Guerrero's arms trembled as if he had done a hundred push-ups. Maybe two hundred. His feet hurt, and his legs ached from ankle to groin. The last of his bottled water had run out hours ago—or was it days ago? Judging time in a place like this was impossible; it could be noon or midnight, and he would never know. He owned no watch, so the only thing he could use to gauge the time was the emptiness of his stomach.

Going by that measure, he had been down in this stinking cave for years.

He had found water pooled in natural cups and once in a deep lake. He discovered the lake by falling in it before he realized it was there. He skirted the water and continued on, after which he thanked God for not letting him drown. Swimming across the lake of black water would have taken every last ounce in his dwindling store of courage. The glassy, obsidian surface of the underground reservoir mocked him with its stillness. He could very easily picture waterborne demons, subterranean devils, and hideous, multitentacled creatures living in its black depths. Water zombies, for example.

At first, he had been afraid to drink the cave water. As long as he could remember, the priests had been after the boys not to drink water from stagnant pools. They described a dozen diseases that would eat your brain or leave giant worms in your belly if you did.

But thirst finally overrode caution, and Juan had begun to sip—and, when his brain stayed unrotted, gulp—water whenever he found it. The water smelled like the school's chemistry lab and tasted like licking a galvanized tub, but it did the job. *What if my brain rots out of my head later?*

"Who said there'd be a later?" he asked Armando.

The good news, Juan felt, was that the cave had continued in a more or less straight path, sometimes narrow, sometimes wide. It did not resemble a forest trail or any kind of trail at all. The earth had somehow split open, or water had hollowed out a jagged cut into the center of the mountain. Juan was a little fuzzy on the geology of cave formation, but he knew that the fissure was natural, not man-made, from its ragged and random nature.

The really good news was that he had heard no sign of Miguel of the Purple Ear since he'd entered the cave. His gamble to duck into the cave had paid off, at least a little.

"Now, if I can just get out of here." He passed fantastic structures of glittering stone in long columns that reached down from the ceiling and up from the floor, some joining together like tall candles that dripped frozen wax. At times, he would stop and marvel at chambers ribboned with sheets of rock that wiggled across the roof of the cave.

As he fought his way ever onward, Juan found himself crunching through loose gravel one minute and slipping over smooth rock the next. The tunnel wound back and forth, up and down, forcing him to duck, crawl, climb, slip, stumble, and fight for forward progress.

And now, after hours, or days, or weeks, or years of this halting, grueling march to nowhere, Juan's flashlight had dimmed to a feeble yellow glow.

His rasping breath bounced off the stone walls of the narrow tunnel. That, plus the scrunching of his sopping, mud-caked tennis shoes, was the only sound. He braced his free hand against the wall for balance and concentrated on putting one foot in front of the other. His arm shook.

"Well, Armando..." He huffed, gasping for breath. "Does this cave ever end? I'm tired of this." He listened, but Armando did not answer. "That's okay, brother. I will be joining you soon, I think."

The idea that he would die in this dark hole had been flickering at the corners of his mind for several hours. He'd managed to stamp out the thought, killing the embers before they burned out all hope. Now, he found the flames of doubt growing stronger, and he cried like a baby. *I don't want to die here!*

A puff of air cooled the tears on his cheek. Juan stumbled and barked his knees on the rocky floor of the cave. He was too tired to curse the pain. He remained on his knees for a long, slow minute, trying to catch his breath. He rested on a slanted floor, the walls squished around him like a half-collapsed cardboard box. The floor dropped off to his right, disappearing into a narrow crack, while the ceiling nearly touched his head when he stood.

He worked his way to a standing position and shook his

flashlight. It flared for a second then went dimmer than it had been before. When the flashlight died, he would be in perfect blackness.

Not long now.

Another breath of air, this one stronger, brushed his cheeks.

Wait. Blowing air?

The entire time he had been down in this hateful hole, not a single breeze had stirred so much as a hair on his head. Now, when he concentrated on it, he could feel a definite touch of air gusting and breathing through the tunnel.

Juan forgot his sore body, sore feet, and aching tummy. He launched into a feverish scramble, clawing along the cave floor with extended hands. The flashlight clattered against rock as he bolted forward.

He went so fast he missed a change in the elevation of the floor and tumbled into a larger chamber, his body spitting from the squashed tunnel into a space as big as a classroom at the mission. At first, he barely noticed the regular walls and flat, dusty floor. Had there been snakes all over the floor, Juan would have ignored them too.

All of his attention was fixed on the opposite wall, where a man-sized hole framed a view of stars and the purple sky of twilight.

CHAPTER 28

YEAGER CRANKED THE WHITE 1972 Chevy pickup three times before it caught, stuttering and roaring. Smoke erupted from the tailpipe and fogged the rear of the vehicle before the 350-cubic-inch motor settled to a steady idle. San Felipe owned the truck; faded green paint on the doors displayed the mission's name and a silhouette of the bell tower.

He pulled the knob for the headlights, slipped the transmission lever into drive, and fed it some gas. The old truck jounced forward over the rough ground behind the mission. Yeager drove it around front and stopped next to Victor, a shape in the darkness sitting on the hood of the beat-up Toyota.

"We make a hell of a team, huh?" Yeager yelled through the open window. "Charging into battle in a pair of wrecks."

Victor flashed white teeth and gave him a thumbs-up.

They had burned the afternoon arranging for the truck, briefing Smitty and Riley, laying out a cover story for the priests and, finally, clearing the bridge. Deciding to use a cover story was a no-brainer. Yeager did not trust the priests with the real story, not with a potential informant on the mission staff or among the clergymen. If Verdugo found out they were going to hit the Stinger crew, then bring in a helicopter...

"No bueno," Victor said when they discussed it.

"No shit," Yeager said.

"Tell 'em we're just gonna do some scouting. Be back in an hour, something like that."

Yeager agreed.

Now, he double-pumped a fist in the air—trucker sign language

178

for "Roll on!"—and hit the gas. The Chevy rumbled over the gravel yard, passed the repaired Mack, and bumped along the intervening space to the bridge. Once across, Yeager turned left at the main road. If anyone wondered why he was going in the opposite direction to the one Verdugo had gone, they would have to speculate on their own.

Yeager toed the high beams on. The speedometer needle in the Chevy's dash vibrated at twenty miles an hour, jiggled at thirty, then settled at forty. Yeager drove into the pass, the truck's yellow, mismatched headlights showing the way. The road cut through the mountains before winding upward and to the right. Victor's Toyota held steady at one hundred yards back, twin points of light in his rearview mirror.

Was it right to leave the mission with only Riley and Smitty to guard against whatever force Verdugo could bring to bear? That question had been eating a hole in his stomach all day. If Verdugo hit before Yeager returned, odds were the two defenders would be overwhelmed and killed quickly. Too much perimeter, not enough men. Taking away half the defensive firepower would ensure a quick defeat.

Any way he looked at the problem, it always came down to the same solution: get the noncombatants out of the combat zone. How? Transportation via air or ground was the only answer. No way could the sick and elderly, or very young, be taken on a forced march over rough terrain.

He topped a rise, and two cars, parked nose to nose, blocked the road sixty yards away. A steep drop on the left and a thick stand of trees on the right made an effective funnel. There was no way around the blockade. Armed men on either side of the road, four at least, sat in camp chairs around a lantern. One waved his hat, signaling Yeager to come to a stop.

"Let's get the party started," Yeager said under his breath.

His high beams lit up the roadblock like a Broadway stage. The gunmen reacted with at least a small amount of professionalism. Three stayed back at the periphery of the light while one walked forward, left hand blocking the light. All four men wore the same kind of Western clothes popular among young Mexican males: boots, cowboy hats, and plaid or solid shirts with mother-of-pearl buttons that glinted in the light.

"Hola, amigo." Yeager stepped out of the truck, keeping the M4 hidden behind the door panel. The lead man hesitated, and Yeager shot him with a single three-round burst. The Roman candle of flame from the muzzle of Yeager's weapon almost touched the man's denim shirt.

Pivoting his weapon slightly, he took out the man on the far left. Spent brass spiraled and bounced off the pickup's doorframe. The kick of the M4 pounded his shoulder like an old friend.

The first man he'd shot fell away, dropping in a dead heap. Yeager twisted right and squeezed off two quick bursts. Of the men on that side, one died instantly, blood spraying the car next to him in a fan. The other stumbled and tried to bring his weapon to bear. Yeager shot him with another controlled squeeze of the trigger. He searched for more targets with the M4's holographic sight.

Nothing else moved. Elapsed time, from the first *Hola* to the last man down, was under three seconds.

Yeager switched off the headlights to avoid being silhouetted. The blockade's camp lantern gave him enough light to see by. He crouched low and crabbed to the first guard. Dead eyes stared into the infinity of stars above. The gunman to the left moved an arm, hand patting the ground in uncontrolled spasms. Yeager checked on him and found a kid, barely old enough to shave, in an orange-plaid Western shirt. His yellow straw cowboy hat lay several yards away.

Victor pulled up in the Toyota, lights out, and hustled to check the status of the other two blockade guards. "Dang, hombre," he said from where he crouched next to the right of the roadblock. "You in a hurry? You can't wait for backup?"

The kid in the orange shirt twisted on the ground. His eyes rolled in his head, and black blood, thick as paint, welled behind his teeth. His right hand continued to scrabble in the red dirt of the road's shoulder.

Yeager caught the boy's hand in midmotion and held it. It was cold and trembling. The young would-be soldier of the cartel died a few seconds later. Yeager watched him go.

"Help me get these cars moved," he told Victor.

Yeager took the car on the left—a Chevy Impala—opened the door, and shifted the selector into neutral. With a heave, he pushed the Impala back. Its momentum carried it over the edge of the ravine and down, crashing through brush with a scrunch of metal.

Yeager took a last look at the dead youth. He stared at the body for a minute, jaw clenched.

Put it away. Lock it down. He had once told Charlie that if he had any particular ability at all, it was that he could see what had to be done and do it, no matter how hard that thing might be. He had a vault in his mind—a dark, pressurized container, diamond hard, kept sealed by the mass of his willpower and locked in the sub-basement of his soul. In this place, he stuffed memories and images of the men he had killed in battle, compressing the container's lid much as one would sit on an overfull suitcase to get the zipper closed.

He took no pride in the swift and brutal execution of the four men guarding the cartel's roadblock. He found no comfort in the necessity of killing a young man like the one he'd watched die.

"Wassup, homie?" Victor had come to stand beside him. "Ah." He squeezed Yeager's shoulder then echoed his thoughts. "You had to do it, man. You know that, right?"

"It ain't right, Por Que. These people, these kids, they don't know any better. We aren't at war with kids barely old enough to shave."

"Yeah, we are. They the ones threatenin' people under our protection. These punks are killing people by the bushel basket. They done declared war on us, muchacho. I know you feel bad because you all mixed up with this code-of-honor thing, about lettin' the other guy shoot first and all, but you gotta put that aside. Too many people countin' on your ugly gringo ass."

"Thanks for the pep talk, coach." A ghost of a smile tugged at his lips.

"Anytime." Victor slapped him on the back. "Now, go win one for the Kipper, dude."

"Gipper."

"Yeah, whatever. C'mon."

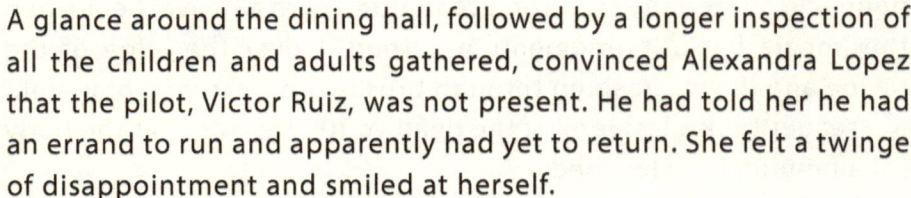

A glance around the dining hall, followed by a longer inspection of all the children and adults gathered, convinced Alexandra Lopez that the pilot, Victor Ruiz, was not present. He had told her he had an errand to run and apparently had yet to return. She felt a twinge of disappointment and smiled at herself.

You're getting as giddy as a schoolgirl with a crush.

She took her tray to the head table, coming to stand opposite the thin and aristocratic Father Dominic. He rose and greeted her with a small bow and a wave of hand indicating the place across from him. "Please, Doctor, have a seat. We welcome your company."

The seating arrangement among the priests and their staff seemed to never vary, and it always reminded Alex of paintings of the Last Supper. Dominic, dapper and dark haired, was in the center of eight seats—the same position as Jesus in the painting. To his left, the round and jolly Father Pepe gave her a sloppy grin and an emphatic handshake. She had never seen the seats next to Pepe occupied.

Perhaps they save those for visiting priests, or staff?

To Dominic's right, the elderly and sometimes acerbic Father Sebastian gave her a mild look and a small nod of greeting. Maybe he was feeling better without the armed presence of Victor and his men. Next to him, Father Dietrich half stood, made a slight, Prussian-style bow, and greeted her by name.

At the end of the table, two of the janitorial and maintenance staff huddled together without looking up. Esteban took care of the cleaning, whereas the skinny guy with a mustache, Gustavo—she heard the kids call him Mocoso—handled most handyman repairs as well as the grounds. Gustavo had a perpetual case of sinus drainage, sniffling and wiping his nose on a handkerchief all day long.

Must be some chemical in the cleaning supplies he's allergic to.

She looked back at Father Dominic. "So I guess Verdugo and his men have not come back."

"That is true, Doctor." The slim priest blotted his lips with a napkin and took a drink of water. "We have heard nothing. Señor Yeager and the short man—Victor?—have gone to see what they can find out."

"So they should be back soon?"

"It is what we anticipate."

She continued engaging the priests in conversation while at the same time trying to take their measure. Could any of these men be involved in something as heinous as selling small girls into the sex trade? It seemed very unlikely.

Father Dominic had the focused, intense look of a committed Jesuit. Spare. Lean. A black-haired, brown-eyed greyhound. The signs of strain she observed around his eyes could well be ascribed to caring for the children, and now the patients, under San Felipe's roof. A man like Dominic would take that responsibility very seriously.

Then there was Pepe. Was it not always the happy, smiling types who turned out to be the biggest monsters? Pepe spoke, his merry eyes alight with a twinkle of good cheer. "So did I tell you, Doctor, about why Noah was the best businessman in the Bible?"

"No, Father Pepe, you didn't."

"He floated all his stock while everyone else was liquidated."

She shared a laugh with the round priest while Father Dominic rolled his eyes. "I have heard that joke more times than I can count, Pepe. You need to get some more material."

"You may have heard it, but the doctor has not. Hey, hey, wait. Have you heard this one…?"

No, it would be ridiculous to believe this man capable of any harmful act. Dietrich, on the other hand, had the features and manner of a first-class bad guy. *A Frankenstein in priest's robes.* When she glanced at the tall German, a cold finger tickled her ribs. He looked away when she made eye contact, but she could tell he had been watching her. The tall, blond priest with ice-gray eyes—and eyelashes so white they disappeared—gave her the creeps.

Finally, she considered Father Sebastian just to be fair. He was old enough that the only way to tell his age would be through carbon dating yet was still spry and feisty. Could he be a perpetrator of sex crimes?

Alex hid her smile behind her coffee cup. "Father Dominic. I noticed earlier, at lunch, that there were many more boys here than girls. Why is that?"

"A matter of habit mostly," the priest said after a short pause. "San Felipe was originally established as a boys-only orphanage, and it remained that way for many years. Only in the last few years have we begun to accept young ladies—becoming coed, as it is said." He shrugged and continued. "Also, we have had quite a number of girls adopted lately, which skews the picture."

"Is that normal? I mean to have more girls adopted than boys."

"It is like the pendulum, Doctor." Dominic demonstrated by sweeping a hand from side to side. "Some years it is mostly boys, some years mostly girls, and some years an even mixture. This year, the pendulum has swung to the, uh, distaff side, so to speak."

The priest delivered the explanation in such a matter-of-fact way that Alex's doubts began to evaporate. But they didn't dry up completely.

"I imagine finding homes for all these children would be a very difficult job. Who at the mission is responsible for the adoption process?"

Father Dominic opened his mouth to answer but paused before a word came out.

The deep boom of the big rifle in the bell tower was transmitted clearly through the building's stone walls, and all conversation stopped as if chopped by a cleaver.

"Excuse me, Dr. Lopez," Dominic said, getting up, "but I need to see what is happening outside."

"Of course."

Another *boom* from above punctuated her words.

CHAPTER 29

VICTOR PULLED TO THE SIDE of the road, twenty-six kilometers north of where they'd breached the roadblock. He and Yeager met at the rear bumper of the Toyota.

"Somewhere along that ridge." Victor pointed to a line of blackness discernable only by the termination of stars. "I was traversing this valley, about eighteen hundred feet off the deck. I saw the smoke trail come out of the ridge, 'bout halfway along. After that, I din' see nothin', homes." He struck a gang-sign pose, thumb and little finger spread. "Jus' grab me some air, chu know?"

"Gotcha," Yeager said. "All right, I'll go find out where the bad guys are hiding and ruin their day for them. You go to town for help, Tonto."

"Huh. Funny, dude. Tonto always got his ass kicked. How 'bout you be Tonto this time?"

"Because you suck at crawling through the woods. Unlike someone with my ninja-like stealth."

"Da fuck?" Victor reeled back in surprise. "I didn't know *ninja* meant *elephant* in Japanese."

"It means I'm gonna kick your ass if you don't get outta here," Yeager said.

Victor muttered something when he got back in the Toyota.

"What was that?"

"I said"—Victor leaned his head out the open window—"it must mean *grumpy bastard*. Quit jackin' around, *esse*. Go kill them assholes up on the ridge. I eat a missile tomorrow, I'm crashing my chopper on your head."

Victor hit the gas, and the rickety Toyota sprayed a small gravel storm getting off the shoulder and back onto the road—though the difference between road and shoulder was more suggested than defined.

"Always have to have the last word, don't ya?" Yeager muttered to the taillights disappearing in a dust swirl.

He pocketed the keys to the Chevy pickup, shouldered the M4, and slipped into the brush, following a rocky goat trail. He had a long climb ahead of him, followed by a long sneak through the brush, followed by a close encounter of the automatic-weapons kind. He glanced at his watch using the beam from his small flashlight. It was approaching eleven o'clock. Time bled away faster the longer a project took to complete. As the clock ran and the minutes disappeared, the loss of time sucked at his patience and resolve.

They'd cleared one roadblock already; they could surely do more if they had to. Why not just go get the people, load them all in the trailer—no matter what the doc said—and blast on out of there? Some of them might die, but if Verdugo showed up with reinforcements, some were going to die anyway. Maybe all would. *Needs of the many outweighing the needs of a few, and all that.*

At the five-minute mark, Yeager forced himself to stop and take a breather. Already, the climb and the altitude were taking a toll on his body, especially after a long day on too little sleep.

Resting against a scratchy pine tree, Yeager allowed his breathing and heart rate to come back down. A sickle moon had risen, silvering the trees as if the woods were an overexposed photograph. The night had gone frosty, and his breath fogged in front of him. Something exploded from the trees, and Yeager was rolling in the dirt, hunting for cover, before he realized the *something* was a huge owl taking flight.

So much for normal breathing and heart rate.

The owl ghosted through the forest, a black shape against a charcoal backdrop. No wind blew. No air stirred at all. Aside from some far-off calls of night birds, no sounds came to Yeager's ears.

The adrenaline crash had sapped his strength. He needed to shut down for twenty minutes, recharge the batteries. He found a spot under cover and shut his eyes, huddled into a ball. Yeager took a series of deep breaths, willing his pulse to slow and his senses to expand.

Twenty minutes later, he opened his eyes. Something clicked inside his head. All the doubts, worries, and extraneous thoughts faded out like one of those old TV sets where the picture drew down to a point and disappeared. The entity that was the forest came to life.

In short, he got his ninja on. Yeager slipped through the shadows, on the hunt.

No cell-phone contact, text, or voice. The international operator told Charlie the phones at San Felipe were out of service from the earthquake. Charlie tried Victor's cell. Nothing. It was close to midnight on Saturday, twelve hours after the EPT had confirmed that she was pregnant. *Knocked up. A bun in the oven.*

Filled half with joy, half with fear, Charlie *needed* to know that the father of her child was safe and well and on the way home. She did not want to tell him over a crackly cell phone connection, but she did want to know *what the hell* he was doing. Was that too much to ask?

Only one option was left. It was like carpet bombing to kill a fly, but her choices were limited. Charlie dug in her wallet for an old, worn-out business card. The information of the original owner had been scratched out and new contact information scrawled in the margins: *Cujo*, and a McAllen phone number.

Nuttier than a squirrel on crystal meth, Yeager had told her once. He also said the man had titanium balls the size of coconuts and would charge Hell with a mouthful of spit. After the crash of Cujo's A-10 in Afghanistan, the army hospital had glued him back together with Elmer's and Scotch tape, said he couldn't fly anymore, and sent him back home. He'd shared a hangar with Victor. He continued to fly his light plane illegally on both sides of the border.

Victor said Cujo would never run drugs, but about anything else was fair game, from tax-free booze to "citizens of another nationality seeking, uh, political asylum" in the US.

The one time Charlie had met him, she had seen a slightly built man with shaggy hair and a bandana tied around his head. A sixties hippie, lost in time. Tommy Chong's clone, escaped from the nice home where residents were kept sedated and happy.

But... crazy or not, he had pulled Abel's and Victor's butts out of the fire the last time they were in Mexico. When he'd passed her his secondhand business card, he'd said, "Anytime you need me, just call. Anytime. Yeager and the stumpy Mexican bastard are all I got. Their family is my family."

Well, let's see if he would like to take a vacation to Mexico and fetch my future husband and his stumpy Mexican friend from whatever boys' game they're playing down in San Felipe.

Charlie punched the number and hit Talk.

———————————⇒※⇐———————————

Oscar Cruz wiped the blood from his hands on the motel sheet. He pulled out an extra twenty-dollar bill and tossed it on the bed next to the whore. He had lost control, there at the end, and she had gotten more than she bargained for, so he felt a tip was in order. Fortunately for her, he was feeling generous.

Besides, she should expect such treatment, turning tricks in a truck stop motel for forty dollars. Forty dollars! For a fat-bottomed black whore. Like everything else in this country, overpriced and proud of it. At home, he could have the same, low-quality whore for less than ten US dollars.

Oscar left the bloody mess on the bed, its wet breath bubbling from flattened nostrils, and closed the door behind him. He placed the Do Not Disturb card on the knob and went to his car, parked in the slot in front of the room.

The debacle with Yeager's woman had left him shaken. He had driven for miles, one eye on the rearview mirror, expecting red-and-blue lights to come up behind him at any second. When he became convinced no one chased him, he picked a roadside motel at random near the town of Killeen, Texas. Then he went scouting for a bottle of tequila and a hooker. Oscar found both, used them up, and discarded them. And now he was hungry.

He pulled into line at a Burger King drive-thru lane.

So, what now? Go back, of course. Not now. Not yet. Let the woman relax and drop her guard. In a few days, maybe a week, try it again. And this time, no fooling around. Walk up, shoot the bitch, and get it over with. Maybe torture the kid, just to set the scene for the trucker to come home to.

At the talk box, the squawky voice asked for his order.

"A Double Whopper with cheese. Large fries. A milkshake too. Vanilla."

His stomach rumbled. He had worked up quite an appetite.

Verdugo, six of his lieutenants, and Raul gathered around a map spread across the mahogany surface of his dining-room table. Under the light of the Waterford chandelier, they discussed the best way to crack the nut of the Mission de San Felipe. Cigarette smoke provided the atmosphere, and cognac fueled the discussion. The scene reminded Verdugo of a high-level secret task force assembled in a wealthy patron's house to enact a dangerous assault. *The Dirty Dozen*, maybe.

"Before the phones went down," Raul said, "our man at the mission said there were only four armed men with the group."

"We saw one," Verdugo added. "A hard motherfucker, calls himself Trucker. *Norte Americano gringo*, brown hair, brown eyes, with the chest of a bull. Probably some kind of mercenary hired by the mission."

"How could they afford such a thing?" This came from Pepito, a man who looked like a teacher, with wire-framed glasses, thin mustache, and a corduroy sports coat. He had the manner and bearing of an intellectual. Pepito enjoyed using a power drill to kill children and forcing the parents to watch.

"Obviously, they are lying about the silver." Verdugo looked across the table. "Marvin. I want to know who are these mercenaries."

"Sí, jefe." Marvin Lascone Rosales, the intelligence chief of

Grupo Verdugo, wore casual clothes and had the kind of everyman face that no one noticed. He had a network of spies throughout Chihuahua and Sonora, many cultivated during the time he spent as a policeman. "I am on it. The lack of phone service has made things... difficult. But I will have answers soon."

"Good. Taco, how many soldiers will we have by the morning?"

His logistics chief, Jaime "Taco" Zambrano, oversaw the supply routes for the flow of product headed north. Assigning personnel, setting up safe houses, arranging transportation—all of it fell under his umbrella.

"Again, jefe, the phones are for shit. This has slowed me down—"

"Not your excuses, Taco. Your answers."

"Twenty, maybe twenty-five. Another thirty by the next day."

"Twenty," mused Verdugo. "That's what we had the first time, and they kicked our teeth in." Verdugo choked back the anger. *Calm. I must remain calm. Angry men make bad decisions.*

He lit a cigarette then pulled in a lungful of smoke and let it out. "The Google Earth picture is useless. Not enough detail. Marvin, send a plane over at first light with a digital camera. I want pictures of the layout from all sides. We need to know what we will face once we make our approach through these woods." He tapped the map on the south side, where the forest met the mission compound. "No more attacking blindfolded."

CHAPTER 30

THE CAVE JUAN GUERRERO FOUND at the end of his journey through the mountain turned out to be more than just any old cave. He had fallen beside a fire ring of blackened stones, next to which lay a pile of clay pottery shards. A squared-off opening cut through the wall to his left. The darkness made it impossible to tell where it led.

Father Dietrich had once livened up a boring history class with a film about the early inhabitants of Chihuahua: the Anasazi. They'd lived in cliff dwellings in the Huapoca Canyon and other canyons to the north and west of Madera. He could not remember what happened to them, but he did remember some of the pictures of their dwellings from that movie. This rock cell looked exactly the same.

Except dirtier. The weak yellow light from his flashlight revealed animal droppings, leaves, and a layer of thick dust covering the floor. More bits of clay pot lay tossed in a corner as if left there when the owner moved out. After a second look, Juan found these were not plain after all but patterned with designs on the outside. They were so covered in dust as to be almost invisible.

So where the hell am I? Sorry, God. Where in the world am I?

"Armando? What do you think, hey?" Juan shoved himself up and went to the narrow entrance for a look outside. The stars arched across the sky, and a sliver of moon gave enough light that he could tell he was high on a ridge, overlooking a wide plain. Then...

"Sí-sí-sí!" Juan fist pumped the air and shouted for joy. At the base of the mountain, a good long hike away but within sight, a spatter of lights glowed.

A city or town. Buildings. People. Food.

Juan coaxed a feeble trickle of light from his trusty metal flashlight and found the beginning of an overgrown trail at the foot of the cave. It seemed to wind downward toward the city lights.

"Thank you, Armando," he whispered, wiping at the moisture on his cheek and not caring. "Thank you, God."

Without listening for an answer, Juan set off on the trail, aches and pains forgotten. The cold night air never felt so good, chilling the sweat on his body and invigorating his tired muscles. *If I never see the inside of a cave again, I will be very happy, forever and ever, amen.*

"There you are, you little bastard," a voice croaked behind him.

Juan spun on his heel and blinked his eyes at the apparition coming from the cave behind him.

Miguel—dirty, unshaven, and twice as ugly as the last time he'd seen the man. Sweat and grime caked his clothes. His cowboy hat was missing, but the weapon he carried looked as fresh and new as the day it was made.

The muzzle flashed fire, and an angry bullet whiffed by Juan's cheek. He bolted down the trail as if the crack of the shot were a starter pistol.

———◆———

Ten minutes after two in the morning, Yeager drove the pickup into the mission's front yard. He used the shallow ford in the river rather than bothering with trying to clear the bridge again.

Riley, who had the watch in the bell tower, came down to meet him, standing by the truck's door as Yeager sagged out, more tired than a mule after plowing a forty-acre field.

"That was fast," Riley said.

"Give me a hand, would you?" Yeager leaned over the bed rail and, with a grunt, hefted out a short, tubular device mounted on a block undercarriage. "FIM-92, aka Stinger missile. This one's so old it might have been one of those shipped to the mujahedeen in the nineties. If the battery still works, I'll fall flat on my ass with surprise."

Riley let out a low whistle.

"And that ain't all." Yeager reached in the bed again and brought out one, then two, then three longer, thinner tubes, each with a pistol grip and a flared end. "RPG-7s. Made famous in every action movie since Chuck Norris was a baby, kicking all the other babies' asses. And..." He went to the rear of the truck and dropped the tailgate then lifted out a wooden crate. "To shoot out of the RPGs, one case of four HE warheads for blowing various and sundry shit all to hell."

"Damn."

"Roger that." Yeager put his hands on his hips. "That's what took the most time: humping this shit off the mountain. The damn Stinger alone weighs thirty pounds at least. The rest of this combined probably the same."

"What about the guys?"

"The former owners of this fine equipment? They have joined their ancestors in Bad Soldier Heaven." Yeager shook his head, more in wonder than disgust. "These guys have owned these mountains too long. They've gotten fat and lazy. The peckerheads manning the OP had a big tent up, a campfire, and a boom box going. They were all sitting around, smoking weed and passing around a bottle." Yeager frowned and shook his head to clear the memory. "Any trouble around here?"

Riley pursed his lips. "A couple of scouts poked their nose out of the woods. What's left of 'em is over yonder." He made a vague gesture to the south. "Barrett don't leave much."

"Everybody here okay?"

Riley nodded, tamped his can of Skoal in one palm, and took a dip.

"You good for another couple hours?" Yeager asked.

"Yep."

"Okay, then. Let's get this shit up to the bell tower. Then I need to rack out. I'm done in."

"Gettin' old," Riley said.

"Roger that."

An hour later, Riley scanned the surrounding country from his high perch, trying to keep his teeth from chattering. Frost covered the exposed stone of the parapet. He covered his dripping nose with the same blanket he had wrapped around his shoulders. Behind him, the ladder creaked, and Riley spared a glance. The head of one of the priests came through the trapdoor, followed by the rest of the robed figure.

"Hola, señor." The priest continued in English. "I have brought you some coffee."

"Thank you, Father. You didn't have to do that."

"Nonsense. It was no trouble." He unscrewed the plastic-cup lid of the thermos. "Here, hold this." Removing the stopper, the priest poured a healthy splash of steaming liquid. Riley's nostrils flared at the scent of strong, dark-roasted coffee.

He sipped with reverence. "Ah, man. That's good. Thanks again, Father."

"Please. It is nothing. The least I could do for a man risking his life for us. Tell me, are you Catholic, by chance?"

"Lapsed, I'm afraid."

"Nonsense! No such thing as lapsed, only temporarily missing."

Riley smiled and downed the remainder of the coffee in the small thermos cup. It burned his mouth a little, but he didn't care. "Any more of that?"

"Of course, of course. Here, drink it down. It will keep you warm."

Riley nodded and went back to scanning the country surrounding the mission. The coffee did make him feel much warmer. He sipped more.

"It is so peaceful here," the priest said. "I often come up here, late at night, just to experience the majesty of God. Look at the stars. Amazing, no?"

"Fu—dang straight, Father." Riley yawned and sipped from his plastic cup.

"Makes you feel so small, yes?"

"Mmmm?"

"Here, might as well finish this off." The priest poured the remainder of the thermos into Riley's cup. "It will go cold, otherwise."

"Thanks again," Riley said through another yawn. "I really *am* tired. I need the caffeine jolt, for sure. What about you, Father?"

"Me?"

"Don't you want some?"

"Oh, no, my son. Any more coffee, and I never will go to sleep tonight. Please, drink up. Here, why don't you sit back against the wall there? I can keep watch for a while. No need for you to do all the work. Just show me how to use these goggle things and… there you go, just lay your head back and rest, my son. Everything will be fine."

"Sleep well, my son."

The priest retrieved the cup and thermos. He arranged the blanket to cover the young man, as there was no need for the vaquero to freeze. Besides, the priest's pit of sin was deep enough already that climbing out would take the rest of his life. Adding a needless death would push his debt to God beyond even His tolerance. The priest shivered from the chilly wind blowing through the bell tower.

Pulling a Maglite flashlight from inside his jacket, the clergyman aimed it at the silent and darkened town of Rascón. Finding his reference points in the night proved to be impossible, so he returned to Riley's slumped and snoring body and retrieved the night-vision goggles.

"Madre de Di—!" The priest choked down his curse in midsentence. Looking through goggles gave him an amazing view of the nighttime valley. He found his target in moments. He clicked the on-off switch three times, very deliberately. Immediately, a return flash of a pair of headlights assured him the message had been received.

He scrambled down the ladder and headed for his office. There were many more things to do and not much night left in which to do them. If he did not get away clean that night, the window of opportunity would be all but closed. The priest hurried along dark, silent halls lit only by the occasional low-wattage security light. He passed from shadow to light and back to shadow. At the end of the hall, he went through a final door and disappeared into the darkness.

———◆———

Juan blundered in the darkness. It was more of a controlled fall than a run. The trail—really more of a narrow strip of weed-choked rock and sand—ribboned through thorny vines and predatory trees that snagged his clothing and slapped his face. Behind him, bull-like crashing and thunderous cursing attested that Miguel remained on his trail, as implacable as Darth Maul and twice as ugly.

"I am going to cut your balls off!" Miquel screamed, much closer than the last time he'd made the same threat.

Juan's breath rasped in his throat, and his legs wobbled under him. He clamped a hand above his right hip to calm a stitch in his side. He caromed from a tree he barely saw into another one he didn't see at all, twisted, stumbled... and fell. "Oomph!"

He sprawled face-first onto a loose scree of rock and sand, hands outthrust, the fall burning his palms with gravel and thumping the air from his lungs. Juan cried out, lost in a dark nightmare of forest, pine trees standing indifferent sentinel around him.

There was dirt in his eyes. He couldn't see. Juan pawed at his tearing eyes, blinking and fighting to get one bleary look so he could see where he was. Where was—

Miguel skidded to a halt three meters away, gravel sliding under his feet. In Juan's watery vision, he appeared nothing more than a darker blur against a black forest, a cutout figure of Death outlined in silver starlight. He cackled. "Hah, you little shit. Now what?"

While the narco huffed and puffed upslope, Juan willed his legs to move. Or his arms. Anything. The power lines were down, and none of his messages made it through.

"I may cook you and eat you," said Miguel. "But I think best of all, I will sell you. Little virgin boy like you? I could get maybe twenty pesos, huh?"

Juan's fingers flexed as desperate brain signals finally connected, and his feet scraped the rocky ground. The narco blacked out part of the sky, an eclipse of evil. Stained and gritty teeth shone in the small strip of moonlight filtering through the trees. Shadows shifted as Miguel moved closer. Juan panted.

"I tell you something," Miguel said. The dark patch closed to a few meters, and Juan could see the man's head and shoulders, outlined in starlight. Gravel crunched under his heavy boots. "I would not have followed this far but for the damn bats. The bats scared the shit out of me. I got turned around in there and went to the wrong way then fell down that goddamn slide, you know? Into the shit? Had to use my lighter the whole way. You know how much that sucked? Here. I'll show you." Miguel did something with his weapon that made a metallic clatter.

Juan's hands scrabbled—seeking, searching.

"Step out of there, boy. I can see—"

Juan whipped the first rock sidearm.

"*Ow!* Pendejo!" Miguel reeled as he screamed curses. "Fuck this—"

Juan's fingers closed over another stone, this one bigger. He cocked and threw.

"Goddammit, you little prick. I'm going to beat you to death!"

A third rock, as big as a baseball, rocketed away and found its target.

"Shit! Goddammit, stop!" Miguel bumbled toward him, one arm raised to protect his face.

Juan scrambled backward on his butt. He rolled to his feet at the edge of the track. He found a ready supply of ammunition and loaded his pockets while scanning for a path, a place to run. Back the way he came was no good; the trail ended at the cave dwelling. Miguel blocked the downward trail and was coming on hard, panting and cursing. Behind him, the cliff dropped away into darkness, and on the other side bulked the shoulder of the mountain.

The fat narco bellowed like the enraged demon he resembled. "I see you!"

Three more rocks whizzed from Juan's hand and whacked the

bulky shape, one after the other, as fast and hard as he could power them.

Miguel stumbled, blinded. *Whap!* Another rock hit him high in the side. He twisted, scratching and clawing in the dark.

Juan rammed a shoulder into the big man and... *shoved.*

"You sorry—whoa! What the—" Arms windmilling, Miguel teetered on the edge of the sheer cliff, defying gravity for the briefest of moments. Like a fat, bloated tree falling—Juan pictured Jack's beanstalk—Miguel toppled into space.

His scream echoed through the pines for several seconds before the thud drifted to Juan's ears.

Cristian Guzman straightened in his seat when a light flickered on and off from the mission bell tower. "The signal."

Herman started up his Dodge Ram with the steel cage welded on front. Next to him, Cristian sighed. The relief—dread?—of action smothered the tension of waiting. They pulled out from the alley where they had hidden for the last three hours and made a left turn on the main road. Fifty meters later, they made a right onto the concrete bridge. The same bridge Verdugo had tried to cross.

Herman's first task was to nudge the blocking vehicles out of the way. Doing this with utmost care was important. Banging around and waking people up would ruin everything.

Engaging the steel cage with a gentle kiss, Herman downshifted and eased the powerful truck forward. The cage crunched into the soft metal of the Expedition's front quarter-panel, denting it with a metallic pop. Herman slipped the clutch and teased the accelerator. The rear tires threatened to spin, and he played the clutch and accelerator together, overcoming inertia by applying steady, relentless pressure.

The heavy SUV moved, slowly at first, then it seemed to give up, groaning and sliding across the pavement. Herman pushed it all the way against the side of the bridge.

He backed up and repeated the process with the Land Rover but shoved that vehicle farther forward so that Cristian would be able to maneuver the big truck between the two in a gentle S curve.

"Well done, Herman," Cristian said.

His son glanced over, and a smile tugged at his lips.

An external basement door had been added a long time after the original construction of Mission de San Felipe, midway down the southern wall. A slanted casing of modern concrete supported steel doors, which were mounted on hidden hinges and secured by an industrial padlock with a half-inch-thick hasp. From the side, it looked like a triangle stuck against the wall, with the foot of the casing jutting out six feet from the base of the wall.

Earlier, the priest had convinced the gringo trucker to move the rig to the same side of the mission as the basement door. The driver could not have positioned it better for them had he been in on the plan from the beginning. The rear doors of the trailer almost touched the basement entrance.

Herman brought the Dodge around in a wide, wheeling turn and parked next to the Mack, facing the same direction. He switched off the engine.

Cristian climbed out of the truck. The warning chime dinged when Herman opened his door without removing the keys. For a moment, Cristian worried about the sound then rationalized that the noise from the engine was far louder.

Next to the basement doors, a shape moved in the darkness. The priest. "Come," he said. "We do not have much time. My brothers will soon be awake for Prime. They will wonder where I am and may come looking."

The priest jittered about, glancing every which way at once. His voice sounded scratchy and dry. *He is as nervous as a virgin,* Cristian thought. "That would be very bad. We are ready; let's get started."

The key trembled in the priest's hand when he tried inserting it in the padlock, to the point he could not get it in. *Just like a virgin!* Cristian kept his smile to himself. The priest took a deep breath, stabbed the lock, and twisted. One tug, and the heavy padlock sprang free. The clergyman slipped it off and stood back.

Herman stepped forward, grabbed a handle, and heaved.

Cristian expected a mighty groan from such a monstrous door, but the hinges must have been well oiled. Only the whisper of a squeal indicated the door moved at all. Herman eased it down, letting it kiss the soil. He did the same with the other door.

"Did you bring a light?" the priest asked.

"Sí, we have lights." Cristian pulled a metal flashlight from his hip pocket. "This for now. Some lanterns in the truck."

"Good. Let me see that."

Snapping on the flashlight, the priest led the way down the stone steps to the basement. "Someone may see the light from inside if we turn on the overheads."

Cristian did not bother telling the priest they had already discussed this. The padre was chattering from nervousness, so he let the man babble while he had a look around. He took back the flashlight and shined it along the walls.

Tomb-like would only begin to describe the underground space. It was small, dank, dark, and full of cobwebs, maybe as big as Tia's store but built the same time as the original mission, in the 1800s. The ceiling supports were columns of decaying bricks, the floor stone, and the low ceiling made of lumber blackened by age and smelling of rot, termites, and dust.

Stuffed in corners and along the walls, cardboard boxes sagged in teetering stacks. Now Cristian knew what three hundred years of church records looked like.

But in the middle of the floor, *that* was different. Stacked in two rows of ten and one of six, twenty-six crates squatted under a bare—unlit—bulb in a ceramic fixture. They were wooden, made of pine, and big enough a man with long arms would have trouble reaching from one side to the other. One of the crates, in the partially depleted third row, had no lid.

Cristian moved over for a look inside.

Nested in straw ticking, blackened and tarnished with age but still gleaming, a beautifully engraved teapot reflected the beam of his flashlight into his eyes. Cristian's hand reached for it before his mind told it to. He lifted the teapot from the crate, and its weight surprised him.

"Is it...?" Herman had come up behind him, unnoticed.

"Yes," said the priest, still by the basement steps. "Ninety-five percent pure silver. Just as in each of the other crates. Now, please hurry and get these loaded. We must be gone before dawn."

The priest started back up the stairs, and Herman said, "Where are you going? Are you not going to help?"

The man with the white collar paused and looked back. "No. I have some matters that require my attention. I will join you once you are safely away." And he raced up the steps fast enough to leave a draft behind.

"Well," said Cristian, lacing his voice with sarcasm. "You heard the man. Let us get loaded so we can be safely on our way." He replaced the silver teapot and reached for one side of the open crate. "Here. Get the other side of this. I suspect this bitch is heavy."

"I hope they all are," said Herman.

CHAPTER 31

ONE OF ALEXANDRA'S PATIENTS, SIXTY-SIX-YEAR-OLD Mateo Luzan, started complaining of chest pains and shortness of breath at 4:25 a.m. Saturday. At the time of the earthquake and subsequent evacuation, Señor Luzan's recovery from double bypass surgery had been on track. He'd appeared alert and in good spirits despite having undergone surgery two days before the earthquake. By the time Dr. Lopez finished her examination early Saturday and decided the cause of pain had more to do with post-op stress than real heart trouble, an hour had slipped away.

Too keyed up to sleep, Alex headed to the kitchen for coffee. To get there, she had to go from the girls' dormitory wing and make a left turn at the end of the corridor then a right through the door joining the dormitories to the main mission building. It was a long way to go for a cup of coffee, but the alternative was to return to her room and stare at the ceiling. No way would she be able to go back to sleep—it was a miracle that she had slept at all.

Regularly placed wall sconces, fitted with weak bulbs, threw pools of yellow every ten meters or so—enough light to not bump into walls but not enough to chase away deep pockets of shadow clinging in between. Everything in this place reminded her of a horror movie, like something from *The Mummy*. It wouldn't surprise her to see eyes move in a painting or a ghost float through a solid wall.

At the end of the corridor, a door led to the administrative wing. The left turn toward the kitchens was just before it. A tiny click of the doorknob warned her a split-second before the door flew open and a slim figure in black rushed through it.

"*Aieee!*" Alexandra threw her hands up in panic. A tall man in a black robe grabbed her by the upper arms. She choked back a second scream when she recognized Father Dietrich.

"Dr. Lopez," the tall priest exclaimed in his thick, German-tinted Spanish. "I am so very sorry. My apologies; I was in such a hurry I didn't think to be careful."

"No problem, Father." *No need for coffee anymore. I am wide-awake now.* "I seem to have a habit of running into priests here."

"Are you okay? Is there anything you need?"

"Just coffee. And clean underwear; I may have peed myself. I mean—uh, I..."

The priest smiled. "Don't worry, señora. Priests do not mind some scatological humor. It is the sex jokes we don't get."

"Hah!" She laughed for the first time in days, it seemed. "So why up so early?"

"Have you forgotten your liturgy already, Doctor?"

"Oh! Prime, correct?"

"Yes, it is time for us to pray." He glanced at his watch. "And I'm afraid I overslept."

"Oh, please. Don't wait on my account."

"We are going the same direction." He gestured with a hand for her to proceed.

They walked together in silence for a dozen steps. Alexandra decided this was a good chance to learn more about the adoption practice. With one of the priests parted from his brethren, he might speak more candidly. A hundred questions flew into her mind, but only one jostled out the bottom of the hopper.

"Father Dietrich?"

"Yes?"

"Last night, before the gunshots, I asked who was in charge of adoptions here at San Felipe but never got an answer."

He looked at her, one eyebrow cocked. "You seem very interested in knowing this." She couldn't tell if it was a challenge or an observation.

"Well, you see"—the lie came off her tongue so easily she felt her neck heat—"I have friends who have not been able to conceive.

They have been wishing for a child, but it is just not to be. So I was wondering…"

"If you might find them a suitable candidate from San Felipe."

"Yes. Exactly." *And now I will go to hell for lying to a priest. I'm sorry, God. It's for a good cause.*

Dietrich opened the door at the end of the hall. Ahead and to the right was the kitchen and, to the left, the chapel. He paused and allowed her to go through first. "Let us speak of this later, my child. I'm really very late. Let me caution you: I am afraid that your friends will still need to pass all the requisite background checks and fill out the proper paperwork. We cannot be careful enough when it comes to the safety and health of those God has placed in our care."

"Of course, Father. That will be no problem at all. Thank you so much." She clasped his hands and nearly hugged him.

He wished her well and continued toward the chapel. She opened the door to the kitchen, getting a face full of warm, moist air laced with the delicious aroma of warm bread and potent black coffee. The conversation with Dietrich played through her mind.

The lean priest was always very formal and composed. Yet, when she pressed on the adoption issue, he seemed to get a little flustered. And, come to think of it, why was he rushing from the offices of the dormitory wing? Other than that, the only thing in that direction was the front door. Had he gone to his office, or outside? *Absurd. What possible predawn outdoor task would need attending by a priest?*

Alexandra pursed her lips, thinking. Somehow she needed to cut Father Dominic from the herd and dig out some answers because something was damned peculiar about the robotic Father Dietrich.

Two crates left, and there'd been no problems. Cristian breathed hard from the exertion of carrying boxes heavier than a Mayan temple up the basement stairs. The dust and mold had worked their way into his sinuses, and his nose did not just run—it flowed.

"Ready?" he asked, taking one side of the next-to-last crate.

"Ready."

"Up!"

They heaved together and lifted something close to seventy kilos—the weight of a medium-sized man—of pure silver. *Enough to buy a hacienda in many parts of Mexico, or at least a nice house.*

Cristian struggled at math and had been working calculations in his head since they began loading the silver. He had to restart every time he got lost in multiplication tables. Using the current—or what he could find in a four-day-old newspaper anyway—price of silver, he finally figured out each crate should contain about seventy-five thousand US dollars of metal.

Times twenty-six that would be... six times five is—

He sneezed so hard his entire body convulsed.

The crate slipped.

Crack! The wooden box shattered on the stone floor, bursting apart and scattering a good portion of its contents. Seventy kilos of silver spoons, forks, knives, and serving pieces spilled from the crate.

The next few seconds lasted an eternity.

"That was *loud*," Herman whispered.

They froze like mannequins, ears tuned for the sound of running footsteps, voices raised in query. Cristian moved his eyes first, looking as well as listening. He straightened and turned a full circle, scanning like a radar dish.

"We may have gotten away with it," he hissed. "Quick, start gathering up the loose stuff. We'll pile it in the trailer and then come back for the last crate. Move, move, move. Let's go. *Andale.*"

Cristian scratched up loose piles of tarnished silverware, carrying it bunched in his hands like so many twigs until he could carry no more. Herman did the same and followed him. They piled their cargo in the right corner of the trailer in a loose pick-up-sticks jumble of blackened metal.

When Herman went back for his third trip, Cristian propped his hands on the tailgate of the trailer for a breather, head down, unconsciously assuming the position of someone being frisked by police.

One more crate, and we will be gone. And none too soon. I'm too old for this.

"Who are you, and what are you doing there?"

An electric shock traveled from his scalp down his back. Cristian forced his anus to squeeze tight to avoid an accident in his pants.

Father Pepe, the short, tubby priest, trundled into the circle of light cast by the lantern on the Ram's lowered tailgate. Round head and round body, like an orange on top of a grapefruit, Pepe often laughed and joked with the men in the village, beaming his happy smile.

This Pepe did not look anything like *that* Pepe. Face scrunched in a thunderous frown, he marched forward in a fat man's waddle, rosary swinging and bouncing on his leg.

Cristian's feet grew roots, and a lump the size of an apple lodged in his throat. Fifty years of Catholicism, from the time the parish priest first dribbled water on his head, had trained him to obey and fear men of the cloth. He thought himself jaded and cynical and above such a spiritual burden, but apparently, one angry priest could invoke a paralyzing fear as though flipping a light switch.

"What are you doing?" Father Pepe stopped a foot away, peering at him with watery eyes. "I know you. Cristian Guzman, from the village. Why are you here? Why are you loading this truck?" The chubby man paused for breath, his face dark with anger. "Well? Speak up."

Cristian moved his mouth, but no words came out. He even had a glib lie prepared just in case this should happen, but it remained stuck in the back of his mind. For the life of him, he could not remember it.

The priest looked past him at the stacked crates and loose silver and, if anything, his face grew even more outraged. "Why are you taking the silver? Who gave you this? Are you trying to steal it?"

A shadow moved behind Father Pepe, sliding into the light. Herman. He held a board from the broken crate in two hands, like a bat, and was poised to swing as if he were standing at home plate.

Cristian's tongue unlocked. "No, Herman!"

The board whipped through the air and hit Pepe in the side of the head with a dull, smacking crunch.

"*Uhhnn,*" the priest grunted and went to one knee. Herman cocked his arms and unleashed another swing, harder than the first, using the edge of the board instead of the flat. It chopped into the side of the short man's round head with a *thwock!*

Father Pepe spasmed and flopped onto the ground. One leg jerked uncontrollably. Blood splattered the dust, black in the lantern light.

Herman brought the board up over his head.

"No!" Cristian put out a hand. This time the board broke when it hit. Herman used the stump of it to pound again, and again, and again. It sounded to Cristian like someone driving nails.

Herman stopped. He panted, bent over with his hands on his knees. The priest lay still but for the one leg that continued to jerk slowly. Until it stopped.

Cristian kept his eyes raised, unable to look at the chubby body directly. The mess at the top of Father Pepe's round body remained visible in his peripheral vision. A strange calm came over him, though he started to shake like a small dog in the cold. Never in his life had he killed more than a chicken. He drove a truck and even broke the law of the United States by driving undocumented people. But never this.

A priest. Madre de Dios.

"Come," Cristian said. The word came out like a croak. "We must go. Now."

"We have time to get the other crate."

Cristian swallowed hard and shook his head.

"Yes, we do," Herman said. "Now shut up, and come on."

"What about the priest?" Cristian asked.

"He is dead. There is nothing we can do for him."

"Not this priest—the *other* priest. He was going to leave with us."

"Too bad," Herman said. "He will have to find his own transportation. We will wait for him in Madera." He tossed the bloody board into the brush and grabbed Father Pepe's hands. "For a short time. If he does not come soon, we will take all the silver and leave."

"What are you doing?"

His son flicked a glance over his shoulder. "Taking him to the basement. The longer it takes to find the body, the more time we have to get away. Maybe they will think Verdugo's men did it. Who knows? When Verdugo comes, we may get lucky, and everyone here will die. Now come on and help me with the last crate."

Lucky? Cristian looked at his son and saw him for the first time.

CHAPTER 32

THROUGH THE BULLET HOLES IN the road sign, Juan pieced together the name of the village. Morochic. Ten or eleven makeshift houses clustered around a store, much like Tia Bonita's, guarded by scrawny hens and two scraggly dogs. A dusty gravel road ran through the center of the village.

Yellow dawn spilled over the horizon and flooded through Morochic, lapping against the houses. Juan's shadow pointed toward the hillside on his left, though calling it a hillside was like calling Father Dietrich a little uptight. The trail Juan had descended during the night switched back and forth at a pitch so steep he had to hold onto tree limbs with one hand to keep from sliding off it completely.

A rooster crowed.

Juan fixed tired, gummy eyes on the store. When it opened, he could beg to use the telephone to call Father Dominic to come get him. He dreaded that call but not as much as he dreaded confession. The priest would be angry, and the punishment chores for running away would last a month. The penance for having killed Miguel would last forever.

Dried sweat, caked mud, bat poop, urine, and other smells combined for an odor that took his breath away when the wind shifted and blew his stink back at him.

To his right, the front door of a small house squealed open. A chunky woman in a sack-like dress came out, carrying an empty wash basket under one arm. Her goal, Juan guessed, was the clothesline in the front yard, pegged with colorful shirts and plain jeans. When she saw him, she stopped.

"Who are you?" Her sharp tone brought Juan to a stop. He swayed on his feet. "*Madre de Dios!* What happened to you? Come here, boy."

He stumbled and took a step and then, for some reason, was staring at the sky—a pretty sky, lit by a soft, morning sun, with high, thin clouds sliding by. The woman's round face blocked his view. She was not as pretty as the clouds.

He closed his eyes, and everything went black.

The priest stood between the tire tracks and spun in a slow circle as if he'd somehow missed seeing the tractor-trailer rig.

They were gone. The truck was gone.

Everyone had become concerned when Father Pepe failed to show up for Prime for the first time in twenty-two years. The other priests wanted to mount a search, fearing he might have become ill or suffered a heart attack. The priest had stepped in quickly and volunteered to check outside for Father Pepe.

And he'd found nothing. No truck, no men, no silver.

The priest walked around the outside of the mission in case, for some strange reason, Cristian had moved the truck to a different spot.

Nothing.

They had closed the basement doors and replaced the padlock. Herman's roadblock-busting pickup truck and the Mack truck with, presumably, the mission's treasure were both gone. Nothing was left but tire tracks and scuff marks.

He leaned his back against the mission walls and hung his head, eyes closed and arms crossed.

Several times in the past months he'd felt the hand of God at work in his life. Like Job, tests were placed before him, each of which he failed until he had come to believe that God would have no more to do with him. Weak flesh, weaker character.

The months of tortured conscience, guilt, and depression could not compare to this moment, the feeling of helpless panic that seized his heart and clamped down on his lungs. Just drawing a breath took an act of will, fighting against the stabbing pain of anxiety.

They had a prearranged meeting place set up in case they got separated: an abandoned lumberyard in Madera. The priest had made the contacts in the right places to sell the silver by weight, no questions asked, so it would pay Cristian to wait. But how hard could it be to turn silver into cash? Any pawn dealer or secondhand trader would buy those pieces without a second thought. Or Cristian and his son could set up in a market in a border town and sell the goods at inflated prices to chubby US tourists in baggy shirts and khaki shorts.

All the months of planning were wasted. He had concealed his plans not only from Verdugo but from Verdugo's spy at the mission: Gustavo, the janitor. The man was a pest, always snooping around with his runny nose, reporting back to Verdugo with every tidbit of information so he could receive another packet of white powder.

I have to get out of here. But how?

He could take the mission truck, but last he heard, the man—Yeager—had the keys. Had he returned them? The key box was mounted on a wall in the mission's main office; he would need to stop there and check. *And if they are not there?*

I must go there anyway. The safe is there.

Always, part of the priest's escape plan had been to empty the safe of cash and negotiable instruments in addition to taking the metal stored in the basement. His plan had been to check on Cristian and Herman's progress and then move on to the safe. Then he would come back, hop in the cab next to Cristian, and be gone from this place. Forever.

His head came up, and a new idea took shape. One, get the money in the safe. Two, go to Rascón and buy a car from one of the villagers or maybe pretend to borrow one instead. Bonita had a Nissan Xterra that she used once a month, and she would be happy to loan it to him. With money and a car, anything was possible.

With a plan fixed in his head, the priest levered himself to his feet and headed for the rear door, in the dormitory section. A question nipped at the corner of his mind: was this the latest test from God, or was this the beginning of his punishment for failing to confess his sins and ask God's forgiveness? He'd always assumed he would be judged in the afterlife, and perhaps he might have some small amount of time left to correct the injustices he had done before he met that reckoning.

But maybe not. Maybe he had no time left at all.

Yeager took time to shower and shave before heading to the dining hall. A shower and chow. What more could a soldier ask for? There were worse places to be in combat than at San Felipe, where they had hot water, hot food, and an indoor bunk.

At eight o'clock in the morning, Smitty had the dining room to himself when Yeager came in. He drew a cup of coffee and a plate of eggs and tortillas from the warming tins. Forty kids could make a serious dent in a pile of eggs, and what remained in the corners was dried out but still edible.

Especially with some salsa. Yeager dipped a big helping of hot sauce onto his eggs. "What's the good word, Smitty?"

The grizzly bear slurped his coffee. "Riley's gonna be pissed. I'm goin' up to relieve him, but I'm late."

"He'll probably chew you out in one-syllable words. One or two of them."

"That's all right. The boy says more with two words than I do with twenty." He tipped his cup back and drained it. "Okay, best I go take my beatin' and get it over with. Daddy always said, 'Eat a frog every morning. Anything happens after that will look good by comparison.'" Smitty pushed back his chair and paused before getting up. "Hey, you take the truck somewheres?"

"Truck?"

"The big rig. The Mack."

Yeager raised an eyebrow and shook his head. "No, I got back with the Chevy about three this morning. Hit the sack after that. Why?"

"I went outside to take a whiz on a lizard and have a look around. The diesel's gone, boy. Done dissemappeared."

"Huh. Riley would have seen it leave; maybe he knows. Let's go ask him."

Yeager rolled the last of his eggs in a tortilla and followed Smitty into the hall and to the bell-tower access. By the time they reached the ladder, he had crammed the last bite in his mouth and worked on chewing it down.

"Comin' up, Riley!" Smitty called. "Watch yer ass."

A finger of concern poked Yeager in the chest when Riley didn't answer. It grew to a hand punching him the gut when Smitty reached the top and started swearing.

"The hell, boy? What's this bullshit?"

Yeager topped the ladder and found the slender Texan wrapped in a blanket, slumped against a wall. He blinked groggy, sleepy eyes at the big man crouched over him.

Yeager ignored Riley and Smitty, went to the parapet, and scanned the countryside for Verdugo's men. "The bridge has been cleared." Whoever had taken the truck must have moved the blocking vehicles aside sometime during the night.

Finding nothing else remarkable on the first pass, he took his time and segmented the search area, focusing on one section at a time until he became certain there were no immediate threats. He kept one ear tuned to the flow of talk between the two men behind him.

"Hey, Riley; wake up, man."

Riley mumbled about being awake already.

"No, you were asleep, dude."

He gave another mumble, this one with a question in it.

"Yes way. Man, I'm sorry; I shoulda gotten up here sooner. Why didn't you come and get me if you were about to lose it?"

"Don't know what happened."

"Did you see the truck drive off?" Yeager asked.

"Truck?"

"Big truck. Red. Had a trailer and lotsa wheels."

"No. Saw Yeager in a truck."

"You remember anything after that?" Yeager asked without looking back.

Pause. "No." Another pause. "Head hurts."

"Check him for a bump," Yeager said. "Maybe he fell and hit his head."

"Roger wilco."

Wilco? Yeager grinned, despite the gravity of the situation. Leave it to Smitty to come up with the strangest words.

"No bump," Smitty said. "'Cept this biggun tween his shoulders."

"Okay, then." Yeager blew out a sigh. Was it worth cutting into Riley for falling asleep on guard duty? He was deeply pissed that it had happened, but the younger man was not a soldier in his platoon; he had in fact volunteered for a damn near no-win situation. And based on the look on his face, he was already beating himself up better than Yeager could. "Nothing we can do about it now. Riley, grab some chow and hit the sack. Get solid six hours, minimum. Eight if you can do it. I'm gonna need you at a hundred percent tonight. Check?"

Riley nodded and rubbed a hand down his face. "Sorry, man. I don't know what happened. Last thing I remember was coming back up here after you got back. After that..."

"Don't sweat it. I shouldn't have left you up here all night. Just be ready later."

"Roger that." Riley made for the ladder, looking like a tottering old man.

"Smitty, you got the watch. I'm gonna check with the priests, see what they know. Maybe somebody moved the rig on purpose. If not..."

"You think somebody stole it?"

Yeager's face scrunched up, and he scratched the side of his head. "Can't think what else might've happened. Maybe a village guy took a shine to it, wanted to sell it off for parts."

Smitty picked up the binoculars from the floor where he found Riley. He toed the stack of RPG-7s and the lone Stinger. "I got this. You go on, play Sherluck Domes and find out what's what. Looks like you brought me some toys to keep ol' Mr. Verdumpo happy if he decides to come play."

Yeager slapped him on the shoulder and made for the ladder. "That prick shows his ass, Smitty, you plant a missile up in it."

"Roger missile. Nonlubricated."

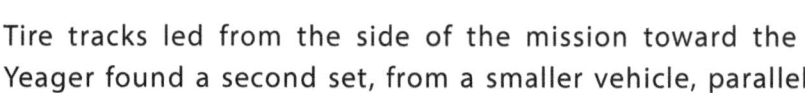

Tire tracks led from the side of the mission toward the bridge. Yeager found a second set, from a smaller vehicle, paralleling the first for a short stretch before they blended and overlapped. The rust-red dust and gravel of the yard showed heavy traffic from the basement doors to the where the trailer would have been situated.

"Well," he said to himself, "somebody loaded something and took off."

A damp patch caught his eye, and he knelt beside it. Touched it with a finger. It came away red and sticky, covered in dirt and...

Blood. And a lot of it. It looked as though someone had kicked dirt over the spot, trying to hide it. Now that Yeager's eyes adjusted to that, he could follow a trail of kicked-over dirt—dampened and darker than the rest—all the way to the basement steps.

The double steel doors were secured with a padlock so big it should have had a wizard's curse engraved on it in hieroglyphics. On the threshold was another patch of blood, also crusted over with dirt. Yeager pulled on the padlock and confirmed it was locked.

He backed out and started a wide circle, studying the ground for any other clues. The blood trail gnawed at him. He had seen enough of them to recognize the evidence of a body being dragged. But which way did it go—from the truck to the basement or vice versa?

Yeager found a broken one-by-six board, stained with blood, ten yards away, hung up in the limbs of a scraggly bush. Blackened blood so thickly covered the piece of wood that it looked as though it had been dipped in burgundy paint. He took a closer look and found strands of black hair caught in the splinters of the board. Yeager winced. Whoever took this beating was either dead or badly hurt.

And might be in the basement.

Yeager broke into a jog for the mission's main entrance. He

would need to track down somebody with a key to that damn big padlock, pronto, in case the victim was still alive.

"Shit. This stinks."

A whole lot of bad things had happened while Riley napped in the bell tower, which seemed like awfully good timing. Had someone planned it that way?

He nearly ran into one of the maintenance guys coming through the front door.

"Gustavo, right?"

"Sí." The man nodded. Scarecrow thin, with a Zapata mustache bracketing his mouth and trailing off his chin, Gustavo wore a gray work shirt and dark-gray denim pants.

"Do you have a key to the basement?"

"No, señor, only the priests. We are not allowed there."

"Where's Father Dominic?"

"In his office, señor. That way—"

But Yeager had already bolted past him. He found Dominic tapping at a keyboard, eyes narrowed in concentration on a glowing monitor. "Basement. Now. I'll explain on the way."

Dominic blinked but followed him without saying a word. In the hall, when Yeager turned left to retrace his steps, the priest said, "This way is quicker," and led him to the right. Yeager explained what he had found as they hustled through the stone hallways, the echo of their footsteps bouncing back.

The priest murmured a prayer and unlocked a deadbolt on an unmarked steel door near the kitchen. The door swung inward, revealing a set of wooden steps leading into a darkened space. A damp smell of mildew puffed out. Dominic toggled a wall switch, and a brace of lights came on over the stairs.

Yeager pushed past and took the steps two at a time. Another wall switch at the bottom activated three bare bulbs spaced along the middle of the basement.

He saw the body immediately and recognized Father Pepe in the next instant. The priest was dead. Of that, he had no doubt.

"Dominic," he called, "it's Pepe. He's been murdered."

He glanced back up the stairs in time to see the door at the top swing closed.

"Dominic? What the hell?"

The lock engaged with a click.

CHAPTER 33

JUAN SNAPPED AWAKE AND SAT up, breathing hard. A dream of being crushed by a million kilos of rock fell apart. The light of a new morning sliced through a high window.

A high window?

Juan realized a number of things at once: he was in a bed, under covers, in a room with faded posters of Milli Vanilli and Eminem on the walls—a girl's room, judging by the dolls on the dresser, the makeup, and the hand-drawn pictures of ponies, all of it covered in a thin layer of dust. And he had no clothes on under the covers. And he was clean. No smell.

Hunger pains stabbed at his belly, and he had to pee like crazy.

He gathered the blanket around him and stood. Too fast. Dizziness made him sit back down until the darkness around the edge of his vision went away. When he tried it again, he had much more success as long as he used one hand for a brace.

Wearing the blanket like a cloak, he went to the bedroom door, which was opened a crack. Sounds of a woman humming and rattling pots and pans drifted from the far end of the house. A door halfway down the hall stood open, and from the tile, Juan guessed it was the bathroom.

Moments later, he confirmed that guess by slipping into it and squeezing the door closed behind him. He used the toilet and then washed his hands. A hollowed-out, eye-blackened face stared back at him from the mirror.

I'm a starving clown. Scary. Best to not look at that anymore for a while.

When he left the bathroom, he nearly ran headfirst into a

mountain of shapeless cotton. He backed up and looked into the face of the woman he had seen when he'd first entered the village.

"You are awake? Already? I'll bet you are a hungry boy, no?" Her expression had gone from angry and suspicious to more like Tia Bonita's—an elderly aunt with a heart of gold.

"Sí, Tia, very hungry."

The woman laughed and led him to the kitchen, keeping up a hailstorm of words. "You can call me *la tia* if you want. Tia Marisol. I like that. Where did you come from? You looked like somebody dragged you behind a horse along a trail of shit and—*aieee!*—the smell. Your clothes I have washed; they are hanging out to dry now, but we may never get the smell out, *la chingada!* Sit there, *mijo*, at the table. I have some pan dulce ready. You start on those while I fix you some eggs."

Tia Marisol shuffled to the stove. Pinched flesh bulged around the tops of blue house shoes too small for her feet. A faded cotton-print dress, more like a tablecloth, came to her ankles, and she had black hair, pulled back and tied with a band. Now that she was not scowling at him, Tia Marisol had a pleasant face with a big nose and laughing eyes.

Juan stuffed in a mouthful of sweet bread before she had taken two steps. The smell of food sent his stomach into a growling fit.

Over the next hour, Marisol worked his story out of him, allowing him to speak in short bursts between her running commentary. He described living at the orphanage and going to school there and how he snuck away to explore the cave. She tut-tutted when he told of falling down the bat-poop slide and being in the dark and having to find his flashlight. With a full belly, and safe in her home, he became more creative in his retelling, speaking of red-eyed bats and narrow passages, white hands reaching from pools of water and ghostly chains rattling in distant parts of the cave.

At the last part, she shook a finger at him. "Now, don't you lie to me, Juan Guerrero, or I will smack your ass for you. Don't you think I won't. I raised four children, and I have nine grandchildren, and I don't put up with that kind of bullshit from anyone. Yes?"

He hung his head and hid a smile. Already, he could tell, her bite would be much less painful than her bark. "Sí, Tia Marisol. But the part about traveling through the cave is true. I came out in some Anasazi dwellings above." He pointed in the general direction of the cliffs.

"Rascón is on the other side of the mountains, mijo. The tunnel must go all the way through. Your orphanage is many kilometers away, by road. Much too far to walk."

"But…" He bit his lip to keep it from trembling. The thought of going back through the cave made his insides knot up. The food in his tummy rolled around. "How will I get back?"

"You leave that to Tia Marisol, mijo. I think I know just the way."

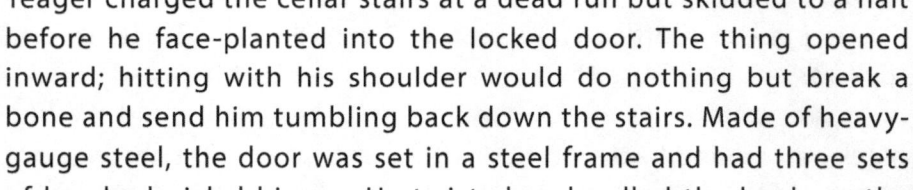

Yeager charged the cellar stairs at a dead run but skidded to a halt before he face-planted into the locked door. The thing opened inward; hitting with his shoulder would do nothing but break a bone and send him tumbling back down the stairs. Made of heavy-gauge steel, the door was set in a steel frame and had three sets of brushed-nickel hinges. He twisted and pulled the knob on the inside, which did nothing—a dummy knob, made to be a handle and nothing more. The lock, a double-cylinder deadbolt, required a key.

"Goddammit, Dominic! What kind of game are you playing?" Dead priests, missing trucks, enough money for guns and ammunition. All of it added up to… *What? What the hell does it add up to?* Yeager shook off the thought. He kicked the door. Hard. "Shit!"

Yeager gave the handle another frustrated jerk, but the door fit so tight it did not even rattle in its frame. "This is bullshit." His hand fell to the butt of his .45, and for a wild moment, he was tempted to pull it and shoot the lock in some kind of wild Hollywood stunt. Sanity flushed the instinct down the drain before he could act on the impulse.

Shooting point-blank at a steel door would be a spectacular way to die.

"And no tac radio." He pictured it, sitting in the base charger in his room. "You're gettin' old and stupid, boy."

Yeager checked the hinges. He picked at the pin in the middle hinge, shoving a fingernail into the gap to try and work it loose. Three fingernails later, he gave up.

"I need a hammer and a punch," he said to the hinge. "That'll fix your ass." Yeager jogged down the stairs, muttering to himself, scanning the floor for a toolbox or a workbench. "A screwdriver. A nail. Something."

In one quick check of the perimeter, he found nothing useful, just boxes and boxes of molding paper, wooden Christmas ornaments, and a Nativity scene piled in one corner. He thought he hit pay dirt when he found a double-door filing cabinet, but it held nothing but erasers, pencils, and crayons.

The only other exit from the basement turned out to be the one to outside.

With the goddamn Padlock of Doom on it. Which means...

Yeager went to the body of Father Pepe, who lay perfectly straight in the middle of the floor. Father Pepe wore a monk's robe, belted at the waist with a braided rope. A crucifix on a beaded rosary hung from the belt. It looked as though whoever left him had taken a minute to arrange the body, placing his hands together on his chest and straightening the priest's robe. If not for the gory mess at the top, the body would appear to be peacefully sleeping.

Next to the body, a broken crate and loose straw filling made an untidy pile. The wood of the crate was the same as the bloody board he had found in the bushes. Whoever had killed the priest had taken a board from the crate to use as a weapon.

"All right, Columbo, but who killed him? Dominic?" Yeager shoved that thought aside and, with a silent apology, inspected the priest's clothing for something he could use on the hinge, like a penknife or a coin. "Or how about a set of keys to the lock?"

But apparently Pepe did not believe in carrying metallic objects of any kind, not even a St. Christopher medal. The cross at the end of the rosary was made of wood—simple, blunt, and extremely unhelpful.

Yeager tried the crate next. Maybe a staple or nail could be worked loose and would be hard enough to loosen the hinge. He dug into the boards, twisting at them to see how they were put together. Metal jingled on the floor, and a flash of bronze caught his eye.

It turned out not to be bronze after all, but rather a tarnished silver butter knife, half-buried in the straw packing material. It had an ornate handle, and when he picked it up, he found the thing weighed twice what he expected. Yeager rubbed at the surface, which didn't much change the discoloration, but he strongly suspected the piece was real silver and not silver plated.

And the evidence of the broken crate hinted that more of the same had been stored here.

A crate of silverware? Just one?

Yeager angled his head to catch the light across the basement floor. Sure enough, now that he knew what to look for, he could just make out a rough outline of a cleared patch in the dust, roughly twenty or thirty feet square. On one side of it, a trampled line of footprints went from the storage space to the basement stairs.

Sitting back on his heels, Yeager scratched his chin. The priests had something—silver, antiques, or whatever—stored in crates in the basement. That was how Dominic could afford to write a big check to Victor for supplies. Somebody found out about it and stole it—probably with that weasel, Father Dominic, helping. Pepe got in the way, and they bash his head in. Or he was one too many accomplices.

Whatever the story, Yeager figured he wouldn't get any answers sitting around in the cellar. Taking the butter knife and a board from the crate, he jogged to the top of the stairs. Setting the point of the knife in the narrow gap between the hinge pin and the hinge, Yeager used the board as a hammer. Three solid whacks, and the tip of the pin popped loose. From there, it was only a matter of using the knife to pry the remainder of the pin free of the shaft.

The top and bottom hinges went quicker, and four minutes later, all three pins were out. The door, however, fit tightly in its frame and refused to budge.

Yeager worked the knife into the doorjamb. Careful not to push too hard, he used the blade as a pry bar to wiggle the door free a quarter inch at a time. He worked from top to bottom, pulling the door evenly so as not to let it twist and jam in the tight frame.

The soft metal of the butter knife kept trying to bend whenever he put too much muscle on it. The stress of jiggling the knife at just the right tension to keep it unbent melted sweat patches under his arms and down his back.

When the door came free, it happened quickly, falling off the hinges and tipping back. Yeager dropped the knife and got his hands up just in time to keep from getting crushed. With a deep grunt and a curse, he twisted out of the way and let gravity take the door where it wanted to go.

Crash! The steel door bounced and banged down the staircase, cracking some treads along the way before slapping the concrete floor with a rattling *boom!*

That ought to get somebody's attention.

Yeager didn't wait to find out. He took an extra second to shove the butter knife in his back pocket then headed for Dominic's office at a dead run.

CHAPTER 34

ALEXANDRA LOPEZ FOUND HER SURGERY patient sitting up in bed, eating a bowl of porridge. The girl had more color in her face and flashed a brilliant smile when Alex came into her room. That one look warmed Alex down to her toes.

"And how are we feeling today, Emelita-bonita?"

The girl giggled. "That's not my name!"

"I'm a doctor, and I can change your name if I want. Now, lie back and let me check your tummy."

Marta, even with a minor concussion and blurred vision, had remained on duty despite Alex's demand that she rest. The nurse kept up with dressing changes and maintained Emelita's chart, so Alex found nothing unexpected during her exam.

"So tell me about the last girl who was adopted." Alex sat on the edge of the bed and kept her tone light, concealing her interest in the answer. "What was her name?"

"Irene."

"And when was Irene adopted?"

Emelita bit her lip and looked at the ceiling. "Uh, last month, I think?"

"And do you know the name of the family she went to?"

"No, Father never tells us that. He just comes and takes away the children who get adopted, and they leave."

"So how do you know they are going to a good home?"

Emelita gave her a strange look, and her eyebrows creased in a frown. Alex wished she could take back the question; she had introduced doubt and fear into the little girl's worldview.

"Father says so," Emelita said in a serious tone.

"Of course." Alex patted her hand and fixed the warmest smile she could manage on her face. The girl did not seem fooled. "So what did Father Sebastian tell you about Irene?"

"Father Sebastian?"

"Yes, Sebastian. The priest in charge of adoptions?"

"No, silly!" Emelita giggled again. "Father Sebastian is a meany."

Alex blinked. She had spoken with Dominic a short two hours ago, and he had named Sebastian as being in charge of the adoption function. "If not Sebastian, then who...?"

"Father Dominic," Emelita said as if the answer were plain as day. "He's so nice."

Father Dominic snagged his backpack from his office and headed for the main doors at a brisk march. He did not know how long Yeager would remain locked in the basement, but there was no longer any doubt; Dominic's time at the mission was up.

It had ended when Yeager burst into his office, demanding to see the basement. Good timing, in one sense—Dominic had just finished typing his *mea culpa* on his office computer. He did not expect his confession to generate forgiveness, or even understanding, but it just felt wrong to leave without an explanation.

The morning sun blinded him, and he stumbled for a moment, squinting, holding an arm over his face. When his eyes adjusted, he angled for the bridge and set off with long strides.

Dominic silently cursed, again, the betraying organ between his legs. That same organ had tempted Eve with the fruit of forbidden knowledge. How long had it taken for Adam and Eve to lose the Garden of Eden? Months? Years?

For him, the Garden was lost in a matter of weeks. Not long ago, he'd taught an English class in Guerrero. It was a free class, open to anyone who wanted to come, but mostly consisted of future migrants: men and women who wanted the rudiments of the language so they might better blend in when they made the trek north. At the time, he thought Lola had the same goal.

She claimed she was nineteen years old, though he found out

later she'd lied about that as she had everything else. She was petite and small waisted, with a dancer's legs and intelligent, laughing eyes. Her peasant blouse strained with melon-sized breasts, never confined by a brassiere.

She executed his seduction in six weeks, staying late after class to help him clean up. Bending over in front of him. Brushing him with a hip, a breast, or just a light touch of her hand. Kneeling in front of him and asking for a blessing, apparently heedless of the way her top gaped open, revealing swelling globes tipped with brown bullets.

His blood heated to a point, and he forgot his oaths, forgot his calling... forgot God.

After his first indiscretion, he had spiraled down a drain of depravity that made him shudder now to think on it. Lola had teased him along with one sexual act after another, incrementally adding layers of wickedness until his lust-addled brain could no longer remember a time of abstinence.

Only later, when the first envelope of photographs arrived, did the truth sink in. Sharp fangs of remorse bit deep, so hard his breath failed. Lola met him one last time, laughing at his gullibility and how clumsy and awkward his lovemaking was.

Then came the demands. Lola's employer, at the time unknown, threatened to expose him should he not comply. And at first he seemed so... reasonable. Cash. A small amount at first, which snowballed until Dominic was forced to start liquidating silver pieces from the basement collection.

Then the devil had upped the stakes. The blackmailer, a shadowy face in a dark room, had said, "I have some childless friends. They would like to adopt a girl between the age of twelve and thirteen. If you could perhaps arrange something like that, then maybe we can lose some of the pictures."

A childless couple. How could he have been that stupid? After that, the requests for a girl came every few months. Year after year. Each child he dropped off at a house on the outskirts of Ciudad Guerrero killed his soul a little more, for he knew by then they weren't going to childless couples.

The look in their eyes when he told them he had found them a family...

A few months ago, he had finally told his tormentor, "No. Expose me. Show the pictures. I don't care."

The man stepped out of the shadows, and Dominic recognized him, knew instantly who he was from the man's blond hair and scarred throat.

Verdugo.

"I have heard rumors," the killer hissed, "that San Felipe was gifted a century or so ago by a wealthy benefactor. A large amount of silver."

"No, I—"

Verdugo punched him in the stomach, and Dominic fell to the floor, vomiting and trying to ease the super-hot star that had exploded in his midsection.

"Fuck your no, pendejo." Verdugo stepped on Dominic's ear and pushed his face down so that his cheek was pressed into the puddle of warm muck he'd spewed. "I want either the silver or the next girl you have ready for delivery. You have ten days to comply."

But he had not complied. Against an onslaught of escalating threats, Dominic had held firm. Then came the earthquakes. Verdugo's men shut down all the roads and stole all the supply trucks coming from either Madera or Guerrero. A thought continued to revolve in Dominic's mind: why didn't Verdugo just come take what he wanted? He had the men and the guns to destroy San Felipe ten times over, so why try starving him into submission?

Those questions would have to remain unanswered. Dominic bit down on the inside of his mouth until blood ran, wiping away the memories of past sins. All he had to do was borrow Bonita's car and run.

He came to the door of Tia Bonita's store and paused for a moment to find the expression he wanted and get it fixed on his face.

It was time to leave.

Yeager came out of Father Dominic's office. His eyes, which Alex normally found warm and kind of sad, had gone hard and cold. He looked violent and frightening in a way she had not seen before.

"Doctor, have you seen Dominic?"

"No, I was just—"

"Thanks," he said, brushing past her. "If you see him, stay away from him."

Alex stared at the man's broad back as he stalked away. Yeager stopped and turned around. "Dr. Lopez, we need to gather everybody for a strategy session. I'd like you there." He glanced at his watch. "Eleven o'clock. Dining hall."

Without waiting for an answer, he spun on a heel and left. She stared at the space where he had been, not sure if she wanted to be angry... or scared.

Yeager got his tac radio first, switched it on, and pressed the talk button. "Smitty, you up?"

"Go for Smitty," came back in an instant.

"Did you see Father Dominic leave the building?"

A short pause. "That the skinny guy with black hair? Yeah, I saw him hike over to the store a little while ago. Not sure, but he might've tooken off in a car right after."

"Clarify."

"'Bout ten minutes after he went in the store, a white Toyota SUV came out from behind there. I weren't payin' a lot of attention, but it coulda been him drivin'."

"Damn," Yeager swore to himself. He slung the M4 over one shoulder, his battle harness—with full mag pouches—over the other.

"Was I supposed to stop him?" Smitty asked.

"No. You couldn't know. Listen, I'm going to send somebody up to keep an eye out for you. I need you in the dining hall in thirty mikes. Copy?"

"Copy."

On the way back to Dominic's office, Yeager checked his cell phone for the millionth time. No signal. He mastered the temptation to sling the electronic paperweight down the hallway.

How did people function in the old days?

He could not check on Por Que, he could not call Charlie and let her know what was up, and he could not reach de la Cueva and ask for some backup. Yeager stuffed the phone back in his pocket. Had he held it a moment longer, he might have crushed it into plastic shards.

Funny how quickly a person got used to having backup at the other end of a field radio or satellite phone. In Afghanistan, even in the hairiest, wildest parts of Way the Fuck Nowhere, he had telecommunication gear good enough to call the moon. Admittedly, sometimes the wind had to be just right and Jupiter in the house of Mars for it to work, but when it did, he could order up a couple of A-10s with shit-hot pilots who ached to lay a big pile of whup-ass on any target he designated. Not to mention the surveillance drones, spy planes, and even balloons with cameras attached to their underbellies that would come runnin' when he whistled.

Here, he could not even get a Google Earth picture. It was like fighting with Black Jack Pershing in the chase for Pancho Villa. Worse than that, it was like hunkering down in the Alamo with Davy Crockett, Jim Bowie, and Travis Barrett.

And look at how well that turned out.

What was it Sgt. Masterson always told me when I would gripe about not having the right equipment, or enough of it? "You got your rifle, dontcha? That's all a marine needs, boy, so shut up and get your ass downrange before I kick it there."

"Oooh-rah, Sarn't."

Dominic's office looked much the same as Father Sebastian's. A single, simple desk, two guest chairs, and a low couch made up the furnishings along with a three-drawer file cabinet of plain gray steel. A computer monitor—the old CRT kind—took up one corner of the desk. Other than that, the top was completely clean. A safe, about the size of a dorm-room fridge, stood behind the desk, door open. It had been emptied of everything except dust bunnies and a paperclip.

Yeager sat at the desk, set his rifle on top of it, and started rummaging through the drawers. His jostling bumped the mouse, and the computer's screensaver kicked off. The display showed a text document opened up, cursor blinking at the bottom.

Yeager scrolled up and began to read.

———✦———

Tia Marisol waited by the passenger door of the dusty Jeep Cherokee and waved to Juan to get in. Before Juan could react, she crushed him a mother-bear hug. Up close, she smelled of baked bread and a trace of some flowery scent. He blinked eyes that had gone all watery and hugged her back, though he could barely get his arms around her.

She broke away and held him by the upper arms, shaking him a little but not hard. "You be careful, Juan Guerrero. Otherwise, Tia Marisol will come find you and beat your scrawny ass until it is black and blue and purple. *Entendido?*"

"Sí, Tia."

"No more climbing through caves. You want to come visit me, you come like a civilized person."

Juan was not sure he heard correctly. "I can… come visit?"

"You better, you little stinkbug. My youngest daughter went away to college many years ago, and all my grandchildren are far away. No one comes to visit anymore, the shits. You come back, I'll make you a nice flan, no?"

Juan turned away and took a quick swipe of his sleeve across his burning eyes. "Sorry. Must be the dust."

"For me too," she said with a sniff. She leaned in the open door of the Jeep. "Now, Jorge Mendoza, you listen to me too. You take care of this boy, and make sure he gets back to the orphanage, no?"

"Sí, Marisol, of course." Jorge Mendoza lounged behind the leather-wrapped steering wheel and fiddled with a bit that had come loose. He looked bored but indulgent, or at least not willing to piss the woman off.

Juan stifled a giggle. Nobody would want to piss Tia Marisol off; it would be like kicking Godzilla in the butt.

As Tia had explained to him, Señor Mendoza sold grapefruit all over the valley, driving the back roads from village to village. Juan could not remember seeing him in Rascón, but that was not strange. He rarely paid attention to the comings and goings of people passing through the little town.

"Get in, Juan Guerrero, get in," Tia urged him. "Why are you standing around here? Move, move, move." She slammed the door behind him and backed away.

Señor Mendoza cranked the engine, shifted gears, and shot away, all before Juan had gotten his butt planted in the seat. He craned his head out the window and looked back. Tia Marisol—a white shape in a sack dress—waved from a cloud of red dust. He waved back and kept waving long after she'd disappeared from sight.

CHAPTER 35

"HERE'S THE DEAL." YEAGER STOOD at one end of the head table in the dining hall. Seated around him were Dr. Lopez, Smitty, Riley, and the two priests, Sebastian and Dietrich. Riley still looked groggy and tired but better than he had that morning.

The kids had been given lessons and left to study in their classrooms, and the eagle's nest in the bell tower was manned by one of the maintenance staff.

Yeager tapped the table with a knuckle, organizing his thoughts. Breaking the news of Dominic's betrayal would be bad enough, but the rest of the situation smelled like a dead skunk in a pile of manure. On the bright side, at least Victor wasn't around to hear about his mother's cousin.

"Here's the deal," he said again. "First, you need to know: Father Pepe has been murdered."

Yeager let the outcries of disbelief wash over him. The priests and the doctor tried asking questions at the same time, shouting over each other to be heard. Smitty looked stunned, whereas Riley just looked as though he wanted to puke.

Finally, the tiny doctor stood up, and her voice overrode the others. "How could you not tell me? An injured man—"

Yeager held up a hand and cut her off. "Doc, his head was bashed in. I hate to put it out there all blunt like that, but I've seen enough to know. Pepe was gone long before I ever got to him. Now, if y'all will settle down, I'll give it to you the best I can."

The doctor sat, arms crossed, and her frown could have frozen his nuts off from six feet away.

"Father Sebastian," Yeager said, "does the mission have a treasure of some kind locked in the basement? Silver maybe?"

The old priest's eyes got wide. "Yes, but how did you know? It is a secret."

"Not anymore." Yeager went on to explain the missing truck and the empty basement and, knowing this last part would throw more gasoline on the fire, told them of Dominic locking him up and driving away.

"Que?" Sebastian bounded to his feet. His face reminded Yeager of a kettle left on the boil too long; he half expected to see steam coming from the priest's ears. The old man launched into a tirade entirely in Spanish, so fast Yeager caught only one word in three.

"Read this," he said when Sebastian paused for breath. From his back pocket, he pulled several folded sheets of paper. "I found this letter on Dominic's computer and printed out several copies."

The document, written in Spanish, had taken a while for Yeager to puzzle through—he spoke the language better then he read it—but once he got started, the contents left him stunned.

He waited while the group read the letter. By the end of it, Dr. Lopez openly wept. He knew exactly how she felt. He had to drag the words from his throat when he spoke. "For the non-Spanish readers in the room, the letter is Father Dominic's confession. He fell into a honey trap, orchestrated by Verdugo. Verdugo has been blackmailing Dominic—first for cash and later"—he grimaced—"kids. Girls specifically."

"Motherfucker," Smitty growled. Riley nodded, holding the table in a white-fingered grip.

"Roger that," Yeager said. "But that's not the end of it. Once the earthquake hit, and our pal Verdugo put a stranglehold on traffic, Dominic had a vision, or more like, uh..."

"An epiphany," Riley said.

"Exactly. An epiphany. He decided to take the mission's treasure and escape to another life."

"Pardon me." Dr. Lopez held up a hand. "What treasure?"

"I'm not real sure where that came from." Yeager fixed the older priest with a look. Sebastian appeared to have aged ten years in the last ten minutes; any worse, and the doc would need to check the old man for heart failure. "Father? Any comments on the treasure?"

Sebastian looked at him for a long moment. Dietrich shifted in his seat, and Yeager caught his eye. The German knew something, but it appeared he would defer to his older colleague. Smitty, Riley, and the doctor held their silence, studying the priest.

"The first non-Indian in this valley," Sebastian said at last. His voice cracked, and he swallowed. "The first settler who came here was a man named Octavio Mariscal Pedraza, who was distantly related to a powerful family, though he came from poor circumstances himself. In 1832, four years before your battle of the Alamo, Pedraza came here with an intention to settle."

Sebastian looked up with reddened, watery eyes. "To make a very long story short, Pedraza found silver ore in several locations. He struck it rich, as you would say. He did many good things with his fortune, one of which was founding this mission. When he died, he passed on a large part of his worldly goods to the care of the clergymen here with the proviso that it not be sent back to the mother church but be used here exclusively. He donated both coinage and the furnishings of his home, all cast in the silver dug from his mines."

"Rudy Aguilar told me the founder was an ancestor of de la Cueva," Yeager said.

"Yes, this is true. De la Cueva's family is a branch of Pedraza's family tree." The old man slumped in his chair, clearly tired of the subject. "The family benefitted from the remaining estate. The de la Cuevas are the only ones who have lasted to this day."

"So how much we talkin' 'bout?" Smitty asked.

Sebastian shrugged. "What does it matter, if it's gone?"

Dietrich spoke for the first time. "When I first learned of this stockpile in the basement, the price of silver was very high. Out of curiosity, I weighed the boxes in which the goods were packed. I calculated, just by weight, somewhere around three million dollars, US."

"Ho. Lee. Shit." Smitty's mouth hung open in exaggerated

surprise. Yeager had expected a big number, but the amount still shocked him.

"And this is just weight," Dietrich said. "Many of the pieces are antiques, and their value is well beyond their weight in metal."

"Dominic didn't drive the damn truck," Smitty said. "I saw him leave in Toy-yoda."

"According to the note, he made a deal with somebody from Rascón to drive the rig. He didn't say who." It was Yeager's turn to shrug. "We can find out easy enough. It's a small town."

"Cristian Guzman," Dietrich said with conviction. "He was once a truck driver. I saw him visiting with Dominic in his office last week."

"That's a side note, far as I'm concerned," Yeager said. "I suspect Verdugo's headed back here, and this thing with Dominic doesn't change that one bit. We need to figure on gettin' outta here. Now Victor Ruiz"—the doctor looked up sharply at the mention of Victor's name, but Yeager continued without pausing—"is making a run for de la Cueva's. He'll load up the Huey with avgas, strip everything else out, and make the hop over the mountains. We can evac the most critical patients when he gets here. You good with that, Dr. Lopez?"

"If I must move them, then yes, that is the best way."

"Where to? I'd rather avoid Madera if I could. The place is owned by the cartels."

Lopez pursed her lips and tapped a long fingernail on the table. "Hermosillo. In Sonora."

"Okay, we'll have to see if Victor can make a hop that far." Yeager scratched the back of his head. "I don't think we have a choice. I think that snake is coming back and coming back hard. He didn't look the type to take an ass whippin' gracefully. Anybody disagree? Hell, this ain't a dictatorship; if one of y'all have a better plan, speak up."

Dietrich cleared his throat. "I would tend to agree with you, Herr Yeager. I have heard stories of this man, and from those tales, I would deduce that Señor Verdugo has a history of doing very bad things to his enemies. I do not believe we can risk staying."

"Sebastian?"

The older priest showed a little life, though he still looked fragile and shaken. "Yes. What is here to keep safe? Stone walls? No, if the children are in danger, we must go."

Smitty and Riley gave him a thumbs-up. "I don't wanna ride in no jelli-copter though," Smitty said. "I had enougha that in Viet Nam. I'd rather taken a beatin' with a briar switch."

"We'll have to see how many trips Victor can do. In the meantime, we have one Chevy pickup with a leaky head gasket and four bald tires." He looked at Dietrich and tried a rueful smile. "Couldn't y'all have spent some of that money on better transportation?"

"I believe the priests here have tried to be frugal." The stern German didn't return his smile. "For the most part, the money went to general upkeep and to the education and care of the children. This is not like most orphanages you would see in this country. Here, the children are better fed, clothed, and educated—"

"And sold into sexual slavery!"

At the doctor's words, Dietrich flinched as though struck by a whip and went silent, bowing his head over his hands.

"Even if it was the work of another man, you should have known," Dr. Lopez said.

"So," Yeager said into the uncomfortable silence, "let's say we get ten, twelve people out by air. What about the rest? Can we hide some in Rascón?"

Sebastian shook his head. "If Verdugo comes and finds no one here, he will search the village. If he finds us there, he will punish the people who have given us sanctuary. I do not think it would be wise."

"What about vehicles? We have one pickup here. Can we borrow more from the townspeople?"

"At most, three or four," Sebastian said.

"Hmm. Maybe another fifteen or twenty people. A few more if we cram them in like sardines. What about walking? How far to the nearest place with a real police force?"

"Madera—"

"Madera police are likely in Verdugo's pocket," Yeager said.

"But it's the closest place, Señor Yeager." Sebastian held his palms up, a look of helplessness on his face. "Even so, it is 150 kilometers by road. A bad road, at that."

Smitty's barrel-chested laugh boomed out. "That's a long hike. I changed my mind. I wanna ride the whirlybird."

"Are there any maps of the area available?" Yeager asked.

"Sí, we have maps," Dietrich said and rose to his feet. "I will get them for you."

He moved like a man twice his age. Yeager had a moment of sympathy for the German; it was hard to find out your brother and friend had double-crossed you the way Dominic had. Was Dr. Lopez right? Should the priests have realized what Dominic was up to?

All those innocent little girls. Yeager clenched his jaw. *And how do I get the rest of them out of here?*

Juan Guerrero yelled and grabbed for the hanging strap over the door when the fruit seller, Señor Mendoza, took a hairpin turn so fast the Cherokee tried to come up on two wheels. Juan couldn't decide if he wanted to be exhilarated or scared to death. For the entire trip, Señor Mendoza had driven as if chased by demons from a nasty hole under Hell.

Juan held on and prayed to God, Armando, and any saint whose name he could remember. Twice, they had been stopped by cartel thugs at roadblocks, and both times, Juan's throat had squeezed closed. The guards had acted as if Mendoza were an old friend; they laughed and joked with him and waved him through after taking a small sack of grapefruit.

When Juan mentioned it, the dumpy man showed him bad teeth in a crooked grin. "I drive all over these mountains for many years now. Some of these boys I have known since they were smaller than *you*."

They took another scorching turn in a swirl of dust, and Juan blinked in sudden recognition. He knew this stretch of road. His heart doubled its already fast thumping. They were close to the mission! He never would have believed in a million, million years that he would be happy to get back to the orphanage. Something about being lost in the cave and nearly dying had scared him down to his toes. All he wanted was a plate of hot food and his bed. Even putting up with the punishment chores would be worth it.

When they rocketed through the mountain cut and the village of Rascón appeared in the valley below, Juan had to wipe a sleeve across his watery eyes. The cluster of homes along one side of the road had taken on a golden glow from the late-afternoon sun, and the mission cast a shadow so long it nearly touched the river.

"There you are," said Señor Mendoza. "Home at last, hey?"

"Sí." Juan nodded. *Home at last.*

CHAPTER 36

ATHER SEBASTIAN AND YEAGER STUDIED an atlas of the region surrounding Rascón. Yeager's blunt fingertip traced potential routes through the mountains as he listened to Sebastian give him the pros and cons of each.

His earpiece crackled static. "Car. Coming in hot," Smitty drawled, then after a two-second pause he added, "Two people inside. One looks like a kid."

Yeager, already headed for the front door, pushed the talk button. "Copy. Two people in a car."

When he reached the entrance to the mission, Father Sebastian joined him. They watched a Jeep Cherokee cross the river in the shallows, avoiding the blocked bridge. *Coming in hot* might have been an understatement, Yeager noted. Twin rooster tails of spray jetted up when the Jeep hit the water, and a bow wave crashed over the windshield.

"That guy's insane," Yeager said.

"Jorge Mendoza." Sebastian grunted, his mouth set in a frown. "He sells fruit."

Yeager glanced at the priest. "Bad guy?"

"No." Sebastian grumbled something in Spanish that sounded like, "He needs to go to church more often."

The Cherokee braked hard and slid to a stop in front of them, dust rolling past in a small cloud.

"*Juan*," Sebastian barked. "Where have you been?"

For an old man, Sebastian could be pretty spry when he wanted. The priest bounded to the passenger side of the car and yanked at the door handle. A small boy spilled out and would have fallen but for Father Sebastian catching him by the upper arm.

"What have you been up to? Where have you been? Why are you riding with Juan Mendoza?" The priest gave the boy a little shake after every question.

"Give him a chance to breathe, Padre." The short, potbellied driver stood on the Jeep's doorsill and spoke from the other side of the car.

The kid looks familiar. Long, skinny legs, thin face. Stubborn expression. Fishing pole! That's it. He's the one with the fishing pole who bolted when we drove up. Juan Guerra? No, Guerrero.

"I have been through the mountain!" The boy jerked his arm loose and stabbed a finger to the northeast. "Through a cave, all the way to Morochic."

"Morochic?" Sebastian snapped. "Do not lie to me, Juan Guerrero, or it will go badly for you."

"*Es verdad, Padre,*" the driver said. "He was on the other side of the mountain. A woman of the village, Marisol Martinez, told me to bring him back here. I have been driving all day from Morochic." He grinned, showing a mouthful of yellow teeth. "We do not like to disappoint Señora Martinez."

"Through a cave?" Father Sebastian said, his face showing skepticism.

"Sí, Father," the boy said. "A long walk in the dark, through bats and zombies and—and all kinds of evil things."

"Zombies! Pssh. Now I know you are lying to me. Come to my office so I can get the cane. You need a good swat to cure that Devil's tongue of yours."

"Wait a second, Father." Yeager held up a hand and went to one knee in front of the boy. "Hey, little man, tell me more about this cave, would you? You think you could show me where it is on a map?"

"Sí, señor." Juan's eyes held a gravity beyond his years. "Of course."

Pepito, Taco, and Raul had joined Verdugo and Marvin at the main house and were once again grouped around the dining room table. Aerial photos, maps, and ashtrays littered the surface, and smoke fogged the room. Tequila and cognac glasses left sticky rings on the polished wood.

Fifty-eight men of the Grupo Verdugo, stationed in various houses throughout Tomochi, were waiting on the *go* word from the leaders gathered there.

"So somehow," Verdugo said in wrap-up, "this shit-licking priest, who says he's broke and won't pay money, finds enough cash to hire mercenaries to bring in a truckload of supplies. And he tells me: *No, Verdugo, I will not supply the girls you need either.*" He studied the map for a brief pause. "What has changed? Has Dominic grown some balls? Decided to cheat us of our product, our tariff, by hiring a private army?"

Raul said, "You think this cocksucker priest who sells the little girls to us has some *buried treasure*. And now he's found God?" He spat on the floor for added emphasis.

Pepito frowned. "Why are you so pissed at this guy?"

"It is a goddamn priest, hombre." Raul threw up his hands. "A fucking man of the cloth!"

"What's the plan, boss?" This came from Pepito.

"I want whatever they have hidden at the monastery. We need to make an example as well. They have defied us and hired soldiers of fortune, and many of our men are dead because of it. I want everyone up there dead, down to the smallest chicken." Verdugo tapped an aerial picture of the southern approach to the Rascón valley. "We leave before dawn. We drive to here and park. We will infiltrate these woods and cross the river where our scouts have marked it. Then we will split into two groups. One will cut above and behind the mission on the east. The other will attack the south side of the building. They will breach the south entrances and the main doors, which face west, toward the village."

"And the group here, behind the mission?"

"They will have the high ground, so they will provide suppressing fire and ensure no one escapes. There are no exits on the north side, so we will not need to cover that side." Verdugo sipped his cognac, letting the fiery liquor numb the ache in his throat. "Marvin, you and Pepito will lead the overwatch group. The rest of us will be with the attack group. Comprende?"

"What about the bell tower?" Raul asked. "The sniper there, he kicked our ass last time."

"Leave the bell tower to me. Okay?" He collected a series of nods from each man around the table. "Bueno. That is settled. Tomorrow, we find out what this priest has that is so valuable." He settled back in his seat with a grin and held his glass up as if in toast. "Then, we will cut his dick off and feed it to him."

Yeager gathered Riley and Smitty in the bell tower so they could poke holes in his evacuation plan. The descending sun marked a solid gold line rising on the hillside above the village, leaving everything below in deep shadow. A heavy bank of troubled clouds covered the horizon to the east, but for the time being, the sky directly above remained clear blue, turning purple.

He convened the meeting in the tower for two reasons. One, they could have privacy from any spies employed by the cartel, and two, they could keep a lookout on the countryside.

Plus, the view was nice. "So here's what I'm thinking—"

"Listen." Riley held up a hand.

Thirty seconds later, Yeager heard it too. "You're like my damn dog, Riley. Ears like radar."

The stutter of rotors beating the air strengthened and echoed from the surrounding hills, making the helicopter's direction hard to pinpoint. Yeager rotated his head until he could confirm the sound came from the north.

"Dang," Smitty said. "I hope it's that midget Mexican, Cruz." He picked up the captured Stinger missile and started giving it a once-over. "But juss in case..."

"Hold your fire," Yeager said when the military-green Huey split the gap between the hills and thundered into the valley. "See that duct tape on the nose? Por Que stuck that on to keep a panel tight."

"Burning hot damn," Smitty yelled. "We gots us *air support!*"

Victor's voice fuzzed in his ear, the tac radio nearly drowned out by the noise of the chopper. "Looo-seee," he sang. "I'm ho-o-o-me!"

"Bring it on in." Yeager waved at the short figure wearing aviation sunglasses. "Never thought I'd be glad to see you."

The helicopter swirled dust as it settled to the ground in front of the mission. Almost before the skids fully engaged, the side door slid open, and five men hopped out. All wore the type of Western wear typical of men from rural Mexico, from white cowboy hats to silver-tipped riding boots. They also carried an impressive loadout of personal firearms.

"I brought some friends," Victor radioed. "A present from de la Cueva. Just call me Santo de Claus."

Yeager keyed his mike. "More like Jaime the Christmas Elf."

"Don't be a hater, dude." Victor flipped switches and shut down the whirling blades. His passengers ducked and trotted clear of the rotors. They milled around in the gravel yard of the mission, some looking at the bell tower and pointing, others stretching and bending out the kinks.

"Too many for up here," Yeager said. "Gather your new buddies, and meet me in the dining hall."

"Roger that. Be there in ten. I gotta piss so bad I'm gonna need two dicks."

Charlie accepted Judy's offer to spend Saturday night at her place on the condition that she, Charlie, would buy the takeout. Her friend used the refrigerator to chill wine and nothing else. The only knob on the stove that wasn't frozen stiff was the one she used to heat the teakettle.

As a consequence, Charlie's car smelled of broccoli beef, moo shoo pork, sweet-and-sour chicken, and hot, greasy egg rolls. Charlie was rooting in the egg-roll sack, giving in to temptation, when her cell phone rang. She fumbled the phone with slippery fingers when she tried to answer, and it jumped into the car's floorboard.

"Damn." Charlie pulled over to the side of the road and managed to snag the jingling thing just as the ringer quit. The caller ID was blocked. "Damn again."

While she was pulled over, she took advantage and fished out an egg roll, stamping down her guilt at eating one before anyone else got the chance.

Hey, I'm eating for two now. That excuse always works.

So of course, when she pulled back on the road, her phone rang again. Juggling the wheel and the half-devoured egg roll, she managed to get the phone to her ear.

"Herro?"

"This Charlotte? Charlotte, it's me. Cujo. You called me. The other day, you know?"

"Cujo! Yes, hold on. Wait a sec, let me pull over."

"Sure, no problem."

Charlie rolled onto the shoulder of the two-lane highway, loose debris crunching under her tires. "Listen, here's what's going on..." After she'd laid out the story from start to finish, Cujo said nothing for a moment. Two cars, back-to-back, *whooshed* past and rocked her SUV. She finished off the egg roll and found a napkin in one of the takeout bags to wipe the grease off her hand.

"So," Cujo said, "you want me to fly down and see what's up? Maybe haul Yeager's butt home if he don't have a ride?"

"Exactly." She tensed, realizing the enormity of the favor she was asking. "It's just that—"

"Sure. No problem."

"Uh... what? What was that?"

"I can be there by morning."

"Are you sure?"

"Yeah. Well, see..." His voice lowered to almost a whisper. "I'm already in Mexico, so that part ain't a problem."

"In Mexico?" She winced at her reflection in the mirror. *Damn, I'm beginning to sound like a moron.*

"Yeah, looking for a, uh, a part." A longer pause this time. "For my plane. I found it here in Juarez."

"A part? Will it fly?"

"Oh, yeah. It's not... it's not that kind of part. It's an, uh, an accessory. Y'know?"

"Okay," she said, drawing it out. No way in hell did she want to know more. "So you know where this place is?"

"Naw, but I can find it. San Felipe de Cristo, south of Madera. Easy-peasy. I'll call you when I find 'em. Okay?"

"Uh, okay. And thanks."

"No problem, Charlotte. Yeager and Victor are the closest thing to family I got. I'll get 'em back for ya. Cujo out."

With that, the phone went dead in her hand. She looked at the screen to confirm he had terminated the call, blinked, and put it away. Checking the mirrors, Charlie engaged the transmission, put on her signal, and pulled smoothly back onto the highway.

What a strange man. Or let's say it a different way: what a strange man for me to pin hopes on for flying down and finding Abel, lost somewhere in the ass end of nowhere.

Strange or not, Cujo was the best option she had, so she would have to trust him to do the job.

And if he doesn't?

Shrugging, Charlie snagged another egg roll from the bag and bit into it. *I may just have to go down there myself and drag that man's butt outta whatever playtime fun he's having. Some things you just have to do yourself.*

In the meantime, one more egg roll wouldn't hurt.

CHAPTER 37

YEAGER TOOK STOCK OF THE new recruits in the dining hall: five vaqueros, young, fit, and tough as beef jerky. They carried an arsenal of ranch weapons, everything from a bolt-action hunting rifle to an honest-to-God Winchester .30-30. For sidearms, Yeager saw a collection of worn .38 Smiths and two Colt Single Action Army revolvers in tied-down holsters.

"They know the drill, and they signed up anyway," Victor said. "De la Cueva gave a speech, and these guys volunteered."

"Understood." Yeager addressed the group in border Spanish. "You men know what we're up against?" A few nods. "Good. First thing, Smitty here will outfit you with some newer hardware. More firepower, *entiende*? Smitty, you got this?"

"Roger dodger." The big man stood behind Yeager, the Barrett cradled in his arms. The volunteers had been eyeing him ever since they walked in.

"Okay. After that, give these boys the nickel tour. You already know their assignments, so once they're set up, put 'em to work."

"You got it, boss," Smitty said. "Hey, any of you fellers *habla* Texan?"

A man in a red denim shirt and blue-checked bandana tentatively raised his hand.

"*Como se llama*, Red Shirt?"

"Eduardo, señor."

"Excellenta-mundo! *Vaya con* thisaway, Eddie. Bring your amigos."

As they filed out, Yeager shot a look at Victor. "You think they'll understand one word in ten he says?"

"Sure." Victor shrugged. "As long as he uses lots of hand gestures."

"How many can you airlift out of here?"

"Patients? Six, maybe eight if they like it cozy. You put 'em in stretchers, and it takes up all the cargo space, you know? Where to?"

"Doc says Hermosillo. I checked it on the map; it's about two hours away, maybe three."

"No problem. I can do that in my sleep."

"Speaking of sleep," Yeager said, "how much have you had?"

"Since we got here? Ten, maybe twelve minutes."

"Great."

"I can fly; don't worry."

"I'm not worried about you flying. I'm worried about you crashing. Why don't we let Riley take the first run? Way I figure it, we'll need three or four loads to get all the sick people and the littlest kids out of here."

"Sure," Victor said through a yawn. "Sounds like a plan. Then what?"

"We keep loading people on the chopper till Verdugo stops us. Any left over, we take a little hike through the mountains." Yeager took a few minutes and sketched in everything that had happened since Victor had left. "And I'm sorry, buddy, but it looks like your mom's cousin is bent." He handed over a folded copy of the priest's confession.

Victor refolded the paper after skimming it. "Aw, shit." His face worked through a number of emotions. When he did speak, he was uncharacteristically laconic. "Well, damn. I never liked that part of the family anyway. Fuck it. Drive on."

"Oooh-rah." Yeager clapped his friend on the shoulder. "Okay, man. Go flop out for a few hours. I'll get the first load headed out of here. Who knows? Maybe we'll get lucky and everybody gets out on the chopper."

Sodden gray clouds rolled in before dawn on Sunday morning. Tendrils of drifting mist brushed the mountaintops surrounding the mission. Alex yawned and watched the helicopter settle to the ground in the front court, close enough the thunder of its engine vibrated her teeth.

Victor sat beside her on the makeshift barricade surrounding the mission's main doors. In contrast to how tired and miserable she felt, he appeared happy and well rested. She had been up all night, prepping two loads of patients for air transport, assisting Señor Yeager in packing medical supplies, and getting her own kit ready to go.

"Last flight for Riley. Looks like it's you and me, Dr. Alex." Victor bumped her with his shoulder, bringing a smile to her face. "Off into the wild gray yonder."

Drops of rain spat in singles and pairs, enough to be annoying but not enough to make anything wet. A nippy wind blew the dust raised by the chopper rotors over them.

Alex rubbed grit from her eyes. "I have to say I will miss this place. A beautiful country. Too bad it is infested with the likes of Verdugo and the cartel people."

"Eh. Be even prettier, they had a Taco Bell in the village."

"Shut *up*, Taco *Bell*." She rolled her eyes and nudged him with a shoulder in return. "I have to get the last of the patients ready to go. Are we going to have a real pilot, or do I have to ride with you?"

"Ow, querida. You have a sharp tongue, you know that? Cuts me right here." He pointed at his heart.

"Somehow, I think you will live."

She levered herself up with a hand on his shoulder, groaning as she did it. She shooed him away with her hands as if brushing off a fly. "Now, go do pilot stuff, Taco Bell. Get us to Hermosillo in one piece, and I'll buy you a café con leche at this place I know near the hospital."

"Sí, Dr. Alex. For a café con leche, I'll fly you all the way to El Paso."

She still had a smile on her face when she made it to Emelita's room in the girls' dormitory wing.

"Guess what, Emelita-bonita?" Alex sat on the girl's bed and patted her hand. "You get to go on a helicopter ride. Would you like that?"

Emelita's eyes lit up as if she had hit the Christmas jackpot. She squeaked out a single word. "Really?"

"Yes, and go to a real hospital in the big city."

The girl's face fell. "A *big* hospital?"

"Yes, with lots of doctors and nurses. Why, I'll bet they have a television in the room, and do you know what else? I'll bet they have ice cream for special little girls who have had their appendix taken out."

"What's ice cream?" Emelita's nose scrunched up in confusion.

"You never had ice cream? That's terrible! Well, you will love it; don't worry. Now, do you have a backpack or a bag? We need to get you packed up to leave."

During the night, Father Sebastian had withdrawn into a shell of misery and silence and refused to participate in any conversation having to do with strategy. Yeager had pulled Dietrich aside, and together they decided to move the kids out of the mission in the morning whether or not Verdugo showed up. Ferrying people out by helicopter was taking too long.

Riley told Yeager that after dropping off patients at the Hermosillo medical facility, he had to stop at the local airfield and tank up the chopper, adding another hour to the round trip. On the first run, he had burned another hour talking to a local police captain about their fear of Grupo Verdugo. When he'd asked for some support, the captain had shrugged and said it was out of his jurisdiction.

"He said he'd call the federales," Riley said. The slim Texan leaned to the side and spat. "I don't see much comin' of that."

"Me neither."

Yeager had pulled aside the recruits from de la Cueva and given them the team designation Task Force Rascón. Rather than try to remember their names, he assigned each of them a call sign: Alpha, Bravo, Charlie, Delta and Edward. Since Edward was the guy in the red shirt who understood a little English, and his name was really Eduardo, Yeager designated him team leader and gave him Victor's radio headset.

The crew's first task was to scavenge ladders from the shed and set them up inside the dormitory quadrangle. Using these, the men could scramble to the roof of the mission and vector to any point along the parapet.

Next, they had to seal the back and side entry points into the mission. The men set to it with a will, scrounging lumber and tools from the shed and laying a solid wall of timber across the doorframe then securing it with three-inch lag bolts.

This effectively sealed in the occupants, leaving them only one exit at the front, so Yeager had the men of TF Rascón take sledgehammers to the chapel wall on the north side and make a new doorway while he worked on a surprise for the front doors. Father Sebastian came out of his funk long enough to wail about the damage but threw up his hands and wandered away when he saw they were determined.

Verdugo had originally come from the south then retreated in the same direction. Dietrich believed that was where his base of operations lay. Odds were, when he came back, he'd come from the south. Leaving through the north side, they could avoid being seen or fired upon.

However, since God didn't hand out guarantees, he had the men board over the new opening with a sheet of plywood, held in place by only a couple of concrete anchor bolts. A few spins of a wrench would free the obstruction in minutes.

Now, in the weak light of a gray morning, Yeager frowned with more pessimism than he'd had the night before. Something foul tickled his spine and overtorqued the bolts on his patience. He could feel the *badness* coming, the same way he could feel the weather change.

"Try to catch a nap," he told Riley. "As soon as Victor quits playing patty-fingers with the doctor, he'll take the next run."

Riley nodded and shuffled away, head down, while Yeager went to find Dietrich. They had thirty-two kids left in the mission, aged ten and up. The smallest children had already left, packed around the patients and nurses on the two helicopter trips to Hermosillo. Nurse Marta had agreed to reach out to the Catholic Church in that city to find a place to put the children until the crisis had passed.

Getting the remaining kids ready for a two-day hike through the mountains was Dietrich's job. Each person had to carry his or her own food, blankets, extra clothes, toilet paper, candles and personal items. The bigger kids were tasked with hauling the cooking utensils and extra water.

Inside the mission, pandemonium reigned. Yelling kids raced the halls, high on the excitement of going on a hike.

"Where's my underwear?"

"I need a *mochila*!"

Shouts dopplered down the corridors, followed by giggles, cackles, and squeals. A quick scan through the dorm rooms showed Yeager the kids were nowhere near ready to travel.

This ain't good.

Yeager found Dietrich in his office, consulting a clipboard and making marks with a yellow pencil.

"ETA on moving out?" Yeager asked without preamble. He had to fight the impulse to snarl it. *No use biting the man's head off; it won't make him move any faster.*

Dietrich glanced up. "An hour, Herr Yeager. The children have all been fed and are dressed for travel. All that remains is to assemble the few remaining items on my list and gather the children for a backpack check. This should not take long."

"I don't know where you get your optimism, Father. It looks like a Chinese fire drill on acid back there."

Dietrich stretched a smile across his blocky teeth. "I know these children, Herr Yeager. They will be ready despite all the commotion."

Yeager checked his watch. "One hour, Padre. We move then, ready or not."

Verdugo got out of the car and stretched. The chilly breeze cut through him after the warmth of the car's heater. Moist clouds covered the sky and deadened sound. Trees lined both sides of the road, the green of pines mixed with the gold and yellow of oaks.

Doors up and down the country road thudded closed as his sixty men assembled near the tree line. Some coughed and snorted phlegm while others clattered their weapons, checking chambers and racking slides. A hawk circled overhead, slipping in and out of the mist.

Raul appeared through the trees, returning from a scouting trip. His lieutenant jumped over a trickle of water in the ditch next to the road, holding his tactical rifle high for balance.

"They have a helicopter, jefe," Raul said when he came up.

"A helicopter? How the hell did they pay for that? Dominic is wasting my money, Raul. Another mark against him. How many men?"

Raul shrugged his slender shoulders. "I saw one man—the trucker—and the pilot speaking together. A second pilot took over for the first pilot, who went inside. Another man was in the bell tower. So four men that we know about, though I don't know how much help the chopper pilots will be."

"Pilots? Not much, I wager."

Marvin joined them, lighting a submarine-sized cigar. "Pilots? Who has pilots?"

When Raul explained, Marvin said, "No, pilots are not warriors. They sit in a chair and push buttons. Was the helicopter armed?"

A good question, Verdugo thought.

"No," Raul said. "Nothing I could see."

Marvin pulled in a mouthful of smoke and let it puff out as he spoke. "Well, then, there you go. We will concentrate our covering fire on the sniper in the tower, and you should be able to walk up without even a mosquito bite."

Verdugo grunted a sour laugh. "I changed my mind. You lead the charge, Marvin."

"Oh, no, jefe. I always thought it was the leader's place to be out front." Marvin laughed and waved his cigar in a circle. "I am the chief of *intelligence*, amigo. It means I don't lead charges."

"Let's move," Verdugo said. "They will be carrying whatever

treasure they have on the helicopter. We need to get there before they take off with it."

Smitty had the tower watch again, and when he reported, "Movement right," Yeager wasn't surprised. They were lucky they'd made it this far without interference. He left his coffee cooling on the dining-hall table, snatched his rifle, and headed for the front at a dead run.

"Report," he said, keying his mike as he ran.

"Juss one or two wiggling around back in the trees. All I can get is a glimpse. Three hunnert yards, jumping from cover to cover. Want me to light 'em up?"

"Hold fire until you have a shot."

"Roger. Holdin' it. I gotta say, it's big and hot and ready fire, though."

Yeager banged through the main doors and vaulted the stacked layers of rice and beans. In the forecourt, Victor had the Huey spooling up while the doctor helped a small child into the cargo bay. He ducked under the blades and hustled up to the pilot's-side window. Victor had left his tac radio for Eduardo, which meant Yeager had to deliver the message in person.

Victor pulled back a window and mouthed, "What?"

"We got contact right—your left," he yelled. "You gotta lift, now!"

Victor nodded and jerked a thumb over his shoulder. Yeager got the message and went around to the far side of the helicopter. The doctor was shoving a bag into place and didn't see him until he grabbed her around the waist and lifted her into the cargo bay. He heard her *yelp* over the roar of the engine winding up.

"Company coming, Doc! Move your ass!"

He registered her big-eyed look of surprise an instant before he slammed the door closed and flipped the latch. Yeager thumped the metal skin of the door, signaling to Victor that he was all set, then hunched over and ran for the mission doors, expecting a bullet to catch him any second.

As if in answer to his expectation, the ground burst ahead of him with the impact of one round, and a flat *crack* slapped his ears from the close passage of another.

Above him, Smitty opened up with the Barrett.

CHAPTER 38

HIS SCOUTS OPENED FIRE WITHOUT waiting for orders. The rest of his men heard the gunfire and ran for the scene of the action. After that, Verdugo's attack plan fell apart in bits and pieces. The younger men in his crew bounded ahead through the forest like young hounds on the scent of a fox, leaping over fallen logs and dodging limbs along the way. They showed *some* discipline by not yelling or calling out, but with shots already fired, voices were hardly needed to alert the enemy.

He grabbed Raul by the arm and jerked the smaller man to a halt. "Stop this," he hissed through clenched teeth. "We must gather and hit them at once or lose the initiative." The popping of small-arms fire echoed through the forest, followed closely by the dull boom of the sniper's heavier rifle. "Dammit! The overwatch group is not set up. Get those *pendejo* assholes under control. *Go!*"

Raul nodded and raced ahead. Verdugo came on at a steadier pace, lungs laboring in the thin air. Too many cigarettes and not enough exercise had taken a toll on his endurance. Not that it mattered; this hiking through the forest would be over soon. A quick dash under fire, and they would take the mission regardless of lack of covering fire, and from then on, it would be a massacre.

The similarities to the historical attack on the Alamo weren't lost on Verdugo. It had taken thirteen days for Santa Anna to overwhelm the defenders of that mission over a hundred and eighty years ago. This mission wouldn't last thirteen minutes under assault from his heavily armed pack of hounds.

As long as we don't attack piecemeal.

The whine of a helicopter engine spooling up charged his blood with adrenaline. He sucked in a painful gulp of air and quickened his pace.

The first indication Alex had that they were under fire was a sound like a rock thrown against a tin roof. A hole the size of her index finger appeared in the cargo-bay door next to her head. Already sprawled on Señora Gutierrez's legs, she yelped and fell on another patient, Señora Ochoa, who moaned in pain.

"Sorry!"

The old woman howled, and someone else called out in surprise. Emelita screamed and started crying when two more bullets punched through the chopper's body. Alex kept her head down and straddled the old lady in an awkward three-point stance.

"What's happening?" she yelled toward the cockpit. Panic threatened to loosen her bowels while her stomach seized up in a spastic knot.

Victor flicked a glance back and grinned. "They're shooting at us. Don't worry. Couple more seconds, and we'll be gone."

The maniac almost seems to be enjoying this. Alex balanced carefully and crabbed sideways across her patients to the cockpit opening. Struggling and swearing, she managed to work her way into the left-hand seat. The engine had been spinning up in volume and vibration, and the rotors whirled into a blur.

Victor pointed to a headset lying on the armrest, identical to the one he wore. She put it on, and the noise cut off as if by magic.

"The boys are laying down some suppressing fire now." Victor's words came to her through the intercom. He sounded distracted and a little bored, as though it were just another day at work. "That'll keep the incoming fire down until we lift off—*huhn!*"

A smack on the glass window on Victor's side punctuated his sentence. The pilot flinched and hunched over the controls. Alex's pulse skyrocketed.

"No! Are you all right?" Alex grabbed Victor by the upper arm and pushed him back. "Were you hit? Let me see."

"No time," Victor gasped. "Just a scratch."

He pushed her off and wrapped his right hand around the control stick, keeping his left arm clamped to his side. Teeth clenched, sweat beading and trickling from his black hair, Victor manipulated the controls, and the chopper broke contact with the ground.

Another smack on the windshield, and glittering shards burst in near the pilot's face. Victor cursed and flinched. Something sparked over Alex's head where the bullet hit. She ignored it, her attention staying fixed on Victor, willing him to be okay.

The helicopter vaulted into the air as if catapulted straight up then heeled over in a gut-wrenching pull to the right. The sky wheeled, and red cliffs loomed in her window, followed by a sideways view of the ground. Her stomach had no idea where it belonged, and she squeezed her throat tight to keep from vomiting.

Cries of alarm from the cargo bay, including the high-pitched shriek of one little girl, tore at her instinct to provide comfort and aid, but at this point, there was not one thing she could do about it. The helicopter swayed and jerked through the air so violently it was all Alex could do to hang on to the dangling seat belt.

More *spangs* of metal striking the skin of the helicopter vibrated through her feet.

"It's okay," Victor gasped out. "They're... hitting the underside. More... armor there."

He grimaced and rubbed a sleeve across his forehead. It came away with a smear of blood.

Yeager vaulted the low wall of "sandbags" arranged in a semicircle in front of the main door. He started putting rounds into the trees, more by feel than aim. In the courtyard, Victor had the Huey almost up to takeoff speed. All he had to do was keep the bad guys' heads down long enough for Por Que to get the bird off the ground. He would worry about the rest later.

He keyed his radio. "Edward, this is Trucker. Do you read me?"

"—ahead." Edward had started speaking before he pushed the talk button.

"Contact from the south. Get your men on the roof, and provide suppressive fire on the tree line."

"Sí, señor. Uh, señor? Suppress…?"

"Start shooting at the woods."

"Sí. Uh, copy."

The boys of TF Rascón must have been ready. In less than a minute, the volume of fire from the mission picked up. Leaves and twigs danced as rounds chopped through the forest. The cannon-like thud of the Barrett cut through the chatter of lighter rifles at spaced intervals.

"*Go, Por Que,*" Yeager yelled, knowing his buddy couldn't hear him but needing to yell it anyway. "Get outta here!"

The helicopter lifted and lurched a step sideways, seemed to hesitate for a moment, then screamed into the air. Sparks pinged from the underside as the aircraft tilted and swung away. Yeager turned his attention to servicing targets in the tree line and heard rather than saw the Huey thunder to the north, through the mouth of the valley.

"Trucker, you copy?" Smitty's voice.

"Go."

"Over yonder, between them two tall pines, 'bout two hunnert meters off the river, a whole bunch of Injuns has come together for a powwow."

Yeager was too low to the ground to see past the underbrush. "I see the trees, not the men."

"Nolo problemo," Smitty sang out. "I juss wanted you to know I'm fixin' to light 'em up with Ringo, Paul, and George."

Before Yeager had worked out in his head what the big man meant, a smoke trail fizzed from the bell tower with a *whoosh*. The rocket-propelled grenade impacted squarely between two pine trees and erupted in a ball of grungy white smoke.

Leaves, splinters, dirt, and a reddish spray blew out from the impact site, a hellish flower blossoming and shedding its pollen.

Men screamed in pain. The volume of incoming fire dropped off, and Yeager took advantage of the pause to slither inside the main doors and slam them shut. A crossbar had been mounted there in the past, but nobody remembered where it was, so Edward of TF Rascón had scavenged around until he found a two-by-six board long enough to fit across the double doors. It would not hold against a determined attack with modern weapons, but it would at least buy Yeager some time. Plus, he had fashioned a little surprise gift for anyone forcing the doors from the outside.

Verdugo stared at a green, leafy sky.

Why is there no sound? Why am I lying here?

Those questions passed through his mind as abstract musings as if he were wondering why gravity made things fall to the ground. Interesting, but essentially not important.

Raul's face materialized above him, and Verdugo observed his mouth moving. It looked really funny. He grinned and tried to laugh. Things faded away for a while.

Images came and went. A forest. Pine trees. A group of fighters crouched down low between the trees. *Why is that important?* He'd come up behind them to do... something. Maybe if he rested a while, he would remember.

On his way to the tower, Yeager keyed his mike. The priest had been given Riley's tac radio just for this situation. "Dietrich," Yeager barked. "Get your people to the chapel, now!"

"Ja, Herr Yeager."

"I'll meet you there in ten." Yeager scrambled up the ladder and popped through the roof hatch. Riley was already there, next to Smitty, using a Ruger SR-556 to lay down short, controlled bursts. Incoming rounds pinged off the cupola or whined past. Every so often, one would hit the bell with a ringing clap.

Below them, arrayed along the north side, de la Cueva's men lay prone behind a low wall that surrounded the rooftop. They exhibited good fire discipline by popping up, firing, then moving to a new spot before showing themselves again.

Smitty, cheek glued to the stock of his Barrett, peered through his scope. "I think that little present done got 'em flummoxed. They act confused, some shooting and some just millin' around, gettin' shot."

He shifted the aim point of his Barret a hair left and cranked off a round. *Boom!* Up close, the report of the rifle hit like a whole-body slap. Yeager could almost see the molecules of abused air blown apart.

"Like that poor sumbitch," Smitty said.

"Flummoxed is good for us," Yeager said. "We're buggin' out in six minutes. Riley, get to the chapel. You're leading the kids and the priests outta here. Since your Spanish ain't so good, I'm sending Edward and the other guys with you." He keyed his mike and gave Edward the same instructions. The man waved from the rooftop, tapped another man on the foot to get his group moving, and low crawled toward the ladder.

Riley nodded and made for the trapdoor.

"Lead the kids due north," Yeager told him, "along the river. Get that Guerrero boy to show you where to cross the river and how to get to the cave he found. Dietrich knows the drill."

"What about y'all?" Riley stood on the ladder, just his head showing through the trapdoor.

"We'll be along directly. Our job is to slow down the pursuit for as long as possible."

Riley nodded and disappeared.

"All right, Smitty." Yeager patted the big man on the shoulder. "Now, let's buy 'em some time."

"Yeager, you're a crazy sumbitch, you know it? But I think I'm startin' to like ya."

Boom!

CHAPTER 39

SMELLS LEAKED BACK TO VERDUGO first.

Charred meat. Open guts. Loamy earth and fresh sap. Sounds came next, those of men screaming in pain or moaning. Rifles popping and men yelling. Bedlam.

He opened his eyes, and the world blurred into focus like a camera lens, the scene sharpening in front of him. He saw Raul's face over him, frowning, eyes creased with worry. He kept saying something...

"Boss. Boss, you okay? Can you hear me?"

Verdugo waved a shaky hand. "Yes," he croaked. "What happened?"

"You took an RPG in the face. Or the guys in front of you took it in the face; you were just caught in the blast."

"An RPG? Shit."

"Sí, la mierda. I sent Marvin and his group to the north slope to cover the back. That was"—Raul consulted his watch—"ten minutes ago. They should almost be in position."

Verdugo sat up, propping his back against a tree. Through the overhanging canopy of leaves, he could barely make out the gray outline of the mission rooftop. His men were deployed forward on their bellies or behind trees. Ten meters away, a group of twisted bodies lay, some clearly dead, others almost so. One man pushed at the earth with a leg, scoring tracks in the ground while he screamed. His chest was a bloody mess, white tips of ribs poking through the ruined skin.

Verdugo watched as another man died, his lifeblood pumping into the fallen leaves from the severed stump of a leg.

"Jesucristo," Verdugo muttered.

Two men came from the rear and knelt next to Verdugo and Raul. "We brought the missiles, jefe," one said. The men set down two long black cases and started undoing the latches on the sides. The first case held the launching tube for an RPG-16, a newer version of the RPG-7 with four times the range, firing High-Explosive Anti-Tank—HEAT—rockets. RPG-16 HEAT rounds were designed to penetrate a foot of armor plate.

Three rockets nested in foam padding inside the second case.

"They like to play with fire, huh, Raul?" Verdugo wiped a trickle of moisture from his nose with the back of his hand. He saw that it was blood. "We will see how they like our toys."

Juan Guerrero took a seat on the first pew in the chapel with his backpack on his lap, in the middle of a dozen boys. The two rows behind him likewise filled up with children, warned to silence by the scary Father Dietrich, who paced the aisles with a ruler poking out of the hands cupped behind his back.

Also keeping watch was the cook, sitting in the back. The two maintenance men waited by the plywood that covered the new hole in the wall.

Since he had gotten back to the mission, Juan's time had been a whirlwind of questions, commands, and demands. He had managed only a couple of short naps, and sleepiness tugged at his eyes, but the excitement of the moment kept him jazzed awake.

The strong man—El Toro—with the sad eyes had asked him lots of questions about the cave and how to get there. Where was the best river crossing? Where was the trail? How long had it taken him to get through the tunnel? At the end, Juan's throat was dry and his voice rusty.

The big man, who called himself Yay-gurr, had smiled and shaken his hand, treating him like a man. He'd clapped Juan on the shoulder. "Well done, hombre. You may have just saved a lot of lives."

Juan sat a little straighter at the memory.

The chapel doors banged open, and six of the defenders rushed in, led by the skinny Tejano in jeans and a leather jacket.

"Dietrich," the Tejano said. "Everybody ready?"

Father Dietrich said *yes* in his stiff way, went to the front row, and made a gesture for everyone to rise. Juan stood along with the rest in his group and waited while Gustavo and Esteban worked the bolts holding the plywood sheet in place. When the board came loose, the Tejano held up a hand and checked outside.

"Okay," he said after a long look. The sound of gunshots came much clearer than before. The Tejano looked back and said something to Father Dietrich, who repeated the instruction in Spanish.

"Follow me. Keep loose. Don't bunch up, but come quick."

With that, the slim man disappeared through the gap. The Father waved a hand at the first boy in the row, Pedro, and they were moving. Single-file, the boys marched through the gap and into the wet, blowing wind.

A big raindrop hit Juan in the ear, and he flinched at how cold it was. Behind him, the next row of kids, and then the one after that, followed them through the gap. The cook, the maintenance men, Father Dietrich, and the other five fighters brought up the rear.

The Tejano led them into the trees sixty meters to the north of the mission, following a trail that Juan had used many times. It was not his preferred route to the cave, but he knew how to get there going this way. He supposed it was safer than crossing the river out in the open where they could be seen by the narcos and shot dead.

All in all, it seemed like a good plan, and Juan picked up his step, his feet feeling lighter than air, knowing he had helped. *So this is what it feels like to be d'Artagnan.*

The helicopter rocked and bounced through a gray mist. Alex could see nothing six inches past the windscreen except for an occasional patch of cotton gauze drifting by. She had no idea if they would hit a mountain, hit the ground, or continue flying until they ran out of fuel over the ocean.

Blood smeared Victor's sleeve. He remained hunched to one side, sweat trickling from his eyebrow and over his cheekbone. His skin looked as though someone had poured too much milk in his coffee, and his breathing had turned ragged and shallow.

"Are you hit?"

He nodded, straightened up in his seat, and looked to where his right arm pinched his side. Alex scrambled over the center console and, careful not to jostle the arm holding the controls or nudge any of the thousand switches or buttons, pulled open his jacket. It took every bit of her clinical detachment not to gasp when she saw the blood saturating his shirt on the right side midway up the rib cage.

"Can't... breathe so well," Victor rasped. "I think they... got a lung."

"I need to get at this. Can you set us down?"

"Not here," he said. "I don't know... exactly where we are. In relation to the... mountains." He winced as she worked his jacket loose from one arm then the other. "Have to get about... a hundred miles west. Till then. Have to stay over three thousand feet. Go any lower, say hello to Mr. Mountain."

"Okay, this is going to suck for you big-time. Let me get my kit."

"Love the... bedside manner, Doc."

Twisting and squirming, Alex worked her way back into the cargo bay. Most of the patients had settled down. Emelita had pulled the blanket over her head, and all Alex could see was a trembling mound. "It's okay, Emelita-bonita. We're away from all the bad men."

A pair of dolls poked their heads out of the blanket, followed by the girl's doe eyes. She gave a weak smile then retreated under the blanket. Alex didn't blame her. She wished she too could crawl under a blanket and hide.

Grabbing her kit, Alex slithered into the cockpit and, poised on the very small patch of center console not covered with dials and switches, considered how to get at Victor's wound.

"Only one way, Doc." he said. His grin, when he looked at her, was as big as ever, though his breath still came in short hitches. Crusted blood outlined a thin cut over his left eyebrow. "You're gonna hafta. Sit. On my lap. Facing me."

"Oh, I see what your ploy is now, amigo." She put on a cynical frown. "I'm a doctor, not a lap dancer. Are you sure there's not an autopilot?"

"Nope. Never had one on a chopper."

"Fine. Hold your arm up."

He gasped. "Be quick."

Alex twisted her tiny body until she could stretch her left leg across his hips and settle herself onto his legs. He reached around her and latched onto the control stick.

"Hold still," she said.

"Not going anywhere."

She unbuttoned his shirt and pulled it aside. A wound bubbled blood between the sixth and seventh rib, six centimeters left of the sternum. "No wonder you're having trouble breathing. You have a sucking chest wound."

"Like you said. Sucks. For me."

She had nothing in her medical bag specifically made for taping a sucking chest wound, but she had a surgical kit with a peel-off plastic top. Wiping off the blood with some gauze, Alex cleared the surrounding area. She peeled the cover off the kit and trimmed it to size with tape scissors then centered it over the bullet hole. Using short strips of tape, Alex secured it over the wound on three sides. The fourth side she left open to vent excess air.

As soon as she finished her tape job, Victor drew a full breath, and his tense posture eased a little. She realized he had been watching her face, the whole time, from less than ten centimeters away.

"Not the way I had pictured this," he said. "But it works for me."

"Behave." She mopped the blood on his ribs and abdomen with more gauze. "Are you injured anywhere else?"

"No."

She searched his eyes. "Seriously. Are you dizzy? Any blurred vision?"

His default setting seemed to be a goofy grin. "Well, tell the truth, my heart feels a little funny."

"What's wrong?" A moment too late, she realized she had been suckered.

"There's an arrow gone right through it."

"Stop it! You must be well enough to fly if you can make jokes like that."

His smile faded, and a wave of pain washed across his face. "Let's hope so."

※

David Milton Quattlebaum III—known commonly, far and wide, from Afghanistan to Texas, as Cujo—flew his twin engine Cessna C320E Skyknight over the blanket of low clouds covering the Sierra Madres mountain range. This was only the second time he had flown the Cessna since its... *modifications*.

So far, he was pretty pleased with the performance. The 285-HP turbocharged engines could reach 240 knots at max power and had a stall speed in the low sixties. He could climb at nearly two thousand feet per minute up to a ceiling of twenty-nine thousand feet. The Cessna was configured to seat six, but if he wanted, he could pop the seats out and carry a thousand pounds of cargo.

But best of all, the bitch packed some heavy fucking devastation the makers of the Cessna would have never approved.

With his last plane, a Cessna 172, he had concealed a vintage .50-cal under the wing and controlled it using a crude lanyard. The one time he used it—the last time he helped Yeager and Victor, in fact—the machine gun had worked better than he expected. Problem was, the monster recoil had made the plane hard to control and cracked the wing supports in fundamentally bad ways.

With that experience in mind, Cujo had horse-traded his way up to the twin-engine turboprop Skyknight mainly because of the teardrop wingtip fuel tanks the plane carried. Modifications to empty out the tanks and relocate the fuel bladders and piping to the interior of the cargo compartment had taken a month of sweaty and bitchy work.

Running down a pair of Russian-made UB-16-57UMP rocket pods and thirty-two S-5M air-to-ground missiles to go in the pods had taken another three months of ticklish negotiations with some very nasty men in some very unglorious shithole places. The market he'd gone to was so black that light was *afraid* to go there.

Four weeks earlier, in Juarez, he'd taken delivery of the munitions and launchers along with the requisite electronics to arm and trigger the devices. As a bonus, the dealer had thrown in six test missiles with dummy warheads.

He had tightened the last wire nut, tested the electronics, and flown out in the dead of night two days before Charlotte Buchanan's phone call. On the test flight, aiming by the light of the moon, Cujo had shot the shit out of a mountainside, firing three test missiles from each pod. The streaks of fire from the wingtips nearly gave him a hard-on, they were so beautiful.

People sometimes said that he had issues, but he didn't give a fat fart in a fairy tale.

When Charlotte called, he reckoned it was something akin to God's plan. Destiny. Kismet. Cosmic karma. Whatever it was, he had been given the green light to fly into harm's way again, for everybody knew that when Victor and Yeager wandered down to Mexico, really bad manure splattered all over the propeller.

He took off before dawn, not bothering to install the plastic covers he had fashioned to hide the launchers on the wingtips. They resembled the aircraft's original fuel tanks so much that no one would notice in the dark anyway.

Now, with the morning sun flushing the cloud tops yellow-orange, Cujo navigated by GPS to the Mission San Felipe de Cristo at a steady cruising speed of two hundred knots. For the sixth time, he toggled the launchers' arming switch to On, verified the red light, then toggled it back off.

Smiling, Cujo tapped the iPod cradled in the Skyknight's stereo system—another improvement of his—and cranked up "Fortunate Son," by Credence.

He glanced at the GPS to check his position. *Not long now.*

CHAPTER 40

YEAGER AND SMITTY WORKED THE bell tower position in tandem, Yeager spotting while Smitty manned the Barrett. Verdugo's people seemed disorganized, scattered through the edge of the woods where the trees thinned out. Sporadic fire, undirected and poorly coordinated, came from individual locations in the underbrush.

Yeager would spot movement or a muzzle flash or a bright article of clothing against the green-and-gold backdrop and would call out the position and distance, so all Smitty had to do was shift his aim point.

Boom! Heat waves shimmered around the barrel of the enormous weapon.

The wind had picked up and blown away some of the rain clouds, though the ceiling remained low. Gusts blurred the trees and teased at Yeager's hair. He mentally crossed his fingers and hoped Victor could see well enough to fly.

"Last five rounds," Smitty called out, slapping home a magazine.

"All good things must end."

"Ain't that the truth, brother. Ain't had this much fun since one night in a Filipino whorehouse when I got the clap and was robbed and beat to shit by the natives."

Yeager chuckled. "Have to tell me that story sometime. Low, two o'clock, blue shirt, twenty meters past the white-blazed tree trunk."

"Got him."

Boom!

"You at least ruined his day. Whoa! Shit, look out!"

At a shade under two hundred meters, a man stepped out into

a clearing beneath a towering oak and dropped to one knee. He brought to his shoulder a long tube with a venturi nozzle to the rear and a bipod at the front. At that range, the RPG could hardly miss, and if the warhead impacted inside the bell tower, Yeager and Smitty would be chopped to hamburger.

Yeager yelled. "Ten o'clock, RPG, just at the tree line."

"Fuck, where?" Smitty yelled.

Though not as accurate as the Barrett, Yeager's M4 could make that range with ease. He put the Eotech holographic aiming reticule over the shooter's head, to compensate for bullet drop, and squeezed off a round.

And missed.

Yeager bracketed the first shot with three aimed rounds, trying for a quick hit or at least to scare the bejeezus out of the guy before he could fire.

The man lurched. A half second later, a rocket streaked from his launcher.

"Down!" Yeager ducked below the parapet wall, clamped his hands over his ears, and tried to burrow into the solid wood floor. Smitty flopped beside him.

"Goddammit!" Verdugo smacked the tree he leaned against with the side of his fist. Emilio, the man he had tasked to take out the bell tower, toppled to the side after firing the launcher. Verdugo had a bright hope, like watching a football arc toward the goal, that Emilio had scored a direct hit.

But it wasn't. Instead, the RPG round hit the tower about halfway down from the cupola. A cotton ball of dirty white smoke, dust, and brick blossomed outward in an expanding cloud. The crump of the explosion thumped Verdugo's chest a half second later. The impact caused the bell to ring a clear peal through the morning as if calling the faithful.

"Quick, Raul," he called out. "A near miss is almost as good as a hit. They will be out of action for a few seconds. Move!"

The blocking force on the western side opened up with covering fire, peppering the bell tower with dozens of rounds.

"Vaya!" Raul shouted, and twenty men jumped to their feet and pelted into the clear zone. Raul made big overhand circles with his arms and led the way across the open ground between the forest and the mission. When no fire came from that damn big rifle, a cheer started up and rippled through the men in one great outpouring of bloodlust. Finally, they would be able to get revenge on the assholes who had been killing them for two days.

———✦———

Cujo's Skyknight had been built sometime in the '60s and, as a result, did not come equipped with much in the way of terrain-mapping or collision-avoidance avionics. Cujo had "sourced" a Garmin GT 650 for navigation and mapping and had scavenged a Honeywell MK VIII Terrain Avoidance Warning System and its associated radar transmitter-receiver. He'd installed all of it in the Cessna while waiting for his rocket pods to come through.

The problem was, the maps for this part of Mexico were sketchy, so he couldn't fully rely on the Garmin, and the secondhand TAWS acted glitchy as hell. It used a woman's voice, so he named it Glenda after an ex-girlfriend. Also because he thought Glenda was the name of a witch in *The Wizard of Oz*, but he couldn't remember which witch she was.

So now, at Angels-6—six thousand feet above sea level—Cujo committed to a descent into the Sierra Nevada mountain range based on weak intel and a bitchy TAWS. His butt puckered hard enough it made his testicles hurt. He forced his hands to relax on the yoke, wiping first one then the other on his pant legs. Too tight, and he risked oversteering. Jerk on the yoke too hard, and the little plane would do a wingover in a heartbeat, which could be fatal in a narrow canyon.

The clouds swallowed the twin-engine Skyknight, and Cujo's world went gray for a long, long time. He kept his eyes scanning: altimeter, attitude, rate of descent, VSI, check outside. Still gray. Altimeter, attitude—

"Warning. Ground. Five hundred. Feet." Glenda's electronic voice spooked him even though he half expected it.

"I can read the altimeter, bitch."

"Warning. Obstacle ahead. One. Thousand Feet. Pull. Up."

Jesus Christ!

A speed of two hundred knots translated to something like three hundred feet per second, which gave Cujo all of three seconds to pull the yoke back and stand the Skyknight on its tail. He jammed the throttles and *climbed*.

"Warning. Obstacle ahead. Two hundred. Feet. Pull—"

The warning cut off midsentence, presumably because he'd gone over the obstacle. Either that, or he'd flown into a mountainside and was already dead but didn't know it.

"A little more warning next time, huh, Glenda? Would that be too much to ask?"

Cujo tipped the nose back down, his GPS telling him he was almost right on top of the village of Rascón. He reduced speed and bumped the flaps down a notch.

This time, Glenda kept her mouth shut, and Cujo broke out of the clouds at six hundred feet—in time to skim so close to a mountain he must have left paint from his port wingtip on the rocks.

"So now you won't talk?" *Sulky bitch. Gonna get us both killed.* "Whoa. What the hell?"

Cujo popped into the San Felipe valley right in the middle of a war. A line of skirmishers broke from the tree line, moving on the mission situated on the starboard side less than three hundred feet ahead.

He killed his speed even more, hands dancing between throttle and flaps and yoke, then jinked the Cessna starboard so he could make a close pass on the mission. Charlotte said Yeager and Victor had come down here with a truckload of supplies to support the mission-slash-orphanage. If he had to guess, Cujo would say his friends were the ones defending the mission. Only Yeager could piss off that many people in so short a time.

One look into the bell tower confirmed it. A guy who could only be Yeager—flannel shirt over a T-shirt, light-brown hair, lumberjack shoulders—stood there with his mouth hanging open. Cujo flashed by so fast he had no time to study it, but that one glance was enough for him. The bad guys were attacking his pals.

He toggled the arming switch for the UB-16s. *Looks like I'll get a chance to use my missiles on my first flight. There is a God after all.*

"Come on, Glenda. It's time to light these bastards up."

Smoke poured through the trapdoor like a chimney. The brass bell *bonged!* and threatened to split open Yeager's head, finishing the job started by the concussion of the RPG. Smitty rolled over on his back and groaned.

"Fuck me," the big man said. "Can I go home now?"

"Good a time as any." Yeager pushed up to his knees only to drop down again when a bullet spanked off the bell and chipped rock dust from the wall by his head. More impacts, along the west side of tower, clattered like hail. "Time to unass the tower, Smitty."

"Roger that!"

A blood-curdling yell of pure hatred welled up from the ground, and Yeager popped his head up long enough to see a ragged line of cartel gunmen running full tilt from the trees. He didn't stay to count, but his estimation was: a lot.

"Get down the ladder, Smitty. Leave the Barrett."

They had pre-positioned go-bags in the chapel, complete with semiautomatic rifles, filled magazine harnesses, water, food, and other supplies. They could snag those on the way out, but what they needed at the moment was to *go*.

"Haul ass, big boy!" Yeager said.

Smitty was working his way down the ladder, as graceful as a panda on a bicycle. "Hey, ease up there. The ladder's busted to shit, and there's a fuckin' big hole in the wall. I ain't built for gymnastics."

"You're gonna be built for dead, you don't get to moving."

"Bitch, bitch, bitch." Smitty's voice receded as he disappeared through the lightly smoking trap. "Just like my wife, Yeager."

"You have a wife named Yeager?"

Yeager swung his feet over the edge, nearly stepping on Smitty's hands, and paused there. A droning sound had been working its way into his hearing for the past few minutes. At first, he'd dismissed it as the aftereffect of the bell ringing near his head, but it grew stronger as time passed.

He risked another look over the edge of the wall in time to see a twin-engine airplane, white with a red stripe down the side, dip under the clouds and zoom past at less than a dozen feet away. He blinked, and his mouth fell open when he got a quick glance at the pilot as the plane flashed by: white teeth in a bearded smile, aviator sunglasses, bandana holding down a shock of unruly black hair.

Holy shit. Cujo.

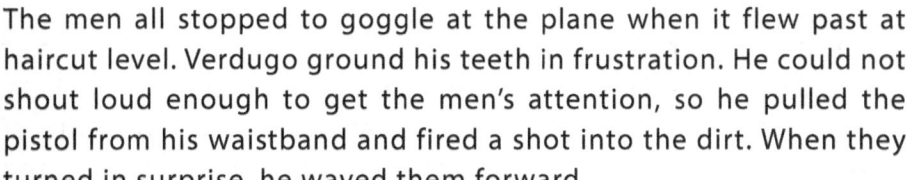

The men all stopped to goggle at the plane when it flew past at haircut level. Verdugo ground his teeth in frustration. He could not shout loud enough to get the men's attention, so he pulled the pistol from his waistband and fired a shot into the dirt. When they turned in surprise, he waved them forward.

"*Go,*" he rasped.

When they started moving again, Verdugo paused by the last tree, putting a hand against it for support. Sounds came to him as if his ears were stuffed with cotton, and his entire face stung as though it had been slapped. He shook his head like a dog, trying to clear it.

Who was that in the plane? And why are they here? And does it really matter?

A single civilian aircraft couldn't do anything. The road twisted too much for it to land, and if the pilot did manage that, anyone inside could be riddled with bullets before the aircraft came to a stop. Verdugo shrugged off the questions and pushed away from the trees only to pause again when the buzz of the plane's engines came to him through the stuffing in his ears.

His men were almost to the mission. Another few seconds, and they would be inside. Should he call some of them back? Have them shoot at the plane? The damn thing could be a scout for the federales or the army.

Or Los Zetas. Damn, it is hard to think with this pounding in my head.

Before he could decide, the plane broke through the cloud cover to the east, over the village, and aimed directly at the mission.

Verdugo squinted to get a better look. Civilian markings. Two engines. And… what were those teardrop shapes on the wingtips? A heartbeat later, both wing pods erupted in smoke and flame. His first thought was that the plane had blown up in midair, then he saw the streaks of yellow-orange fire, tipped with white arrows—

Missiles! The fiery bolts hit the ground in less time than it took to blink. Impacts splattered along the ragged line of his men like some kind of vengeful lightning. Explosions rippled so close together they hammered Verdugo's chest as though God were beating a kettledrum.

Dust and debris fountained up, spreading a ghastly collection of maimed bodies and their equipment like so many wind-tossed dolls. The plane zoomed through the expanding dust cloud, twin swirls of smoke curled through it with its wing wash. The pilot pulled up and skimmed the trees on the hillside behind the mission, passing over Marvin and the rest of his men in the trees.

Shoot it!

He willed his men to kill the plane, fire back, get retaliation, but no one did. He ran for the RPG launcher, but by the time he'd reached it, the pilot had angled skyward and slipped over the cliffs, disappearing into the clouds without so much as a scratch.

CHAPTER 41

Yeager and Smitty grabbed their packs from beside the door, and each picked up a new Ruger SR-556. In addition, Smitty slung a Browning Medallion bolt-action rifle, muzzle down, on his back. A rumble shook the chapel, and plaster dust fell from the ceiling. Yeager and Smitty paused for an instant in the middle of the aisle, between a double row of empty pews, then kept moving.

A chilly wind ruffled the unadorned white-linen cloth draping the altar, and a scattering of leaves danced in from the jagged opening in the chapel wall. The rumble subsided.

Yeager and Smitty looked at each other. Smitty said, "That weren't no earthquake."

"Ordnance. A lot of it."

"You think they brung artilli-airy?"

"Let's hope not." Yeager shrugged his pack higher on his shoulders. "C'mon." He checked for enemies the old-fashioned way: by sticking his head outside then jerking it back. When no one shot at him, he gave Smitty a nod and hit the opening at a dead run. The big man lumbered behind him, huffing and churning across the ground. A buffalo ran quieter than Smitty did.

The gap between the trees that identified the trailhead was almost a straight run from the chapel, and Yeager made it in seconds. He held up and waited for Smitty to pass him.

"Damn, Smitty. You're puffing so hard you sound like a freight train."

Smitty jogged a few more steps then put his hands on his knees and gulped air. "Don't worry 'bout me... you ugly jarhead. I'll be there... when the time comes."

Yeager settled to one knee and took a long look behind them. From that angle, the mission appeared peaceful except for the rising cloud of dust and smoke from the far side of the building. The bell tower, too, looked a little worse for wear, canting slightly forward, chipped and streaked by bullet strikes.

To his left, the village of Rascón appeared to be either asleep or vacant. Even the chickens had run for cover. To his right, the screen of trees and the back of the mission complex blocked his view of whoever had taken the high ground behind the buildings and dropped suppressing fire on them.

Which means their view is equally blocked.

The pall of dusty smoke from the other side of the mission confused him. Somebody had set off some damn big explosions to make that much of a cloud, and he had a strong suspicion Cujo was somehow to blame. The man's pathological need to destroy things was downright scary at times. *I'm glad he's on my side.*

"We may have gotten out clean, Smitty." Yeager pitched his voice low, nearly a whisper. If the enemy was still on the other side of the mission, they wouldn't hear him if he yelled, but he saw no reason to tempt fate. "I don't think they know we've run away. Let's hold up a moment in case they spotted us."

"Sure." Smitty mopped his face with a bandana. He found a seat on a fallen tree. "Let's sit a spell and visit. How's your mom and them?"

Yeager ignored him, thinking aloud. "They'll try 'n take the doors, going for the sides first, I imagine. Then they'll hit the front."

"Izzat an evil grin I hear in your voice?"

"One thing I learned in the Stan, it was how to make an IED out of unexploded ordnance. Some of our *allies* were artists with a battery and a block of C-4. Probably practiced on the Russians, then on us."

"So that's where the Stinger went."

Yeager nodded and held up a hand for silence. The drone of a small plane sounded from the west.

Cujo was coming back.

"Shit the fuck, yeah," Cujo yelled inside the closed cockpit. No one but Glenda heard him, but he didn't care.

In Operation Enduring Freedom, he had flown an A-10 and loved every second of it. It seemed as though the narrow cockpit of the Warthog had been molded just for his butt. To Cujo, the A-10 was the ultimate in-your-face, fuck-up-your-day aircraft, and he had been *the* most badass Hog driver who ever lived. In the combat zone, he flew at grasshopper level, engaged the enemy at knife range, and burned through massive quantities of munitions. He had flown one hundred and twenty missions before a sneaky turban-headed mullah jammed a Stinger missile up his port engine and took him out of the war for good.

He missed it every day. But not today. Today, his blood sang with the ponderous thunder of a Wagnerian opera. Twenty or more centuries of Teutonic warriors had contributed their DNA to the fighting spirit of David Milton Quattlebaum III, and all of his ancestors looked on from Heaven with hearty approval at what they had wrought.

He could not have pulled off a better strafing run on loose skirmishers crossing open ground if he'd had a month to plan it. His impression, which was better than any pencil-neck bomb-damage weenie at battalion, was that he had wasted none—not one!—of the eight S5s he'd launched.

A damn near perfect run on a cloudy day at a range so close he'd singed his underpants flying through the dust cloud.

"Fuck, Glenda. It don't get no better than that."

When he pulled up and buzzed the hill, another group of goggle-eyed men peered at him through the trees. He had eight missiles left and an aching desire to hose down the little pissants.

But how to get at them? With the low ceiling, he was damn near *in* the valley before he could *see* the valley. And the wind across the cliff face was downright snarly. The right approach would be lateral, along the hillside from south to north. But that would be a stone bitch because he would have to drop into the valley, orient, then slide to port in order to line up.

"Screw it," he muttered. "Just do it."

Cujo took a close look at the GPS and set up his run.

Verdugo loaded the RPG-16 with the next to last tubular "grenade" in the case. Unlike the RPG-7, its 58mm warhead fit completely inside the tube and did not have a bulbous end sticking out the front. The weapon used a pistol-grip trigger located about a third of the way from the muzzle with a simple lever-type manual safety, left of the trigger guard. The optical sights had hash marks to allow the operator to lead his target, each mark representing an incremental difference in the target's speed.

At the moment, standing in the killing field next to the Mission San Felipe de Cristo, Verdugo could not remember what speed each number represented. All he could think about was how much he wanted that little bastard in the white plane to come back and give him a chance.

Verdugo waited for a full two minutes, rooted in place, while his men wailed in pain or clustered against the mission walls in confusion. More than a few silently added their life's blood to the rusty-red soil.

Nothing. No sound of engines.

Verdugo sighed and trudged toward the mission. He passed craters as big as Volkswagens and chunks of men. He paused at one man lying on the ground—Gregorio or Angel; he couldn't remember—who stared at the sky with sightless eyes. Amazingly, the man had not a mark on him. But for his eyes, you would think he had lain down for a nap.

Raul came to Verdugo as he knelt to close the man's eyelids. "Jefe."

Verdugo got to his feet and slung the launcher over his shoulder like a hunting rifle. "How many do we have?"

"Who can fight? Twelve. Plus all of Marvin's men." He tossed his hand in the direction of the hill behind the mission. "I don't think he took any casualties in the missile attack."

"Get them down here. Their purpose has been served. The doors?"

"The side entrances have been sealed." Raul eyed the RPG. "We will need explosives to breach them."

"The front door?"

"Have not tried it yet."

"Do so."

"Sí, jefe... do you—"

"Sshhh!" Verdugo held up a finger for silence.

The sound came, faint as a butterfly's wings at first then growing into a buzzing bee. Verdugo smiled. "The plane is coming back." He rotated a full circle, hand cupped to his ear. "Which direction do you think?"

Raul stood stock-still for a three count, his head cocked. "South. He's coming from the south."

"Agreed. He will try for the men in the trees. He will not risk firing on the mission."

Verdugo broke into a lumbering run, the RPG cradled in both arms, headed to the rear of the mission and the hill behind it. He had no desire to run into the path of a missile, but he had never fired an RPG at a live target, especially not one moving at more than 120 kph. He needed to get closer.

By the time he reached the rear corner of the mission, his breathing sawed through his open mouth, and his thudding heart sent blood roaring through his veins. He knelt and gathered himself, breathing deep and willing his heart to slow down. The noise of the plane's engines came strongly now; it would only be a matter of seconds before he had a target. Verdugo set the launcher on his shoulder after he verified his backdraft would not hit the building wall and scorch him where he crouched.

He flicked the safety off and took a quick look through the optical sight to make sure it worked. Then he waited.

Today was one of those days when Cujo could do nothing wrong. As if drawn up on a coach's chalkboard, he hit the valley dead center from the south. He spotted the bell tower immediately. A small correction on the yoke, and the nose of the Skyknight lined up with the forested hillside, straight and true.

The only downside: "Warning. Altitude. Two Hundred. Feet."

"Shut up, Glenda. I'm working here." Cujo scratched his beard and did a quick sweep of his instrument panel. Everything nominal, no worries. He would make this pass and expend every missile on the tree line. No reason to hold back, and he had been taught that returning with unexpended munitions while the enemy remained on the field was tantamount to treason.

And after that? That was the problem. Where in hell would he find a stretch of straight road to land the bird and find Yeager and Victor?

Screw it. Worry about it later. Carpe the fucking diem.

Cujo zipped over the last few hundred feet and settled the Cessna's nose on the area where he'd seen the muj—Mexicans. Whatever. Ahead and to his right, the ghostly gray bulk of the mission squatted, a thin smoke trail spiraling from the bell tower like a farmhouse chimney. Small figures moved, and his butt puckered. He would be taking small-arms fire any second.

"Too bad, boys. I'm here to fuck up y'all's day." He punched the firing button mounted on the dash as though it were a video game and he was on his last quarter. Rockets flared from the wingtips— two, four, six, eight—and Cujo pumped his fist in the air. "Wooo! Who do we appreciate, muthafuckahs? Take that!"

A white line of smoke arrowed into his starboard side, and he had one full second to think, "Aw, damn," before the RPG hit the tip of his starboard rear stabilizer and blew it all to hell, shredding the tail, the rudder, and a good chunk of the port-side rear stabilizer.

The nose dipped from the loss of downward force on the tail. Cujo reacted instinctively to the unexpected nosedive and pulled up. The yoke responded with a mushy slowness, like pulling on taffy, so Cujo jockeyed the flaps to gain some lift. The missing chunks of the plane's tail upset the carefully balanced forces of air, gravity, and lift; the Skyknight stumbled through the air like a drunk on a Saturday-night binge.

The best he could manage was a looping, sickening starboard turn. There was no flying straight anymore, nor was there any leveling out, no matter what he tried. The rudder was shot, he had no stabilizers and—he glanced back to confirm—there was a big, nasty hole in his plane.

The ground blurred by on his right, close enough for him to smell the flowers. The plane cut a wobbly circle completely around the mission and passed over the river, then the road. Blocky, tattered homes and buildings loomed in his forward windshield.

"Shit. The village."

Cujo used all of his magic words and a few he invented on the spot to coax another couple of feet of lift. On the way across the rooftops of Rascón, his starboard wing clipped an aerial and sent it spinning.

That's going to ruin somebody's reception.

In front of him were trees, rocks, and dirt.

"Warning. Obstacle. Three hundred. Feet. Pull. Up. Pull—"

CHAPTER 42

"**A**W, DAMMIT, CUJO." YEAGER CLENCHED his jaw and tensed up as if he were about to take a punch to the gut.

The small plane crunched into the wooded hillside above the village with a dull *whump!* A cloud of dust billowed out from the impact site. Unlike in the movies, the aircraft did not burst into a fireball, though smoke curled from the trees surrounding the wreckage. With a ponderous crackling of breaking wood, a wounded pine fell in a heap over the ruined tail section, blotting the aircraft from view.

In the village, no one stirred from their homes.

"Gotta hand it to that dude," Smitty said. "He blew the shit outta the bad guys. You know him?"

The smoke at the crash site thinned, so there was a chance that it came from overheated oil and not a fire. Not so on the opposite hillside behind the mission. A blimp-sized gray cloud billowed to life above the treetops, growing larger every second. At least one missile strike had started a fire.

"Yeah... yeah, I do." Yeager straightened up, took a deep breath, and let it out. "Okay, new plan. I have to go see if Cujo lived through that. I can't leave him—"

"Gotcha, podnah. Nolo problemo. Let's go."

"No, I need you to follow the trail and catch up to Riley and them. Pretty soon, these chumps are going to figure out where we went and be on our trail. If they catch up to the kids..."

"Nuff said." Smitty held up a palm. "I'm on it."

Yeager checked the mission and saw no movement. "Okay,

boogie outta here. I'm going to fade into the bush and find a way across the river, out of sight of Verdugo's people."

"You know how to find the cave?"

A cold wind ruffled Yeager's hair and worked its way into the collar of his hoodie. "I'll find it. If Cujo's banged up, I may have to dig in and lay low. Don't wait for me. Just get them kids through the mountain. Shoot anything that comes up behind you that ain't me. All else fails, I'll hike outta here the long way."

Smitty's frown covered his whole face.

Yeager didn't wait to hear the protest he saw forming. "Gotta run, Smitty. Good luck."

He slipped to one side of the big man, cut right past a sprawling live oak, and moved deeper into the forest. He followed no trail but trusted his instincts to find the quickest route to the river. The feeling of being too late wouldn't leave him no matter how hard he tried to ignore it.

He broke into a trot, dodging trees and ducking under limbs.

Don't be dead, Cujo, you son of a bitch.

Marvin and Pepito came down the hill, followed by twenty-five of Verdugo's soldiers. Two seriously injured men were being carried by their comrades. Several others were bloody but able to walk without aid. All of them looked... beaten.

Goddamn that pilot! "Report," he demanded.

Pepito, his schoolteacher glasses smudged, spoke first. "Three dead. Two badly injured"—he waved vaguely at the two men being laid against the wall with the other wounded—"five or six took shrapnel, mostly splinters. From the trees."

"Of course from the—"

A dull thud from the front of the mission caught Verdugo off guard. More screams, attenuated by distance, jangled his nerves. "What the...?"

He and his two lieutenants jogged the length of the mission, sliding to a stop at the front corner. Yet more smoke and dust fogged the area in front of the mission doors. Three more of his men lay dead on the ground. Raul stumbled out of the smoke and would have fallen but for Verdugo catching his arm. He had a wooden splinter as big as a pencil stuck in the flesh over his right eyebrow. He seemed unaware of it.

"The door..." Raul said. "The door. It blew up."

"Pinche cabron!" Verdugo screamed so loud his throat ached. He walked away, toward the river, and tried to gather himself. This outrage of temper, this level of frustration, was not like him. He always maintained a cool head during a crisis. *Stay calm, speak quietly, command the room.* That's how he'd gotten ahead in La Línea. But this was so much more than just a crisis.

What the hell was going on? First the foiled attack in Madera, then this trucker shows up and chases him off, kills his men, destroys his vehicles. And now they get bombed by a—what, a fucking Beechcraft? A Cessna? With fucking *missiles*?

He walked back to his lieutenants. Pepito had the bloody splinter in one hand and pressed the other hand to Raul's forehead. He jerked the piece loose, and blood drizzled over Raul's eyebrow. The slim man never flinched; he merely mopped it with a sleeve.

When Verdugo spoke, his voice was back to normal. He pulled back one finger at a time to enumerate his points. "These men have booby traps. Sniper rifles. Automatic weapons. A fucking plane with bombs—"

"Missiles," Marvin said.

Verdugo glared, and Marvin shrank back. "Missiles, then. Who are these people? They must be hiding somewhere in this building. I want them rooted out right now. Find that sniveling rat, Gustavo. The janitor. Find out what he knows. Raul, you are the soldier. Gather the men. Send them in quietly, two groups of four at first. They should check everything first. When they make contact, send the remainder for backup. Do *not* kill the priests. Entiende?"

"Sí." Raul nodded and left the group. He waved his arms and started calling to the nearest men. *"Aqui! Andale!"*

A shout came from one of his men by the mission door. "This way, jefe."

Verdugo followed him at a jog through the blast-shattered

doors, made a sharp right turn in the foyer, and proceeded through a small interior door. He entered the chapel, and immediately, Verdugo clenched his jaw to keep from screaming. A hole, big enough for a man to walk through upright, gaped in the far wall. Hidden from all of them, the mercenaries had hacked through the church and made their escape.

Verdugo turned to Pepito. "Have someone bring the cars up. Load the wounded and take them back to Tomochi to the doctor there." Verdugo paused and rubbed his forehead. The man ran a small practice from the back of his house; it would not be able to accommodate all the men who needed treatment. "Better yet, take them to my house; pick up the doctor on the way."

Pepito pushed his glasses up and nodded, grim faced. He peeled away and grabbed the arm of the first man he saw, issuing rapid-fire instructions.

"Marvin, you are my intelligence chief, yes?"

"Of course, mi jefe." A rumpled, unassuming man with plain features—brown hair, brown eyes, slightly dumpy—Marvin could pass for a middle manager in any bland, ordinary business. Outwardly, he gave no sign that he had killed—with knives, guns, and once, a chain saw—more than thirty-seven men, women, and children. Some of them he'd killed while working as a police detective in Chihuahua.

"Then get me some goddamn intelligence," Verdugo hissed and pointed across the river. "Take three men. Check out that plane and see who it is. Identify the pilot. Tail number. Chewing-gum wrappers. Everything. Find out who these people are. *Now!*"

"Absolutely, Verdugo." The normally stone-faced Marvin played a devilish game of poker, but now his sweat-slicked forehead betrayed some anxiety. He looked a little pale. "It shall be as you say."

Raul came through the gap into the chapel and spotted Verdugo. He looked grim and implacable, sooty and smoke blackened, with a blood trail down one side of his face. "We know which way they went." His voice echoed in the chapel. "We found a trail through the woods, and tracks."

"A bunch of kids and old men." Verdugo hurried through the pews to get close enough for Raul to hear him. "They can't have gotten far. Take everyone here not already assigned, and get after them. Go quickly. A thousand-US-dollar bonus to the first man who brings me the head of one of these mercenaries and two hundred dollars for each child."

Some of the men standing nearby heard this and passed on his comment. In moments, all of them were grinning and ribbing each other, ready to go after their quarry.

Verdugo held up a finger. "Two thousand for a priest. But only alive. Anyone kills a priest, I cut off their balls. Now go!"

His wolves streamed from the church, their faces eager. Verdugo smiled for the first time since that morning. In the open with no walls to protect them, the mercenaries' inferior numbers would be outmatched and outgunned. They could be flanked and taken easily. It was only a matter of time.

Too much beer and potato chips. Smitty huffed along the trail, jogging in a kind of a shuffle step so slow a granny with a walker could leave him in the dust. In Vietnam, he had measured out at six-six and 192 pounds. Last month at the doctor, the bill had come to six-five, 296 pounds. He'd shrunk an inch in height and gained more than a hundred pounds in girth.

As he ran—shuffled—Smitty looked for a .223 cartridge lying in the trail. Riley was supposed to leave it as a marker of where to turn off and head for the water. Smitty had been jogging along for six minutes and didn't have much more jogging left in his tank. Pretty soon, he wouldn't have to worry about the bad guys because he was going to die of a heart attack any minute. What'd they call it these days—a mayo cardinal infraction?

The last few days had been... extreme. He couldn't remember a more intense time since—well, hell, since that little tropical adventure, fighting small men in their black pajamas. That war had claimed more than a pound of flesh from him. He'd watched too many friends—no, *brothers*—die, some from enemy action, some by accident, and more tragically, some by their own hands. A big chunk of his soul had stayed behind in that shitty little country, and he had never gotten it back.

But here he was again, deep in the shit and lovin' every stinkin' minute. Except for the running. *Fuck this.* Smitty downshifted to turtle drive and started walking. Which was when he kicked the brass cartridge and sent it spinning into the brush.

"Well, there ya go."

He ducked through the trees on his right and picked up the trail immediately. Within a minute, he made it to the river, which ran swift and nasty but shallow at this point. Slick rocks poked up from the water, just the type to make a guy slip off and break an ankle.

"I ain't a ballerina neither," Smitty muttered, taking the stones one... careful... step... at a time.

There. Easy-peasy. A straight jog across the road, and he found himself at the base of a mountain. People from Colorado would call it a hill, and anybody from the Him-allyas wouldn't even notice it, but to a boy from Texas, this sumbitch qualified as a mountain.

A gentle slope of red rock led up from the road. There was no cover for fifty yards in either direction. Fully as big as a football field, cracked and broken, the rock shelf reminded Smitty of a boat-launching ramp at a lake back in the States. *A damn big launching ramp.* A man could launch a whole fleet of bass boats off this mother; that was for sure. *Just need him some water.*

He climbed the slope, one hand touching the stone, pushing his aching knees more than they liked. Visions of getting shot in the butt propelled him up the hillside faster than a goat. At the top of the shelf, a well-beaten trail cut through a stand of pines diagonally to his left. The trail wandered up the ridge in a gentle climb, cutting a winding path through the trees until it disappeared from view.

Smitty followed the line of sight to the top of the hill and saw a rock cliff breaking through the top of the pines. He estimated the distance to the cliff at something like six hundred yards. The trail continued along the side of the cliff until it curved around a corner of the mountain. He knew the trail continued because on it, a single-file line of kids marched along like the dwarves from Snow White.

"Aw, shit. They didn't get too far, now, did they?"

Behind him, across the road, a thrashing in the brush caught his attention and made him look back.

"Well, ain't this peachy?" Smitty wiped a hand across his sweaty face and unslung the Browning.

The first of Verdugo's men pelted out of the trees. Young, fit, and healthy, the man ran like a deer. Another one just like him popped out of the trees right behind him. Based on the flashes of color, a whole army of little brown men ran right behind them.

Smitty measured the distance from the children and compared it to the speed of the pursuers. Based on his estimations, Verdugo's men would hit the children before they made it to the cave.

"To hell with that." Smitty dropped to one knee and sighted on the first guy crossing the road. He let out a breath and *squeeeeeezed.*

CHAPTER 43

S SOON AS HE SAW the cockpit, Yeager knew it would be bad. The impact had sheared off both wings and crumpled the nose of the small plane like a beer can. Aircraft debris littered the forest, strewn upslope from the impact site to where the fuselage rested, wedged between a boulder and a pine tree. The plane's truncated tail hung in the air, six feet up, suspended over the slope.

A gusty breeze scattered pine needles and carried the sharp tang of aviation fuel and overheated oil. Metal tinged and popped as it cooled. Yeager nearly jumped out of his skin when the fuselage settled a few inches, groaning like a sticky car door.

Yeager circled around a smoldering engine attached to a stub of a wing, one propeller blade curled over the cowling. The other two blades were gone. He climbed on the boulder next to the crunched nose and got his first look through the shattered windscreen.

Cujo was dead. One look confirmed it. Aviation glasses askew, Cujo's head lay across the yoke. Blood had turned his blue bandana into a dark-purple rag. Yeager clenched his jaw and refused to look away. "Cujo, you crazy bastard. Why are you smiling?"

In death, the pilot had the trace of his nutty grin curling his lips at the corners. Or at least that was how it looked to Yeager.

You went out the way you wanted, didn't you? Yeager hung his head, wishing for time to mourn, time to remember. Cujo—he never did learn the man's real name—had always been someone he kept at arm's length. He'd been a little wary of the man's tendency toward paranoia. Having said that, the scrawny little guy never said a harsh word to him or treated him in any way less than a brother.

And now he was dead, watching Yeager's back, saving his ass for the second time in less than a year.

How do I get you home? He studied the problem from his perch on the boulder while droplets of rain struck around him with dull splats. The sky had grown darker, and the air carried a moisture-laden chill. Somewhere in the mountains, thunder rolled. A rifle cracked once, then twice more, the *boom* of its report competing with the thunder.

Yeager took a long look around. No movement in the underbrush, but how long did he have before company showed up?

He maneuvered across the rock until he could get a hand on the pilot's door. No way could he carry Cujo on his back all the way home, but he'd be damned if he would just leave his friend like this. He jerked on the door handle, but the door was stuck tight. He grunted, heaved again, and the door creaked open an inch.

The click and clatter of weapons being readied froze him in place, crouched awkwardly on a boulder with both hands occupied and his ass waving in the air. *Caught like a goddamn Boy Scout.*

"Señor," a man said in Spanish, "please. Put both of your hands in the air, then do not move."

Yeager risked a glance and found himself surrounded by four men, three of them pointing automatic rifles at him. The fourth looked like somebody's uncle or an insurance salesman, except most insurance salesmen didn't carry Taurus 9mm pistols. The men made good use of cover and had spread themselves out. If he tried to make a play, they would chop him to small bits before he could bring any of his weapons into play.

The crack and pop of small-arms fire rose in volume and intensity somewhere to the north. Either Smitty or Task Force Rascón was exchanging fire with the cartel thugs.

Which is where I should be instead of hanging around here, getting caught with my pants down.

Yeager raised his hands.

⎯⎯⎯⎯⎯◆⎯⎯⎯⎯⎯

The helicopter lurched and swayed in a pocket of turbulent air, and Alexandra's stomach threatened to leave her body again. She ignored her own physical distress and kept an eye on Victor. Sweat saturated the man's shirt collar and trickled over his cheek. He maintained a fierce concentration on the instruments and controls, hunched over and breathing through clenched teeth.

As novice as she was, even she could tell his handling of the aircraft had gotten sloppier and less coordinated. Alex doubted he would last another ten minutes, let alone another hour of flying in the choppy air. She had asked him for a map, which she studied, looking for an alternative landing site they could reach within minutes if not sooner.

When they came out of the mountains, Victor reduced altitude to below the cloud cover. Within minutes, clouds had faded altogether, and a brilliant-blue sky domed the world. Below, she made out the winding gray trail of Highway 20 as it wandered north through the eastern edge of Sonora.

A name jumped off the map. "Sahuaripa," she yelled.

"Gesundheit," Victor said.

"No, look." She thrust the map under his nose. "You said we were about here, yes?"

"Uh-huh."

"Sahuaripa is only... fifteen kilometers north of here. Where Highway 20 makes this sharp bend. See it?"

"You need to stop for a pee?"

"No, listen to me! One of my old teachers from med school retired there to run a clinic. It is small, but he has a full surgical suite. We need to get there, fast, and land before..."

"Before I crash, querida?" His grin reminded her of a cadaver with its lips pulled back.

"Before your lungs fill with blood and you drown." She gripped his bicep, or tried to—her fingers would only go halfway around it. "And then, yes, we will crash."

"Good idea, then." Victor coughed and doubled over, his face a mask of pain. It took him almost a full minute to recover enough to regain control. "Let's go to Sahara-wepa. See the sights. Take in a show."

The chopper made a shallow bank to the left, following the ribbon of Highway 20 to the north.

Alex closed her eyes and spoke under her breath. "Hail Mary, full of grace…"

Verdugo found the office wing and set up command in Father Dominic's office, the largest in the facility. One of his men came through, pushing an elderly priest in front of him.

"Verdugo, I found this one hiding in his room," the soldier said.

"I was praying," the old man spluttered.

"Shut up." The soldier shoved the priest to the floor and threatened him with the butt of his rifle. The priest held up a hand to ward off the blow he expected. "Keep quiet, old man, or I'll smash your face in."

"And who is this, then?" Verdugo rose and came around the desk to stand over the priest. "Wait. I remember you. Father Sebastian, correct?"

The old man failed to respond, remaining on the floor with his head bowed.

"Well, Father Sebastian," Verdugo rasped, "what can you tell me about the mission's treasure?"

Sebastian's wet, rheumy eyes fixed on his for a moment, his mouth open and working like a landed fish. "How…?"

"How did I know?" Verdugo shrugged. "Does it matter? No, what matters is that you tell me where this treasure is now."

The priest's mouth firmed into a defiant look before he cast his eyes back to the floor. Verdugo paced in a circle around the clergyman, examining him from every angle.

"You," Verdugo said to the soldier. "Go to my car and get my machete. We will get some answers from Father Sebastian if it takes all day and many of his body parts."

Smitty scrabbled behind a suitcase-sized rock overlooking the drop to the road and the river. On the sloping shelf, two bodies sprawled, limp and still, staining the rock with their blood. The other attackers had fallen back amongst the trees, and he no longer had a clear shot.

In the pause that followed, Smitty loaded three spare rounds into the Browning's magazine. He propped the Ruger next to him and shrugged out of his pack. In an outer pocket, he found a bottle of water and took a long pull, draining a third of it in one go, then capped it and put it back.

A spatter of rain, like somebody shaking a wet tree, darkened the rock for a brief instant before a gust of wind blew it away.

"Only one way you boys can come," Smitty said to himself. "You wanna cross the river right-cheer, and that's up this here ramp. Like stormin' the beach at Iwo Jima. Let's see how many co-joanies y'all got between ya."

The longer the cartel thugs dithered around, the more time the kids had. Smitty figured he'd hold the bad guys here for a while then fade back up the trail. Maybe he'd have to do it all over again at some other choke point, but he'd managed fighting retreats before and knew how to make it as hard as a dog trying dry hump a moving car.

Bullets clipped leaves overhead and sparked off the rock shelf as the cartel people laid down covering fire for a small group that burst from the trees and tried to take the river crossing at a run. One guy yelled and went sideways into the water, his rifle pinwheeling away.

Ignoring the crack and whine of near misses, Smitty sighted then fired and worked the bolt with an unconscious speed, his hand blurring up-back-forward-down. No sooner had he obtained a sight picture than he triggered the round downrange and snapped another cartridge home. The Browning performed like a thoroughbred, its action silky-smooth and crisp. Smitty emptied the five-round magazine in less than seven seconds.

When he took stock, three of the original seven attackers were still moving forward, two at the rock face and one still crossing the road. The guy in the river was thrashing away downstream, and three others were out of the action, either dead or wounded.

Smitty grabbed his Ruger and took the closest guy first, nailing him with a perfect head shot. The man flopped and tumbled down the slope. The guy behind him leaped to the side to avoid being knocked down, saving him from Smitty's next burst.

The volume of incoming fire stepped up a notch as the shooters on the opposite bank of the river found the range and started peppering his sheltering rock with round after round of poorly aimed but persistent fire. Smitty ducked and leaned to one side, trying to lay sights on Jumping Jack Flash, who was scrambling upslope to his left.

Bad shit happens when you're making plans. A bullet caught his left knee and shattered it with a sound like Joe DiMaggio hitting a solid line drive.

"Aw, shit!" Smitty rolled back behind his rock, stunned. His knee went ice cold for a flash then white hot with a stab of intense pain. If somebody had jabbed an ice pick into his knee and rooted around, it would have hurt less. He screamed through gritted teeth and tried not to pass out, though his vision tunneled down to a binocular view of swirling green leaves and gray sky.

Scrabbling, scraping noises came from the rock below.

Smitty pawed his Kimber .45 from its clamshell hip holster, digging at it with suddenly inept fingers. He brought it up at the end of a very long—and very slow—arm, filling the sight picture with the blue cotton T-shirt of Jumping Jack himself.

Boom-boom! He squeezed off an unaimed double tap that took Jack off his feet and sent him tumbling back, out of sight.

One more coming, John Wayne Smith. Get your shit together. Smitty rolled to his right and brought the .45 up with both hands, elbows planted, ignoring the goddamn toad-burning, goat-humping knee. The last guy came up the shelf, screaming some banshee war cry. Smitty saw the top of his head, let it fill his sights until nothing but forehead and black hair showed.

Boom-boom! The shriek cut off, and based on the rough scraping sound of cloth on stone, the last attacker slid a long way before coming to a stop.

Smitty crabbed his way back to his rock, dragging his shattered leg behind him. Using the boulder as a prop, he sat up and pulled his bad leg straight with a grunt. When he got his first good look at the wound, he was nearly sick to his stomach. The lower section of his left leg remained attached to the top by only a twisted pile of bleeding meat. Chips of white bone, grit, and dirt surrounded the wound, and fresh blood washed over it.

"Well, ain't this the shits."

Voices called from the forest across the river. Smitty recognized the sound. Men were planning how to overcome this little obstacle in their path, yelling encouragement and instructions. He doubted they would try a frontal assault again, but one could always hope.

Once they found his flank, he'd be as good as dead.

"All righty, then." Smitty pulled off his braided belt and wrapped it around his thigh, cinching it tight with the buckle. He hissed in pain at first, and his vision blackened for a long moment. When he came back to himself, Smitty picked up his .45, changed out the partially spent magazine for a fresh one, set the thumb safety, and holstered the pistol. He reloaded both the Browning and the Ruger, laying the rifles side by side.

He drank some more water and leaned his head back against the rock. Raindrops pattered around him. Smitty took a hissing breath and willed the pain away. Eyes focused again, he checked for enemy movement. "Let's see how many of you bastards I can make die."

CHAPTER 44

THE FOUR CAPTORS MAINTAINED A good perimeter around Yeager, never coming too close, two in advance, two behind. They marched him down the hill and through the village. Not even a curtain stirred in any of the houses they passed. A dust-colored dog slept underneath a mobile home on the outskirts of town. He looked up and thumped his tail.

Yeager kept his hands atop his head and bided his time. When he saw the blast-shattered front doors of the mission, he smiled to himself. *Somebody got a nasty surprise when they knocked on that door.*

The guy who looked like an insurance salesman called himself Marvin, but that was all Yeager had gotten out of him. Marvin had Yeager's XDM tucked in his belt, along with his KA-BAR knife and pocket trash. One of the soldiers carried the Ruger SR-556 and looked like a kid given a new Christmas present.

After some hunting around, they found Verdugo in Father Dominic's office. Marvin sent in two of the gunmen then shoved Yeager inside, where he came to a halt behind a club chair deliberately positioned in the center of the room, occupied by a priest. He recognized the back of Father Sebastian's head, bowed and silent. Verdugo lounged against the desk, swinging a gleaming machete in fancy loops and swirls like some movie swashbuckler. Blood flicked off the blade's edge.

"A bad day has just become somewhat brighter," the blond-haired leader of the narcotraficantes said. "Look, Father Sebastian. It is our old friend, Señor Trucker."

The priest remained slumped. Like a punch in the gut, Yeager flinched when he saw Sebastian's left hand. Two bloody stumps were all that remained of his pinkie and ring finger.

Verdugo tapped Sebastian on the top of his head with the flat of the machete. "I think we have a new guest of honor to take your place, old man."

The blade Verdugo carried was not some Home Depot special. Wide as a hand at the flattened tip, the squared-off blade tapered to wrist-thin width at the polished walnut handle. Light flickered in its stainless-steel surface, making it gleam like a marine officer's dress saber.

"Move, old man." Verdugo grabbed Sebastian under his arm and lifted him bodily, shoving the priest across the room to slump into the sofa against the wall. When Yeager started forward, the snick of a safety behind him froze his motion.

Verdugo pointed the machete at Yeager then at the chair. "You. Sit." The bandit leader looked to Marvin, who remained by the door. "Send one man to find some duct tape or rope. Leave one on guard with us, and send the other to the group chasing the runaways."

The sad-sack-looking man gave the necessary instructions then came to stand beside a huddled Father Sebastian, who held his injured hand close to his body and rocked. The priest's lips moved in silent prayer.

Yeager was bracketed by Verdugo holding a machete directly in front of him, the guard behind him, armed with a rifle, and Marvin to his right, holding a Taurus 9mm. Marvin held his pistol dangling beside one leg, watching Yeager through heavy-lidded eyes. Yeager didn't mistake that look for a lack of alertness; Marvin was as ready to strike as any viper. One guard remained by the closed door, and a quick glance showed he was no slouch either.

"So, Señor Trucker," Verdugo began.

"His name is Yeager, jefe." Marvin tossed a wallet onto the desk by Verdugo's hip. "Abelard Yeager. He is from Texas."

"*Excellente!*" Verdugo beamed. "Señor Yeager, here is what we are going to do. Once our man comes back with tape, we will tie you to that chair. At that point, I will begin to ask questions. For each wrong answer, I will cut off a body part. You've seen this in the movies, yes?" The gang leader flourished the blade, sweeping it through the air. "In the end, let's hope we have run out of wrong answers long before we run out of body parts. What do you say?"

"I say you're a day-old dog turd that needs to be wiped off my shoe."

"Hah-hah! Very funny. So far, my record is ten fingers, two hands, and one foot. That man was very brave, very tough."

Verdugo toyed with the machete. He flicked his wrist and buried the blade in the desk with a *thunk*. "Let's see how long you last, hey?"

※

Smitty counted six down, two of them wounded, between the woods and the top of the slope. He left the wounded alone not so much out of mercy but more in hope that the enemy would send men to retrieve their pals and give him more easy targets. Or they would scream a while and make their pals crazy-stupid.

Apparently, fraternity and solidarity was not high on their list of virtues, however, for no one stirred from the trees across the road. He would catch the occasional flash of movement, or bright clothing through the gold and green of the forest, but rarely in time to get sighted. Smitty held his fire and waited. The longer he stalled, the more distance the kids put between themselves and the wolves on their trail.

The throbbing of his wounded leg pounded through his hip all the way to his head, giving him cold sweats and shaky hands. Smitty had lost all feeling below the knee, which was a bad sign. He could only hope that when the time came to shoot, he could bear down and overcome the physical pain—at least for long enough to do what he needed to do.

A rustling behind him sent a knife of fear into his heart. Smitty rolled, bringing the hunting rifle around, its muzzle seeking a target.

"Whoa, you old coot." Riley held his hands out in surrender. "Don't shoot."

"What the hell you doing here?"

Riley Amick settled beside Smitty, using the boulder for cover. He carried the F2000 submachine gun in a sling over his shoulder and a .357 in a hip holster. From somewhere, Riley had found a John Deere gimme cap, sweat-whitened and shapeless, which he pushed back on his head while he checked the belt-tourniquet around Smitty's leg.

"I came to see what was keepin' you." Riley released the tension on the belt around his thigh, and Smitty groaned when pins and needles prickled along his calf. "And what do I find? You're laying around, taking a siesta."

"Siesta, my ass. *Ow!* Fuck."

Riley finished cinching the belt then crab crawled around Smitty to get a look over the lip of the hilltop. He slipped the F2000 off his shoulder and cradled it across his arms. "How many coming?"

Smitty stared at the sky and worked on breathing without passing out. "Don't know. Killed me some. Some more in the trees over yonder."

"You figure they're working on how to flank us out?"

"Nah, I figure they're settin' up a tea service with white china and fine linens."

"Can you walk, you grumpy bastard?"

"Can a cow sing *Dixie*?"

"All right, then." Riley checked the chamber on the bullpup and settled onto his stomach. Leaves crackled under him. "Guess we better stop 'em here."

"You dumb country fuck," Smitty growled. "Get back to them kids. Get 'em outta here."

"Kids are in the cave. Ed's got 'em. Him and the boys are on their way to a safe place."

"Well... that's something, I guess."

"Yep." Riley reached two fingers into his shirt pocket and retrieved his tin of Skoal. "That's something."

Smitty tried not to think about how much his knee hurt or how much damage had been done. Assuming they could get out of this pickle, he would need to find a doctor pretty much ASA-and-frickin-P or be called Pegleg Smith from now on. Every time he moved, he opened a fresh can of *Ow-that-fucking-hurts* and poured it from toe to groin.

"They comin' yet?" he asked.

Riley spat and shook his head. "No."

"Goddamn, Riley; quit jawin' so much. You chatter worse 'n a beauty shop fulla women." Smitty leaned his back against the boulder at the top of the rise and loosened the belt around his upper leg to let the blood flow again. The crowd of cartel bushwhackers had gone quiet, and nothing stirred but for the wind shifting through the trees. Somewhere close by, a bird twittered, and water from the trees pattered the ground. A gray, overcast sky muted color and sound.

After tightening his tourniquet, Smitty levered his body around for a look. What he called the launching ramp, the long shelf of rock below them, tapered from a hundred yards across the base to twenty at the top. To the left and right, thick forest acted like a funnel, forcing anyone coming up to either fight through heavy brush or risk being shot to shit on the exposed rock face.

The boulder he used for a shield stood—from the perspective of the attackers—on the left side of the funnel. Riley had crabbed over to the right side of the lip, without any handy boulders, and had taken up a less secure position there.

"The way I figure it," Smitty said, "they'll pin us with a feint from across the river while a bunch of them boys come through the trees on your side."

"Why my side?"

"They'll go back to Rascón, to the river crossing they know. Back there, they'll hump on over and climb the slope where it's safe."

"Any idea how many?" Riley shifted the washed-out green cap back and scratched his forehead.

Smitty shrugged. "Best I could tell from the tower, could be forty, could be twenty."

Riley worked the dip in his mouth and spat.

"One thing I know for damn sure." Smitty waited until Riley

looked at him before continuing. "Cain't a one of them sumbitches get past us. You hear? One gets by, they can find where the kids went."

Riley nodded. "Remember the Alamo."

CHAPTER 45

EVERY SCENARIO YEAGER RAN THROUGH his head ended up with him getting shot or chopped up. *Take out the guard at the door, and Marvin shoots me. Take out Marvin, and the guard shoots me or Verdugo buries his machete in some body part that I'd rather keep.* He could get one for sure, maybe two, but spaced out as they were, three would be impossible.

Verdugo leaned his butt against the desk in front of Yeager and toyed with his fancy blade. He was saying something to Marvin, but Yeager tuned him out. Taking a bullet would be okay; he'd been shot before. It wasn't fun, but unless they instantly disabled him, he could function long enough to... long enough to what? Not get out alive—that was too much to ask.

But maybe long enough to kill Verdugo. Now that would be worth it. With their leader gone, the power vacuum should throw the narcos into a tailspin. He grimaced. Thinking of tailspin made him think of Cujo augering into the hillside.

Take a bullet for Cujo? Definitely worth it.

Yeager glanced at Father Sebastian and caught the old man looking at him. In the instant before the priest lowered his head, he passed Yeager a look that said... something. The only thing he could be sure of was that the priest's docile, beaten-down look was an act. The fierce, in-your-face priest he had seen standing up to Verdugo was still in there, tamped down, waiting to explode. The question was: what did the old man have in mind?

The priest looked at him again and flicked his eyes to the guard behind Yeager. He did the same thing twice more, focusing on Yeager then flicking his glance back. Yeager nodded, a tiny incline of his head. Did he read that right? It seemed to say: *Take out the guy behind you.*

Verdugo chopped into the desk again, apparently enjoying the act of destruction. The gang leader had the body of a wrestler: thick shouldered and powerful. He stood a head taller than Yeager and matched him pound for pound.

Yeager noted that whenever he stabbed the blade into the desk, the weapon was taken out of play for a brief second. Father Sebastian must have noticed the same thing—on the next downswing, he made his play, flying off the sofa like a scalded cat. He screamed a wordless sound of pure fury and wrapped both arms around Marvin in a furious bear hug. The dumpy man crashed into the wall, a look of comic surprise on his face.

Yeager didn't hesitate. Spinning out of the chair, he grabbed the heavy piece of furniture and swung it around, shouting with effort. The chair moved through the air with exaggerated slow motion at first, gained momentum halfway through its arc, then slammed the door guard with the impact of a freight train. The man hunched to the side and tried to raise a blocking arm when he saw the oak chair coming, but the velocity of it broke his arm, crunched into his ribs, and smacked the side of his head.

The guard's eyes rolled up in his head, and he crumpled. Yeager was already moving, ducking back to his left, instinctively reversing his motion just in time to avoid the downswing of Verdugo's glittering blade. Off balance, Verdugo stumbled past, and Yeager clubbed him in the back with a doubled-up pair of fists.

Verdugo grunted, but he was a big man and he didn't go down. He bounced off the wall and slashed the machete horizontally through the air, catching a piece of Yeager's shirt and scoring a red line across his stomach. Yeager jumped close and pinned Verdugo's blade-wielding arm between them. He hit the gang leader with a pile-driver fist to the nose, which Verdugo shook off. He shoved Yeager back as easily as pushing off a child.

Jesus, this guy is strong. Yeager stumbled back, tripping over the downed guard and going down. The man's weapon was trapped beneath his body—no way to get to it. Yeager rolled to his feet, back against the desk, where he grabbed the first thing that came to hand: the computer monitor. He threw it at the charging gang leader. The monitor snagged on its cord halfway there and fell to the floor.

Verdugo slashed, fast as a snake, but Yeager propelled himself into a back roll over the desk. The blade whipped overhand and thunked into the wood behind him.

From the corner of his eye, Yeager saw Father Sebastian flinch when Marvin pushed the barrel of his pistol into the priest's side and fired. Another muffled shot, and Sebastian jumped again. The priest held Marvin in a literal death grip and refused to let go. The unassuming face of the cartel killer had a frustrated look of impatience, as though wondering how this old man could be so damn pigheaded.

Yeager picked up Dominic's desk chair with a King Kong yell and heaved it across the desk, forcing Verdugo to duck. The massive chair hit him a glancing blow and knocked the gang leader to one side. Yeager used that extra beat of time to take one long stride to his left and hammer Marvin between the eyes. The small man went over backward, carrying Father Sebastian with him.

Verdugo paused and faced him from across the desk. He seemed to have forgotten the pistol in his waistband and focused on hacking at Yeager with his shiny blade. Blood trickled from the blond man's flattened and clearly broken nose. "You have no chance, Trucker." He flicked the machete in a glittering arc. "I have been killing people with this for a very long time."

The other guard would be on his way back, and Marvin was down but not out. Yeager had to end this. *Now.*

Yeager threw a stapler at Verdugo's head. Verdugo flinched and ducked. Yeager followed the throw by leaping the desk and bull-rushing the gang leader. He slammed into Verdugo with his full weight. The blond man stumbled backward but not nearly as much as Yeager had hoped. Not only was he strong, but Verdugo was also fast and capable.

Yeager grabbed the man's right wrist, freezing the machete, and punched low, hitting Verdugo in the groin. Verdugo tagged him with a left hook to his ear hard enough to make spots dance before his eyes. He nearly blacked out, and his legs went loose, but he held onto the cartel man's wrist.

The hold only lasted a second. Verdugo snapped a short jab under his ribs, then another. When Yeager flinched and tried to cover, his opponent's left cross came out of nowhere and caught his chin.

Yeager felt Verdugo's wrist slip free. He blinked and struggled to focus. A blur of motion and color swirled before his eyes, and Verdugo's form took shape in front of him. A dull ringing in his ears blocked out any sound, and he gasped for breath.

He sensed more than saw the machete coming around and got his left arm up just in time. The blade caught him in the forearm, down by the handle. It made a sound like whacking the head off a fish. Had it cut him farther along the blade, with the full force of the swing, it would have cut his arm off. The partial blow chopped a divot in his forearm, striking bone and numbing him from wrist to elbow.

Just as with the desk, the blade was immobilized for a brief moment.

Close enough to smell Verdugo's breath, Yeager head butted the taller man in the chin, snapping his head back. Yeager popped a hammer-like fist into the cartel leader's scarred throat. He drew back and slammed it again, then again.

Cartilage snapped, and Verdugo's eyes bulged. He grabbed his neck with a free hand and slid to his knees, choking. Yeager twisted the machete loose and spun to check on Marvin.

In the corner of the office, Father Sebastian lay across the semiconscious Marvin. Yeager had no way of knowing how often Sebastian had been shot, but the priest clung to the cartel man with the grip of the possessed. He simply refused to give up.

Yeager took two long steps and brought the machete down overhead in a vicious swing. Marvin had a half second to see it coming. The blade *chunked* into his head and split it in half.

Sebastian rolled to his back and blinked at the ceiling. His skin had gone ghost-white underneath his olive complexion, and his ordinarily tidy white hair splayed around his head.

"Father." Yeager took the priest's hand. His grip was clammy and weak.

The priest focused his eyes on Yeager's for a brief moment. "Take care… of the children," he whispered. Sebastian rattled a final breath, and his eyes settled on a place far away from this Earth.

"*Vaya con Dios, Padre.*" Yeager gave the priest's hand a last squeeze.

The door handle turned, and Yeager pulled his XDM from Marvin's belt, spun on one heel, and fired two shots at the cartel soldier who stood in the doorway, blowing him backward. The roll of duct tape the man carried fell to the floor and rolled away.

Verdugo's face had gone red, and he gasped like a fish out of water, scrabbling at his neck with both hands. Yeager cradled his throbbing, wounded arm against his chest and stood over the cartel killer, jaw knotted. The gang leader clutched at Yeager's pant leg, but he kicked Verdugo's hand away. "Sucks to be you, don't it?"

Yeager used a spare shirt and the roll of duct tape to bind the wound in his forearm. Blood saturated his makeshift bandage, and the wound burned. The cut went deep into the bone, and he was pretty sure the arm was broken, maybe even some tendons cut. He could barely flex the fingers of his left hand, which could mean really bad things, or it could be the pain from his forearm blocking the nerve impulses. At least, as far as he could tell, no arteries had been hit.

Yeager gathered his things from the desk and his pack from the floor. He laid a throw from the back of the sofa over Father Sebastian then lowered the priest's eyelids and said a quick prayer.

Six minutes later, he was ready to leave. On the way out, he stepped over Verdugo's dead body.

Now that the shock had worn off, Yeager's arm hurt with a throbbing ferocity. He tucked his left hand in his pants pocket and tried not to move it. All he had for the pain was some Tylenol, which he dry swallowed on the way to the front door.

Yeager found a car in the courtyard with the keys still in it. A Land Rover, probably Verdugo's. *Why not take the best?*

He looked north, toward the spot where the kids should have gone. A misty rain coated everything with a thin film of moisture, and his breath fogged. All sounds of firing had ceased, which was either a very good thing or a very bad thing. One way or another, he needed to find out what happened.

He would have to come back and take care of Cujo at some point, but at the moment, time pressed on him with the weight of an anvil. During the session inside the mission, he had been aware of the muted crackle of small-arms fire.

Now he heard nothing.

He drove across the bridge and turned left, accelerating hard enough the tail end of the SUV spun for traction on the wet pavement. In less than two minutes, he came to a spot in the road scattered with bodies. To his right, a slope rose to a hilltop, its rocky surface dotted with more dead men. Yeager parked the Land Rover fifty yards past the rock shelf, where the tree cover started again, and got out.

The car's door thumped in the silence. A crow cawed in the distance, and the rain turned from a mist to a drizzle. Yeager climbed the hill, working his way from tree to tree, his eyes scanning the brush. He caught a movement on his left and froze then moved on when a squirrel bounded away and spiraled up a pine.

At the top of the hill, he worked his way to the right, back toward the shelf. He took a long moment to study the scene when he came to a clearing. Including the eight he had already seen, Yeager counted another ten bodies surrounding a boulder.

Brass littered the ground as profusely as the fallen leaves from the trees. Burned gunpowder lingered in the air. The earthy smell of fresh blood, as sharp as raw copper, assaulted his sinuses.

Smitty and Riley had made a last stand.

Yeager eased from the trees and slipped up to check Smitty first. The big man lay on his back, arms thrown wide. Yeager couldn't count the bullet wounds on his body, there were so many. Beside him, his bolt-action rifle lay where it had fallen, bolt open and locked back. Smitty clutched the Ruger tactical rifle by the barrel. The weapon's buttstock was matted with the hair and blood of a muscular, dark-skinned man two feet away, whose skull was caved in.

J. W. Smith had taken a lot of killing.

Yeager thought Riley was dead, too, until the slim man stirred. Yeager rolled him over gently, and Riley focused his eyes and blinked. His mouth moved, but no sound came out. Yeager leaned closer, and Riley breathed out one word. "None."

"None? None what, Riley?"

Riley swallowed and worked air down into his lungs. "None. Got. By."

The Texan smiled and died.

CHAPTER 46

YEAGER CAUGHT UP WITH THE orphans deep in the cave and nearly got shot by one of de la Cueva's men when he came to the end of the snaking trail of children. Once he established who he was, the man he'd code-named Bravo ducked his head and looked apologetic.

The children treated the journey like a holiday, laughing and marveling at the sights. They had maneuvered the "poop chute," as Juan called it, with ropes and flashlights, then tromped through the guano with plastic bags tied around their feet. Yeager had none of those advantages, and by the time he caught up to the group, he stank and his butt hurt from sliding down the chute.

Not to mention his arm jabbed knives of pain so sharp it felt as though it would split in two pieces. Father Dietrich irrigated and sanitized the wound, wrapping it with clean bandages. Yeager took one look and glanced away. The meat of his arm was laid bare to the white of his ulna. He was relieved to find he could flex his hand, and his grip was stronger than it had been a few hours before.

"You will need stitches," Father Dietrich said. "Best for now to leave it open. A doctor will need to look at that bone."

The group bedded down with blanket rolls in a large cavern that dripped moisture from stalactites into a deep pool in the chamber's center. A Coleman lantern provided enough light to negotiate the camp inside the cavern.

Yeager posted a guard on their back trail, more for his own peace of mind than any real belief that Verdugo's men were still behind them. He found Juan Guerrero sitting with some other boys, pointing at the dark water and speaking to a ring of attentive faces.

"And over there," the boy said, "a swamp zombie came out of the water, and I hit him, with a rock, like this!" He demonstrated by jumping up and making a baseball-throwing motion, whipping his arm forward. "My rock hit him right between the eyes." He pointed to that spot on his own head.

"You are so full of shit," one of the bigger boys said, though he didn't sound completely sure of himself.

"Hey, Juan," Yeager called.

"Sí, señor?"

"This cave," Yeager said in his border Spanish. "It is good that you made it through to the other side. You saved a lot of lives with your bravery."

"Gracias, señor." The boy grinned, and he looked so proud Yeager wondered if the shirt buttons would pop off his chest.

Yeager motioned him over and, when Juan came close, crouched in front of him and said in a voice only loud enough for the boy to hear, "You should become a writer, you know? Then you could tell stories like that all the time and make a living at it."

Juan tried to hide a smile by looking at his toes.

"I have a boy," he said, louder. "'Bout your age. Lives in Texas. You want to come visit sometime?"

Juan blinked and glanced around as though wondering if Yeager were still speaking to him. "Who? Me? Come to the United States?"

"For a visit, at least."

"I... I, uh..."

"Just say yes, Juan."

"Yes, señor."

Yeager nodded and walked away, leaving behind a mumble of excited voices.

Father Dietrich sat at a camp stove, heating water for coffee. Next to him, the Coleman lantern hissed and glowed with an incandescent light. Yeager hunkered down across from the priest and brought him up to speed on events at the mission. Dietrich took the news of Father Sebastian's death in silence. He bowed his head, and Yeager waited while the German fingered his rosary and murmured prayers.

"We have other issues, Father," Yeager said when Dietrich looked up.

The priest cocked an eyebrow in question.

"The silver," Yeager said. "And Dominic. Both are gone."

Father Dietrich shifted and looked into the darkness. He cleared his throat and met Yeager's eyes then looked away. When the priest spoke, it was only after a glance at the children. Yeager had to lean forward to hear him.

"It is time for a full confession, Herr Yeager. You deserve that." Dietrich poured a handful of grounds into the boiling pot. The aroma of coffee made Yeager's mouth water. "The silver should be in the hands of Don de la Cueva by now."

"De la Cueva?" Yeager sprang to his feet and loomed over the priest. "What in hell are you talking about?"

"Please." Dietrich held up his hands and kept his voice pitched low. "Allow me to explain." The German took a deep breath, and Yeager resumed his seat.

"Six months ago, de la Cueva was approached by a silver merchant in Madera, who offered to sell him some antiquities that had come into his possession. When the old don got a look at the pieces, he immediately recognized his family's heirlooms. He knew at once these came from the mission."

"So?"

"Please, Herr Yeager, this is a long tale. De la Cueva has—*had*—a pledge to the mission to provide it funds. Should the priesthood there wish to sell any of his family heirlooms to raise more money, they agreed to offer them to him first. He didn't want these pieces of his history to be bartered on the open market, plus he had a family interest in maintaining the mission his ancestors founded.

"He traced the sale back to Father Dominic, which he found very suspicious. Being an influential patron, de la Cueva had access to the archbishop, so he approached him and suggested something fishy was going on at the Mission San Felipe de Cristo. The bishop agreed to look into it."

Dietrich sipped his coffee. In the white glow from the lantern, his face looked even more macabre than it did in natural light.

"Even that would have probably not amounted to much more than an audit of the mission's funds. But something else came to light at that time…"

"Something else," Yeager prompted.

"Yes, Herr Yeager." Dietrich sighed, and his mouth took on a flat line before he continued. "Father Pepe reported to the archbishop that Dominic had been seen in the company of a woman of, ah, loose morals. Pepe followed him on one of his trips to town and observed him enter this woman's home. At the door, he witnessed Dominic and the woman embracing. In a romantic way."

"So you're saying he caught Dominic having sex."

"Caught?" Dietrich shrugged. "He suspected. Dominic had begun to act very strangely, and Pepe grew very concerned that Dominic had been compromised. So they sent for me."

"You?"

"I am something of a… specialist."

"A specialist?" Yeager asked.

"Ja, Herr Yeager. A church investigator."

"You have those? Investigators?"

Dietrich inclined his head. "Coffee? Here, I will pour. So yes, I was assigned to the mission to see what was happening. I went in undercover, so to speak, to find some answers. Was Dominic siphoning funds from the orphanage? Or was he just going behind de la Cueva's back? Was his involvement with this woman compromising his ethics? These were questions we preferred to find the answers to before the press and public found out.

"At first, I found nothing out of the ordinary except that Dominic appeared strained and would not answer questions about the church finances. I never saw him with the woman, but of course, after reading Dominic's letter, I understand now that the affair had been terminated. That the damage was already done."

"What about the silver?"

Dominic held up a hand. "More coffee? No? All right. Sometimes in my position, I am forced to do things to which I do not like to admit. In this case, I entered Dominic's office and accessed his computer without his knowledge."

"You broke in?"

Dietrich sighed and nodded. "By the emails and documents I found, I determined that Dominic had been selling artifacts to fund his future plans for fleeing the mission. I did not know why, or when, he planned to leave, just that he did. Then the earthquake hit, and things were thrown into chaos. Soon after, the silver merchant who brought the first artifacts to de la Cueva contacted him again, saying that Dominic wished him to take several hundred kilos of silver at one time. This information was relayed to me by the archbishop. We all agreed that Dominic planned to move all the silver at one time and, ah... how do you say it in American movies? Make a break for it?"

Yeager nodded and flexed his left hand. He swallowed more Tylenol with a sip of cold coffee.

"But how was Dominic going to get that much silver out of the mission?" Dietrich said. "No one could figure out that part of the plan. Until Dominic engaged the assistance of one of his relatives with a helicopter to bring in supplies."

Yeager glanced up sharply. "Victor."

"Indeed, Herr Ruiz." The priest ducked his head and looked away. "And at first, though it pains me to say it, we suspected he might be part of Dominic's plan."

"I can see it. Go on."

"Well, the helicopter plan fell apart when we learned we needed a dialysis machine and couldn't fly it in. Dominic immediately proposed using a truck, and Herr Ruiz volunteered your services."

"And"—Yeager's voice came out flat and hard—"I'll bet you thought I was in on it too."

Dietrich dipped his head and gave a thin-lipped smile. "I apologize for that assumption, Herr Yeager. If it is any consolation, I very quickly decided we were wrong about that assumption."

Yeager waved it off. "Go on."

"We decided that de la Cueva should provide the truck and the logistics to get it in and out of Madera and to assist you with getting to it. That way, we could maintain control of the truck full of goods coming in and going out. De la Cueva planted a GPS device on the trailer and agreed that when it moved out of Rascón, his men would follow and intercept it. I agreed to keep track of Dominic and report when he left the mission and to follow him if possible."

"Well, I'll be damned," Yeager mused. "Real James Bond stuff."

"But as you know, Herr Yeager, things became so much more complicated when Verdugo arrived on the scene and phones went out. And Father Pepe." Dietrich sighed. "I never would have guessed they would take it that far. Very tragic."

Yeager sipped the last of his coffee and sat back on his heels. "And our part in all this? Me? Victor? Riley and Smitty?"

"Forgive me, but at first I could not know if you were part of the plot or just innocent victims caught in the same web." Dietrich gave him a wintry smile, without humor. "I soon figured out that you had been duped into your role. If it is worth anything to you, know that you have saved a lot of lives." He glanced at the blanketed forms lined up beyond the hissing light of the Coleman lantern.

"So what happens to Dominic?"

"If the civil authorities have not found him, then we will."

"I hate to say this, Father, but the Catholic Church doesn't have a great record when it comes to disciplining priests."

Dietrich shrugged. "I can't argue. It is, as you say in America, above my pay grade."

Yeager stared into the darkness for a long time.

CHAPTER 47

D R. ALEXANDRA LOPEZ BALANCED A tray in one hand and opened the door to Room 3 with the other. Her patient sat up in bed, reading a trashy Mexican romance novel. He raised his eyebrow when she came in.

"What's that? More medicine?"

"The very best kind." Alex set the tray on the bedside table. On it, two cups steamed, thick with milk and coffee. "Not as good as that place in Hermosillo, but good enough."

"I get treatment like this, I'll get shot more often."

"No, you will not! No more getting shot for you. It took me three hours to fix the damage that bullet did, and you died on me twice."

"And you brought me back," Victor said. "I heard it was the mouth-to-mouth."

Alex felt a flush build in her cheeks, and she sipped her café con leche.

"So," Victor said. "When do I get out of here, anyway?"

"Oh no." Alex patted his hand. "Not so fast. You're not going anywhere until I know you won't tear any stitches."

"Got to, querida. I have some friends in trouble still."

"Not anymore." Alex considered how much to tell him but decided the whole thing at once would be best. "It's been all over the news, plus I talked to the commander of the federales in Hermosillo once you were stable. The Grupo Verdugo has all but been wiped out in the Rascón valley. All the children are safe, and so is your friend, Señor Yeager."

She hesitated. "Two other Americans were killed. Smith and Amick."

Victor paused, the coffee cup suspended before his lips. He slowly lowered it. His hand found hers and squeezed it. He looked toward the window, though the curtains were drawn and he couldn't possibly see outside.

Alex held his hand for a long time and pretended not to notice when Victor wiped at his eyes with a sleeve.

———⮞✦⮜———

Oscar Cruz sat in the interview room of the New Braunfels Police Department with his hands cuffed to a bracket in the table in front of him. He had been waiting two hours in the same place. They had taken his picture with a digital camera and left without saying a word.

He did not know what had caused the arrest. He had been coming back from the pizza takeout place when two squad cars pulled in front of his motel-room door and held him at gunpoint, cuffed him, and jailed him. They spoke English so fast he barely understood a word of it.

He jumped when the door banged open, and a giant gringo in a Stetson hat lumbered into the room, shoulders almost as broad as the door, followed by a petite Hispanic woman. The man shut the door and held a chair for the small woman then sat down and laid his cream-colored hat on the table.

The man wore a round badge on his chest and had a holstered .45 auto in a hip holster, so he was obviously a policeman of some kind—a blond-haired cop with light-blue eyes and the rough good looks of a cowboy movie star. He set a manila folder on the table next to his hat. The woman wore a conservative suit and frameless glasses, her dark hair pulled back in a ponytail.

"Howdy, Mr. Wallach," the man said. "Or should I say, Mr. Cruz?"

They knew his real name. Cruz cursed to himself. He had hoped the Wallach ID would hold up better.

"I am Ranger Sam Cable," the cop said. "This here is Mizz Domingo. I am told you speak pretty good English, but just in case, this lady is an interpreter. Mizz Domingo, would you interpret that, please?"

Fortunately, the woman spoke fluid Spanish. The man's Texan accent was thicker than mud, and Oscar could barely understand a word he said.

The cop waited while Domingo translated, then said, "Mr. Cruz, you are under arrest for the assault of LaTonya Delmonte in the Motel 6 on Interstate 35 in Georgetown, Texas, two nights ago." He paused for translation. "I won't go into great detail, but we have your rental car on surveillance leaving the parking lot, we've got blood evidence that I feel pretty damn sure's gonna link you up with the crime, and Mizz Delmonte has positively ID'd you in a photo lineup."

Cruz said nothing, but a pressure started to build in his head, a brewing kettle that roared in his ears. This was about a *whore*? Unbelievable. He strained to listen to the rest of the translation.

"Now, ordinarily the Texas Rangers wouldn't be asked to the party on a simple assault case, but... in your possession were several pieces of evidence that indicated you meant to bring harm to a peaceful, law-abiding family here in the state of Texas." He consulted the file in front of him. "Abelard Yeager and Charlotte Buchanan. Ring any bells?"

The roaring pressure squeezed against the back of his eyes, and Cruz breathed hard through his nose.

"No?" The cop seemed to think his down-home charm was cute. He kept throwing looks at the translator, who would hide a smile and look away. "Anyway, I have a report about a break-in at the Yeager residence. This happened right before Mizz Delmonte was assaulted, just a few miles away."

The cowboy tapped the folder and cocked his head to one side. "You got inside their house for some reason, I guess. What were you up to? Robbery? Kidnapping? And I hear you shot their dog. Man, that's cold. Anyway, I sent a technician down to collect some fingerprint evidence and the bullet recovered from the pup, which I imagine will fit the gun we found in your possession. The way I figure it, we'll get a positive hit on all that, too, tying you to the crime like ropin' a heifer."

He paused while the woman caught up. Oscar rocked in his chair. Of all the stupid...

"But even that wouldn't normally interest the Texas Rangers. Just so happens, our little fingerprint search turned up an interesting fact. It seems you, Mr. Cruz, are wanted in Monterrey for a few outstanding warrants. Apparently you've been a bad boy in two countries. An international criminal is what you are. Funny, you don't look like all that. Does he, Mizz Domingo? No, don't translate that." He leaned back in his chair and laced his hands behind his head. "Now, I know a feller in Monterrey, a police captain named Obregon. So I give him a call, and guess what he tells me?"

Cruz stopped rocking and stared into the man's blue eyes. They had gone from warm and friendly to ice chips.

"Don't wanna guess? Well, he tells me that, besides these warrants, the Sinaloa Cartel wants your ass pretty bad. Something about a bunch of dead people at their distribution center outside of Monterrey."

"I had," Cruz started, then his throat seized, and he had to try again. "I had nothing to do with that."

The cowboy cop shrugged. "Don't mean much to me. Here's my position. Now, I got all this physical evidence. I could bring this case to the grand jury and get you set for trial here in the US. But. My witness, Mizz Delmonte, is a... a lady of unfortunate reputation. She won't make a good witness. And going to trial is always tricky. Anything could happen. So I'm inclined to just send you back to my friend Captain Obregon and let him deal with you."

Oscar's eyes watered, and his anus squeezed tight. The roaring in his ears had turned to a whine, and he felt cold and hot at the same time. "No," he whispered.

"What was that?"

"No, I said." Oscar's throat felt coated with sand. "I will confess. To anything. Please, señor, do not send me back. The Sinaloa. The Sinaloa people are everywhere. They will find me and—and do things. Bad things." Oscar groped for the words to make this man understand how bad it could be, but his mind was blank.

"I hear what you're saying there, Señor Cruz; I really do. But a promise is a promise. I told Captain Obregon he could have you. Can't go back on my word now, can I?"

The tall man scraped back his chair and stood. He gathered his hat and folder then held the chair for the translator. The ranger opened the door and stood aside for the smaller woman. "Wait up a second there, Mizz Domingo. I'd like a word."

The cop, one hand on the doorknob, looked at Oscar. He tipped his head in a nod. "Y'all have a nice day."

The door closed, and the lock clicked.

EPILOGUE

CHARLIE WORKED A CROSSWORD AND watched the evening news. After she got the call from the Texas Ranger, she felt better; however, she asked Judy to go with her to check out the house. She wanted to make sure everything was secure and no unwanted visitors hung out in the shower or the attic.

After the all-clear, she and David had gingerly settled back into their routines. The only difference: her gun rested on the end table next to the sofa, where she sat with her feet tucked up under her.

David tended to stay close by, she noticed. He lay in the middle of the floor with a book—something with dragons and wizards—propped in front of him on a pillow. Rascal curled on the sofa next to her, his shaved scalp looking faintly ridiculous.

When the phone rang, she checked the caller ID and had to catch her breath when she recognized a Mexico number. "Hello?"

"Hey." Abel's voice shot a flush of relief through her system so profound she couldn't think of anything to say.

"Hey back." David looked up at the sound of her voice. She nodded and mouthed *Abel*. "Where are you?"

"A quaint little spot called Morochic. It's somewhere south of Madera. Best I can tell, the whole town is run by a tyrant called Marisol."

"What are you doing there? I mean, what happened? Did Cujo find you?"

Charlie listened to a silent hum, and her heart sank. "He saved our asses," Abel said finally. "Again."

He gave her the highlights of what had happened, leaving out, she was sure, a number of things he didn't want her to know. She let it go—for the time being.

"So anyway," Abel said, "I don't know where Victor's gotten off to. I can't find him. I did find out from de la Cueva that they have the silver, and the two drivers are in jail. He's agreed to set up a new orphanage at his compound as long as Father Dietrich stays to run it. Although he may have to fight Marisol for custody. She's taken a real shine to this one boy, Juan, who found a way through the cave. The woman's pretty much taken over the care and feeding of all the kids, finding them places to sleep and eat. She may wind up being part of the deal; I don't know."

"And Father Dominic?"

"Still in the wind. I have to hope his past catches up to him somewhere. If not in this world, maybe the next."

"So when will you be home?" she asked.

"As soon as I can find Victor."

"Well... hurry."

"Miss me, huh?"

Charlie swallowed a knot in her throat. Her hand absentmindedly traced a circle over her stomach. "All of us do."

Dawn. High in the Sierra Madres, on a hill overlooking the village of Rascón, a mockingbird landed on the broken-out window frame of a Cessna Skyknight. His head twitched to the side as he studied the interior of the plane. He blinked.

Something moved, and the mockingbird shot away in a burst of feathers, darting for the cover of a manjack tree before jinking right and away.

"Oh man. My head hurts." David Milton Quattlebaum III, aka Cujo, squinted bleary eyes and tried to focus through the pain in his head and ribs. *And legs and hips and feet and goddamn toenails for that matter.* Everything hurt all at once, all over, with the urgency of a six-alarm fire.

"Where am I?" he croaked.

The fuzzy shapes of a number of people materialized through

the trees. A radio squawked. Someone shouted. As the blurry outlines came closer, or his vision improved, Cujo recognized the uniform of the Mexican Federal Police. He remembered where he was. In a Cessna Skyknight carrying a highly illegal modified rocket pod, which he'd expended on an unknown group of Mexican citizens who had been attacking his friends.

"Oh shit," he mumbled when the nearest federale reached the pilot's door and peered in. "I'm in *so* much trouble."

ACKNOWLEDGMENTS

The author would like to thank some very special people who have helped, guided, mentored, and kicked his ass when needed. For critiquing and generally demanding better writing: Susan Stuckey, Kat Krawczyk, Pete Barber, Ross Murdock, Liz Klein, Marsha Hubbell, Pat Haddock, Doi Nelli, Sherry Terry, and many others.

For general support, care, and feeding of the author, I'd like to sincerely thank the Latter Day Dinosaurs, the incomparable Lynn McNamee of Red Adept Publishing and her staff, the Writer's Guild of Texas, and my pals on Scribophile not named above.

And for those times when the author was a crabby bear and needed to be coddled, spoiled, or at least tolerated, special thanks goes to my wife, Margaret, and our spawn, James and Beth.

ABOUT THE AUTHOR

Scott Bell has over 25 years of experience protecting the assets of retail companies. He holds a degree in Criminal Justice from North Texas State University. With the kids grown and time on his hands, Scott turned back to his first love—writing. His short stories have been published in The Western Online, Cast of Wonders, and in the anthology, Desolation. When he's not writing, Scott is on the eternal quest to answer the question: What would John Wayne do?